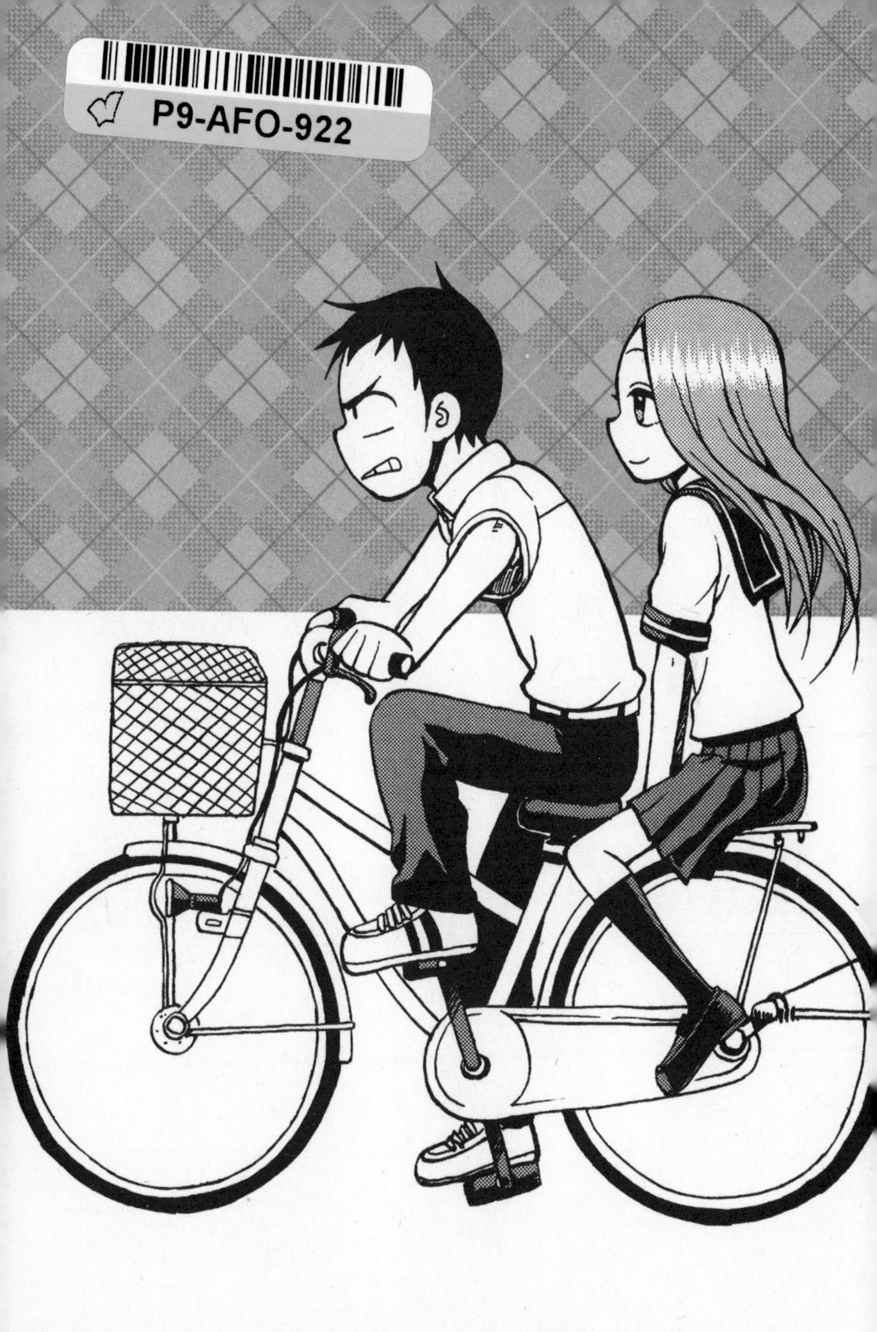

# Teasing Master Takagi-san 2

Soichiro Yamamoto

# Contents

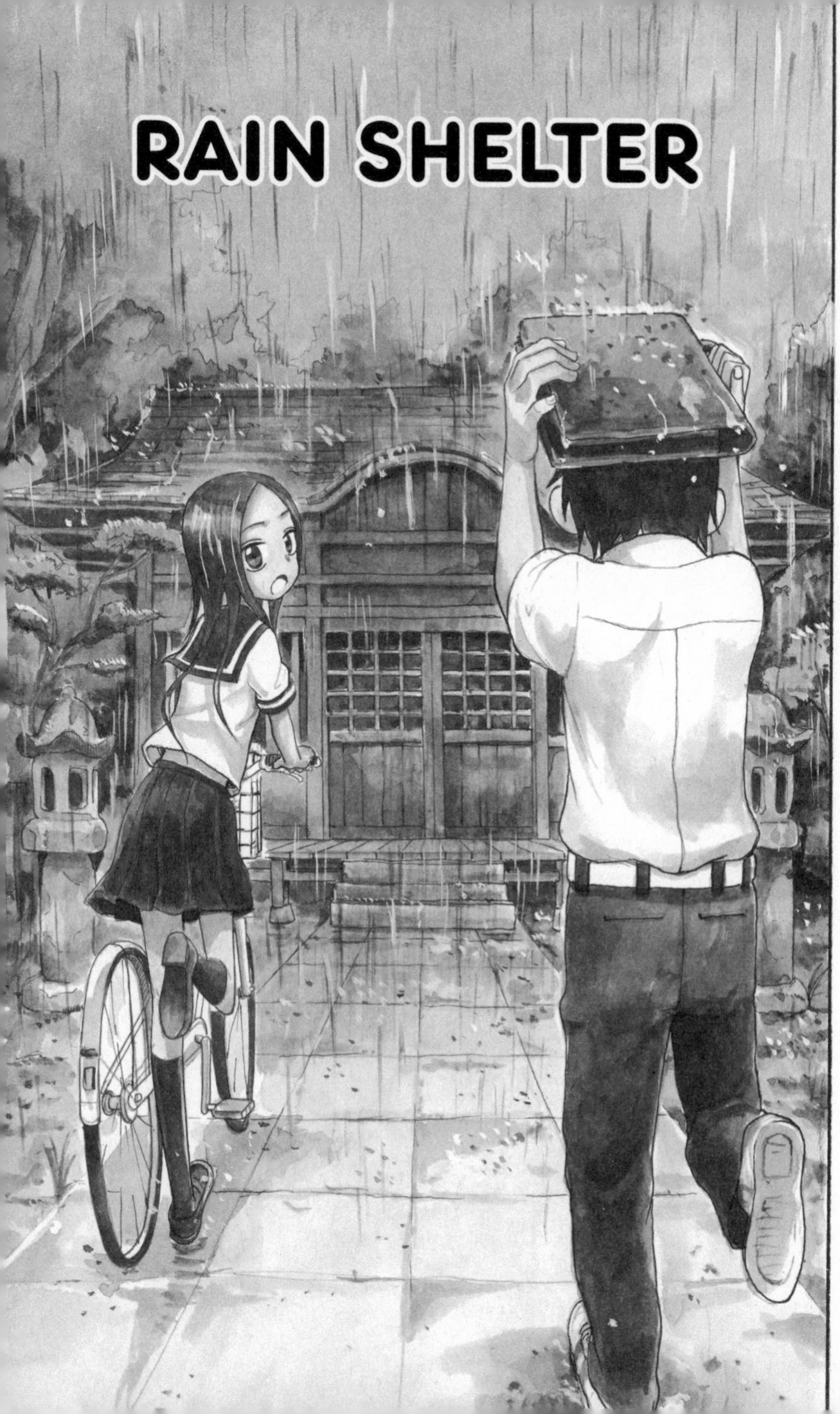
RAIN SHELTER

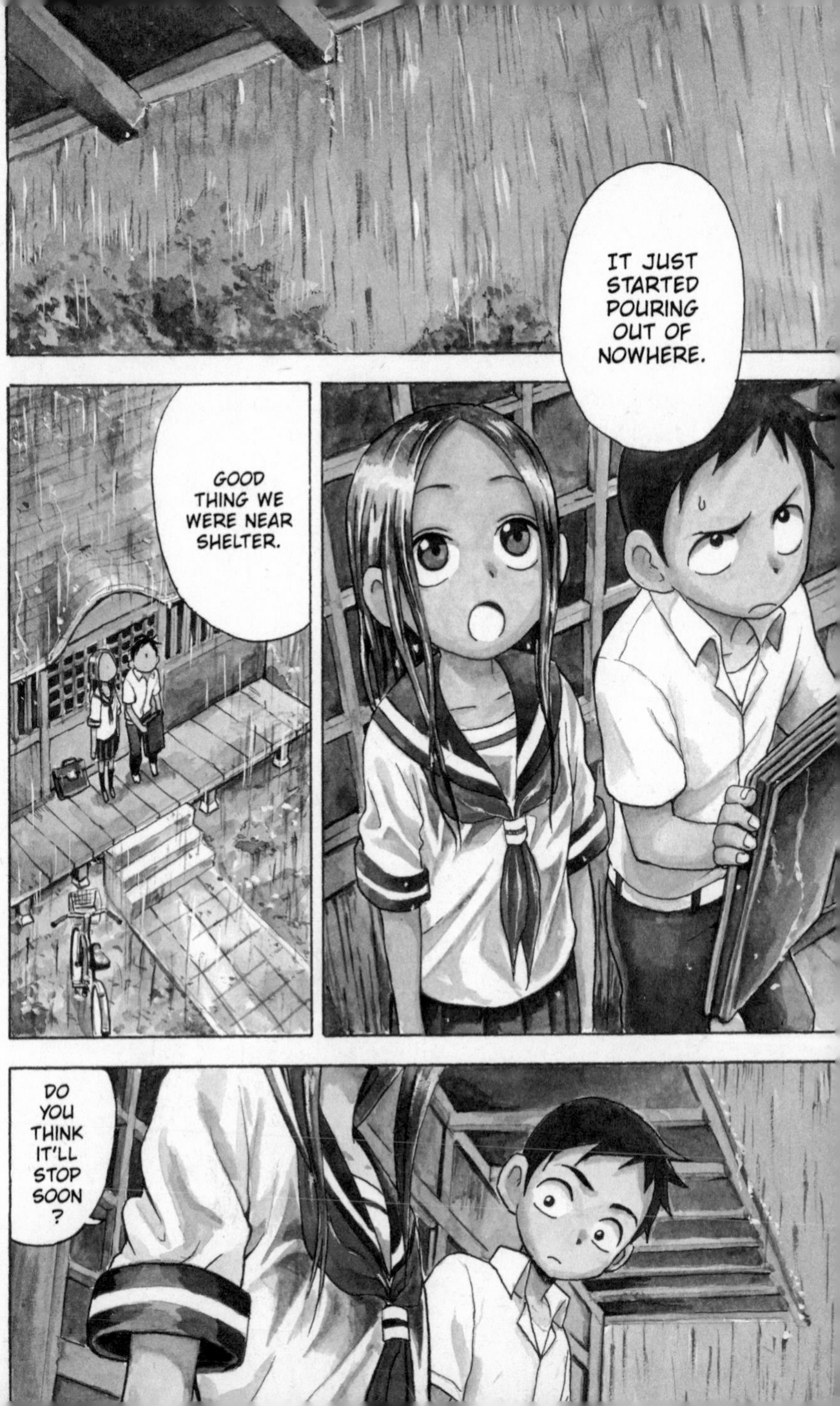
IT JUST STARTED POURING OUT OF NOWHERE.
GOOD THING WE WERE NEAR SHELTER.
DO YOU THINK IT'LL STOP SOON?

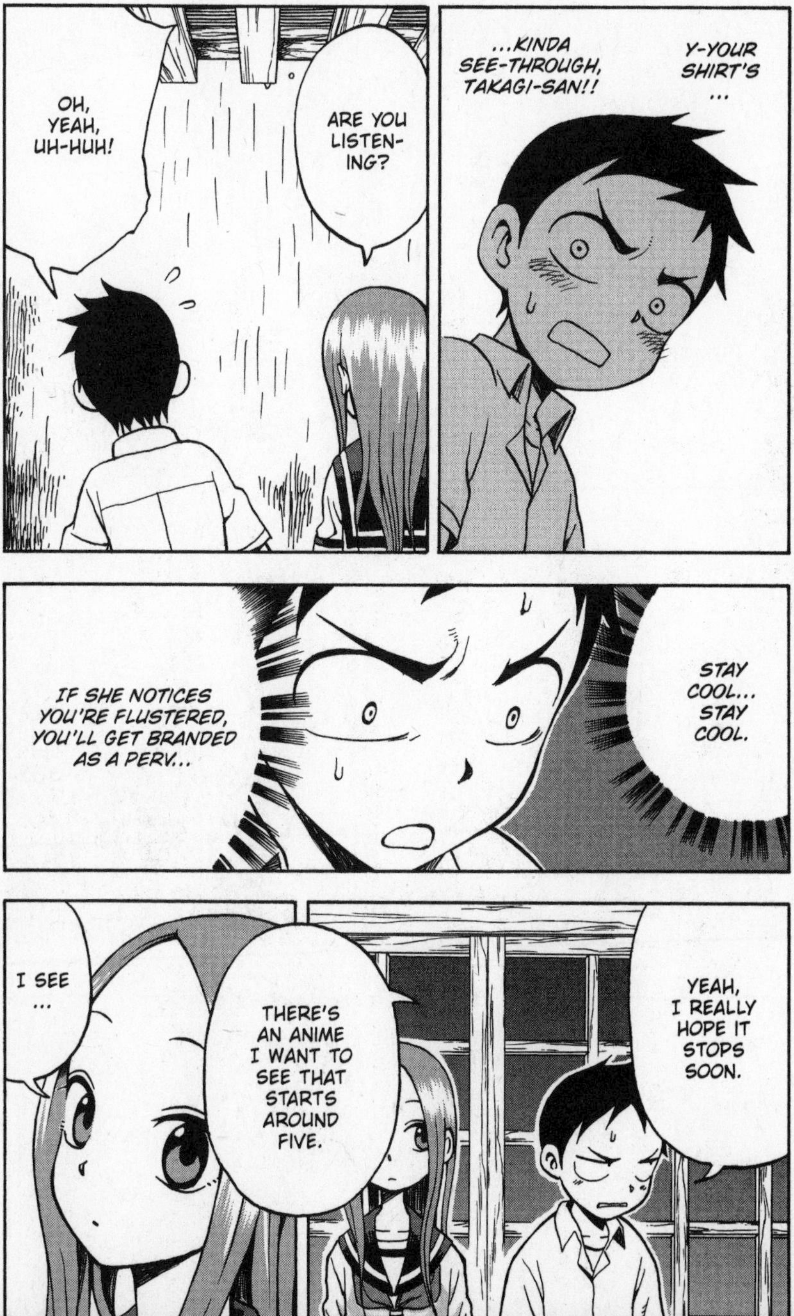
Y-YOUR SHIRT'S ...
...KINDA SEE-THROUGH, TAKAGI-SAN!!
ARE YOU LISTEN-ING?
OH, YEAH, UH-HUH!
STAY COOL... STAY COOL.
IF SHE NOTICES YOU'RE FLUSTERED, YOU'LL GET BRANDED AS A PERV...
YEAH, I REALLY HOPE IT STOPS SOON.
THERE'S AN ANIME I WANT TO SEE THAT STARTS AROUND FIVE.
I SEE ...

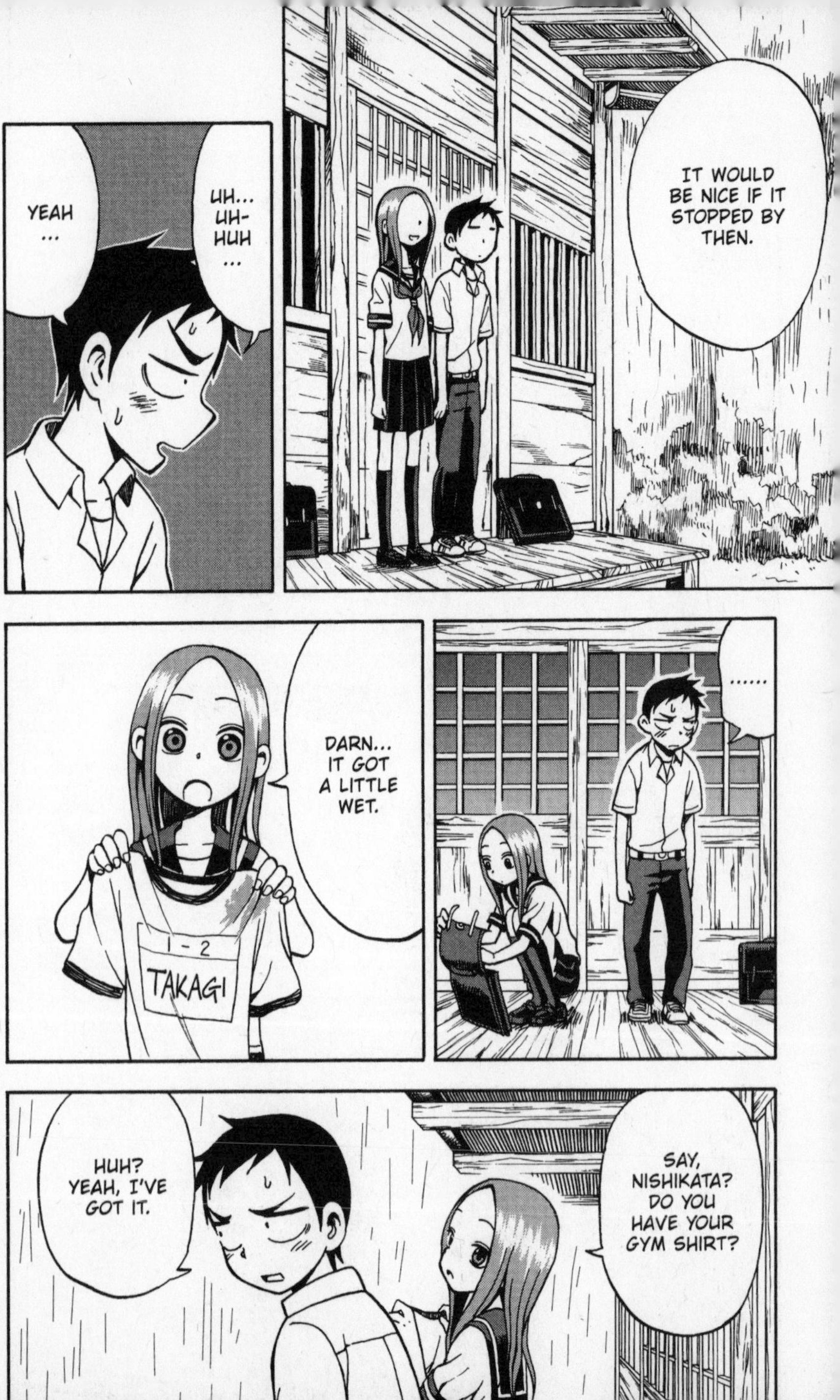
IT WOULD BE NICE IF IT STOPPED BY THEN.
UH... UH-HUH ...
YEAH ...
......
DARN... IT GOT A LITTLE WET.
1 - 2
TAKAGI
SAY, NISHIKATA? DO YOU HAVE YOUR GYM SHIRT?
HUH? YEAH, I'VE GOT IT.

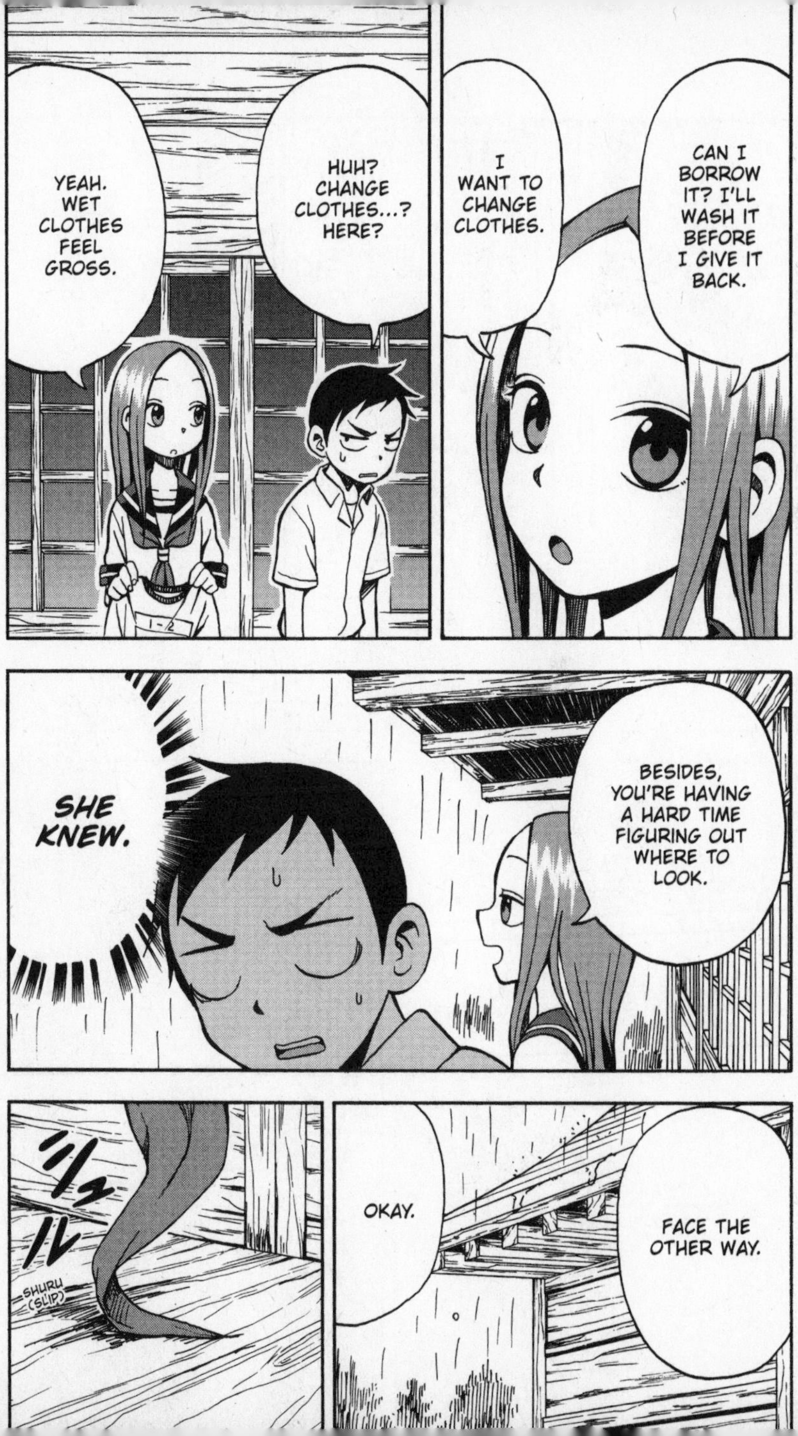
CAN I BORROW IT? I'LL WASH IT BEFORE I GIVE IT BACK.
I WANT TO CHANGE CLOTHES.
HUH? CHANGE CLOTHES...? HERE?
YEAH. WET CLOTHES FEEL GROSS.
BESIDES, YOU'RE HAVING A HARD TIME FIGURING OUT WHERE TO LOOK.
SHE KNEW.
FACE THE OTHER WAY.
OKAY.
SHURU (SLIP)

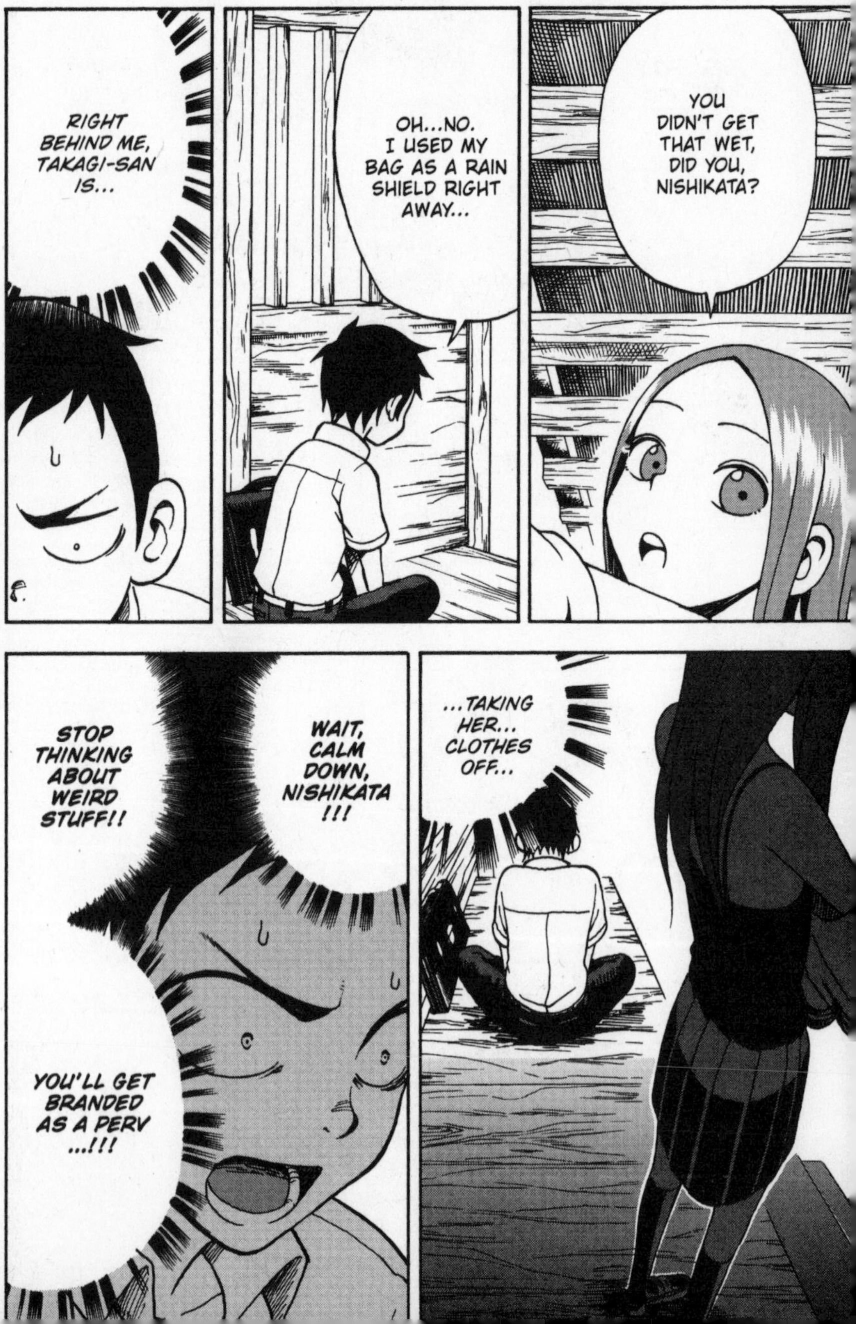
YOU DIDN'T GET THAT WET, DID YOU, NISHIKATA?
OH...NO. I USED MY BAG AS A RAIN SHIELD RIGHT AWAY...
RIGHT BEHIND ME, TAKAGI-SAN IS...
...TAKING HER... CLOTHES OFF...
WAIT, CALM DOWN, NISHIKATA!!!
STOP THINKING ABOUT WEIRD STUFF!!
YOU'LL GET BRANDED AS A PERV...!!!

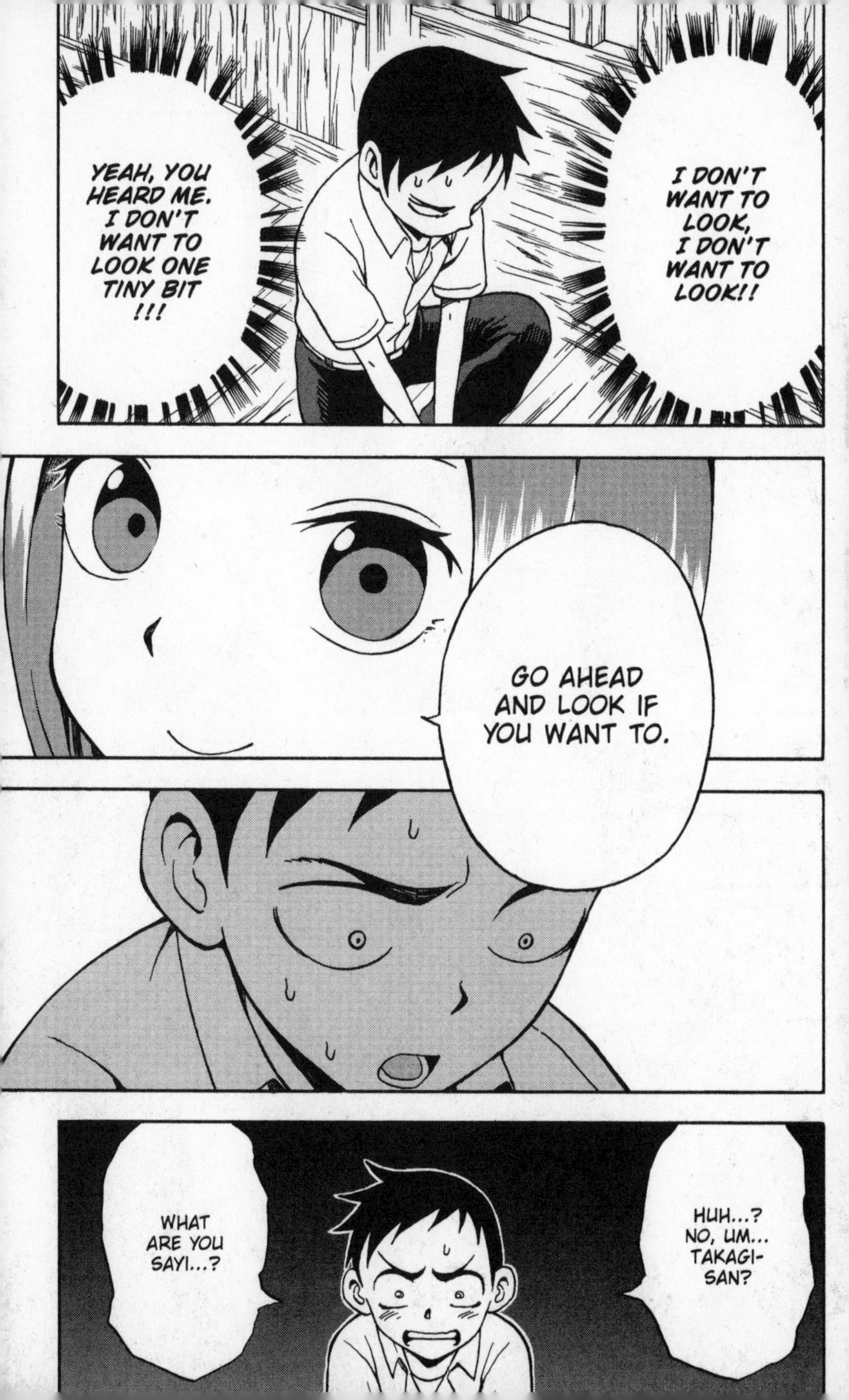
I DON'T WANT TO LOOK, I DON'T WANT TO LOOK!!
YEAH, YOU HEARD ME. I DON'T WANT TO LOOK ONE TINY BIT !!!
GO AHEAD AND LOOK IF YOU WANT TO.
HUH...? NO, UM... TAKAGI-SAN?
WHAT ARE YOU SAYI...?

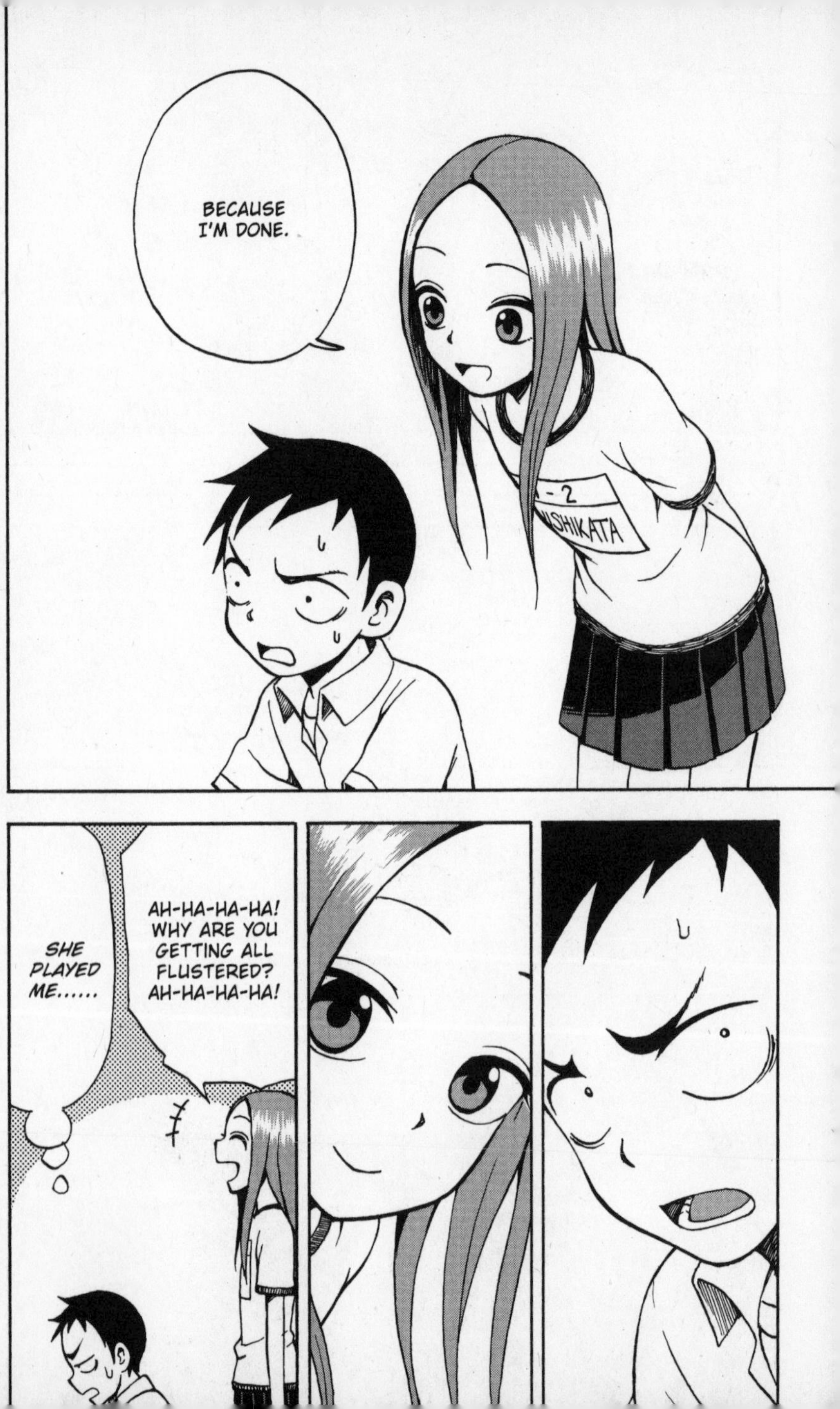
BECAUSE I'M DONE.
AH-HA-HA-HA! WHY ARE YOU GETTING ALL FLUSTERED? AH-HA-HA-HA!
SHE PLAYED ME......

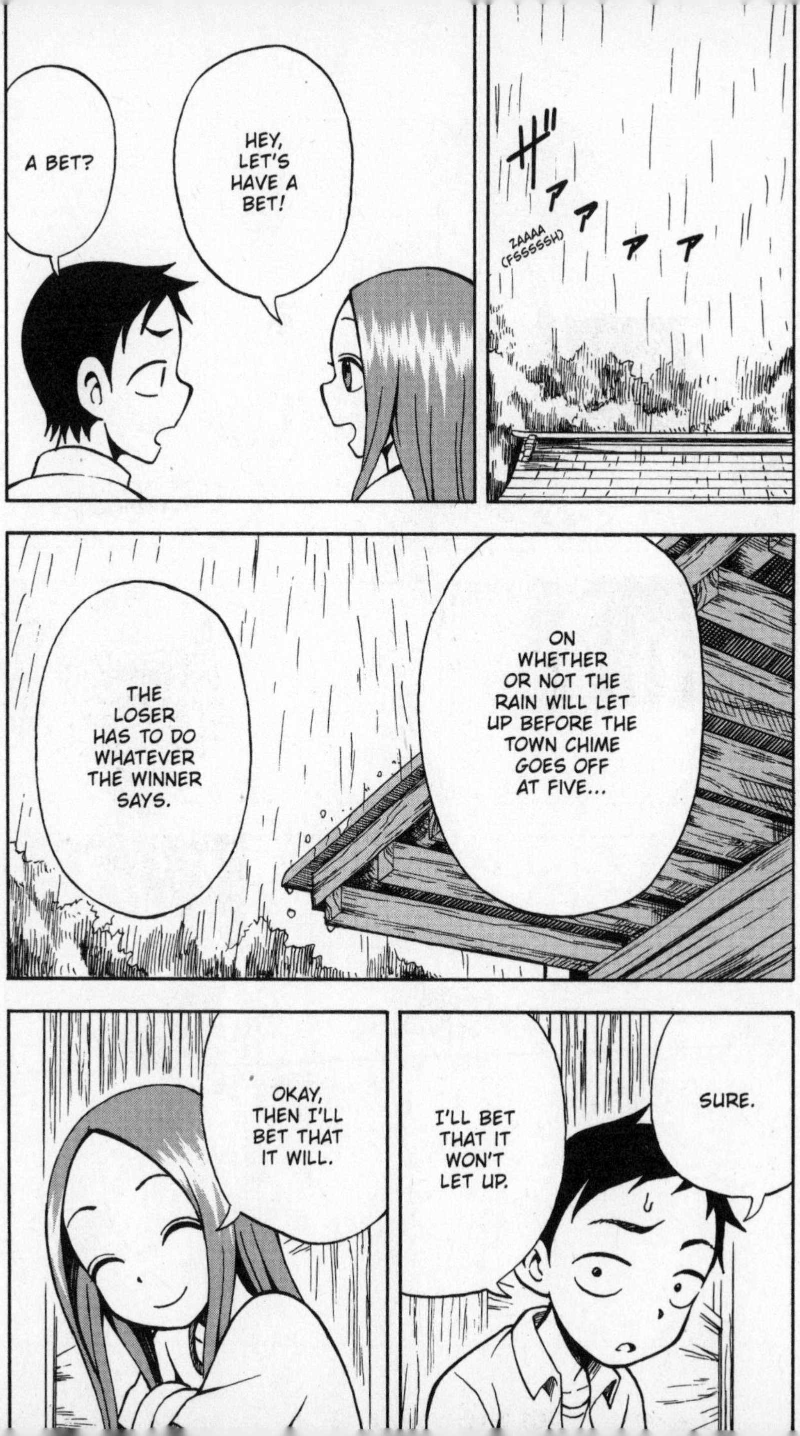
ZAAAA (FSSSSSH)
HEY, LET'S HAVE A BET!
A BET?
ON WHETHER OR NOT THE RAIN WILL LET UP BEFORE THE TOWN CHIME GOES OFF AT FIVE...
THE LOSER HAS TO DO WHATEVER THE WINNER SAYS.
SURE.
I'LL BET THAT IT WON'T LET UP.
OKAY, THEN I'LL BET THAT IT WILL.

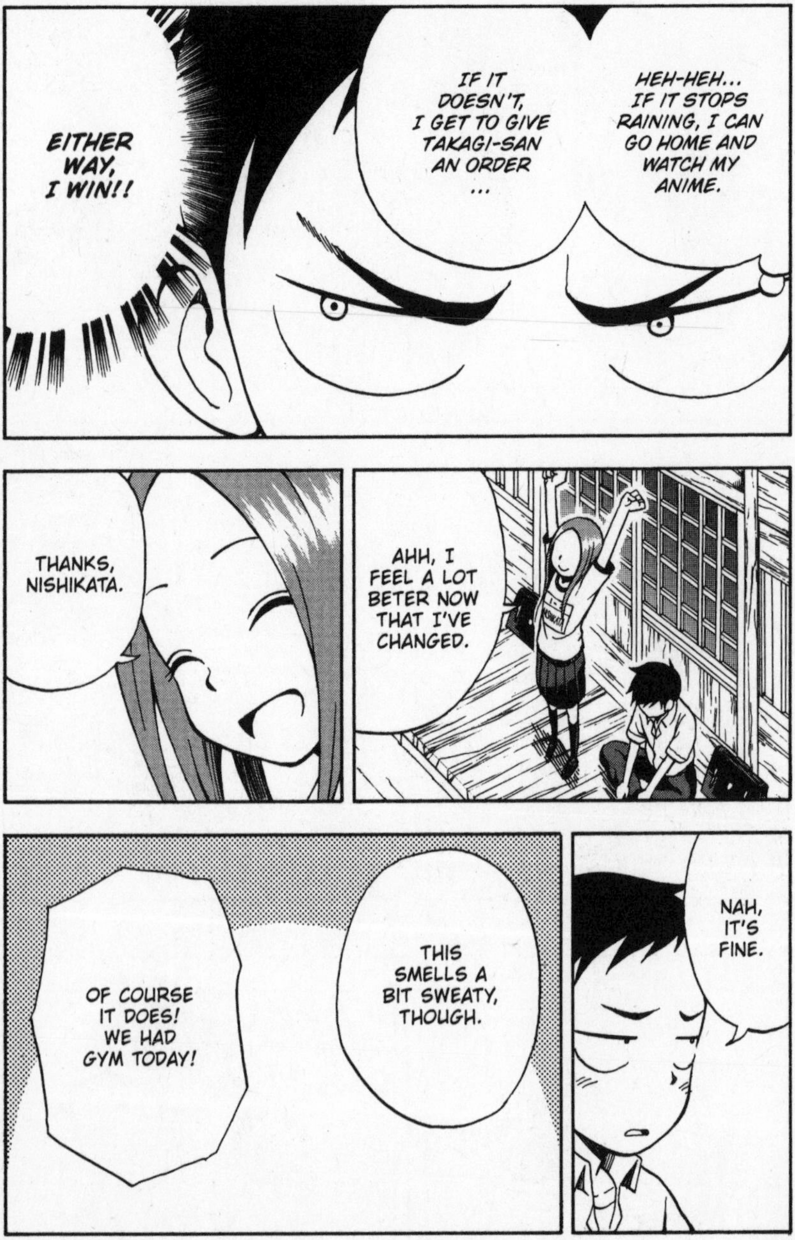
HEH-HEH... IF IT STOPS RAINING, I CAN GO HOME AND WATCH MY ANIME.
IF IT DOESN'T, I GET TO GIVE TAKAGI-SAN AN ORDER ...
EITHER WAY, I WIN!!
AHH, I FEEL A LOT BETER NOW THAT I'VE CHANGED.
THANKS, NISHIKATA.
NAH, IT'S FINE.
THIS SMELLS A BIT SWEATY, THOUGH.
OF COURSE IT DOES! WE HAD GYM TODAY!

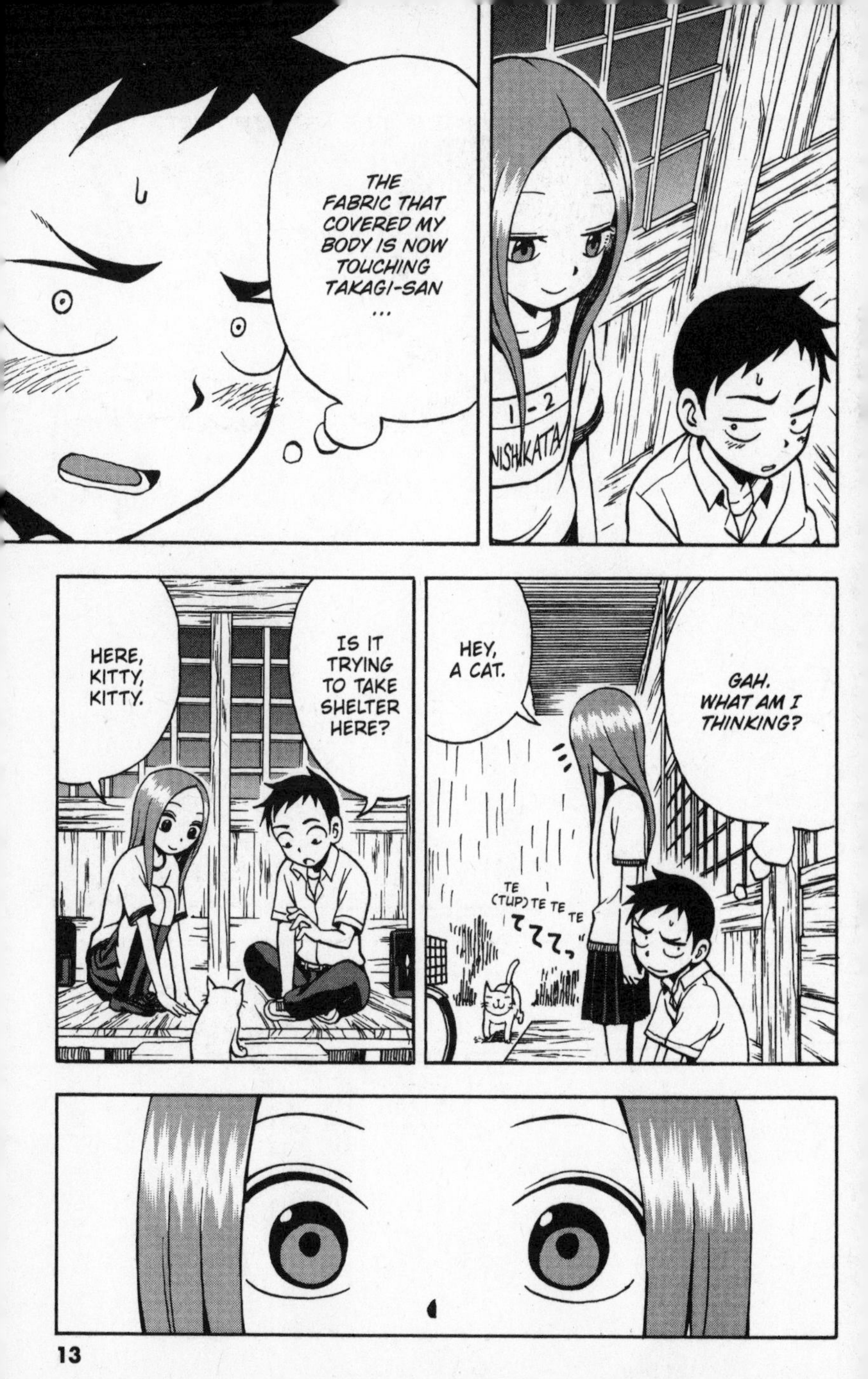
THE FABRIC THAT COVERED MY BODY IS NOW TOUCHING TAKAGI-SAN ...
1-2
NISHIKATA
GAH. WHAT AM I THINKING?
HEY, A CAT.
TE (TUP) TE TE TE
IS IT TRYING TO TAKE SHELTER HERE?
HERE, KITTY, KITTY.

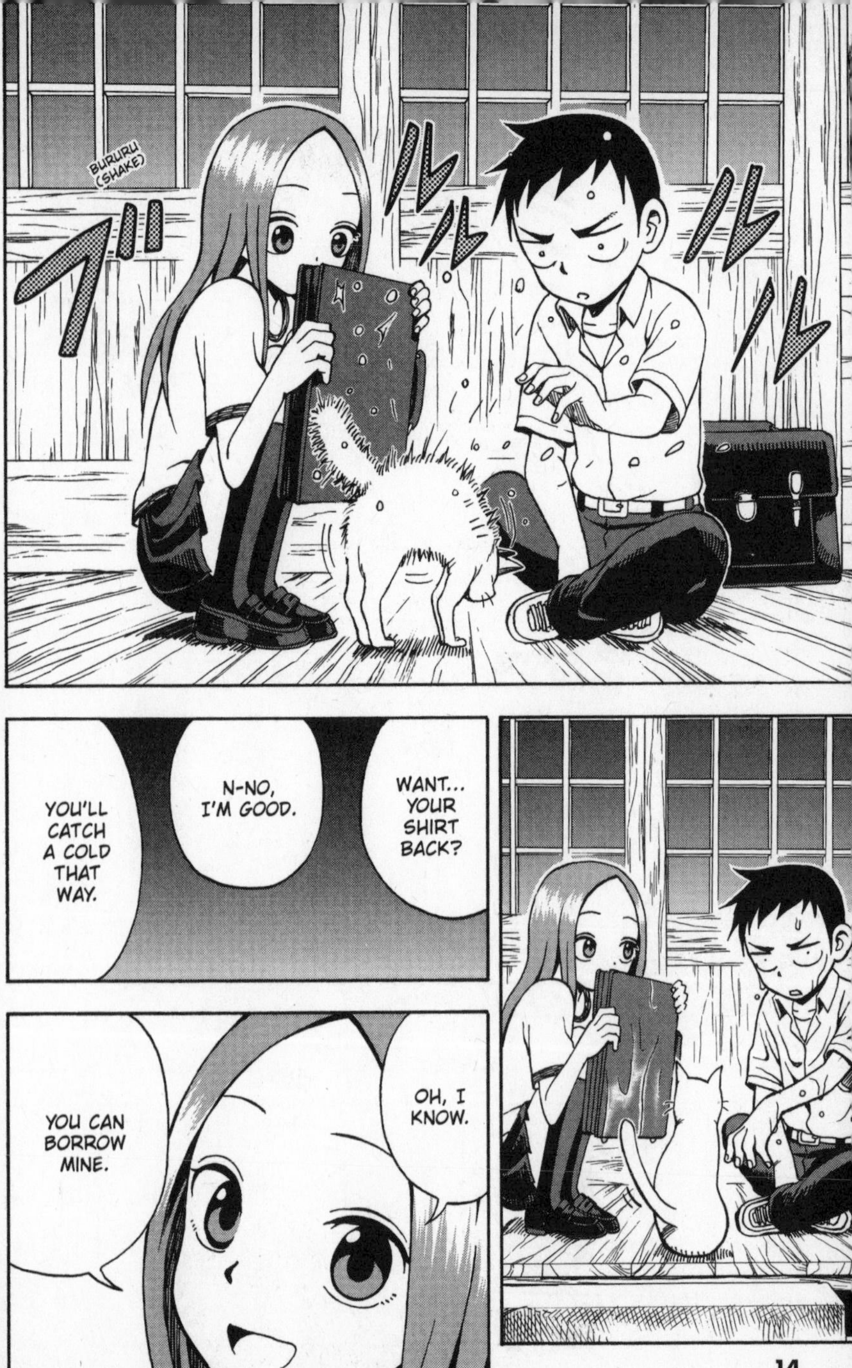
BURURU (SHAKE)
WANT... YOUR SHIRT BACK?
N-NO, I'M GOOD.
YOU'LL CATCH A COLD THAT WAY.
OH, I KNOW.
YOU CAN BORROW MINE.

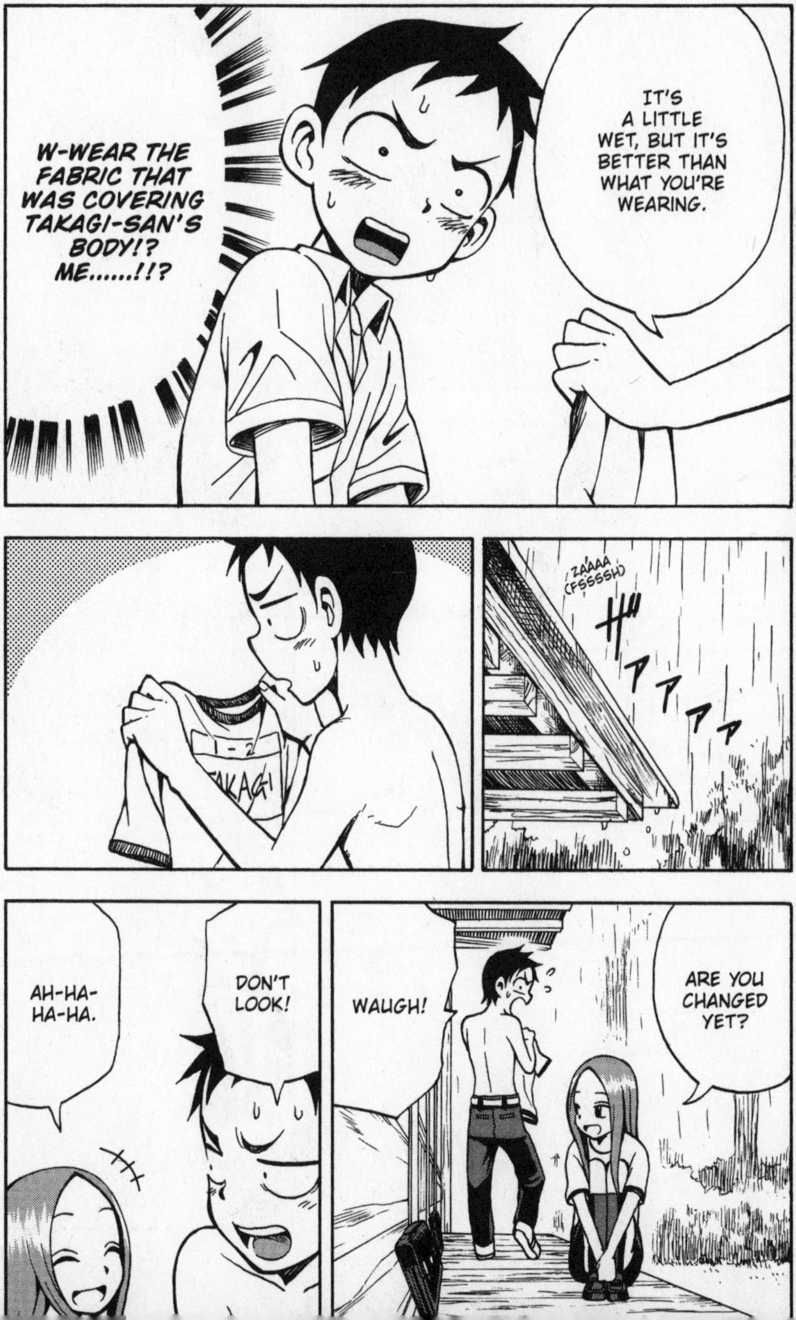
IT'S A LITTLE WET, BUT IT'S BETTER THAN WHAT YOU'RE WEARING.
W-WEAR THE FABRIC THAT WAS COVERING TAKAGI-SAN'S BODY!? ME......!!?
ZAAAA (FSSSSH)
1-2
TAKAGI
ARE YOU CHANGED YET?
WAUGH!
DON'T LOOK!
AH-HA-HA-HA.

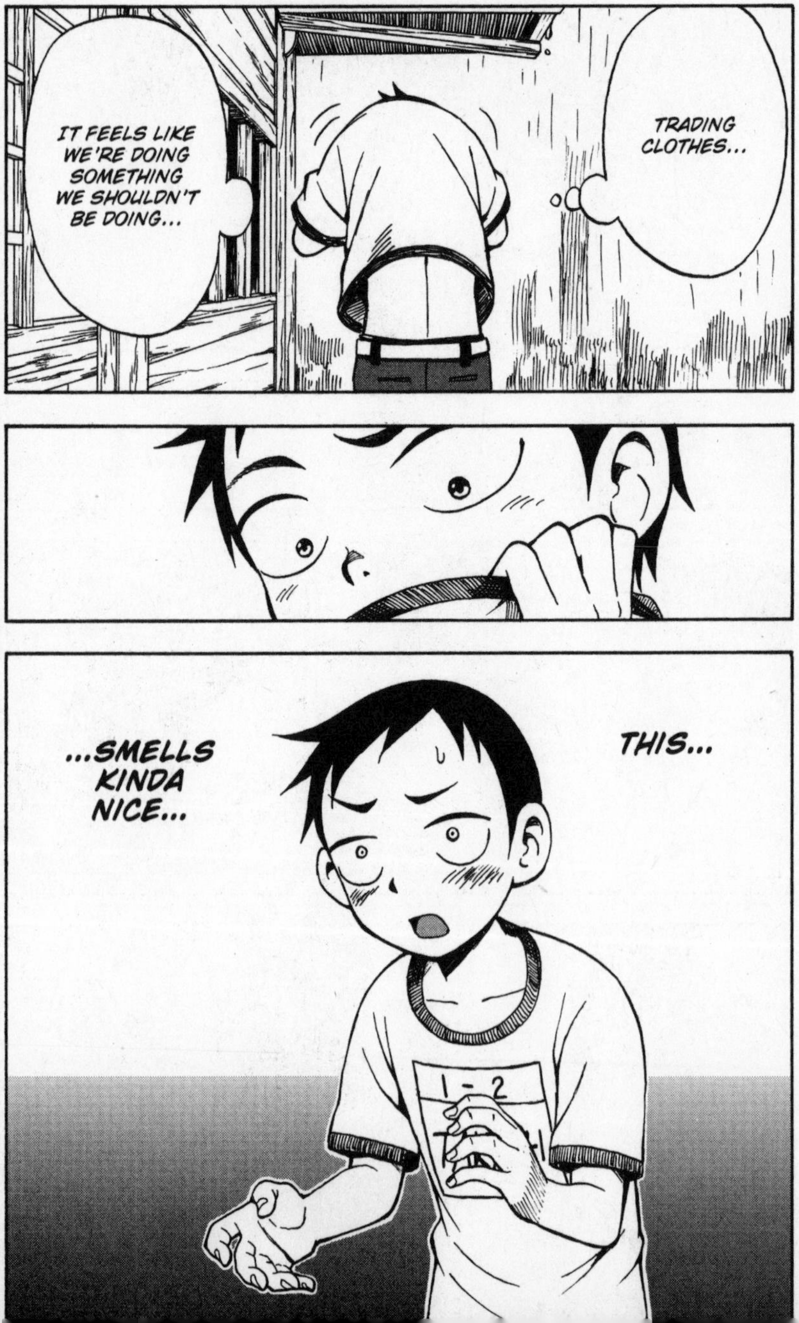
TRADING CLOTHES...
IT FEELS LIKE WE'RE DOING SOMETHING WE SHOULDN'T BE DOING...
THIS...
...SMELLS KINDA NICE...

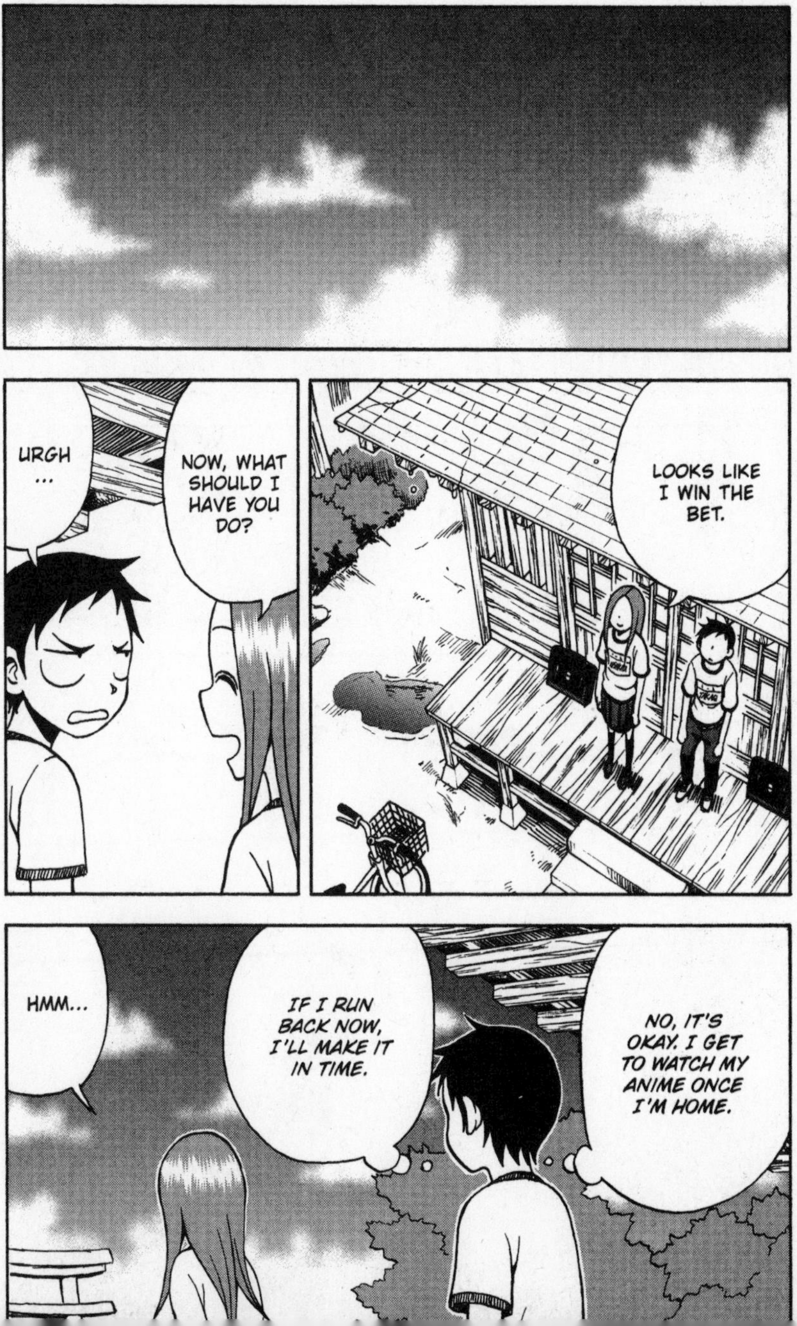
LOOKS LIKE I WIN THE BET.
NOW, WHAT SHOULD I HAVE YOU DO?
URGH...
NO, IT'S OKAY. I GET TO WATCH MY ANIME ONCE I'M HOME.
IF I RUN BACK NOW, I'LL MAKE IT IN TIME.
HMM...

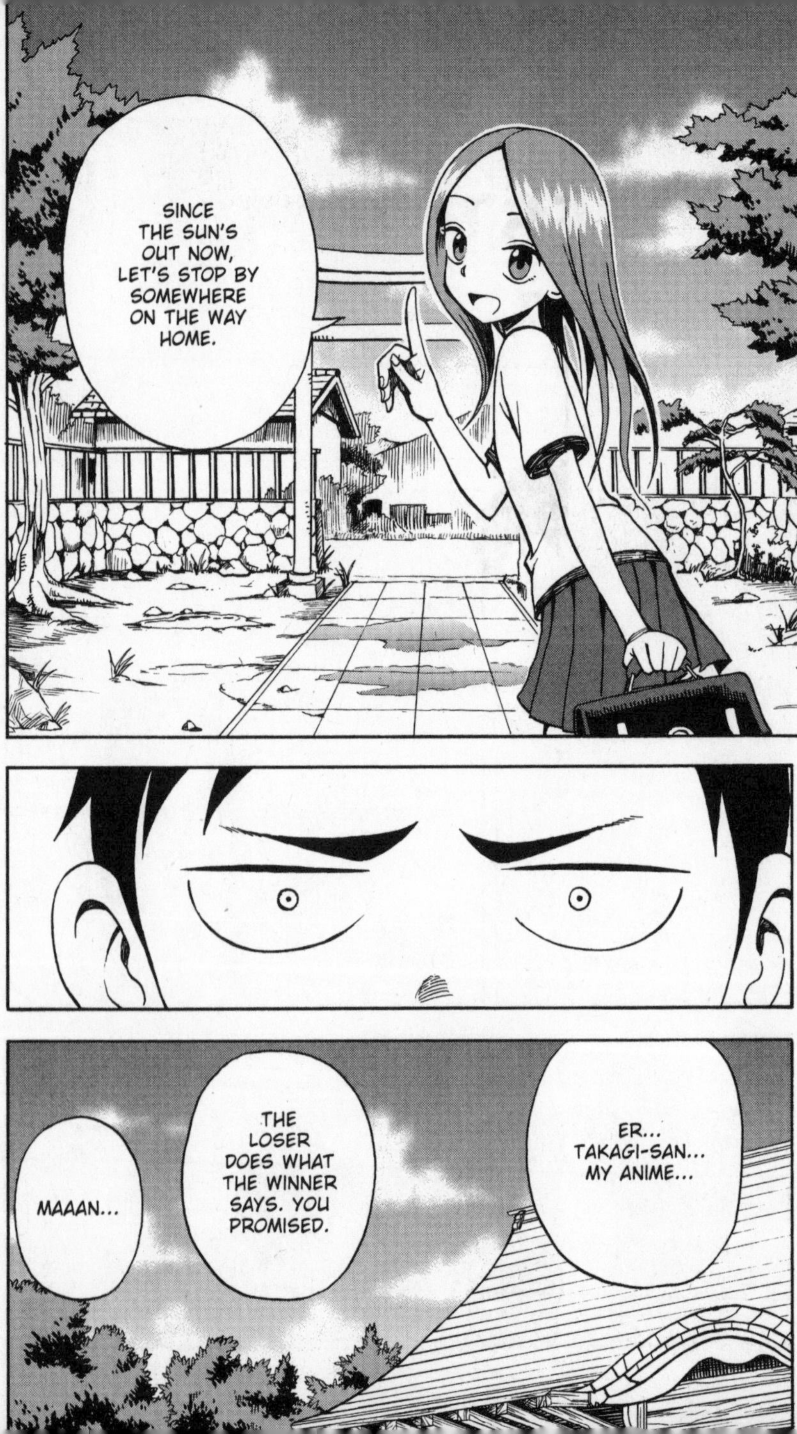
SINCE THE SUN'S OUT NOW, LET'S STOP BY SOMEWHERE ON THE WAY HOME.
ER... TAKAGI-SAN... MY ANIME...
THE LOSER DOES WHAT THE WINNER SAYS. YOU PROMISED.
MAAAN...

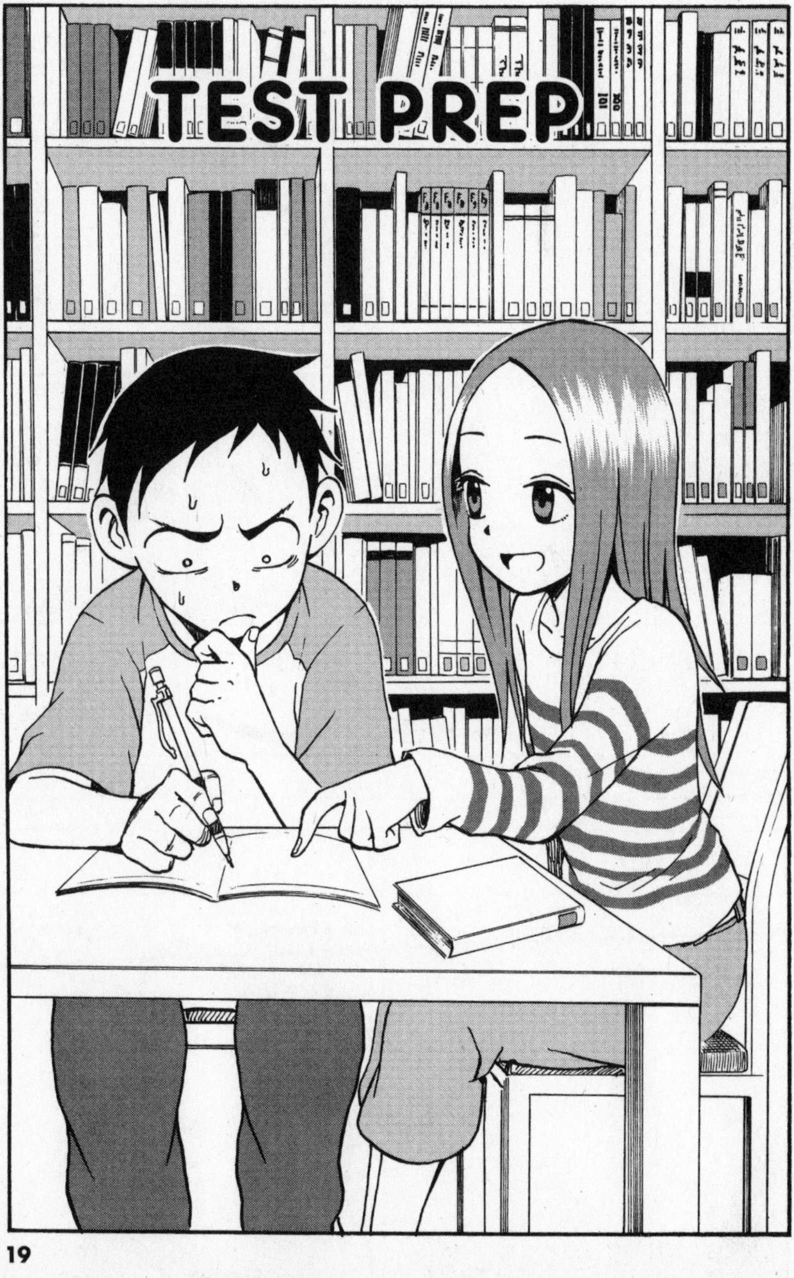
TEST PREP

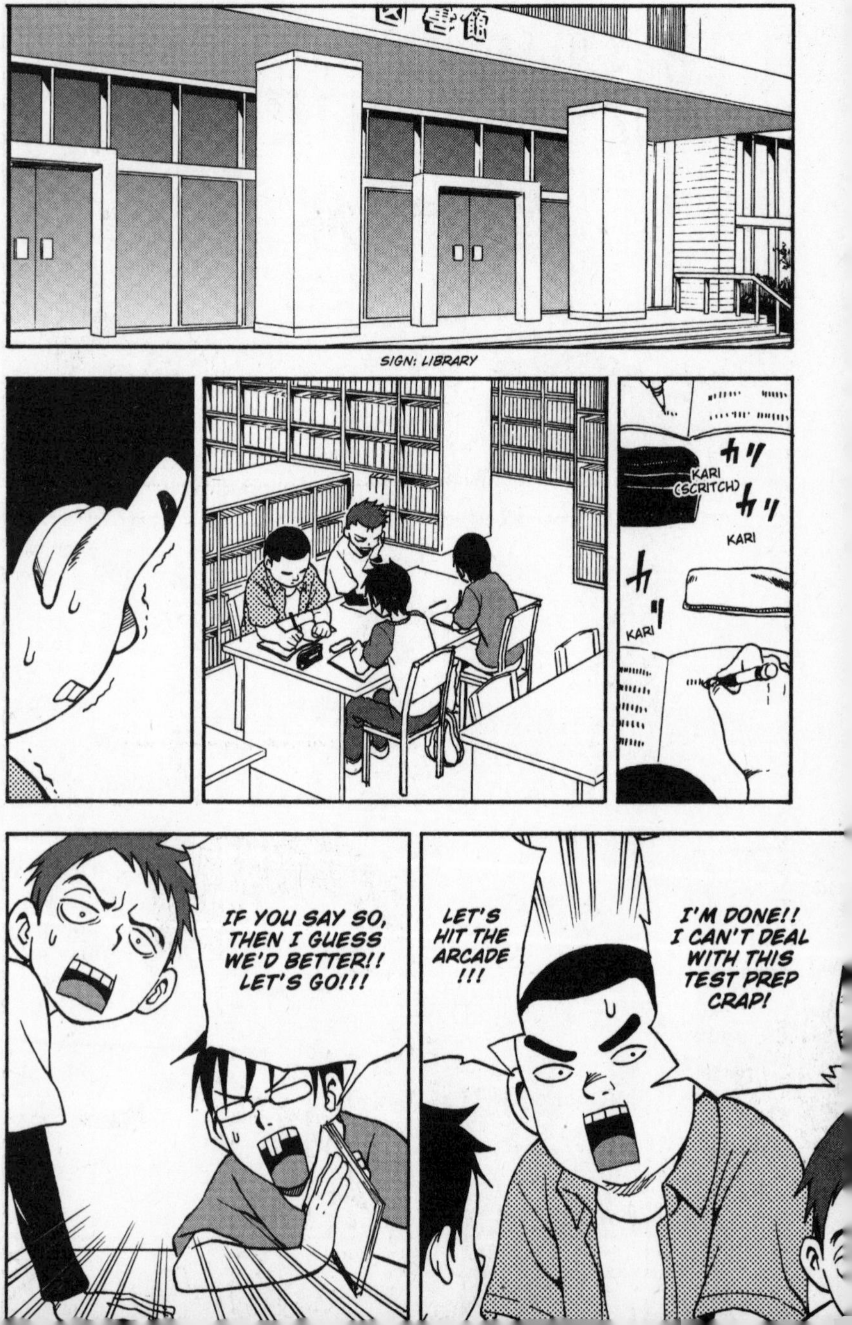
図書館
SIGN: LIBRARY
カリ
KARI (SCRITCH)
カリ
KARI
カリ
KARI
I'M DONE!! I CAN'T DEAL WITH THIS TEST PREP CRAP!
LET'S HIT THE ARCADE!!!
IF YOU SAY SO, THEN I GUESS WE'D BETTER!! LET'S GO!!!

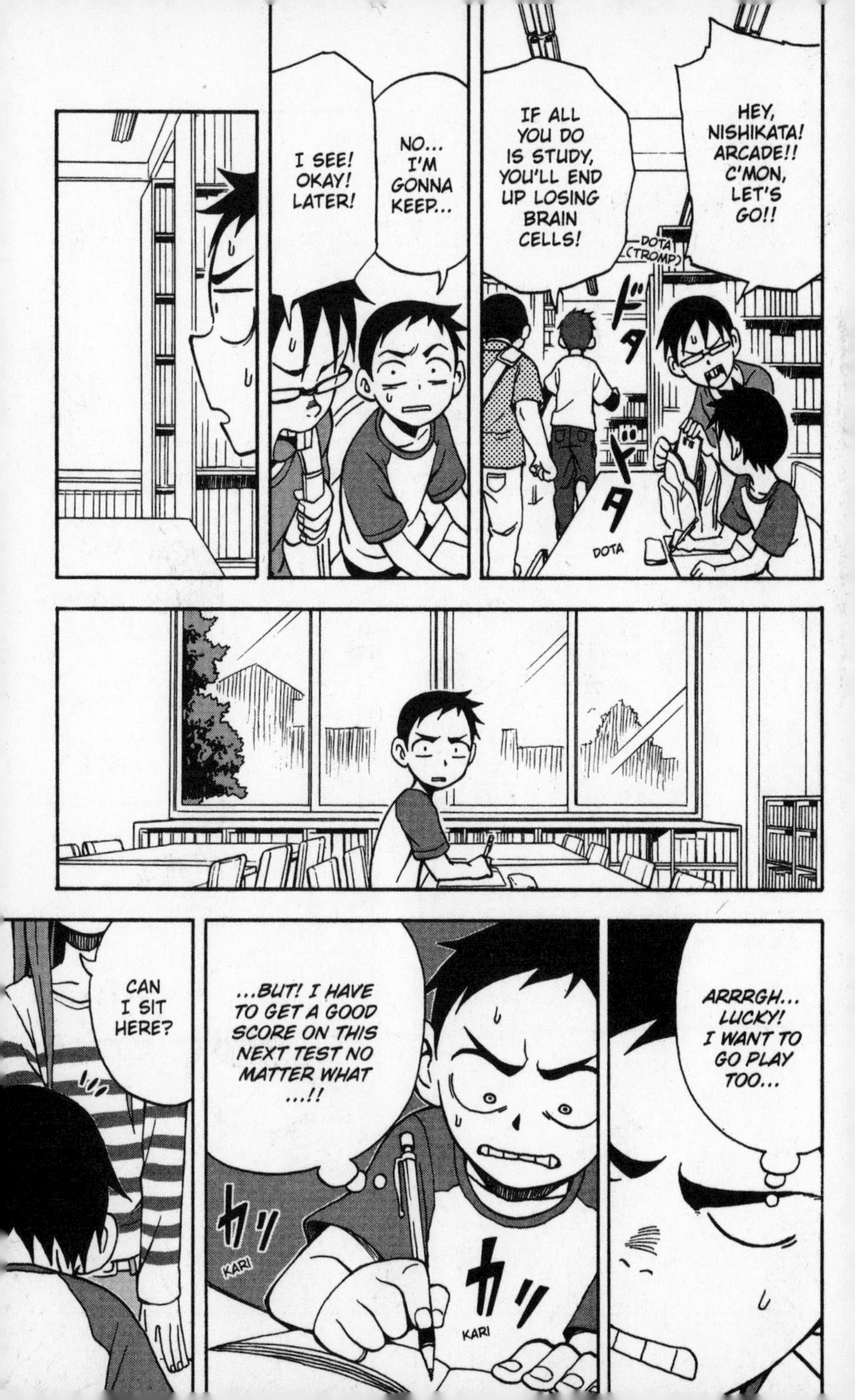
HEY, NISHIKATA! ARCADE!! C'MON, LET'S GO!!
IF ALL YOU DO IS STUDY, YOU'LL END UP LOSING BRAIN CELLS!
DOTA (TROMP)
DOTA
NO... I'M GONNA KEEP...
I SEE! OKAY! LATER!
ARRRGH... LUCKY! I WANT TO GO PLAY TOO...
...BUT! I HAVE TO GET A GOOD SCORE ON THIS NEXT TEST NO MATTER WHAT ...!!
KARI
KARI
CAN I SIT HERE?

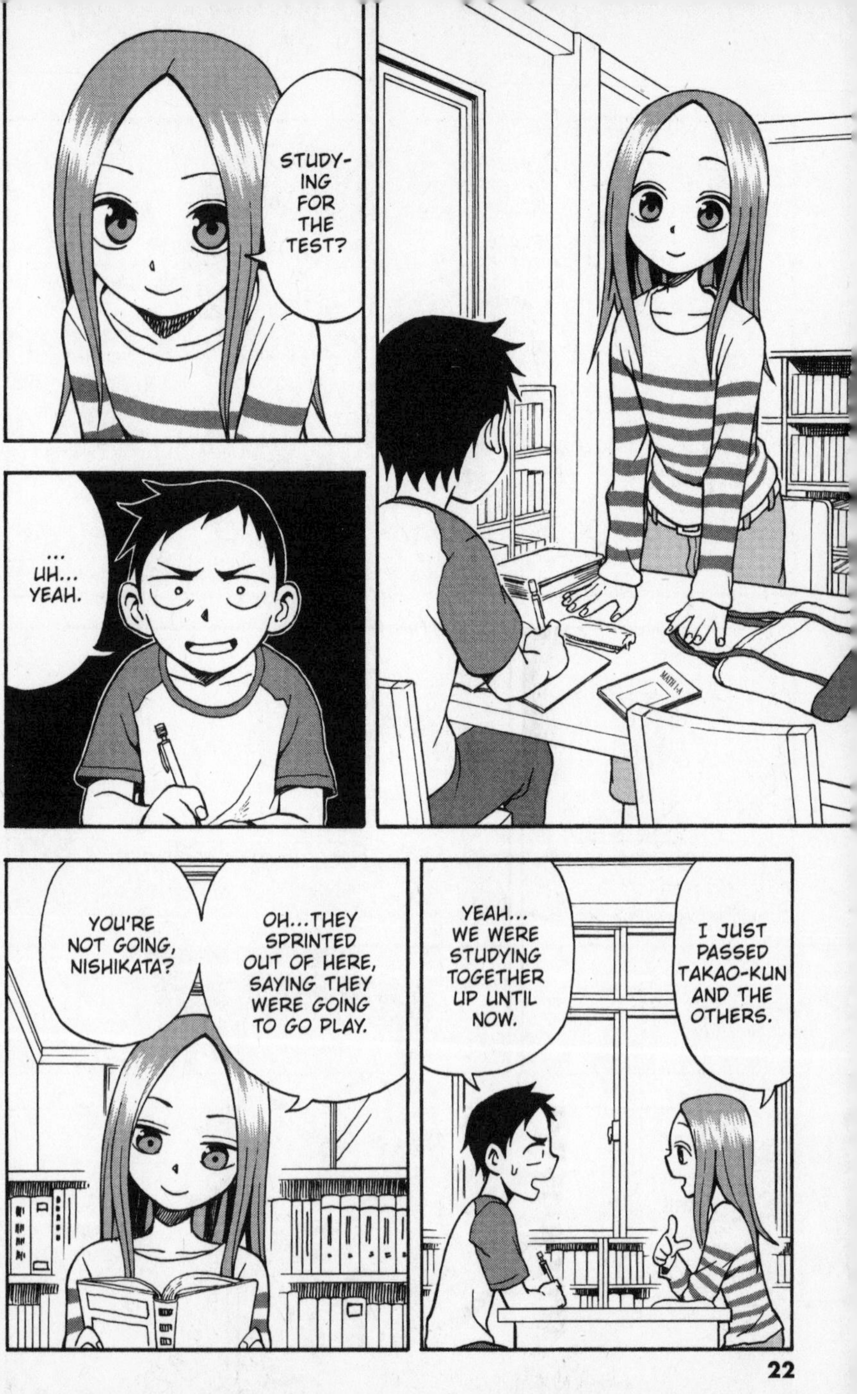
STUDYING FOR THE TEST?
... UH... YEAH.
I JUST PASSED TAKAO-KUN AND THE OTHERS.
YEAH... WE WERE STUDYING TOGETHER UP UNTIL NOW.
OH...THEY SPRINTED OUT OF HERE, SAYING THEY WERE GOING TO GO PLAY.
YOU'RE NOT GOING, NISHIKATA?

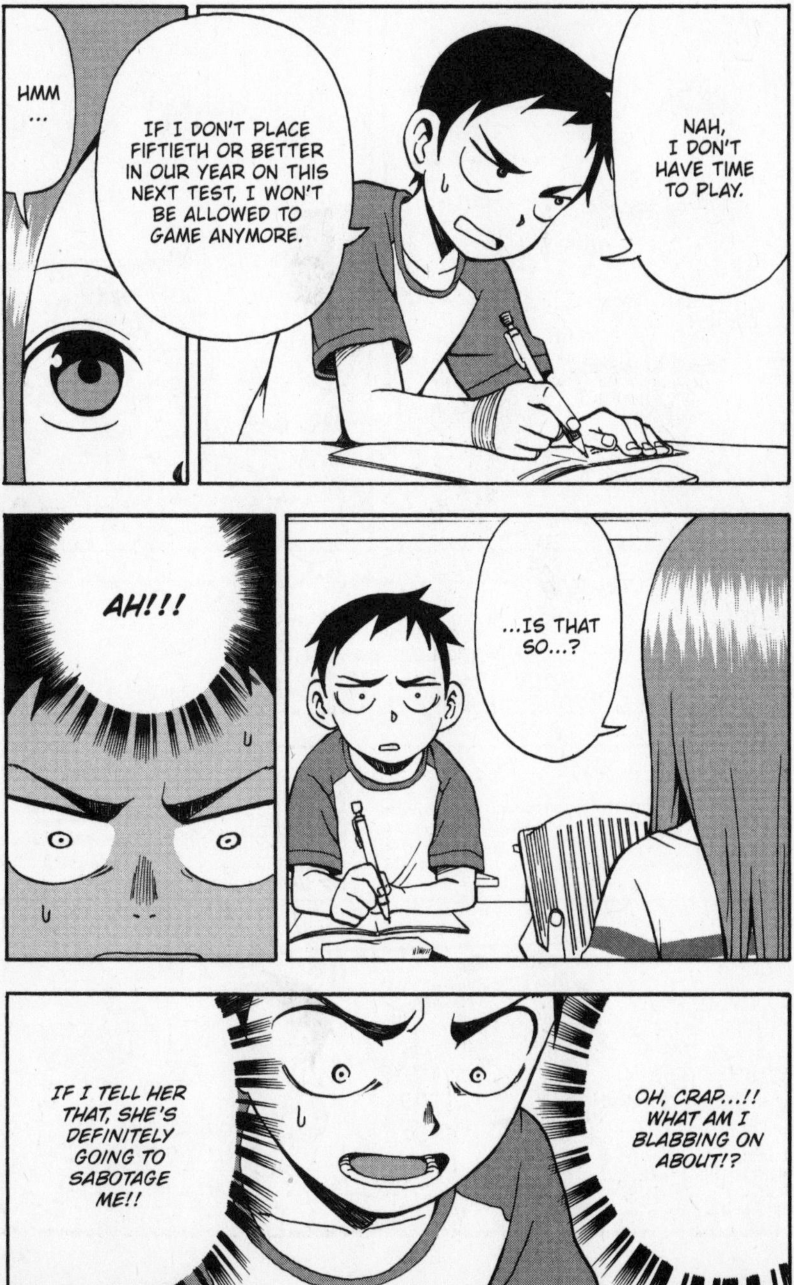
NAH, I DON'T HAVE TIME TO PLAY.
IF I DON'T PLACE FIFTIETH OR BETTER IN OUR YEAR ON THIS NEXT TEST, I WON'T BE ALLOWED TO GAME ANYMORE.
HMM ...
...IS THAT SO...?
AH!!!
OH, CRAP...!! WHAT AM I BLABBING ON ABOUT!?
IF I TELL HER THAT, SHE'S DEFINITELY GOING TO SABOTAGE ME!!

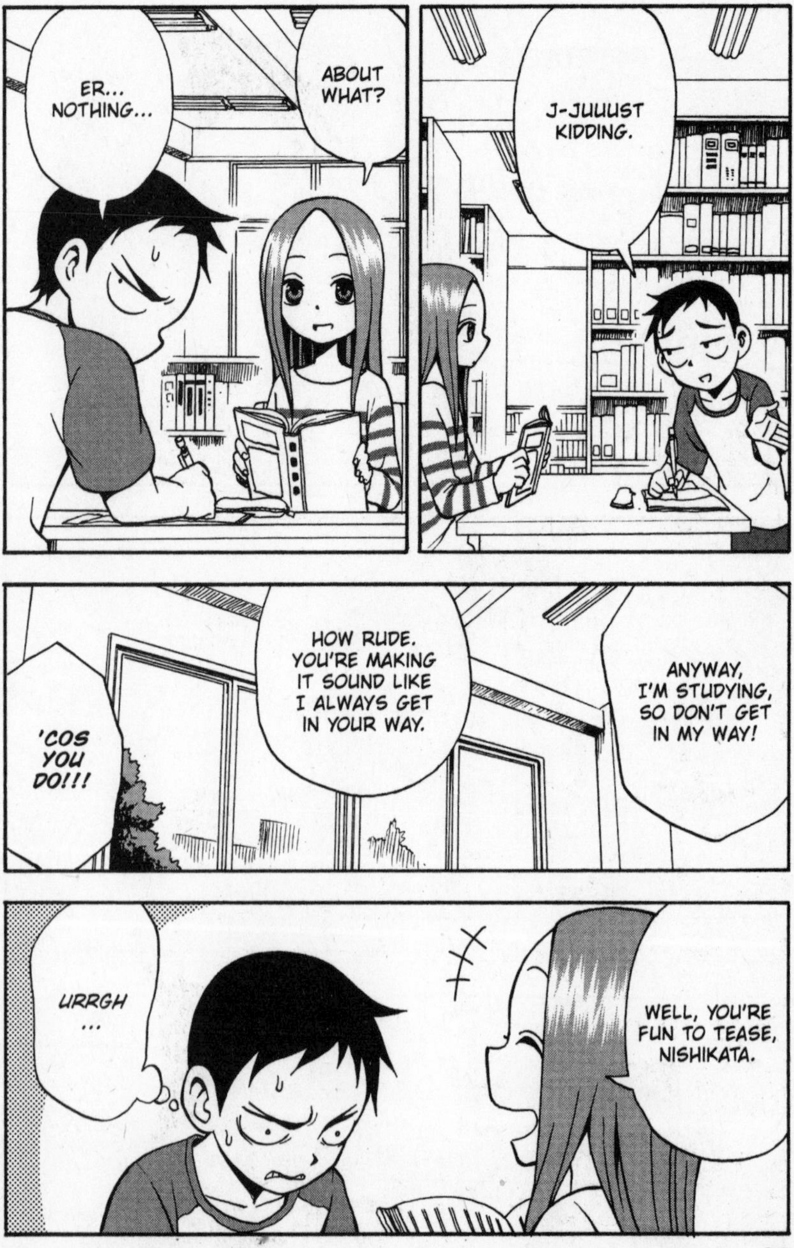
J-JUUUST KIDDING.
ABOUT WHAT?
ER... NOTHING...
ANYWAY, I'M STUDYING, SO DON'T GET IN MY WAY!
HOW RUDE. YOU'RE MAKING IT SOUND LIKE I ALWAYS GET IN YOUR WAY.
'COS YOU DO!!!
WELL, YOU'RE FUN TO TEASE, NISHIKATA.
URRGH ...

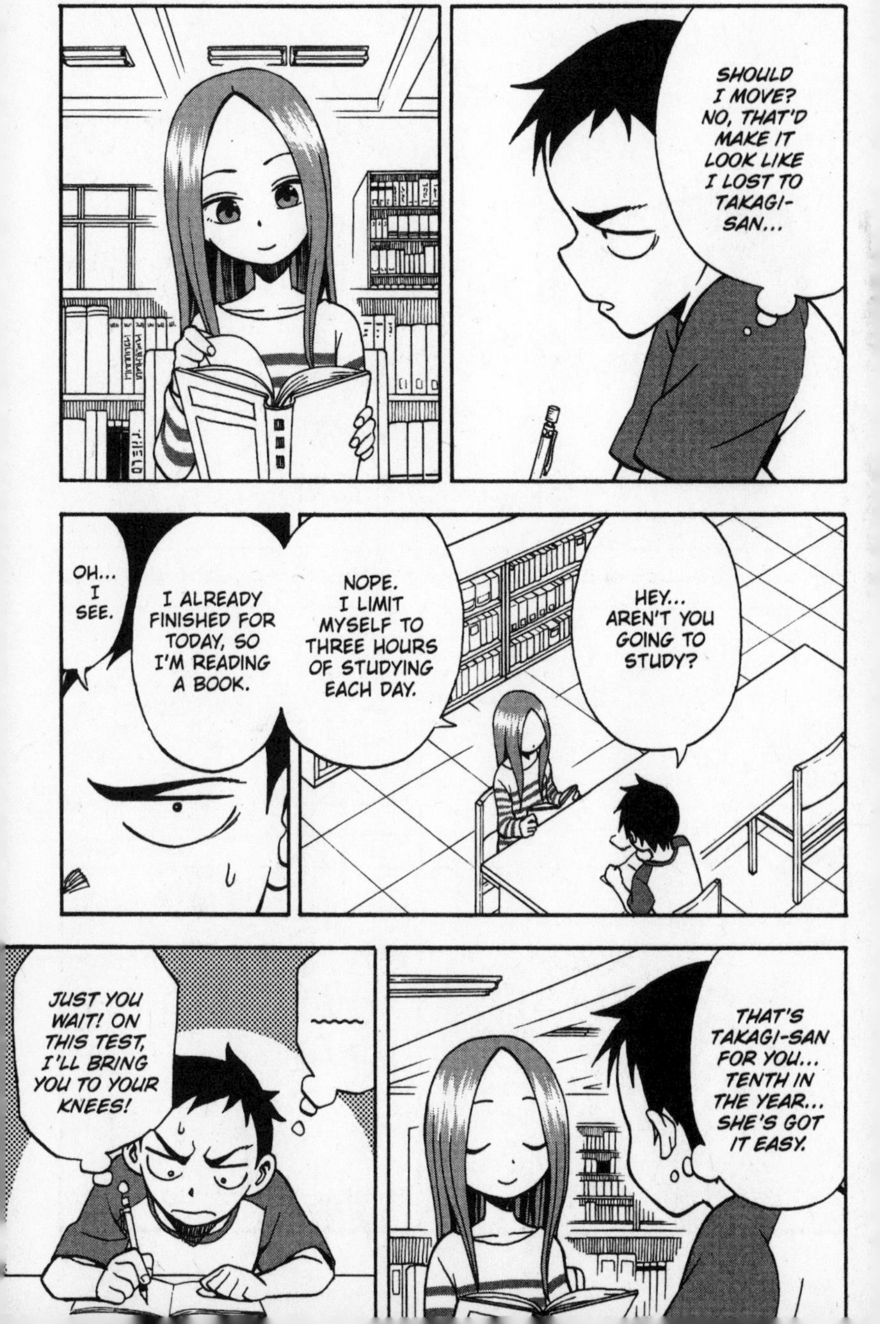
SHOULD I MOVE? NO, THAT'D MAKE IT LOOK LIKE I LOST TO TAKAGI-SAN...
HEY... AREN'T YOU GOING TO STUDY?
NOPE. I LIMIT MYSELF TO THREE HOURS OF STUDYING EACH DAY.
I ALREADY FINISHED FOR TODAY, SO I'M READING A BOOK.
OH... I SEE.
THAT'S TAKAGI-SAN FOR YOU... TENTH IN THE YEAR... SHE'S GOT IT EASY.
~~~
JUST YOU WAIT! ON THIS TEST, I'LL BRING YOU TO YOUR KNEES!
~~~

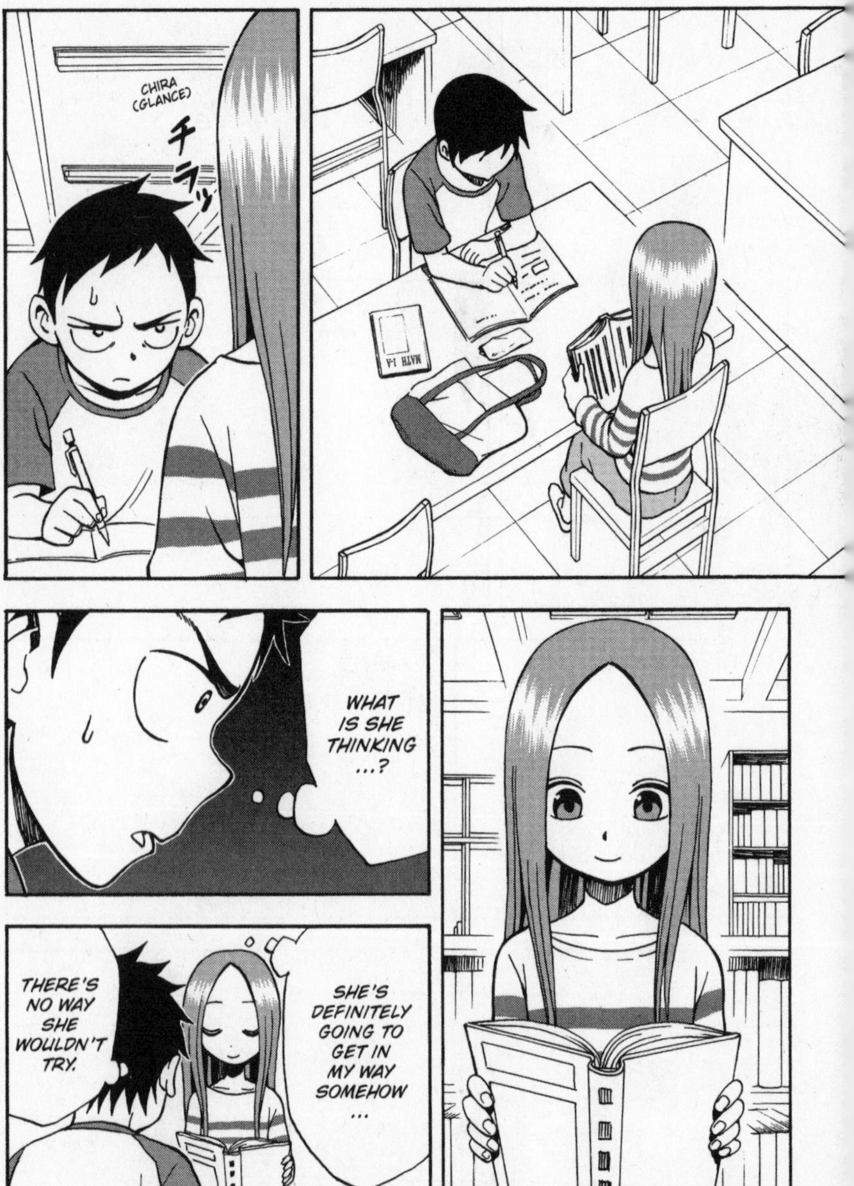
MATH I-A
CHIRA (GLANCE)
チラッ
WHAT IS SHE THINKING ...?
SHE'S DEFINITELY GOING TO GET IN MY WAY SOMEHOW ...
THERE'S NO WAY SHE WOULDN'T TRY.

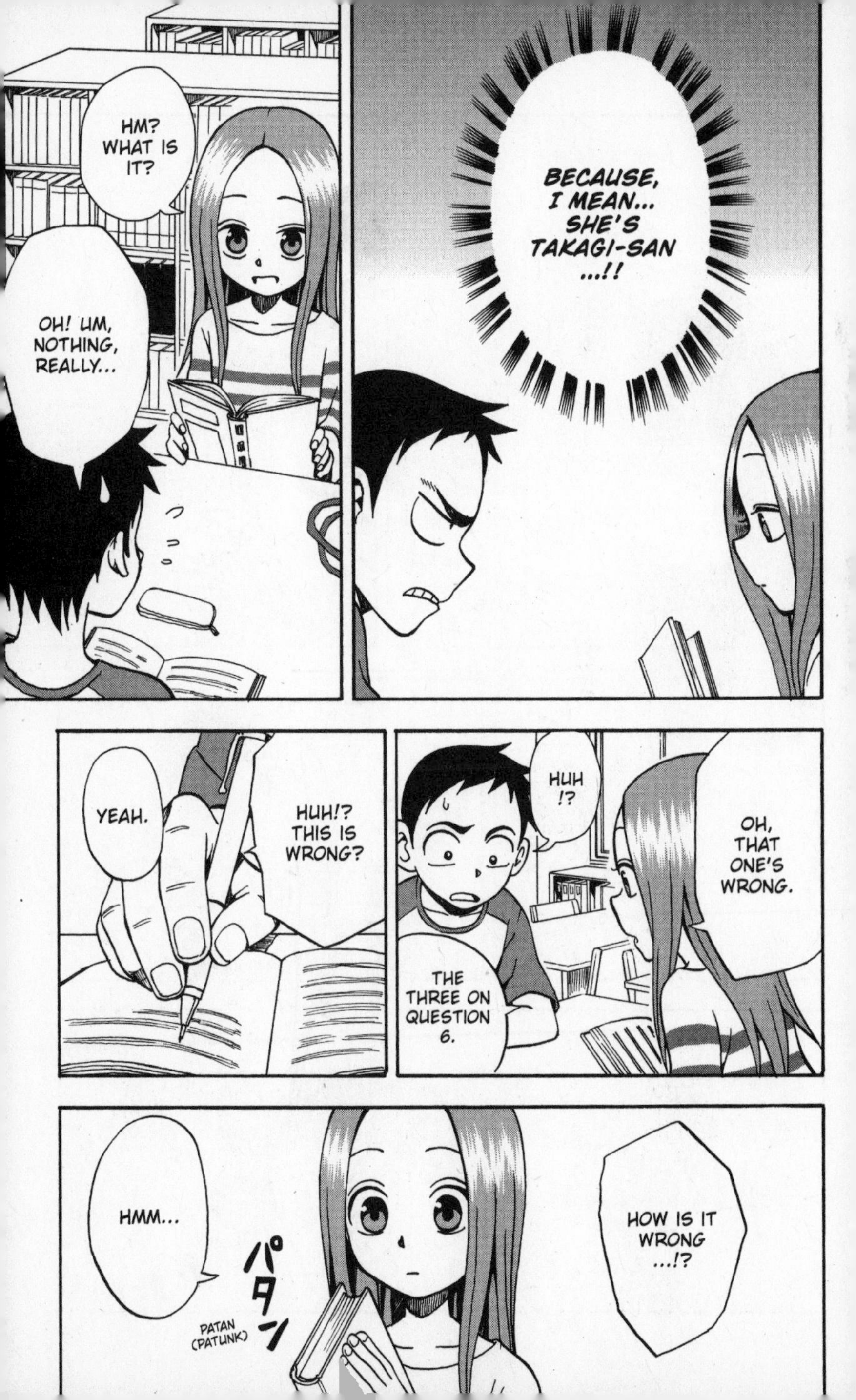
BECAUSE, I MEAN... SHE'S TAKAGI-SAN ...!!
HM? WHAT IS IT?
OH! UM, NOTHING, REALLY...
OH, THAT ONE'S WRONG.
HUH !?
THE THREE ON QUESTION 6.
HUH!? THIS IS WRONG?
YEAH.
HOW IS IT WRONG ...!?
パタン
PATAN (PATUNK)
HMM...

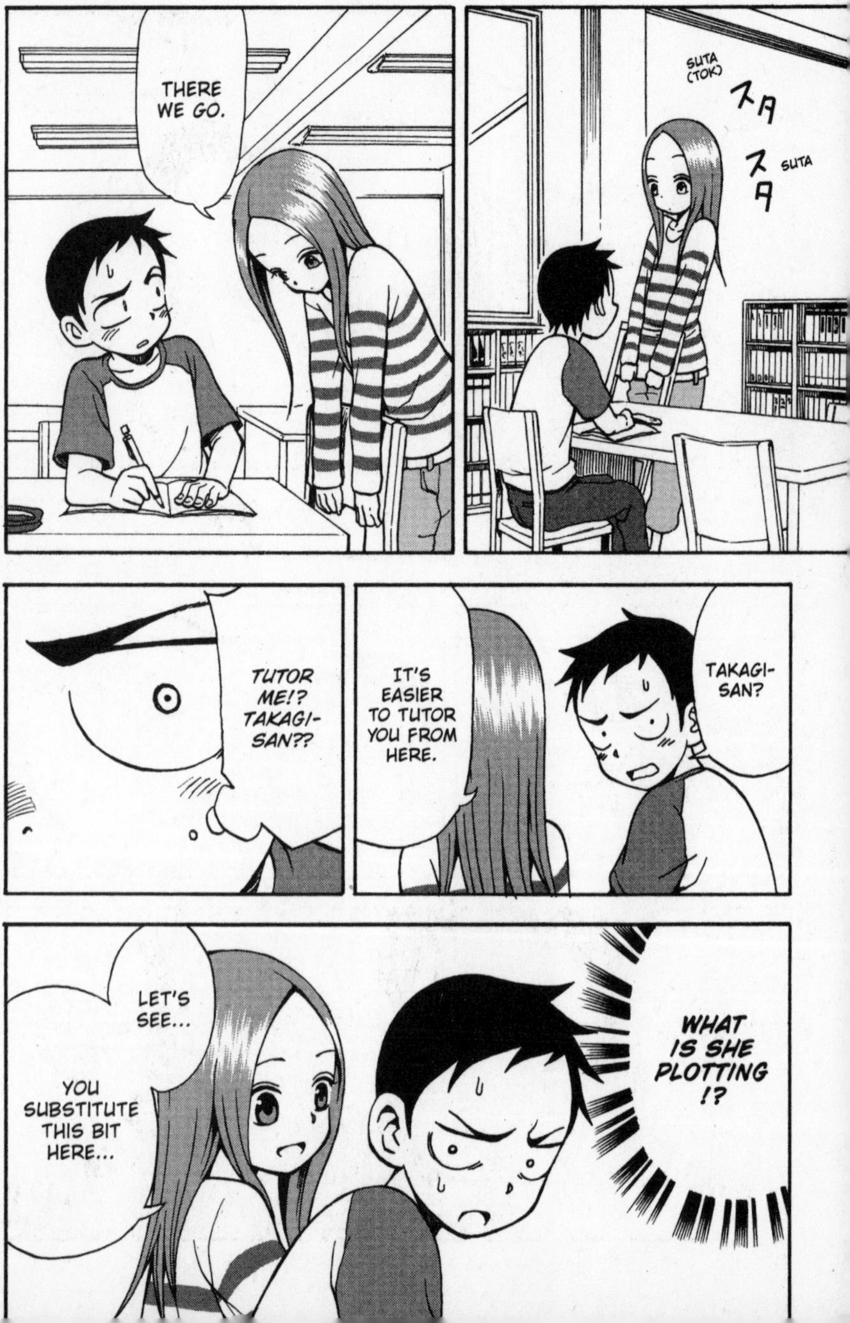
SUTA (TOK)
スタ
スタ
SUTA
THERE WE GO.
TAKAGI-SAN?
IT'S EASIER TO TUTOR YOU FROM HERE.
TUTOR ME!? TAKAGI-SAN??
WHAT IS SHE PLOTTING !?
LET'S SEE...
YOU SUBSTITUTE THIS BIT HERE...

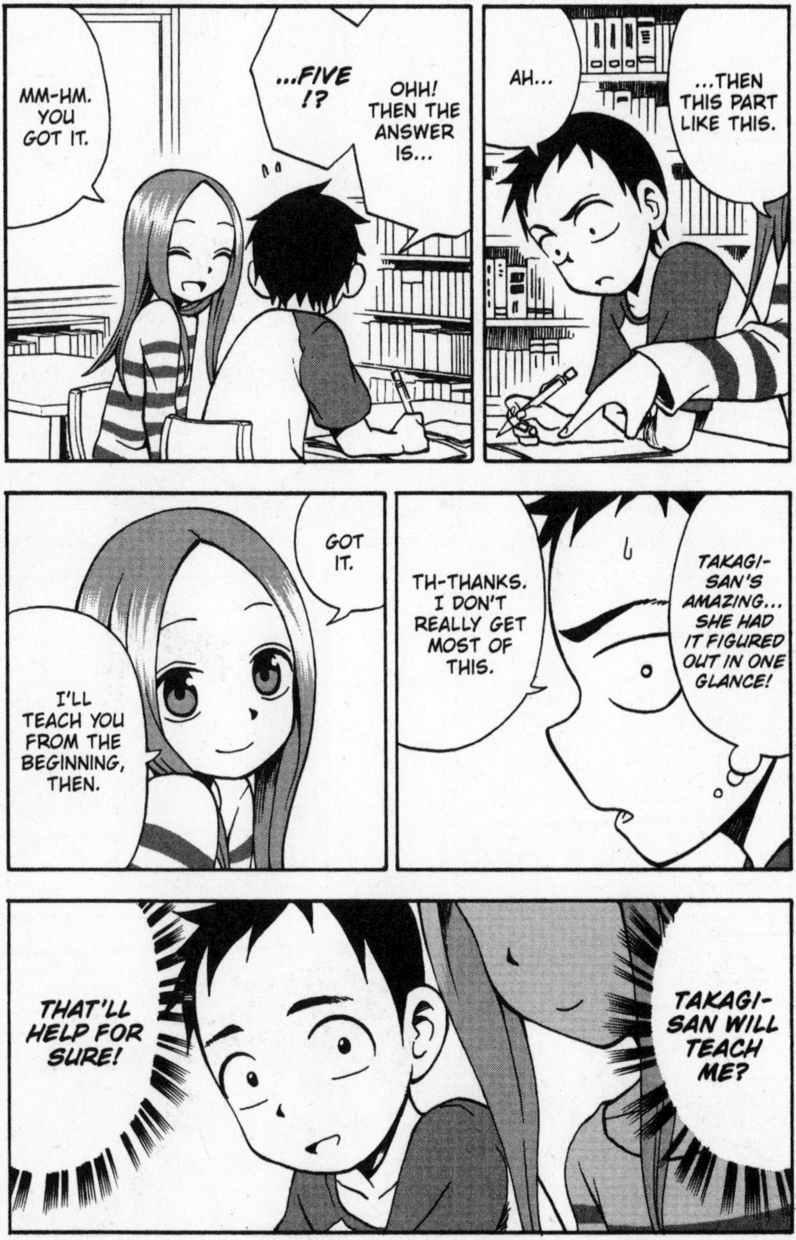
...THEN THIS PART LIKE THIS.
AH...
OHH! THEN THE ANSWER IS...
...FIVE !?
MM-HM. YOU GOT IT.
TAKAGI-SAN'S AMAZING... SHE HAD IT FIGURED OUT IN ONE GLANCE!
TH-THANKS. I DON'T REALLY GET MOST OF THIS.
GOT IT.
I'LL TEACH YOU FROM THE BEGINNING, THEN.
TAKAGI-SAN WILL TEACH ME?
THAT'LL HELP FOR SURE!

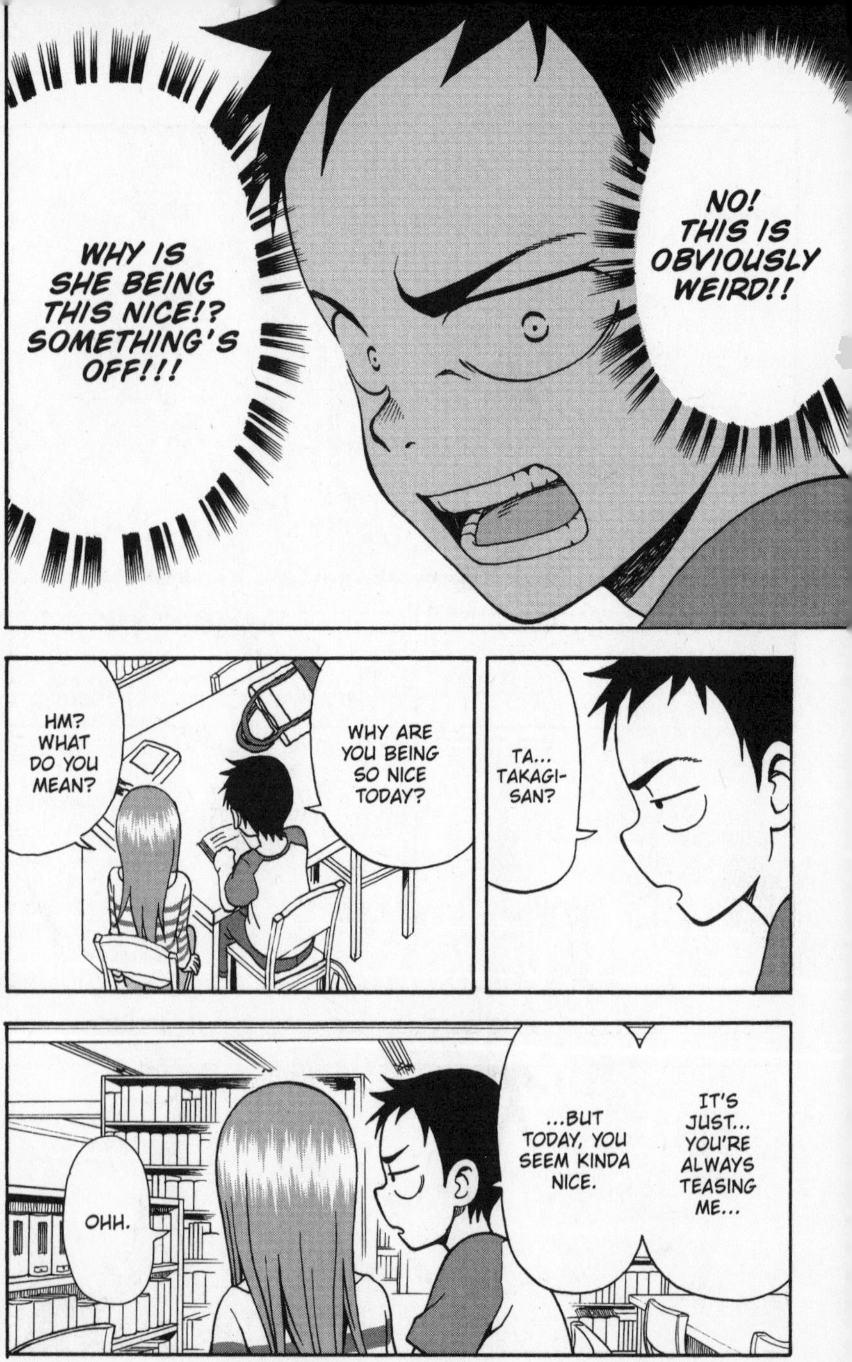
NO! THIS IS OBVIOUSLY WEIRD!!
WHY IS SHE BEING THIS NICE!? SOMETHING'S OFF!!!
TA... TAKAGI-SAN?
WHY ARE YOU BEING SO NICE TODAY?
HM? WHAT DO YOU MEAN?
IT'S JUST... YOU'RE ALWAYS TEASING ME...
...BUT TODAY, YOU SEEM KINDA NICE.
OHH.

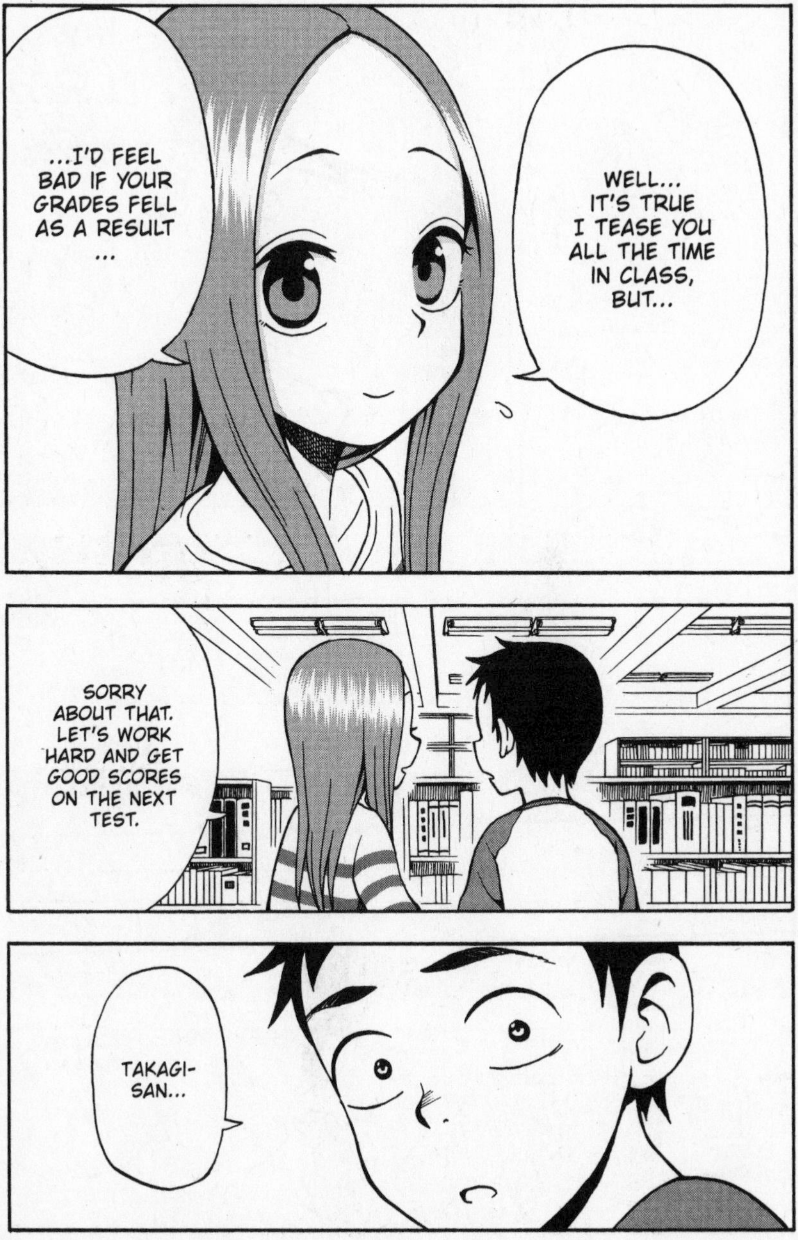
WELL... IT'S TRUE I TEASE YOU ALL THE TIME IN CLASS, BUT...
...I'D FEEL BAD IF YOUR GRADES FELL AS A RESULT ...
SORRY ABOUT THAT. LET'S WORK HARD AND GET GOOD SCORES ON THE NEXT TEST.
TAKAGI-SAN...

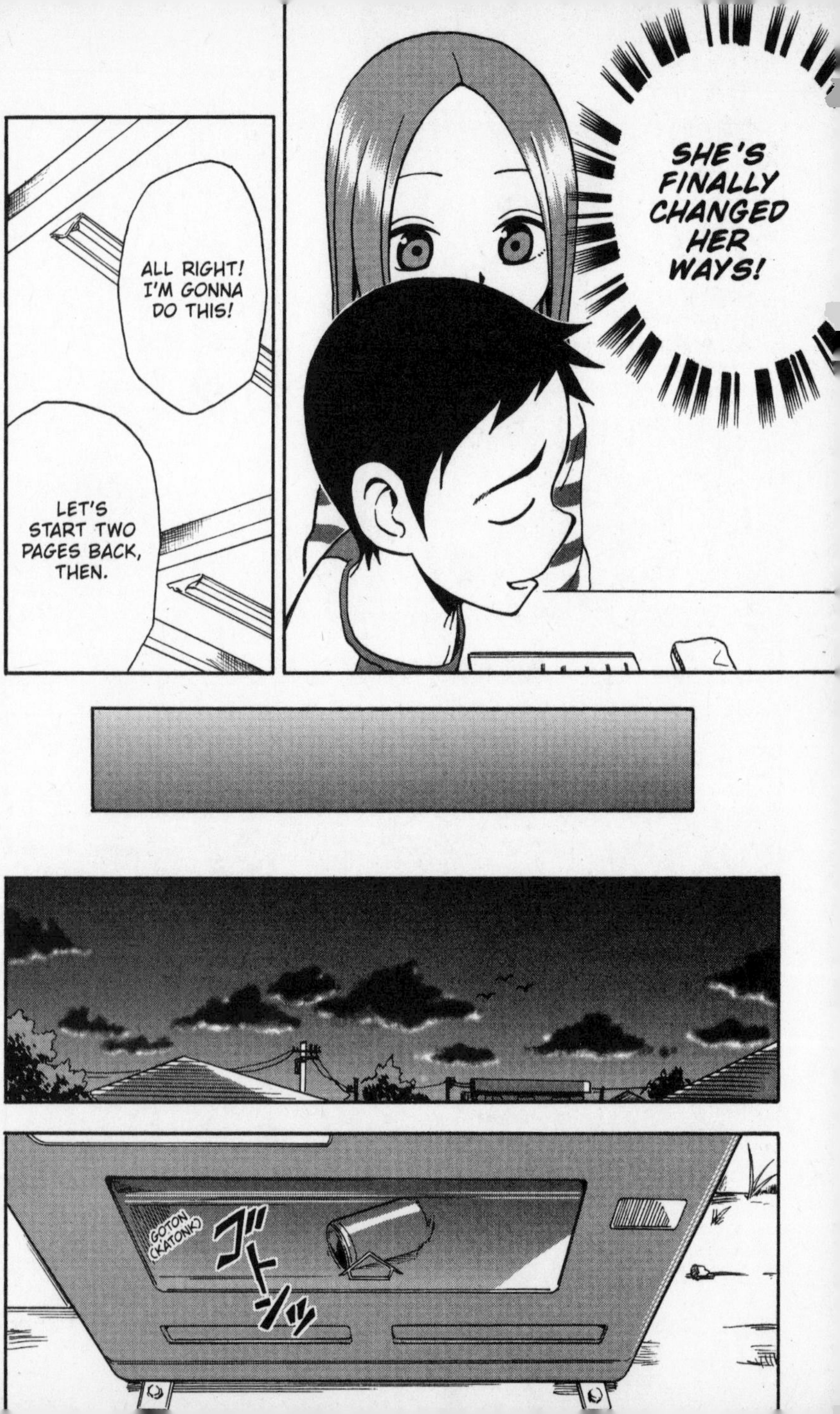
SHE'S FINALLY CHANGED HER WAYS!
ALL RIGHT! I'M GONNA DO THIS!
LET'S START TWO PAGES BACK, THEN.
ゴトッ
GOTON (KATONK)

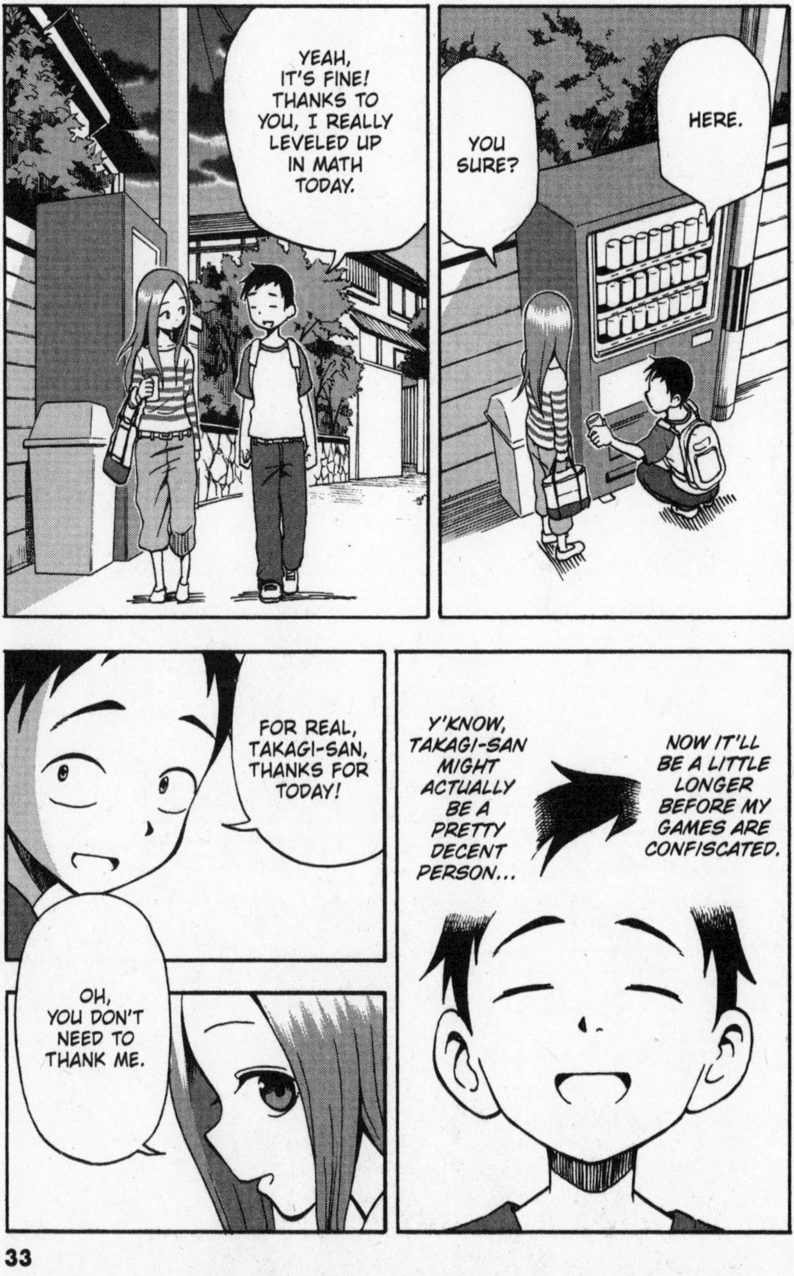
HERE.
YOU SURE?
YEAH, IT'S FINE! THANKS TO YOU, I REALLY LEVELED UP IN MATH TODAY.
NOW IT'LL BE A LITTLE LONGER BEFORE MY GAMES ARE CONFISCATED.
Y'KNOW, TAKAGI-SAN MIGHT ACTUALLY BE A PRETTY DECENT PERSON...
FOR REAL, TAKAGI-SAN, THANKS FOR TODAY!
OH, YOU DON'T NEED TO THANK ME.

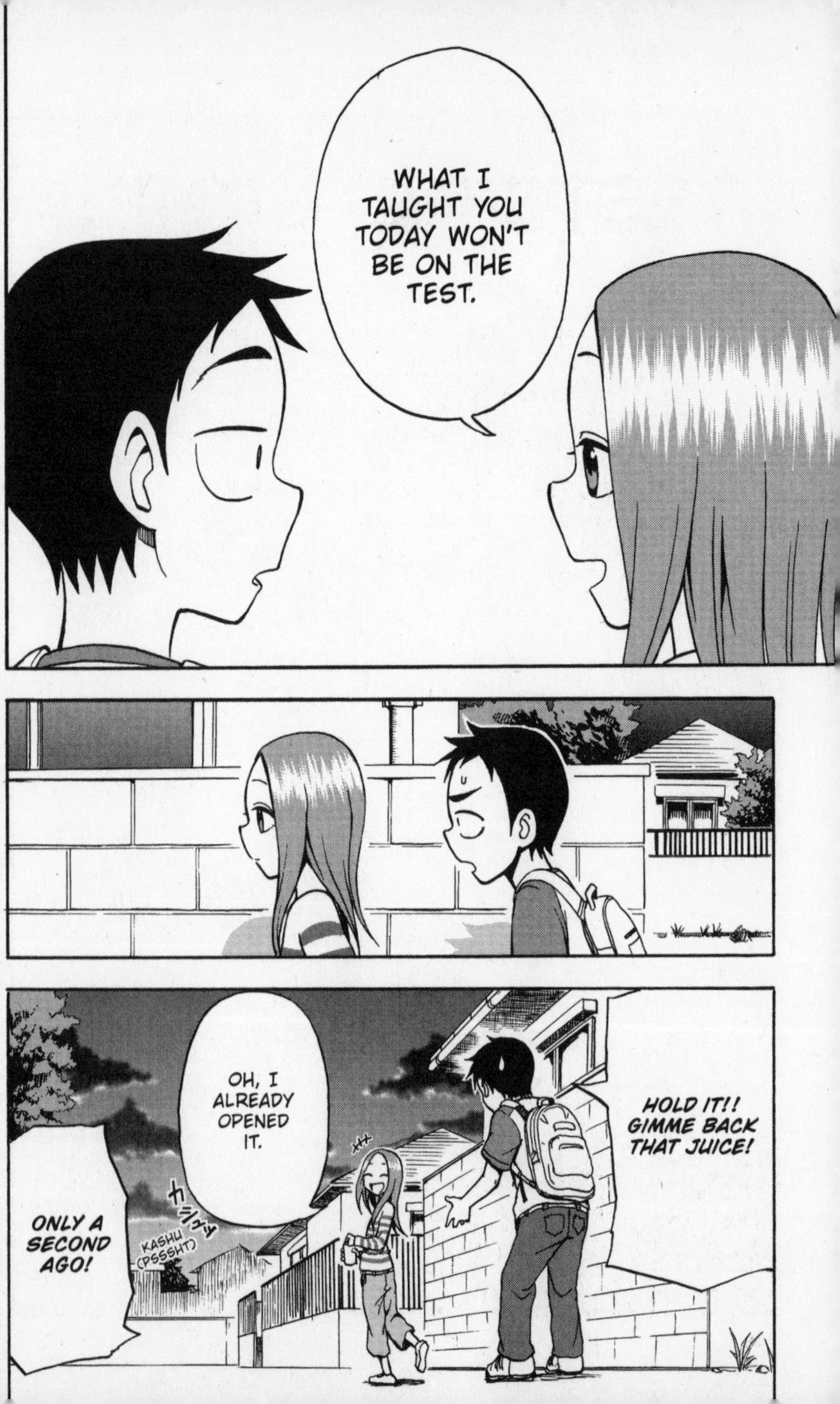
WHAT I TAUGHT YOU TODAY WON'T BE ON THE TEST.
HOLD IT!! GIMME BACK THAT JUICE!
OH, I ALREADY OPENED IT.
KASHU (PSSSHT)
ONLY A SECOND AGO!

# TESTS RETURNED

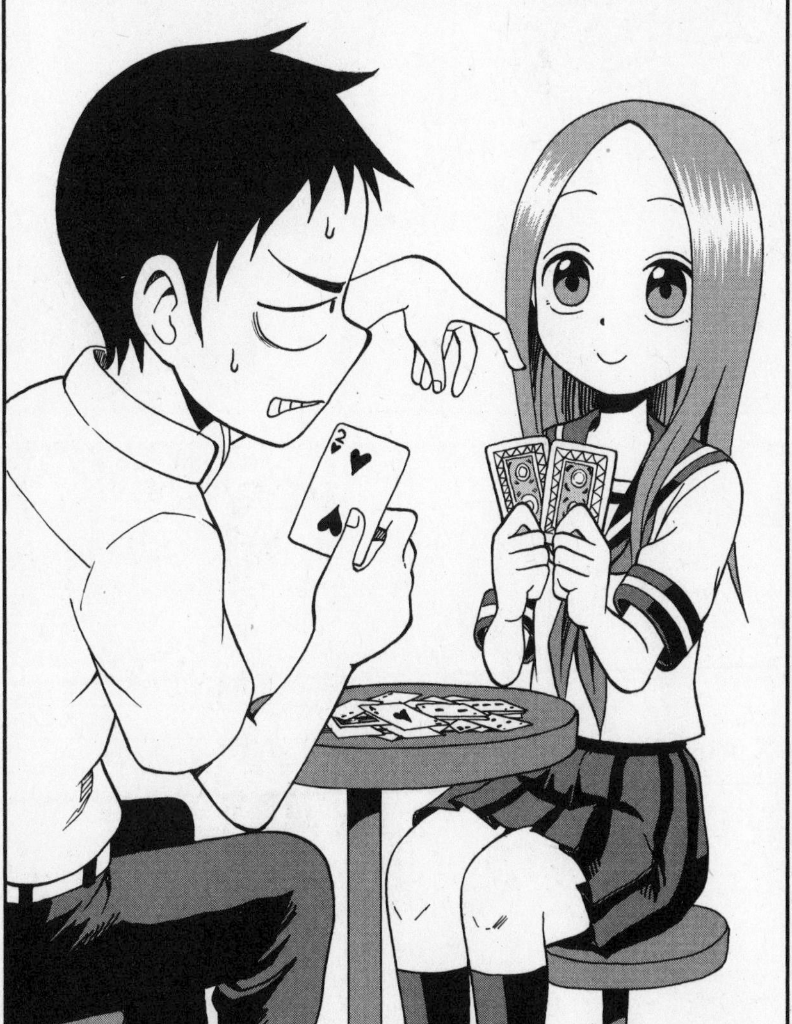

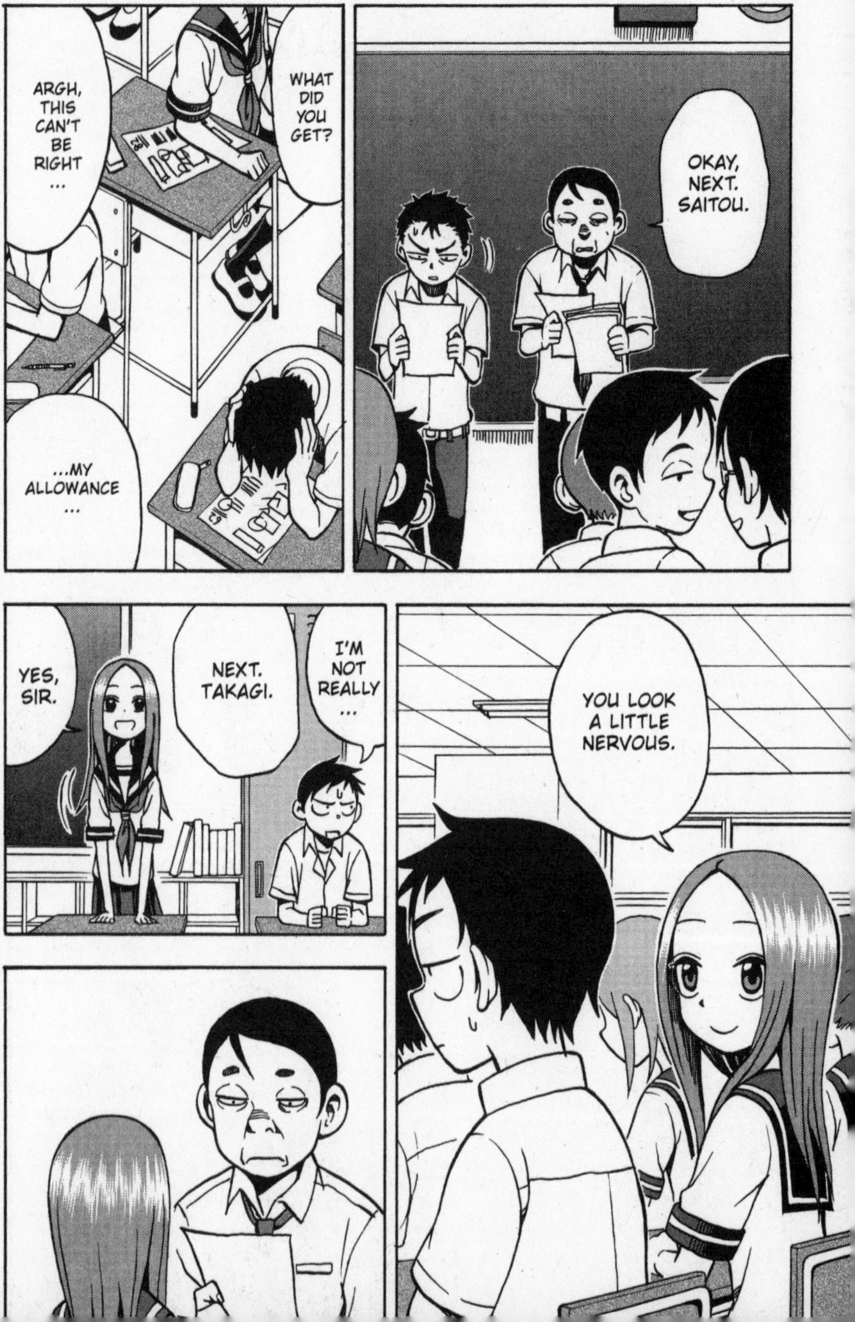
OKAY, NEXT. SAITOU.
WHAT DID YOU GET?
ARGH, THIS CAN'T BE RIGHT ...
...MY ALLOWANCE ...
YOU LOOK A LITTLE NERVOUS.
I'M NOT REALLY ...
NEXT. TAKAGI.
YES, SIR.

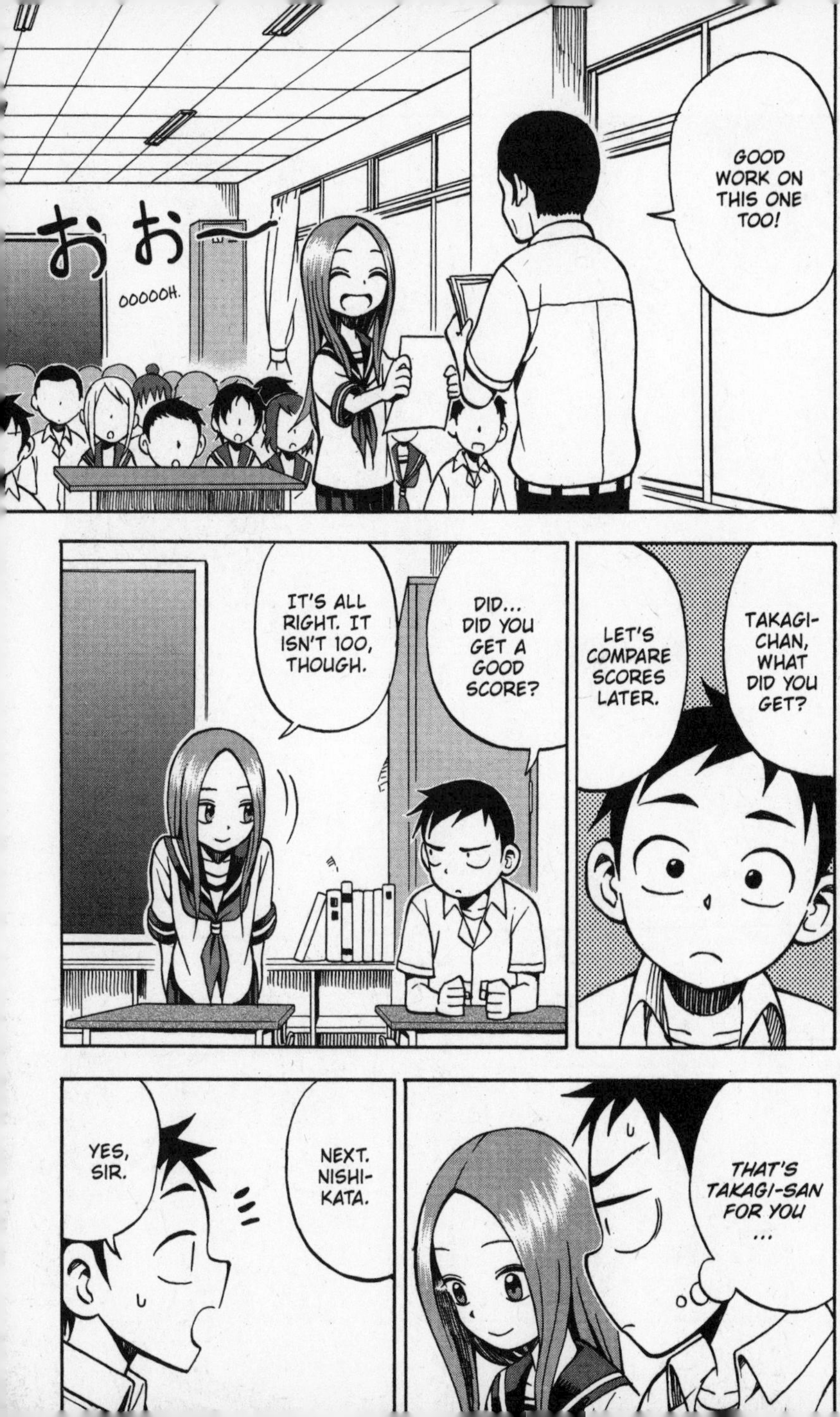
GOOD WORK ON THIS ONE TOO!
おお〜〜
OOOOOH.
TAKAGI-CHAN, WHAT DID YOU GET?
LET'S COMPARE SCORES LATER.
DID... DID YOU GET A GOOD SCORE?
IT'S ALL RIGHT. IT ISN'T 100, THOUGH.
THAT'S TAKAGI-SAN FOR YOU ...
NEXT. NISHI-KATA.
YES, SIR.

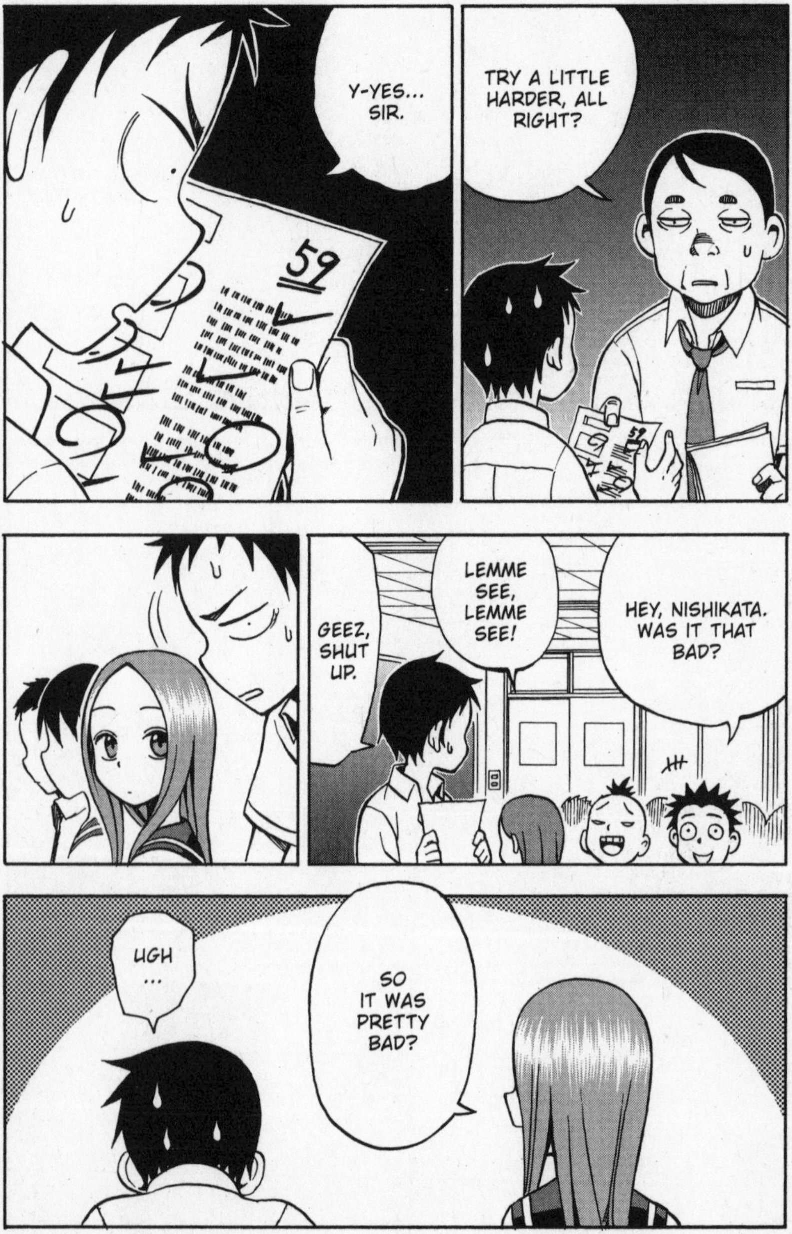
TRY A LITTLE HARDER, ALL RIGHT?
Y-YES... SIR.
59
HEY, NISHIKATA. WAS IT THAT BAD?
LEMME SEE, LEMME SEE!
GEEZ, SHUT UP.
SO IT WAS PRETTY BAD?
UGH ...

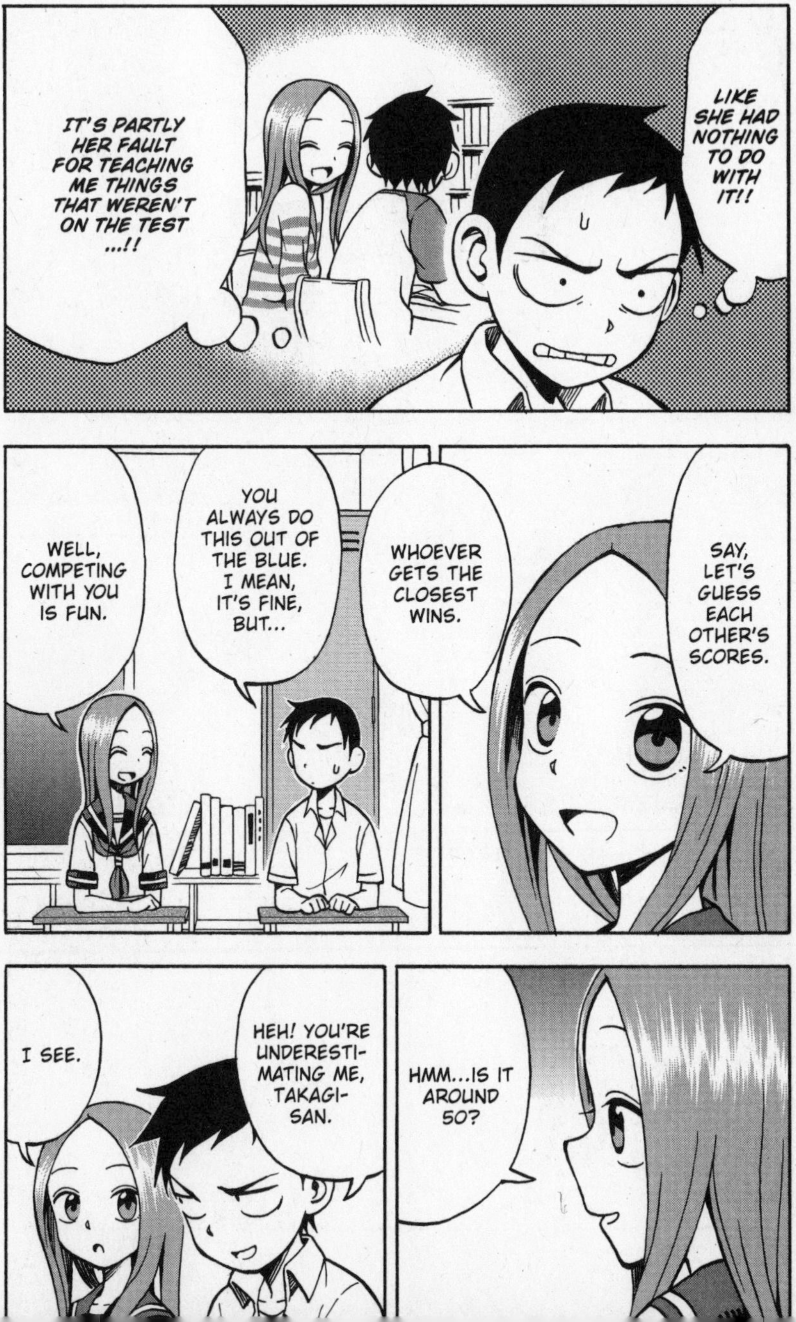
LIKE SHE HAD NOTHING TO DO WITH IT!!
IT'S PARTLY HER FAULT FOR TEACHING ME THINGS THAT WEREN'T ON THE TEST ...!!
SAY, LET'S GUESS EACH OTHER'S SCORES.
WHOEVER GETS THE CLOSEST WINS.
YOU ALWAYS DO THIS OUT OF THE BLUE. I MEAN, IT'S FINE, BUT...
WELL, COMPETING WITH YOU IS FUN.
HMM...IS IT AROUND 50?
HEH! YOU'RE UNDERESTI-MATING ME, TAKAGI-SAN.
I SEE.

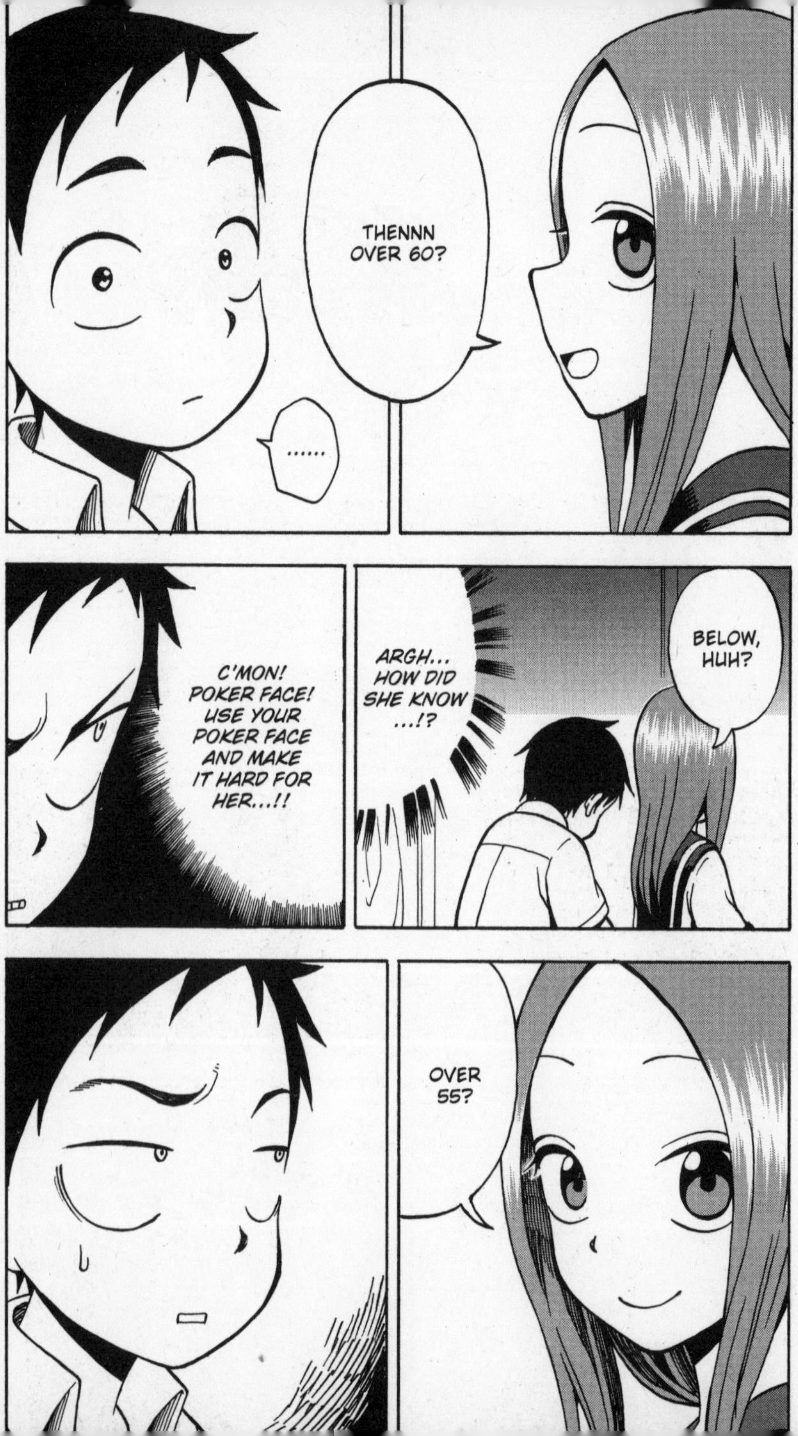
THENNN OVER 60?
......
BELOW, HUH?
ARGH... HOW DID SHE KNOW ...!?
C'MON! POKER FACE! USE YOUR POKER FACE AND MAKE IT HARD FOR HER...!!
OVER 55?

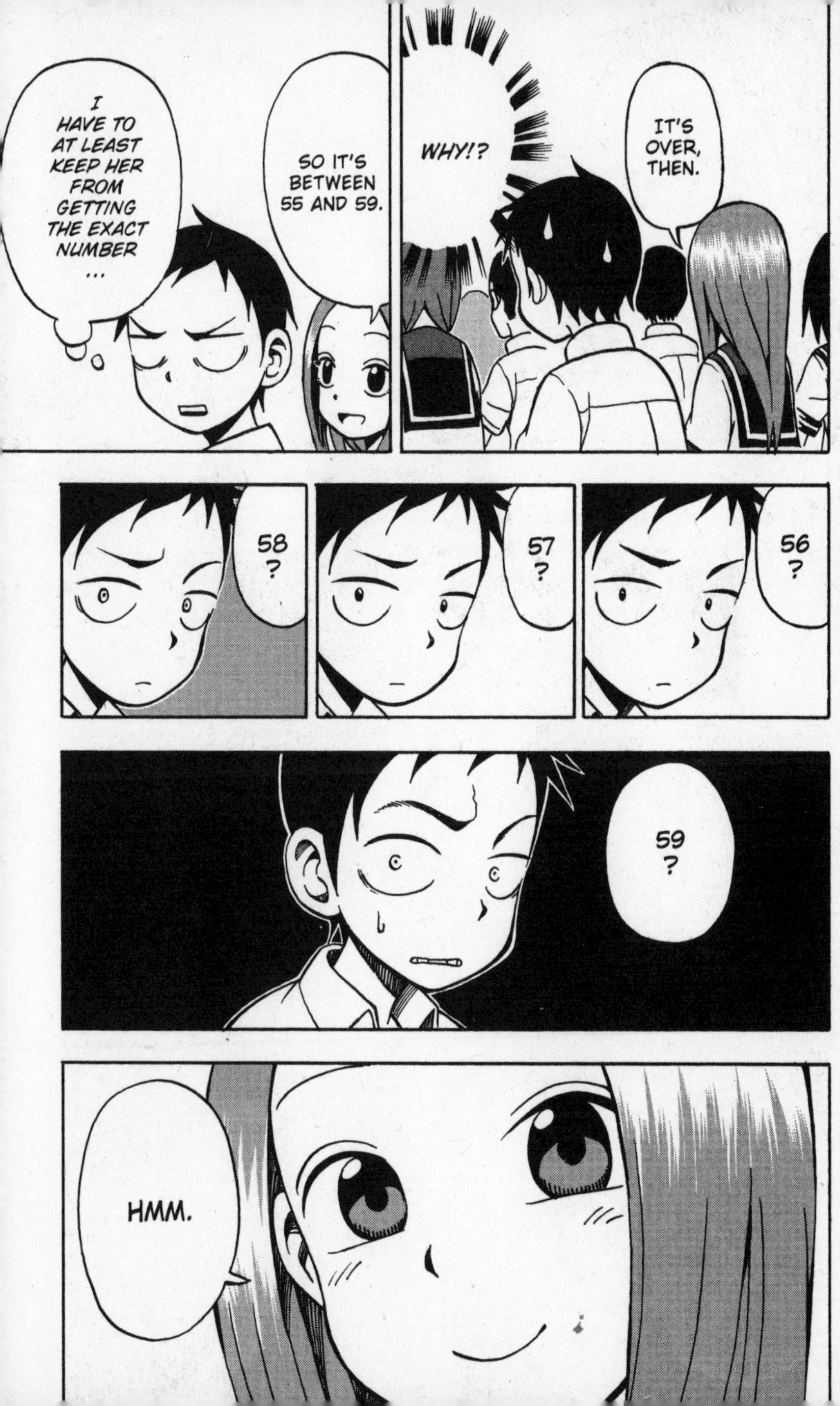
IT'S OVER, THEN.
WHY!?
SO IT'S BETWEEN 55 AND 59.
I HAVE TO AT LEAST KEEP HER FROM GETTING THE EXACT NUMBER ...
56 ?
57 ?
58 ?
59 ?
HMM.

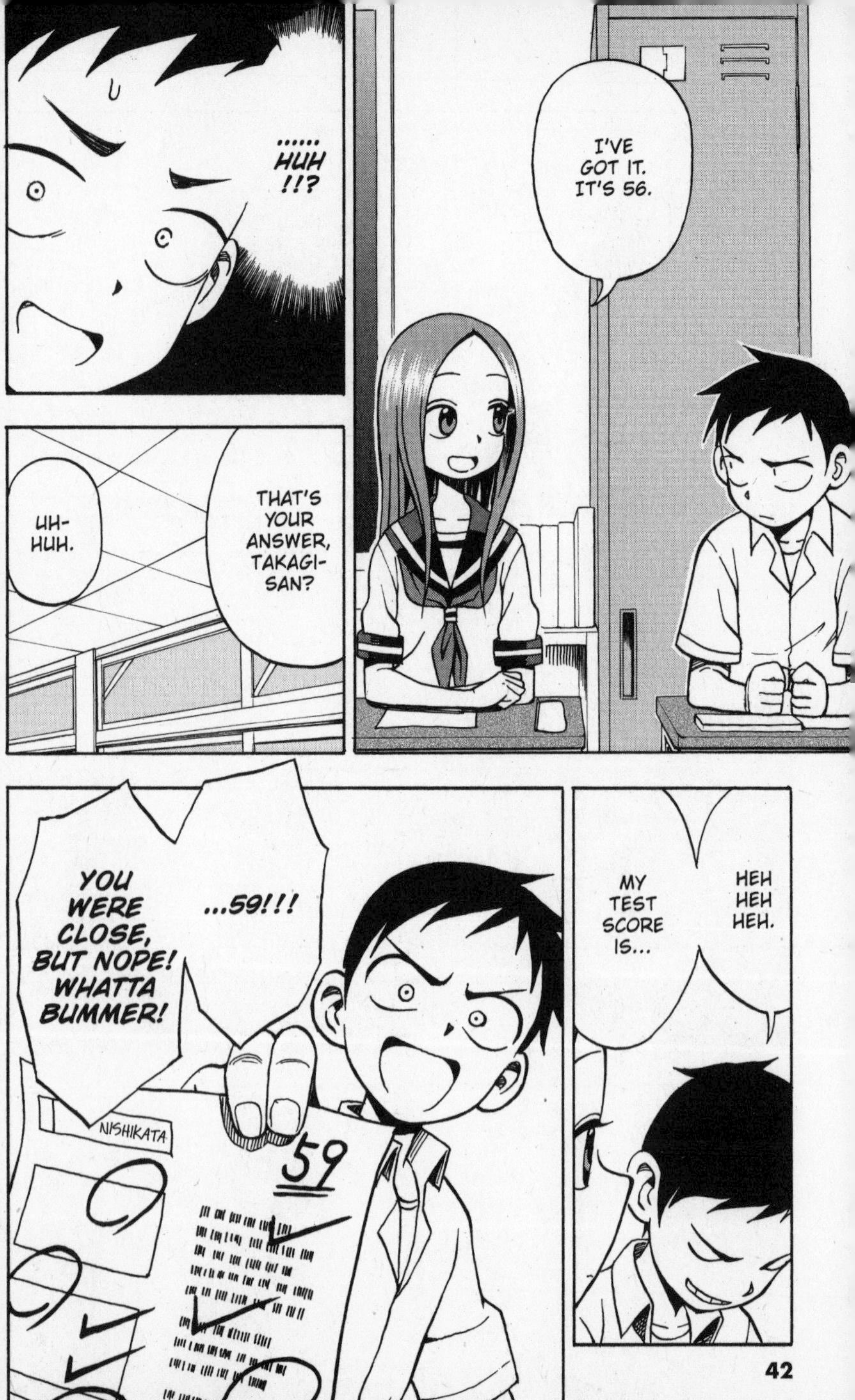
I'VE GOT IT. IT'S 56.
......HUH!!?
THAT'S YOUR ANSWER, TAKAGI-SAN?
UH-HUH.
HEH HEH HEH.
MY TEST SCORE IS...
...59!!!
YOU WERE CLOSE, BUT NOPE! WHATTA BUMMER!
NISHIKATA
59

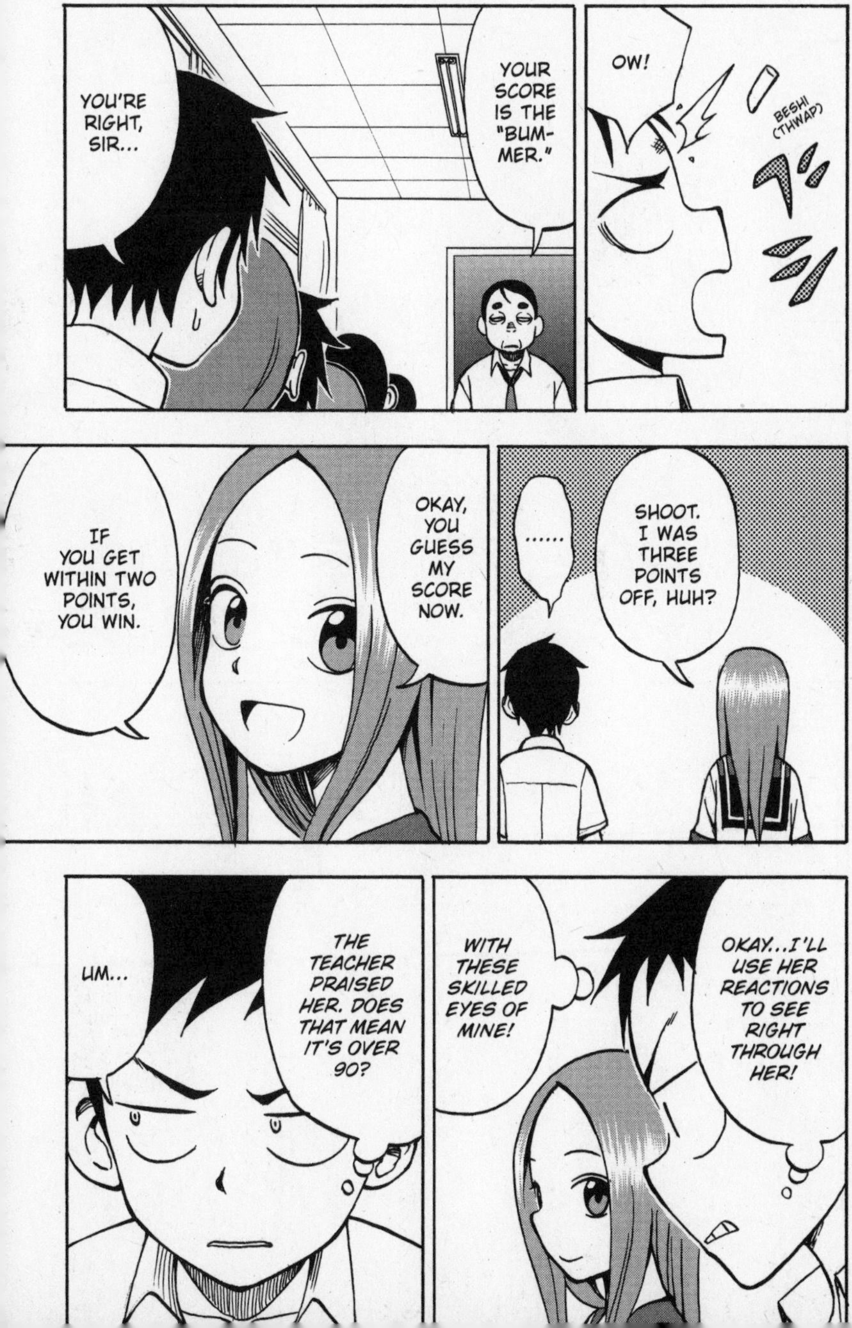
OW!
BESHI (THWAP)
YOUR SCORE IS THE "BUMMER."
YOU'RE RIGHT, SIR...
SHOOT. I WAS THREE POINTS OFF, HUH?
......
OKAY, YOU GUESS MY SCORE NOW.
IF YOU GET WITHIN TWO POINTS, YOU WIN.
OKAY...I'LL USE HER REACTIONS TO SEE RIGHT THROUGH HER!
WITH THESE SKILLED EYES OF MINE!
THE TEACHER PRAISED HER. DOES THAT MEAN IT'S OVER 90?
UM...

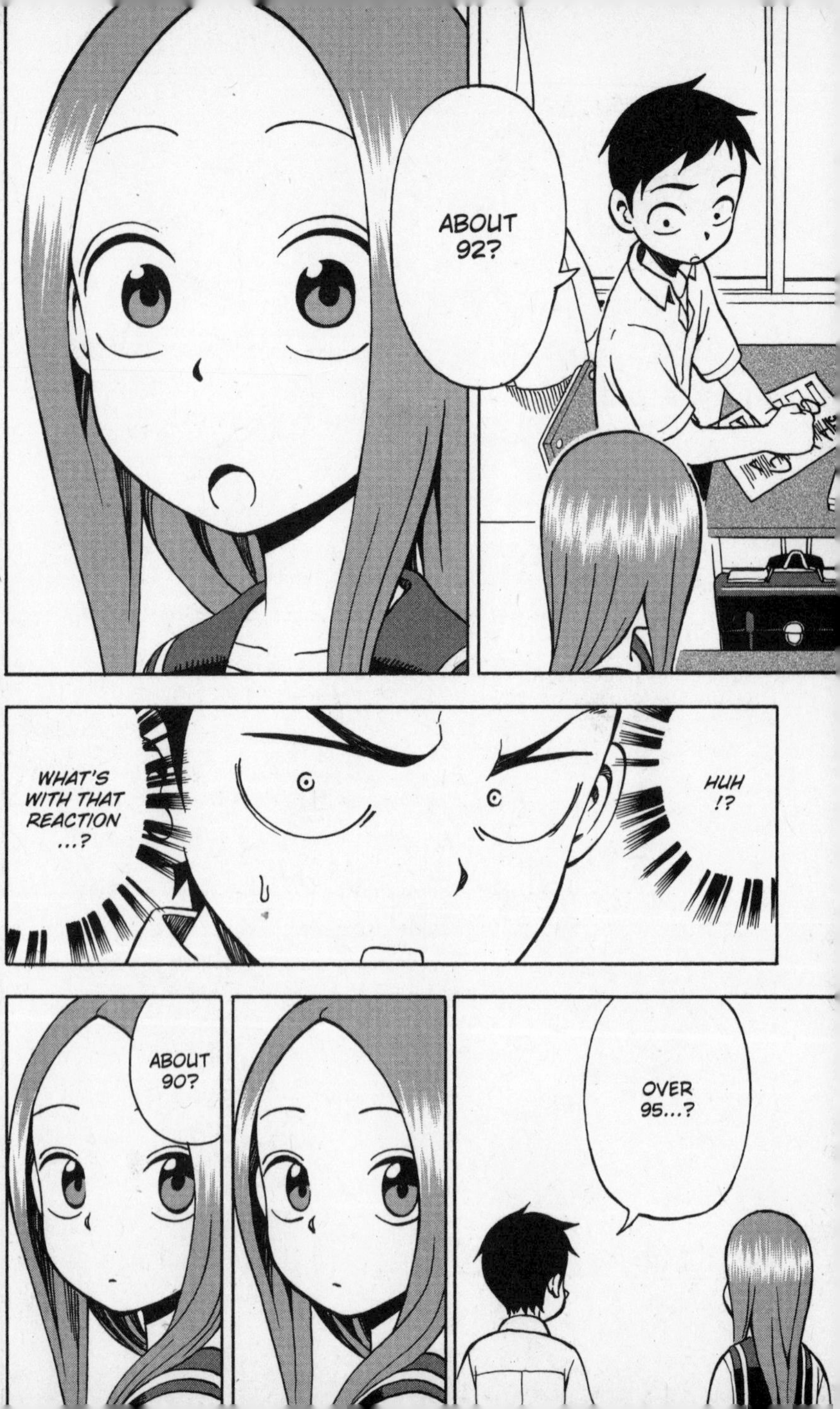
ABOUT 92?
HUH!?
WHAT'S WITH THAT REACTION...?
OVER 95...?
ABOUT 90?

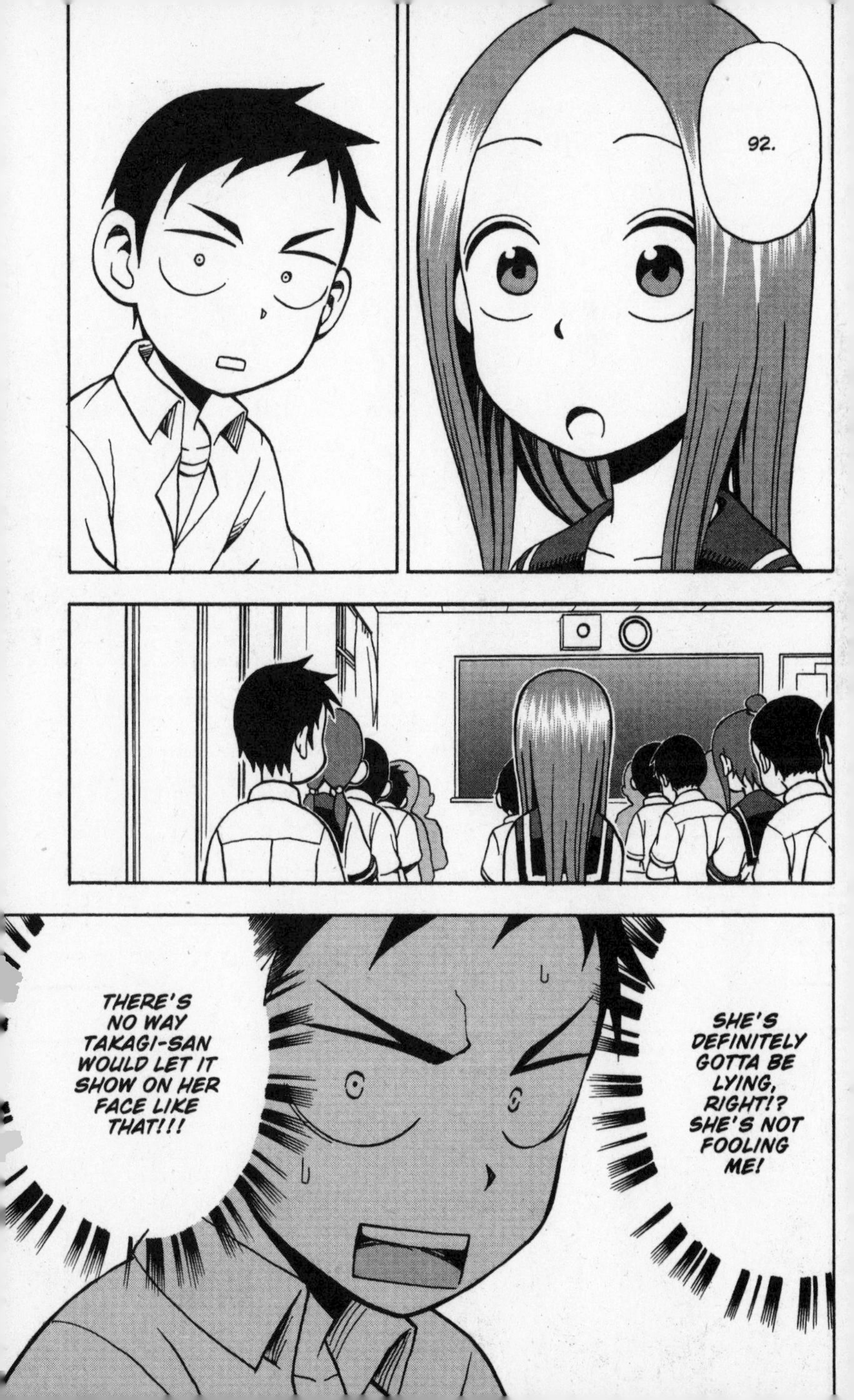
92.
SHE'S DEFINITELY GOTTA BE LYING, RIGHT!? SHE'S NOT FOOLING ME!
THERE'S NO WAY TAKAGI-SAN WOULD LET IT SHOW ON HER FACE LIKE THAT!!!

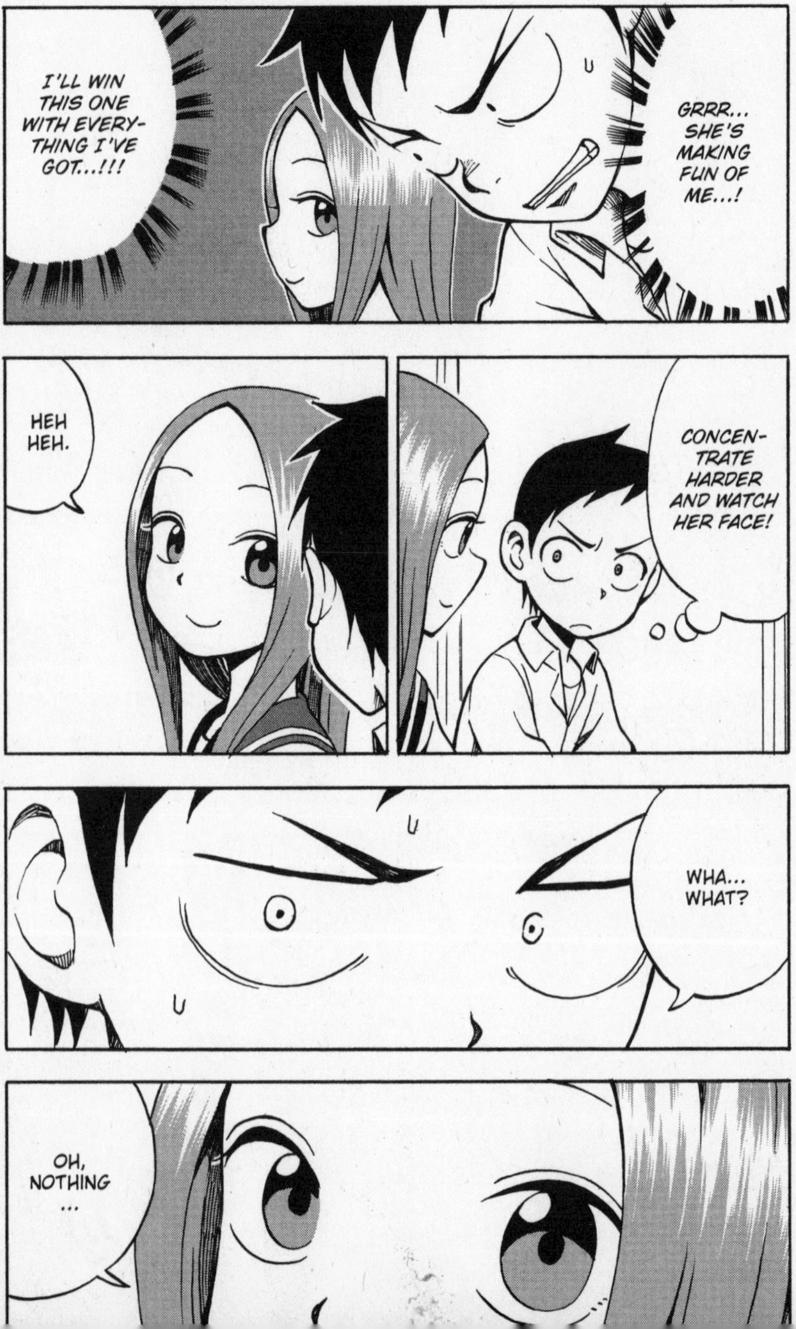
GRRR... SHE'S MAKING FUN OF ME...!
I'LL WIN THIS ONE WITH EVERYTHING I'VE GOT...!!!
CONCENTRATE HARDER AND WATCH HER FACE!
HEH HEH.
WHA... WHAT?
OH, NOTHING...

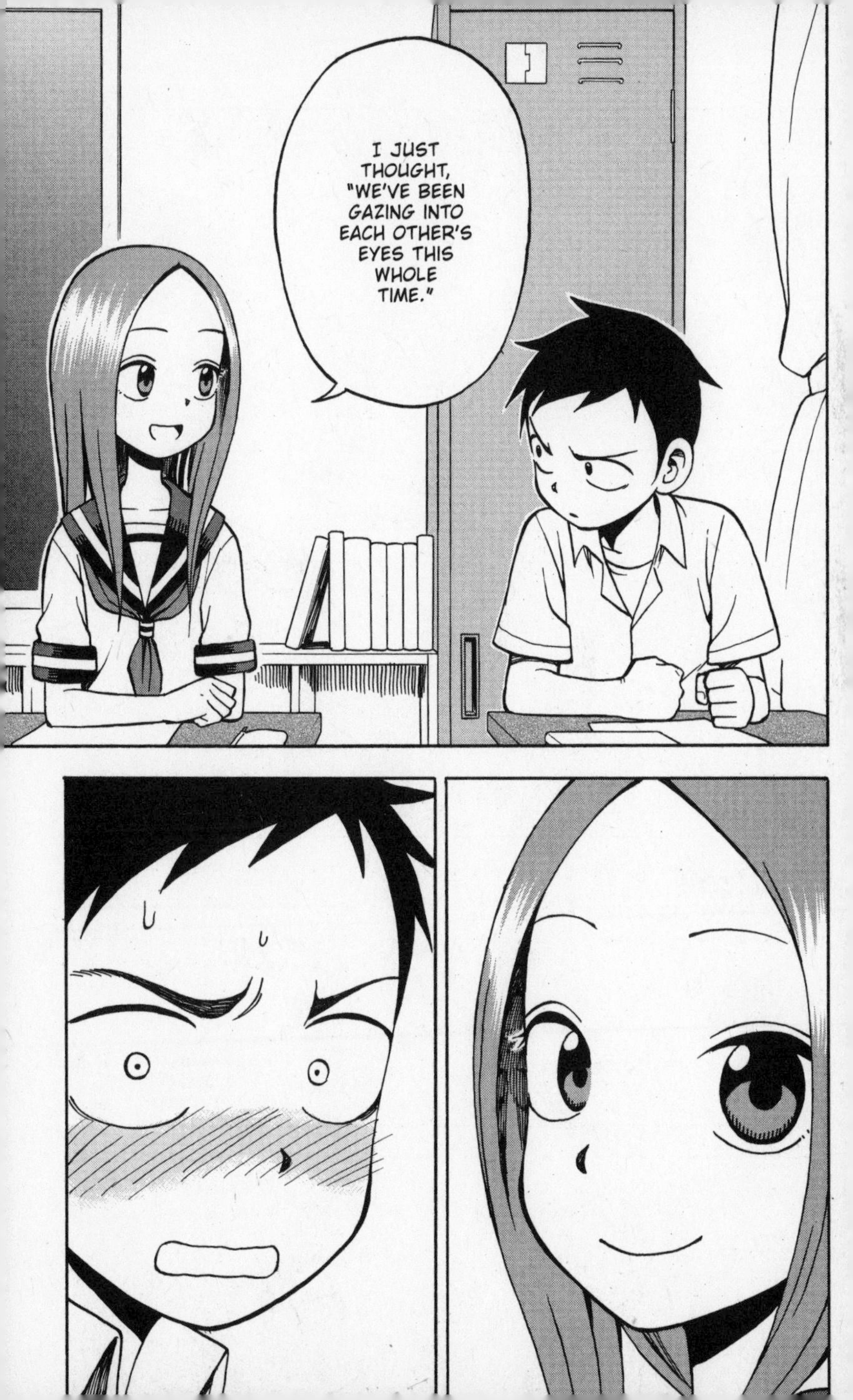
I JUST THOUGHT, "WE'VE BEEN GAZING INTO EACH OTHER'S EYES THIS WHOLE TIME."

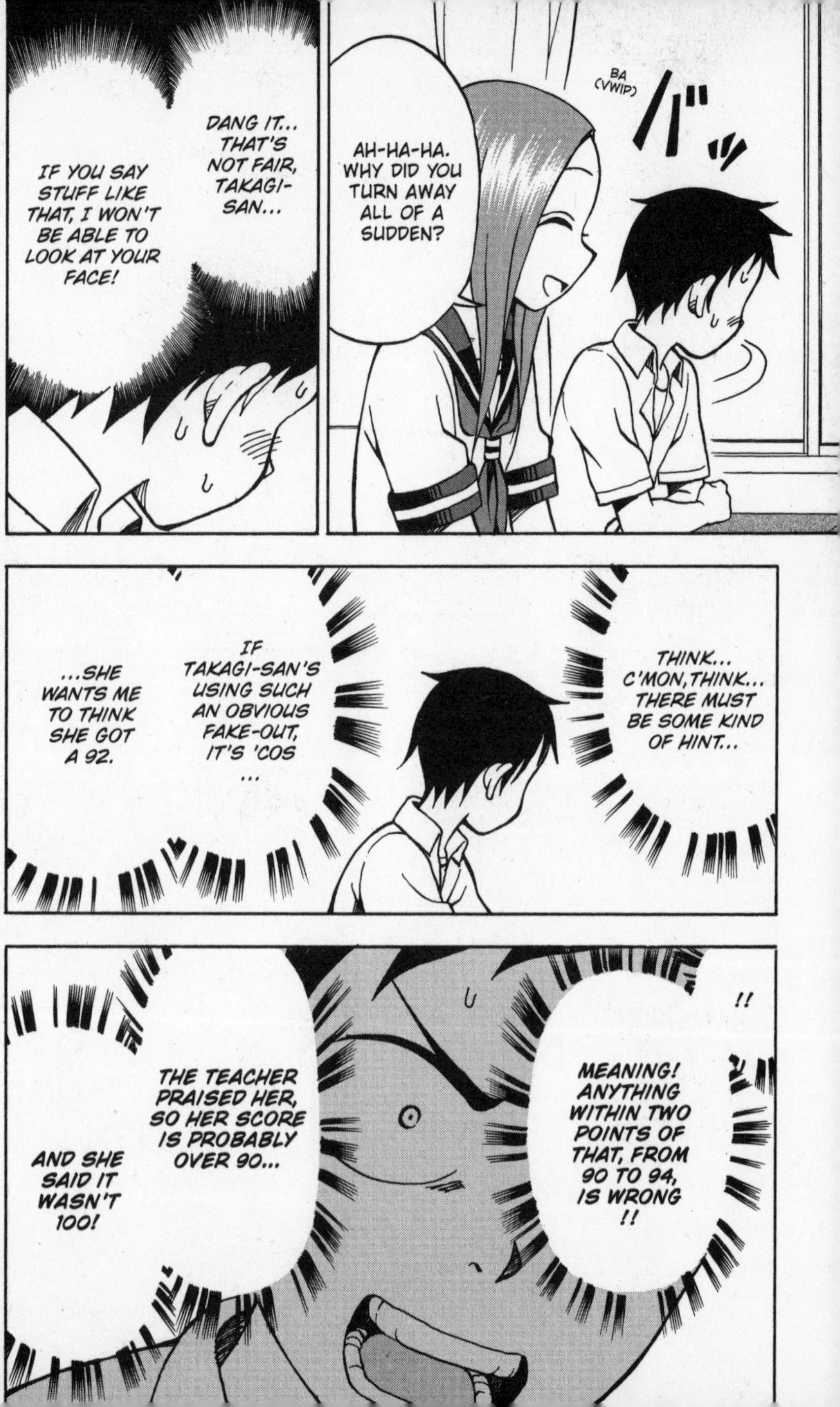
BA (VWIP)
AH-HA-HA. WHY DID YOU TURN AWAY ALL OF A SUDDEN?
DANG IT... THAT'S NOT FAIR, TAKAGI-SAN...
IF YOU SAY STUFF LIKE THAT, I WON'T BE ABLE TO LOOK AT YOUR FACE!
THINK... C'MON, THINK... THERE MUST BE SOME KIND OF HINT...
IF TAKAGI-SAN'S USING SUCH AN OBVIOUS FAKE-OUT, IT'S 'COS ...
...SHE WANTS ME TO THINK SHE GOT A 92.
!!
MEANING! ANYTHING WITHIN TWO POINTS OF THAT, FROM 90 TO 94, IS WRONG !!
THE TEACHER PRAISED HER, SO HER SCORE IS PROBABLY OVER 90...
AND SHE SAID IT WASN'T 100!

PERFECT.

I WIN, HANDS DOWN...!!!

| 100 | X |
| 99 | |
| 98 | |
| 97 | |
| 96 | |
| 95 | |
| 94 | X |
| 93 | X |
| 92 | ← WANTS TO MAKE ME SAY THIS |
| 91 | X |
| 90 | X |

S O M E W H E R E  H E R E

AHA!!!

IF YOU PUT THAT ALL TOGETHER...

TAKAGI-SAN, YOUR SCORE IS...

...97!!!

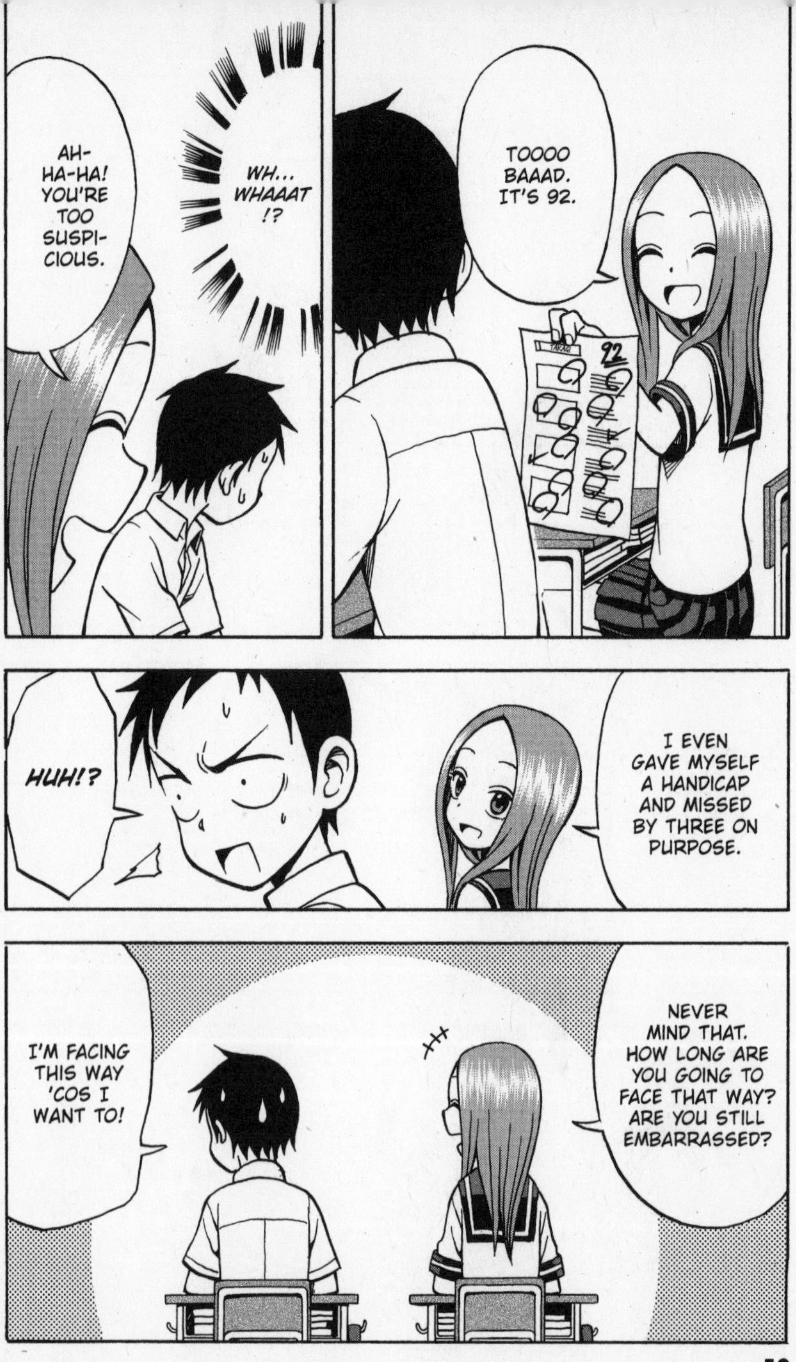
TOOOO BAAAD. IT'S 92.
WH... WHAAAT !?
AH-HA-HA! YOU'RE TOO SUSPICIOUS.
I EVEN GAVE MYSELF A HANDICAP AND MISSED BY THREE ON PURPOSE.
HUH!?
NEVER MIND THAT. HOW LONG ARE YOU GOING TO FACE THAT WAY? ARE YOU STILL EMBARRASSED?
I'M FACING THIS WAY 'COS I WANT TO!

Teasing Master
Takagi-san

# LETTER

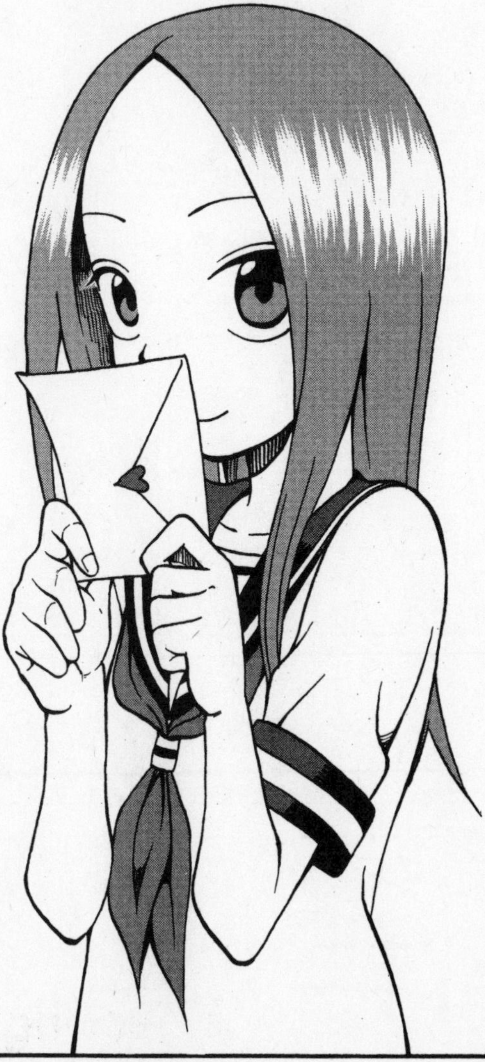

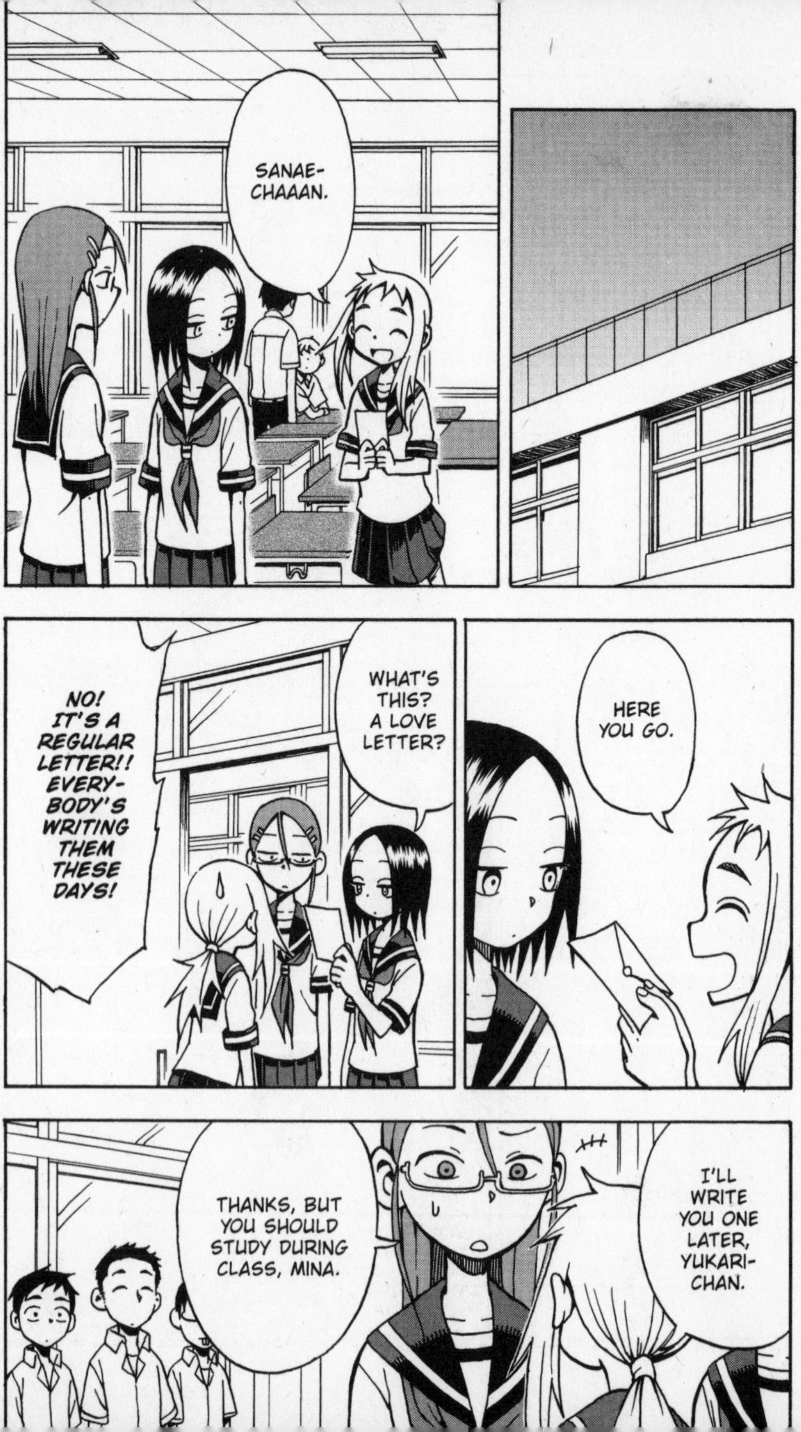
SANAE-CHAAAN.
HERE YOU GO.
WHAT'S THIS? A LOVE LETTER?
NO! IT'S A REGULAR LETTER!! EVERYBODY'S WRITING THEM THESE DAYS!
I'LL WRITE YOU ONE LATER, YUKARI-CHAN.
THANKS, BUT YOU SHOULD STUDY DURING CLASS, MINA.

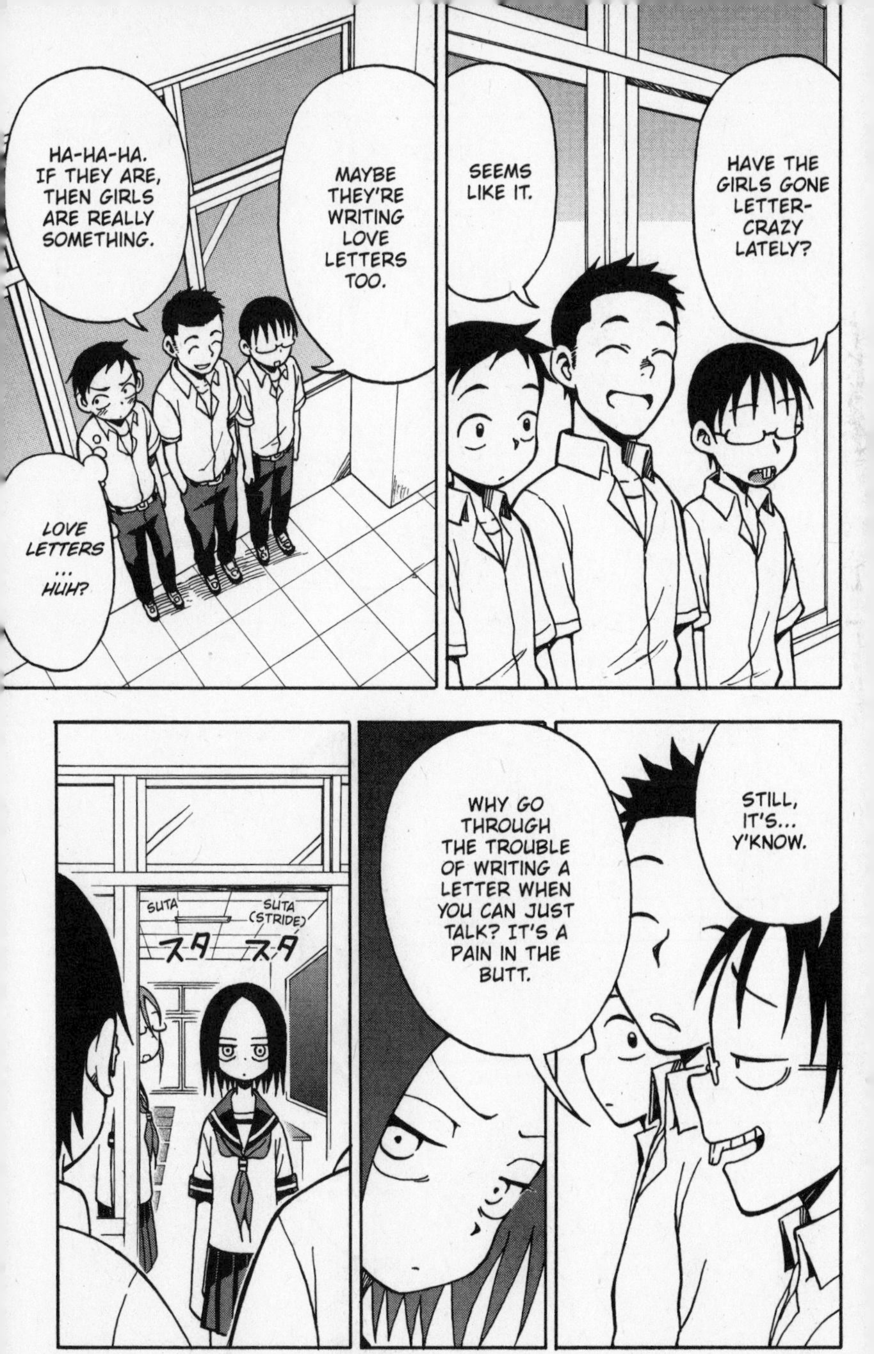
HAVE THE GIRLS GONE LETTER-CRAZY LATELY?
SEEMS LIKE IT.
MAYBE THEY'RE WRITING LOVE LETTERS TOO.
HA-HA-HA. IF THEY ARE, THEN GIRLS ARE REALLY SOMETHING.
LOVE LETTERS ... HUH?
STILL, IT'S... Y'KNOW.
WHY GO THROUGH THE TROUBLE OF WRITING A LETTER WHEN YOU CAN JUST TALK? IT'S A PAIN IN THE BUTT.
SUTA
SUTA (STRIDE)
スタ スタ

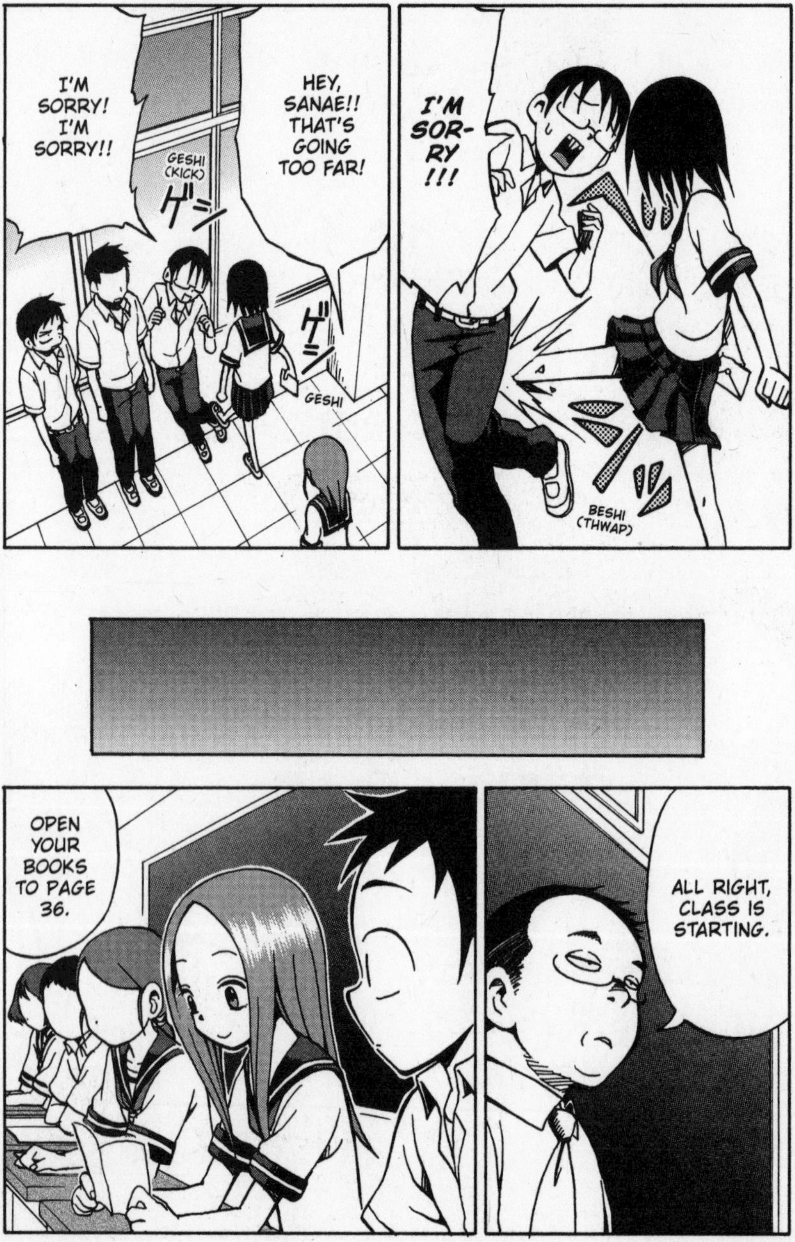
I'M SORRY!!!
BESHI (THWAP)
HEY, SANAE!! THAT'S GOING TOO FAR!
I'M SORRY! I'M SORRY!!
GESHI (KICK)
ゲシ
ゲシ
GESHI
ALL RIGHT, CLASS IS STARTING.
OPEN YOUR BOOKS TO PAGE 36.

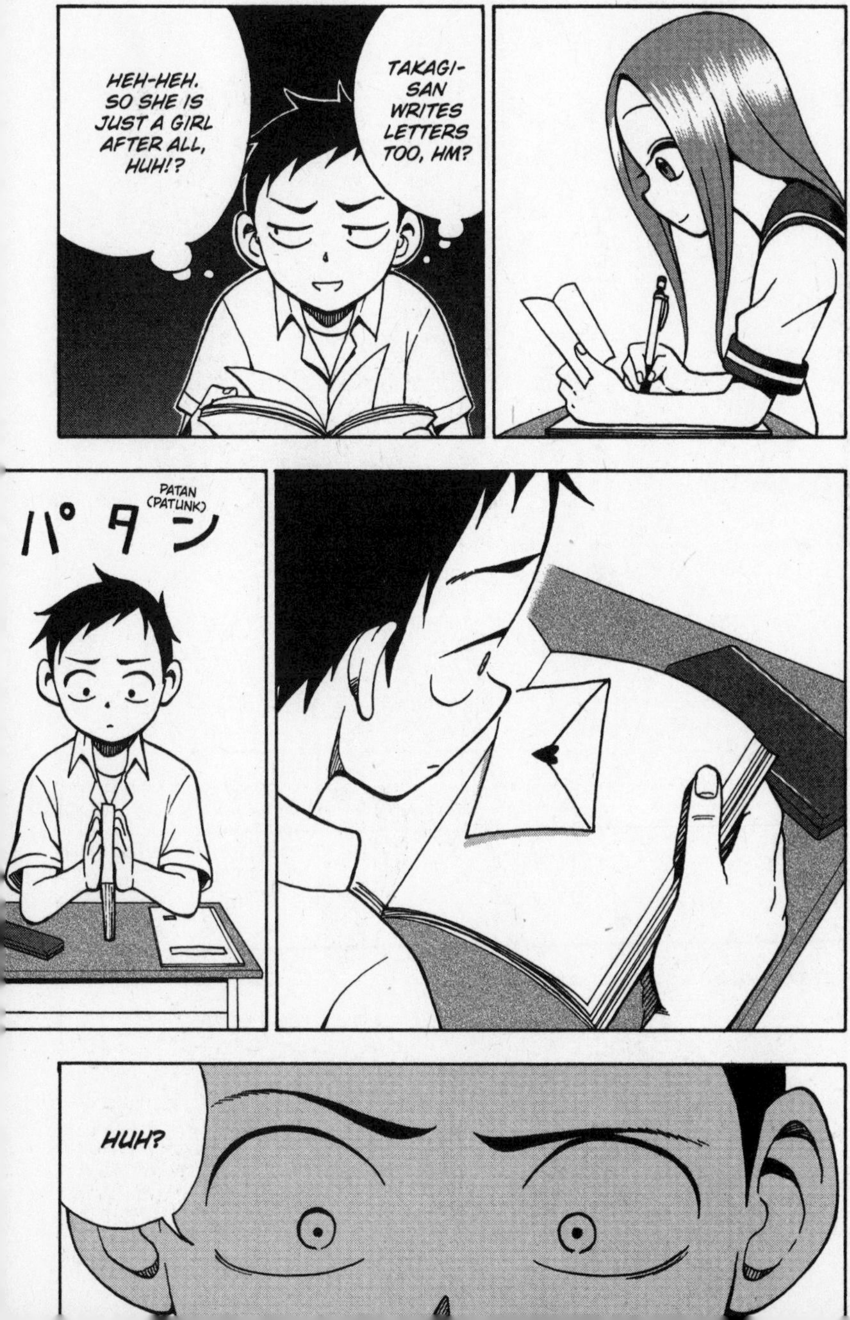
TAKAGI-SAN WRITES LETTERS TOO, HM?
HEH-HEH. SO SHE IS JUST A GIRL AFTER ALL, HUH!?
パタン
PATAN (PATUNK)
HUH?

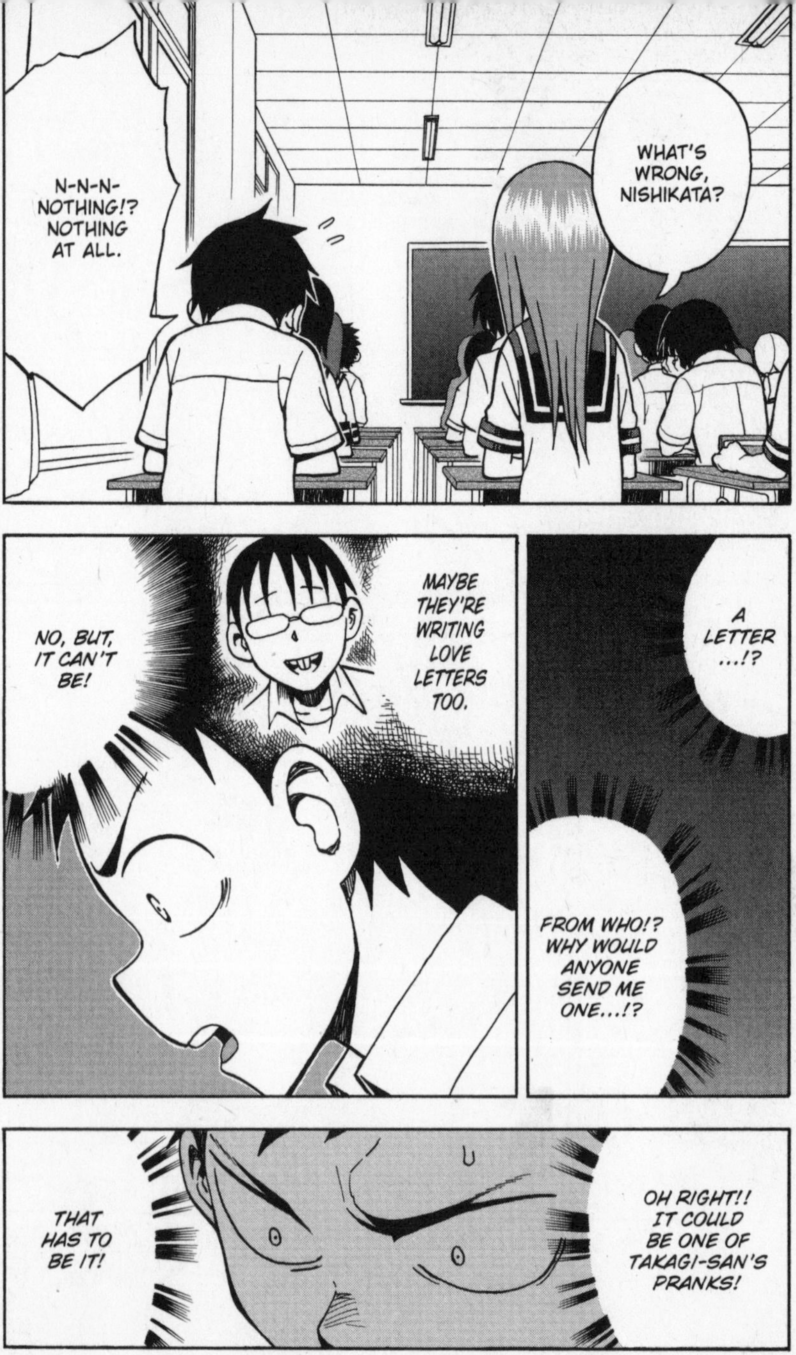
WHAT'S WRONG, NISHIKATA?
N-N-N-NOTHING!? NOTHING AT ALL.
A LETTER ...!?
FROM WHO!? WHY WOULD ANYONE SEND ME ONE...!?
MAYBE THEY'RE WRITING LOVE LETTERS TOO.
NO, BUT, IT CAN'T BE!
OH RIGHT!! IT COULD BE ONE OF TAKAGI-SAN'S PRANKS!
THAT HAS TO BE IT!

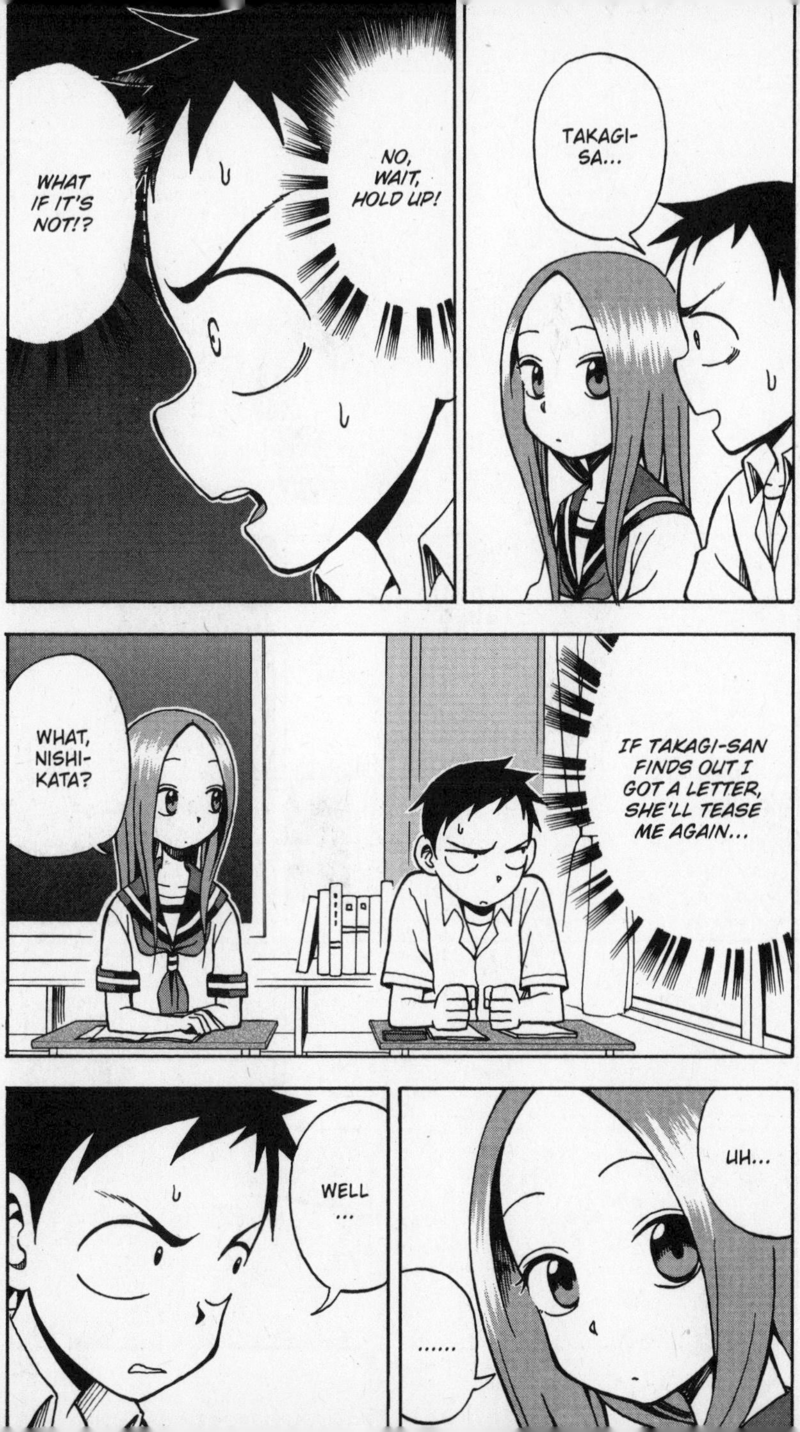
TAKAGI-SA...
NO, WAIT, HOLD UP!
WHAT IF IT'S NOT!?
IF TAKAGI-SAN FINDS OUT I GOT A LETTER, SHE'LL TEASE ME AGAIN...
WHAT, NISHI-KATA?
UH...
......
WELL ...

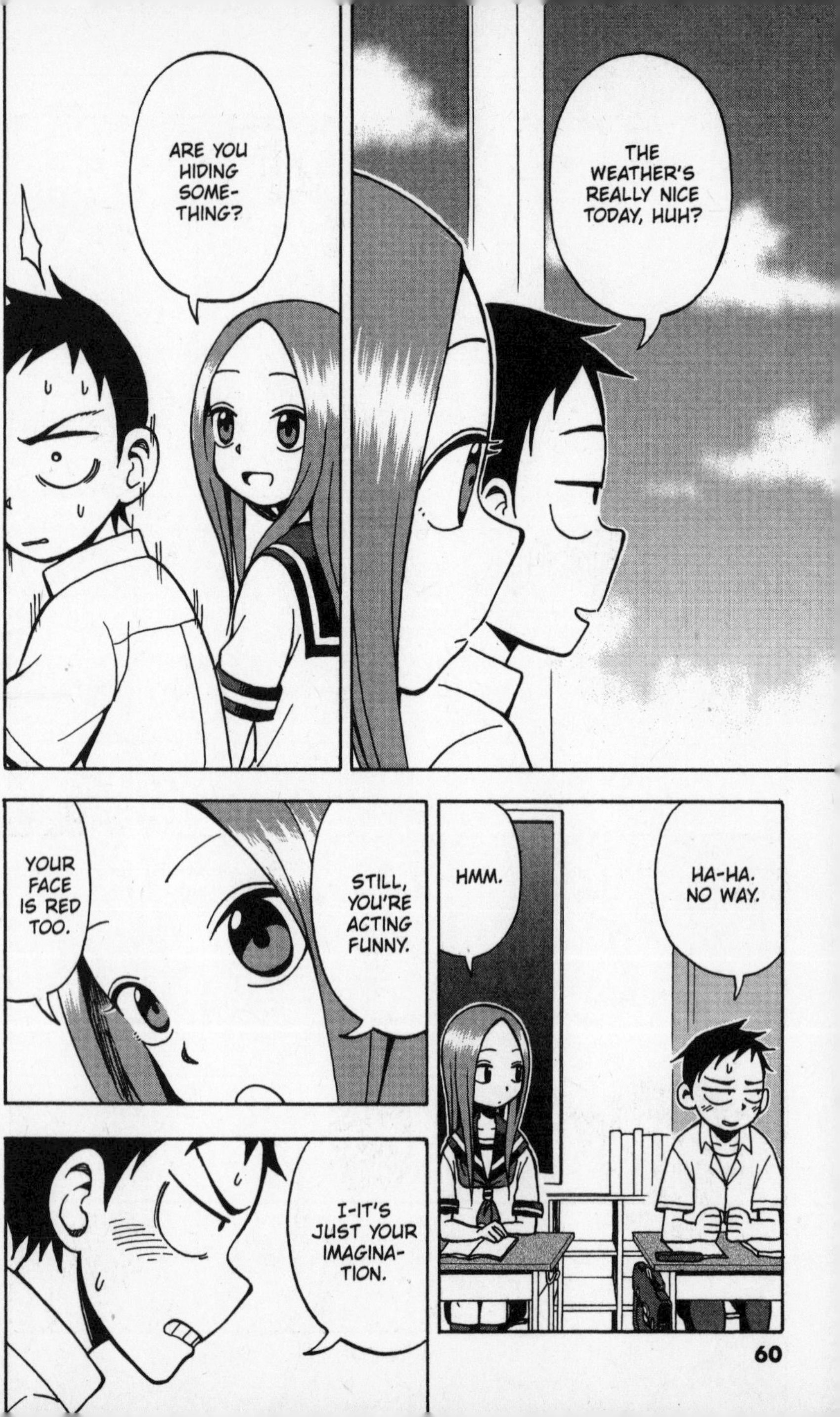
THE WEATHER'S REALLY NICE TODAY, HUH?
ARE YOU HIDING SOME-THING?
HA-HA. NO WAY.
HMM.
STILL, YOU'RE ACTING FUNNY.
YOUR FACE IS RED TOO.
I-IT'S JUST YOUR IMAGINA-TION.

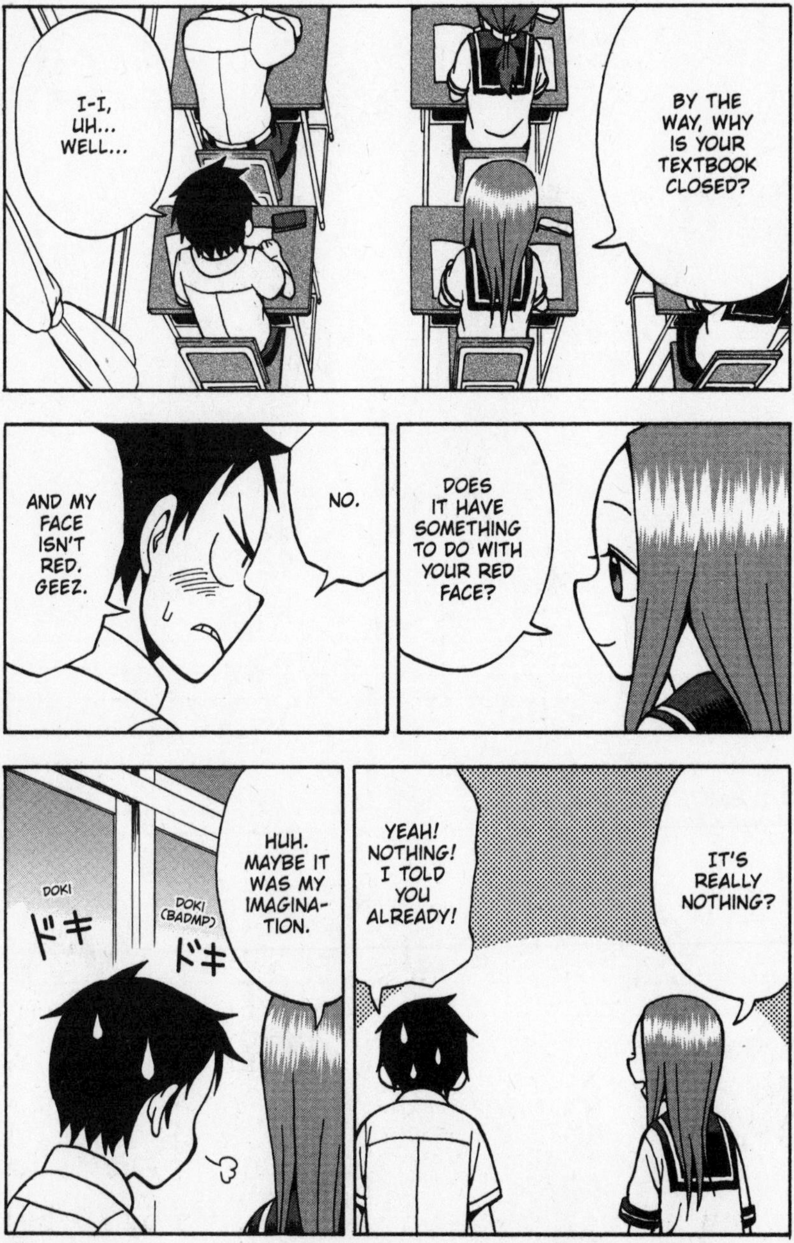
BY THE WAY, WHY IS YOUR TEXTBOOK CLOSED?
I-I, UH... WELL...
DOES IT HAVE SOMETHING TO DO WITH YOUR RED FACE?
NO.
AND MY FACE ISN'T RED. GEEZ.
IT'S REALLY NOTHING?
YEAH! NOTHING! I TOLD YOU ALREADY!
HUH. MAYBE IT WAS MY IMAGINATION.
DOKI (BADMP)
ドキ
DOKI
ドキ

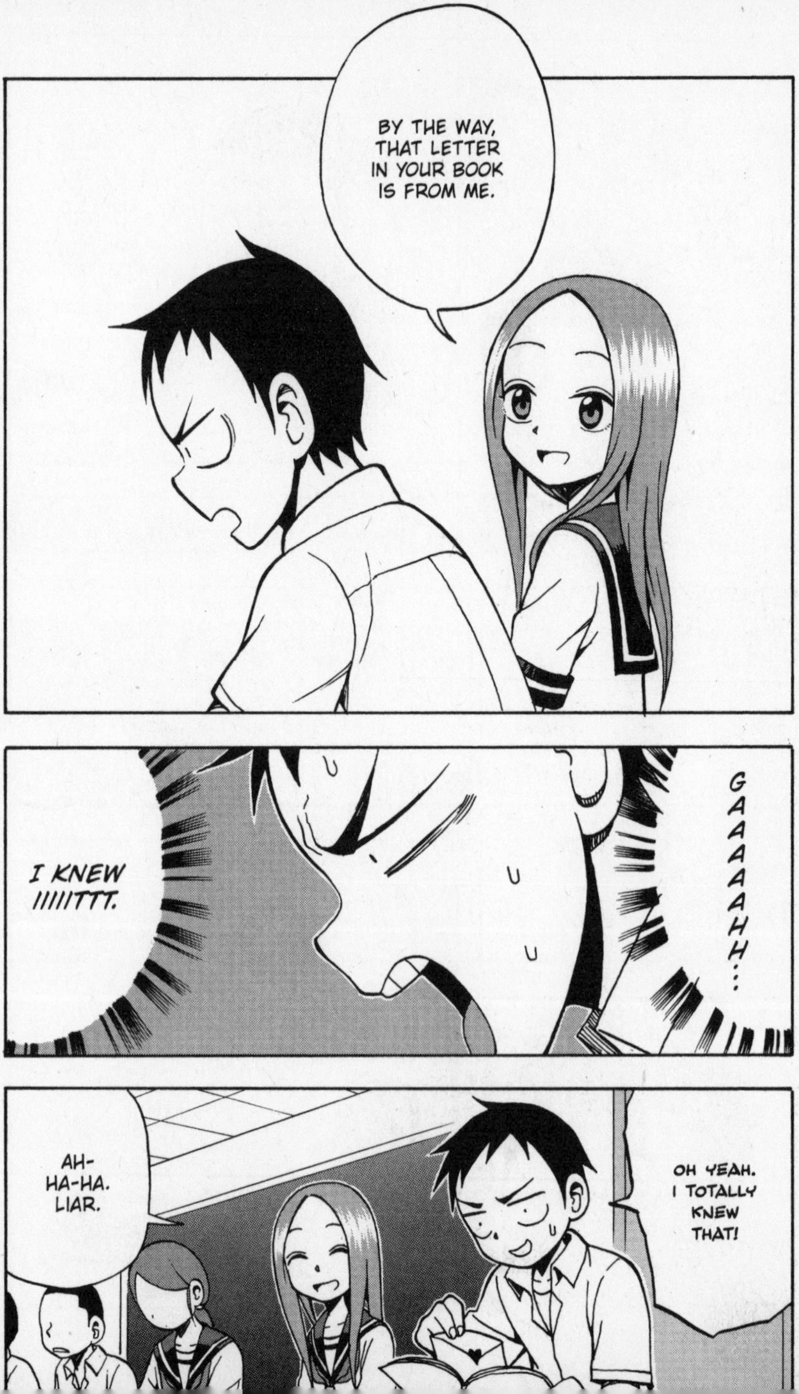
BY THE WAY, THAT LETTER IN YOUR BOOK IS FROM ME.
GAAAAAHH..
I KNEW IIIIIITTT.
OH YEAH. I TOTALLY KNEW THAT!
AH-HA-HA. LIAR.

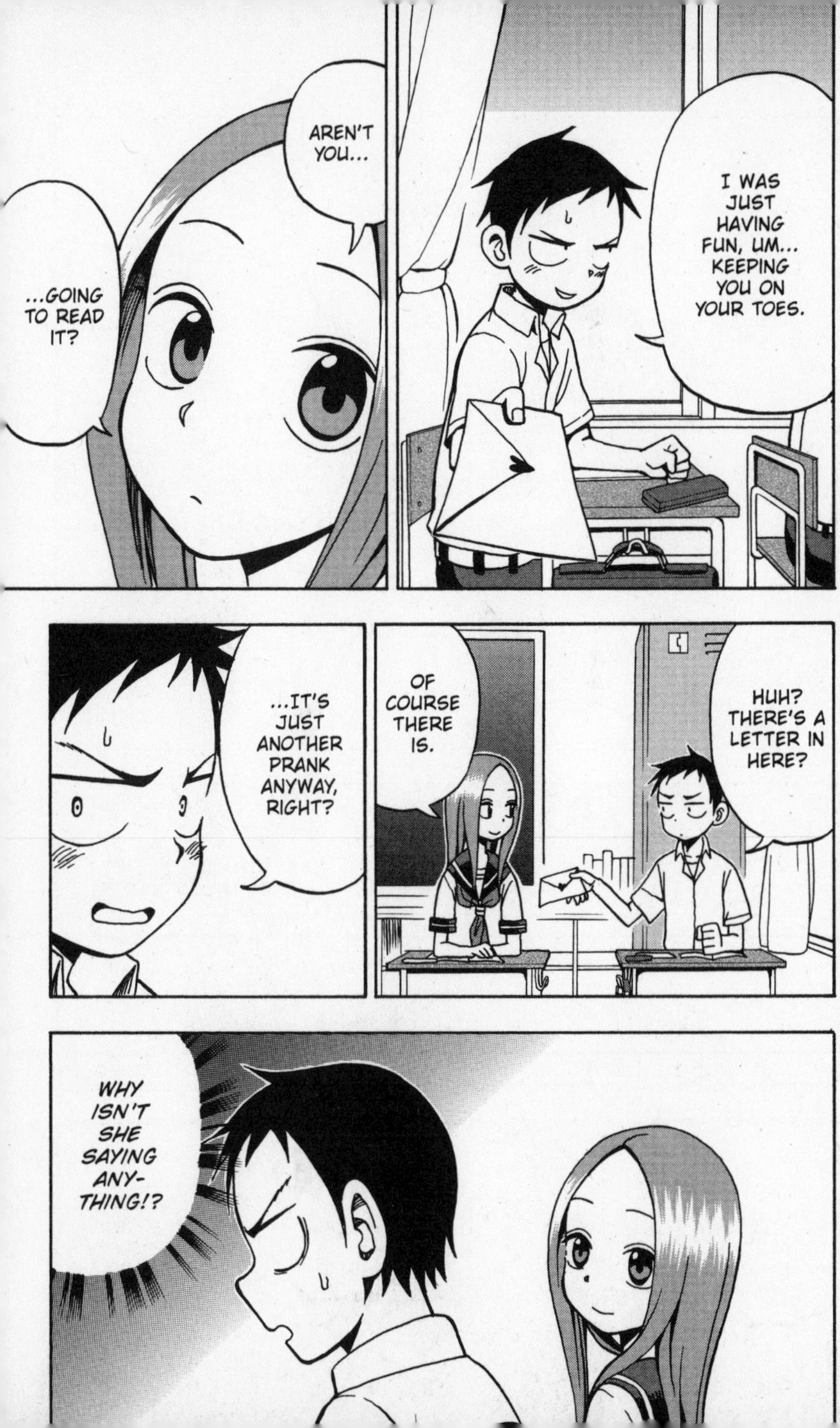
I WAS JUST HAVING FUN, UM... KEEPING YOU ON YOUR TOES.
AREN'T YOU...
...GOING TO READ IT?
HUH? THERE'S A LETTER IN HERE?
OF COURSE THERE IS.
...IT'S JUST ANOTHER PRANK ANYWAY, RIGHT?
WHY ISN'T SHE SAYING ANY-THING!?

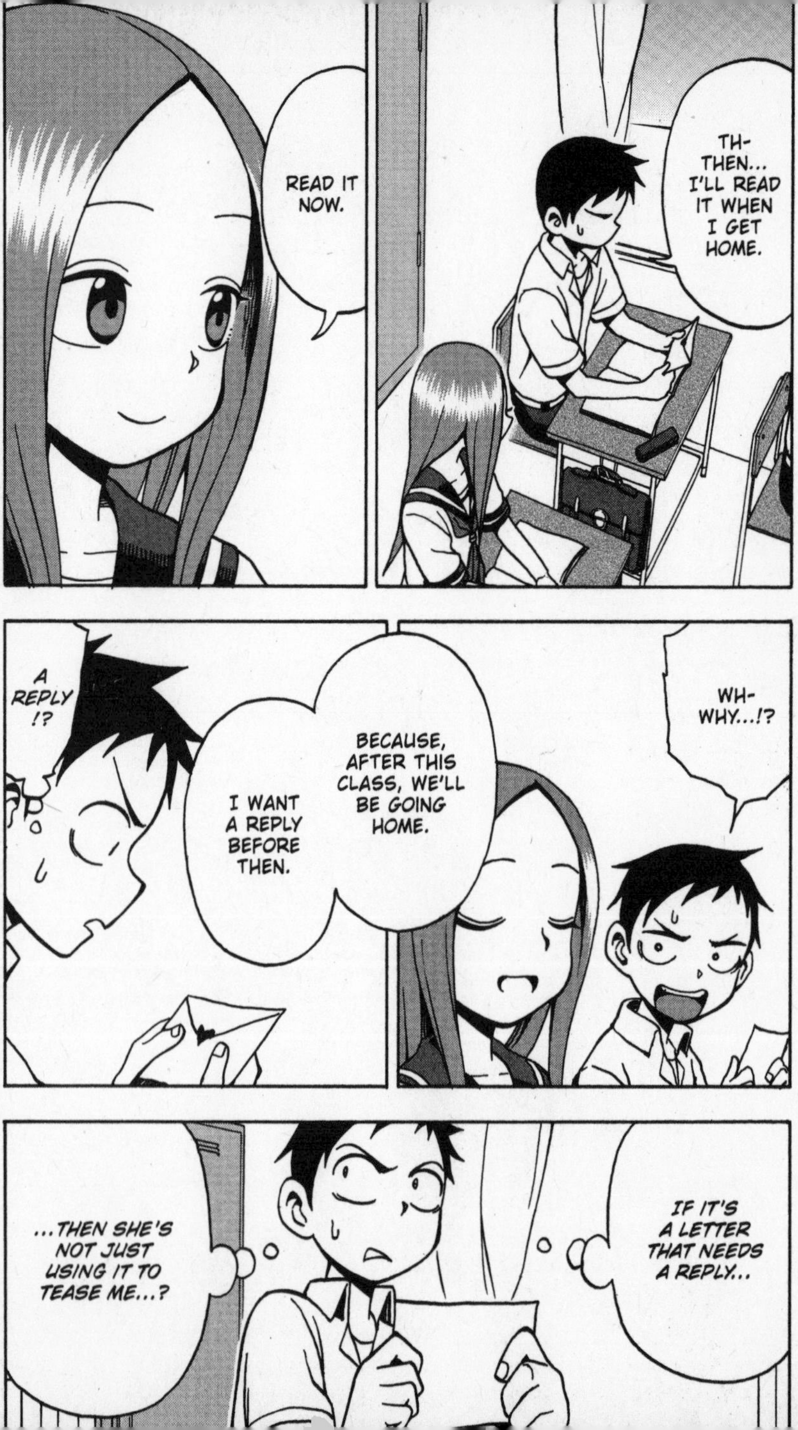
TH- THEN... I'LL READ IT WHEN I GET HOME.
READ IT NOW.
WH- WHY...!?
BECAUSE, AFTER THIS CLASS, WE'LL BE GOING HOME.
I WANT A REPLY BEFORE THEN.
A REPLY !?
IF IT'S A LETTER THAT NEEDS A REPLY...
...THEN SHE'S NOT JUST USING IT TO TEASE ME...?

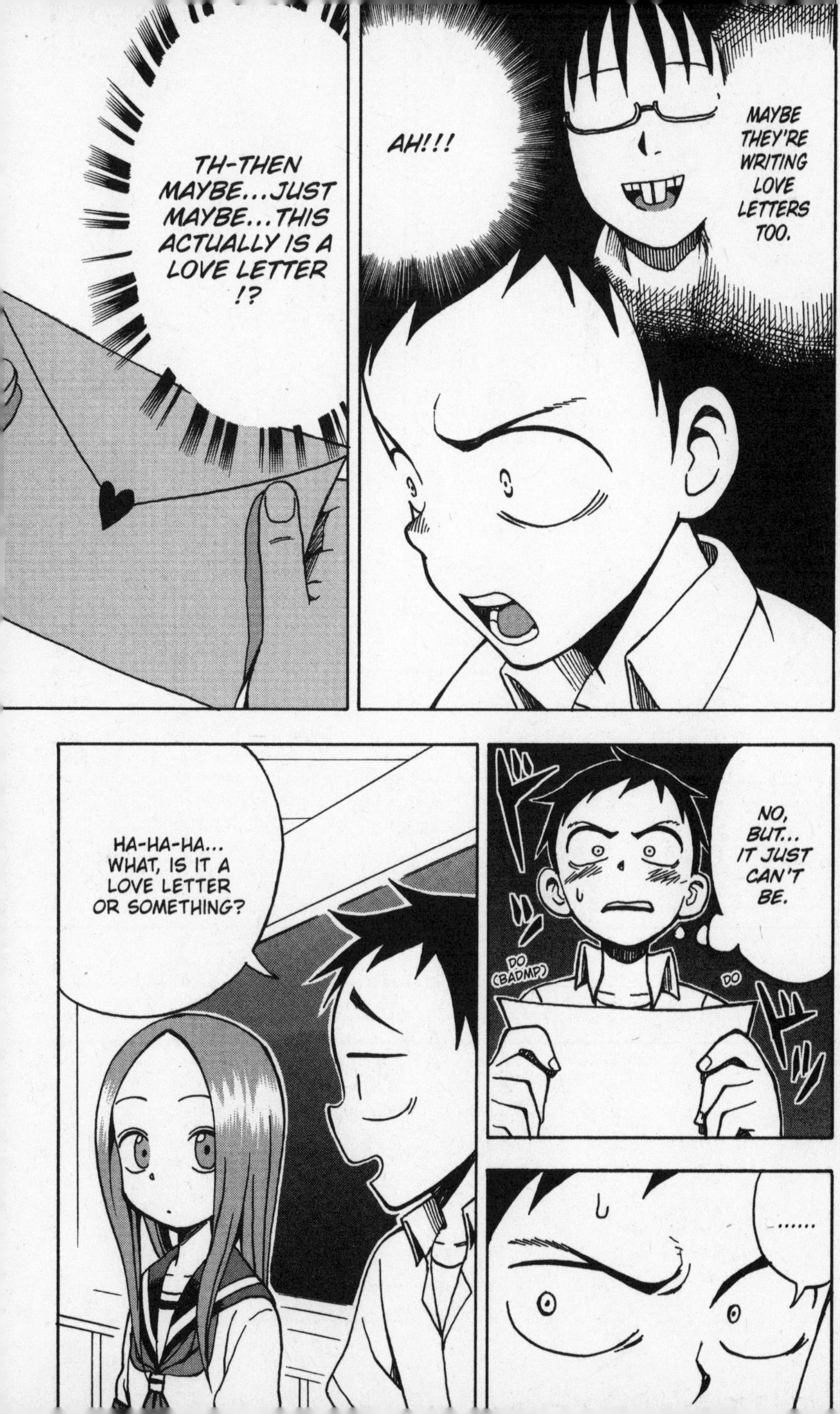
MAYBE THEY'RE WRITING LOVE LETTERS TOO.
AH!!!
TH-THEN MAYBE...JUST MAYBE...THIS ACTUALLY IS A LOVE LETTER !?
NO, BUT... IT JUST CAN'T BE.
DO (BADMP)
DO
......
HA-HA-HA... WHAT, IS IT A LOVE LETTER OR SOMETHING?

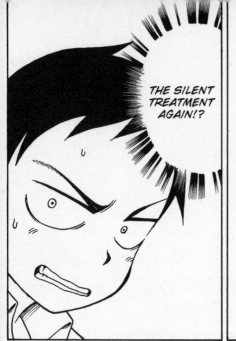

THE SILENT TREATMENT AGAIN!?
YOU'RE NOT GOING TO READ IT?
I-I WILL. I'LL READ IT... I JUST HAVE TO READ IT, RIGHT?
NO...IT HAS TO BE A PRANK. I'M POSITIVE.
THIS MEANS I HAVE TO BE BOLD AND DECISIVE SO I DON'T GET TEASED...!!

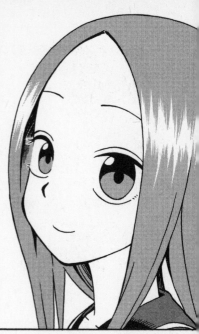

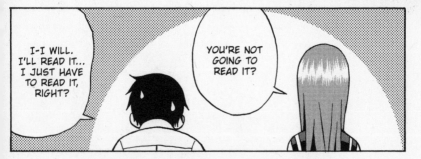

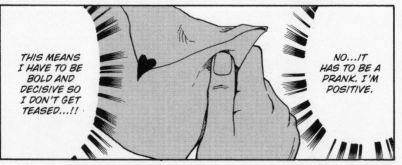

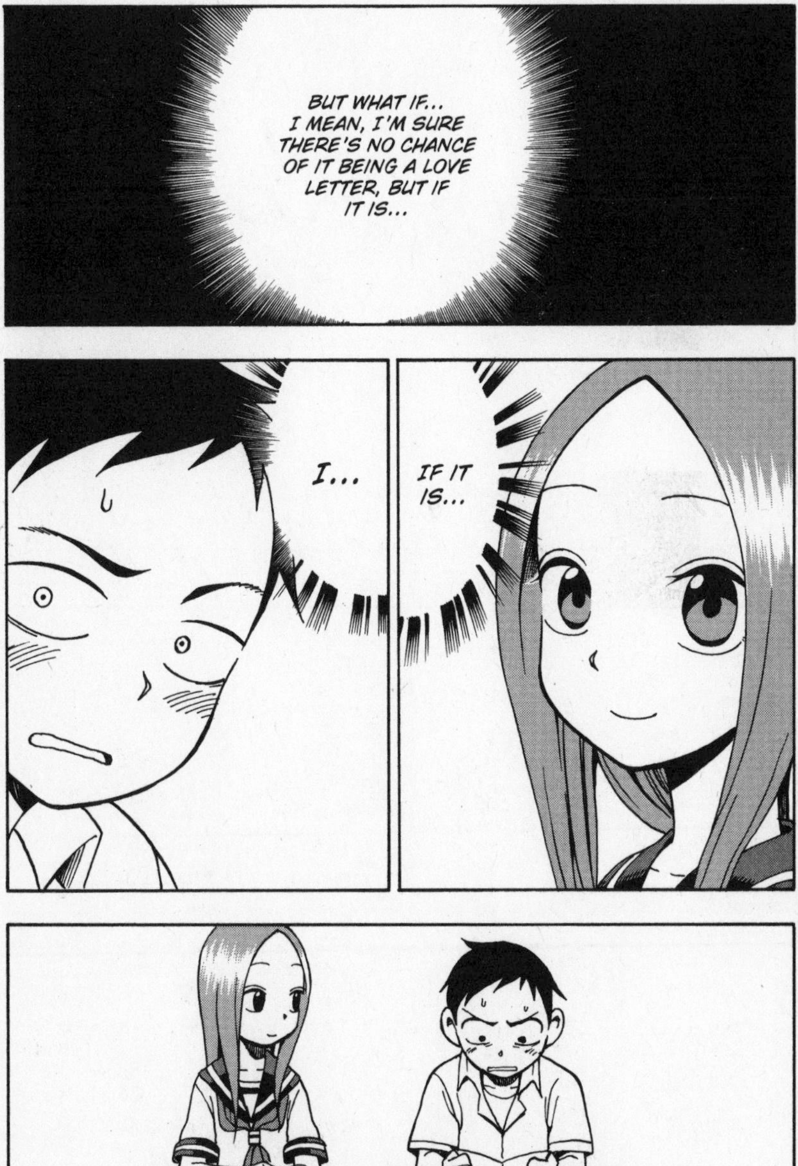
BUT WHAT IF... I MEAN, I'M SURE THERE'S NO CHANCE OF IT BEING A LOVE LETTER, BUT IF IT IS...
IF IT IS...
I...

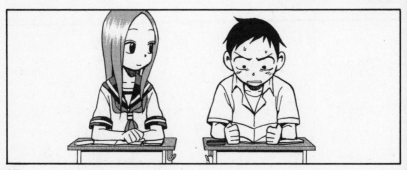

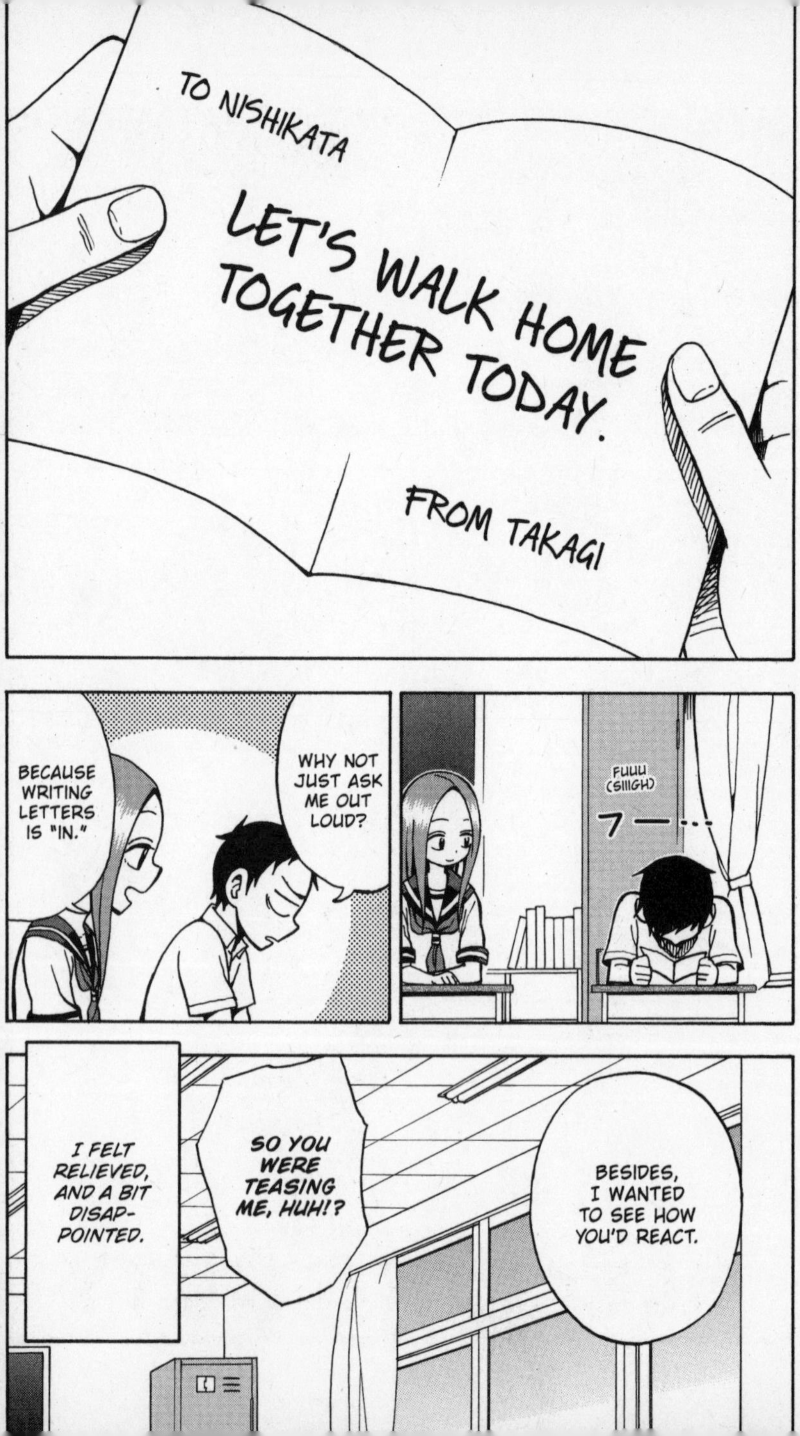
TO NISHIKATA
LET'S WALK HOME TOGETHER TODAY.
FROM TAKAGI
FUUU (SIIIGH)
WHY NOT JUST ASK ME OUT LOUD?
BECAUSE WRITING LETTERS IS "IN."
BESIDES, I WANTED TO SEE HOW YOU'D REACT.
SO YOU WERE TEASING ME, HUH!?
I FELT RELIEVED, AND A BIT DISAP-POINTED.

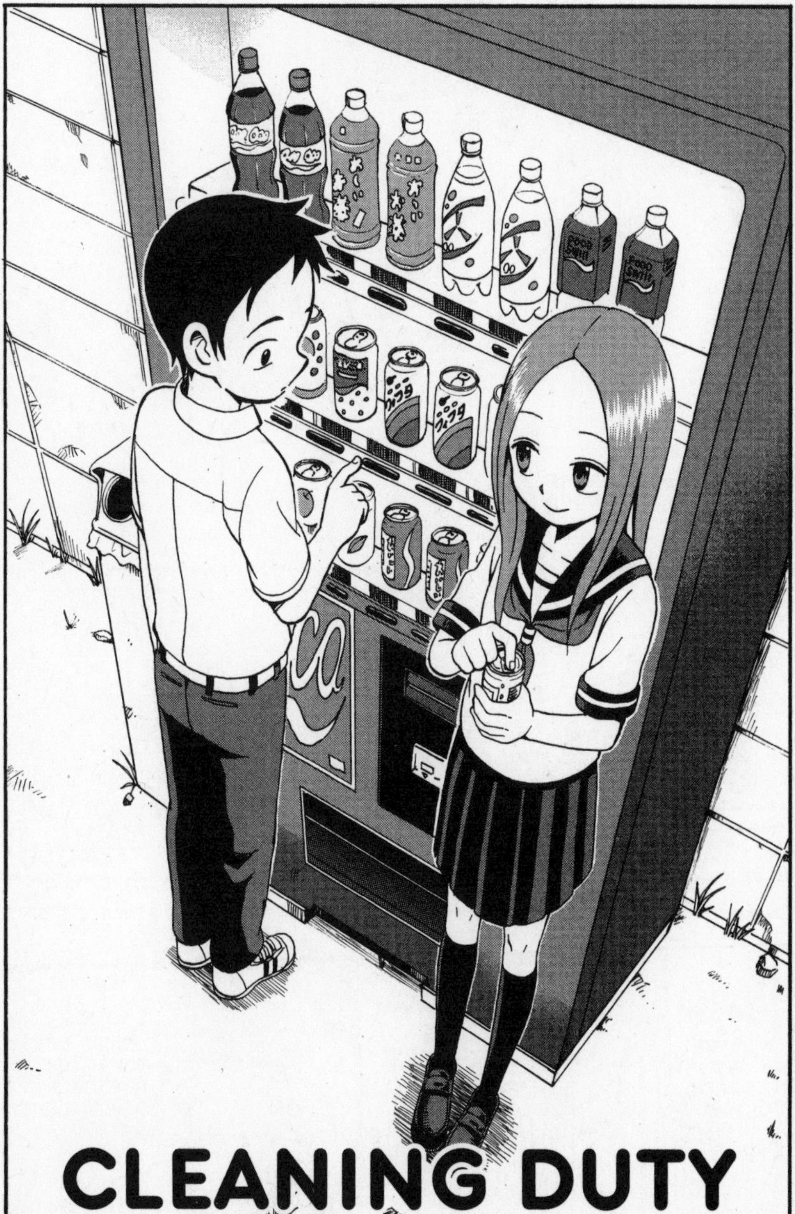

# CLEANING DUTY

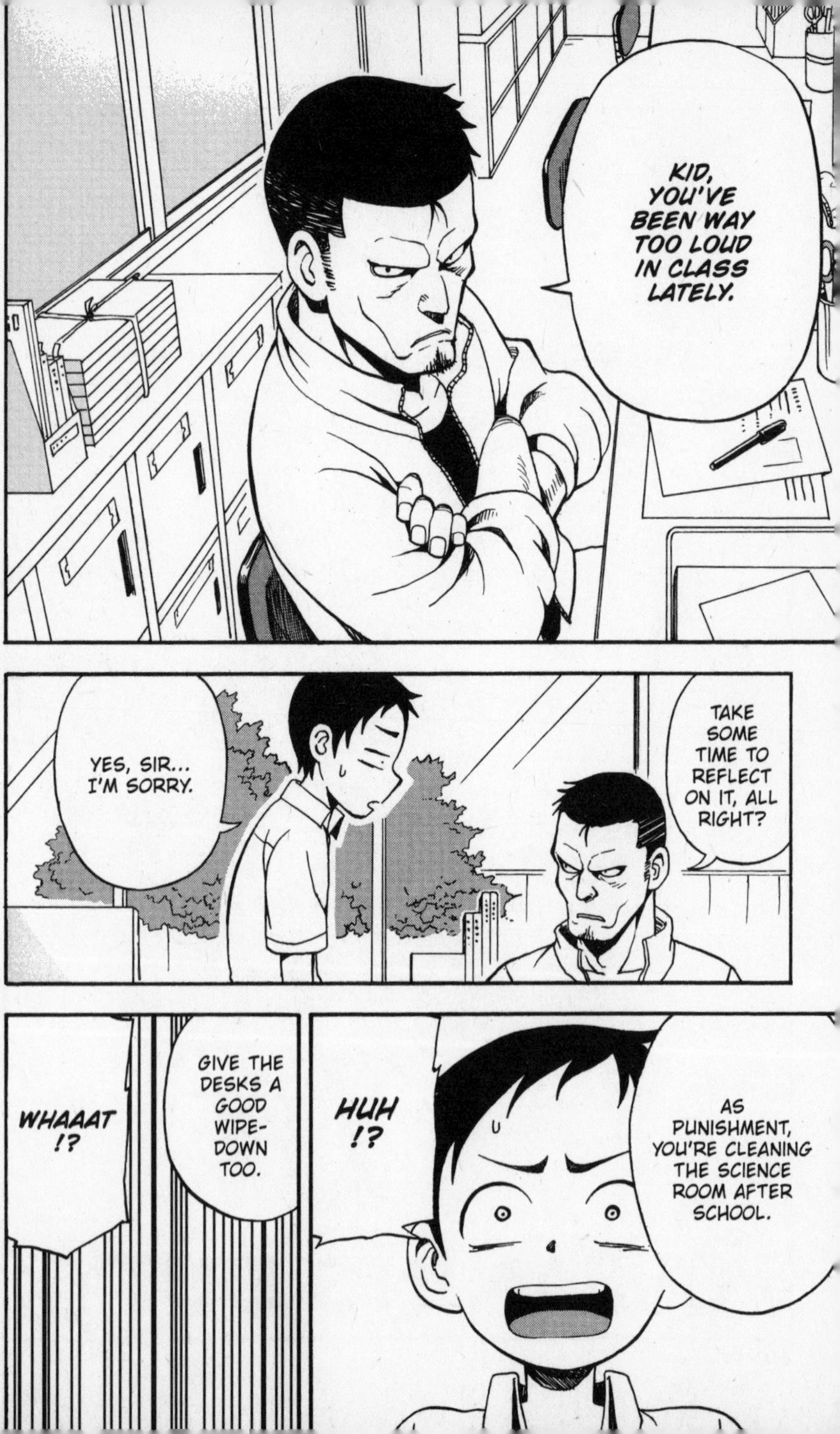
KID, YOU'VE BEEN WAY TOO LOUD IN CLASS LATELY.
TAKE SOME TIME TO REFLECT ON IT, ALL RIGHT?
YES, SIR... I'M SORRY.
AS PUNISHMENT, YOU'RE CLEANING THE SCIENCE ROOM AFTER SCHOOL.
HUH !?
GIVE THE DESKS A GOOD WIPE-DOWN TOO.
WHAAAT !?

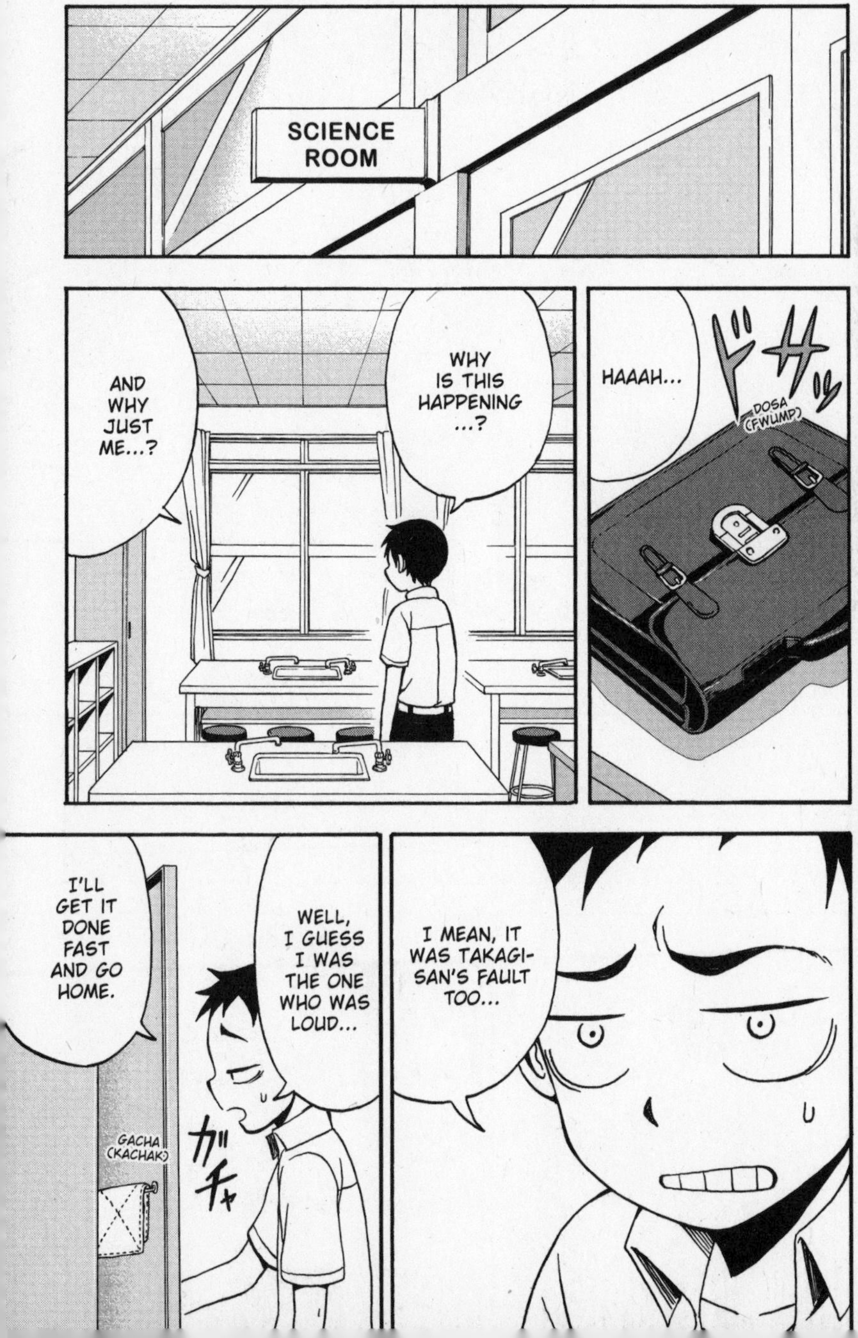
SCIENCE ROOM
HAAAH...
ドサッ
DOSA (FWUMP)
WHY IS THIS HAPPENING ...?
AND WHY JUST ME...?
I MEAN, IT WAS TAKAGI-SAN'S FAULT TOO...
WELL, I GUESS I WAS THE ONE WHO WAS LOUD...
I'LL GET IT DONE FAST AND GO HOME.
ガチャ
GACHA (KACHAK)

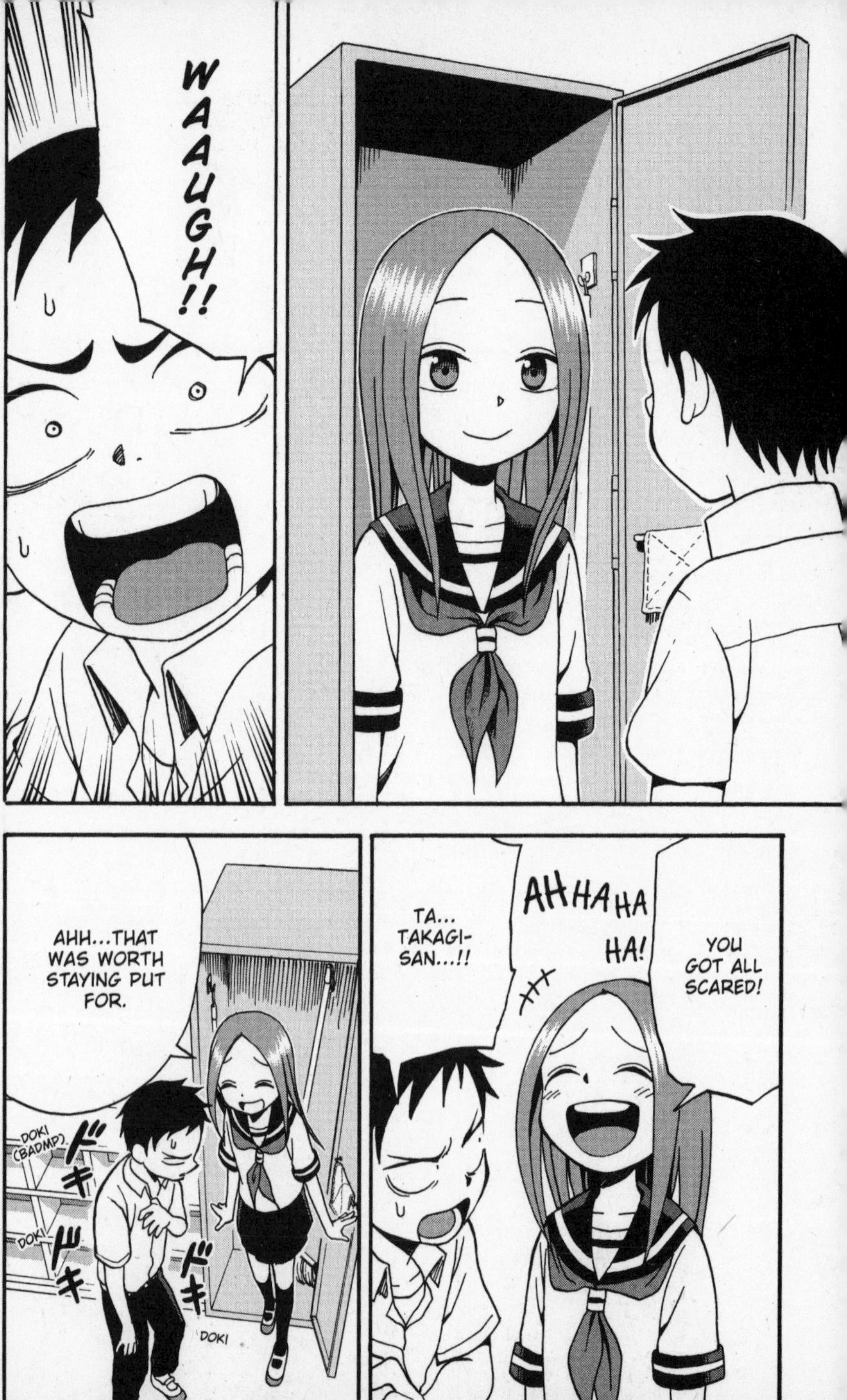
WAAAUGH!!
YOU GOT ALL SCARED!
AHHAHAHA HA!
TA... TAKAGI-SAN...!!
AHH...THAT WAS WORTH STAYING PUT FOR.
DOKI (BADMP)
ドキ
DOKI
ドキ
DOKI

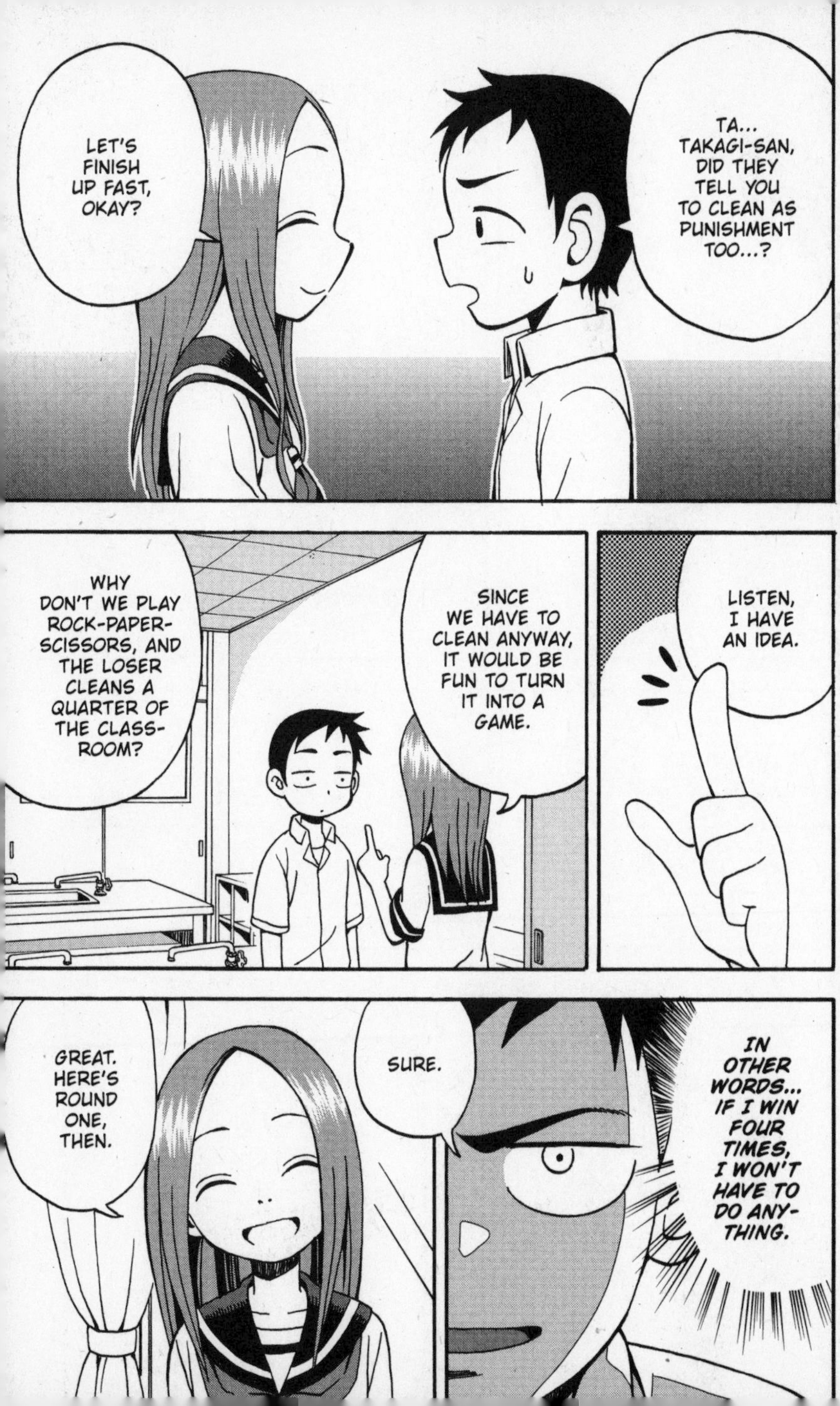
TA... TAKAGI-SAN, DID THEY TELL YOU TO CLEAN AS PUNISHMENT TOO...?
LET'S FINISH UP FAST, OKAY?
LISTEN, I HAVE AN IDEA.
SINCE WE HAVE TO CLEAN ANYWAY, IT WOULD BE FUN TO TURN IT INTO A GAME.
WHY DON'T WE PLAY ROCK-PAPER-SCISSORS, AND THE LOSER CLEANS A QUARTER OF THE CLASS-ROOM?
IN OTHER WORDS... IF I WIN FOUR TIMES, I WON'T HAVE TO DO ANY-THING.
SURE.
GREAT. HERE'S ROUND ONE, THEN.

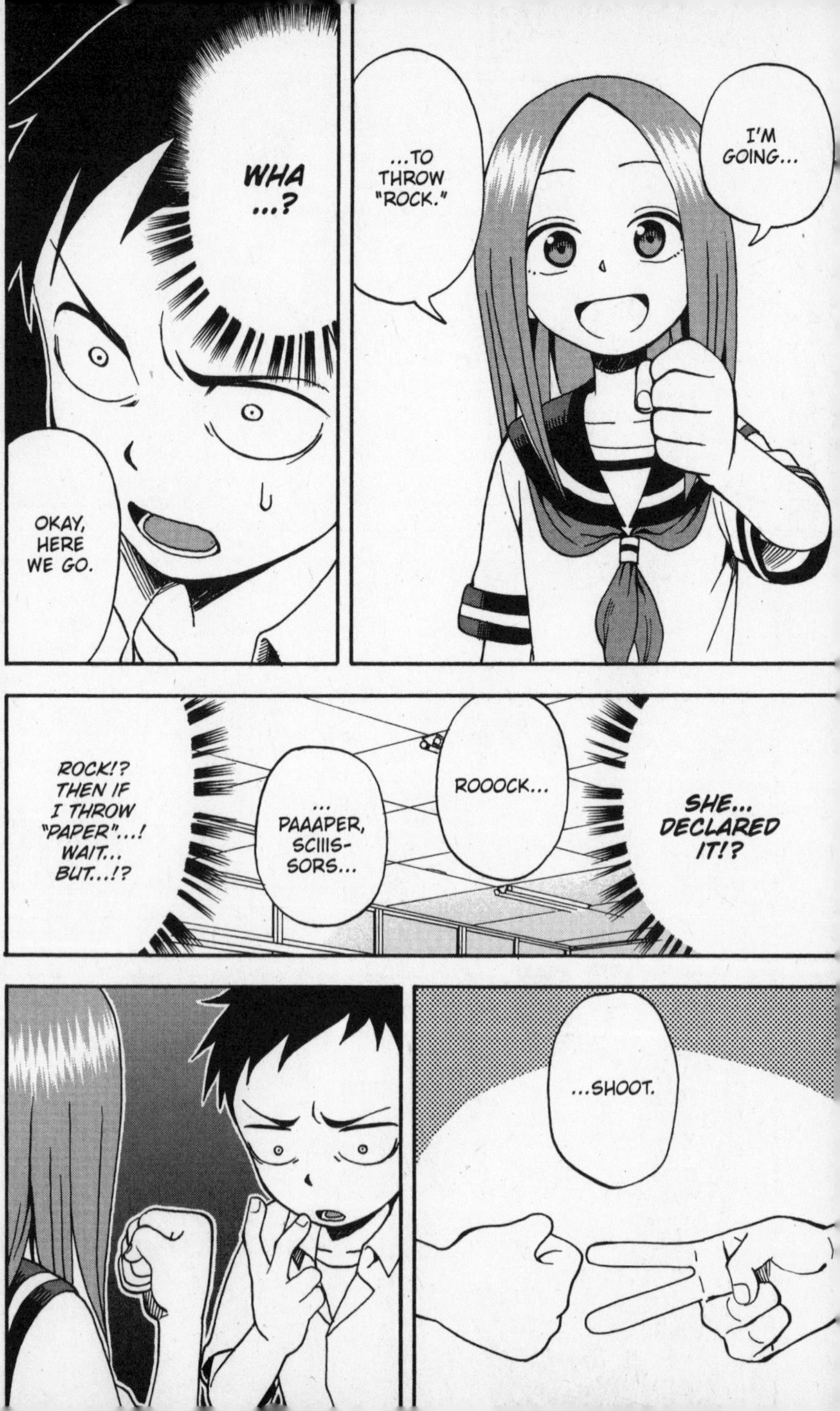
I'M GOING...
...TO THROW "ROCK."
WHA ...?
OKAY, HERE WE GO.
SHE... DECLARED IT!?
ROOOCK...
... PAAAPER, SCIIIS-SORS...
ROCK!? THEN IF I THROW "PAPER"...! WAIT... BUT...!?
...SHOOT.

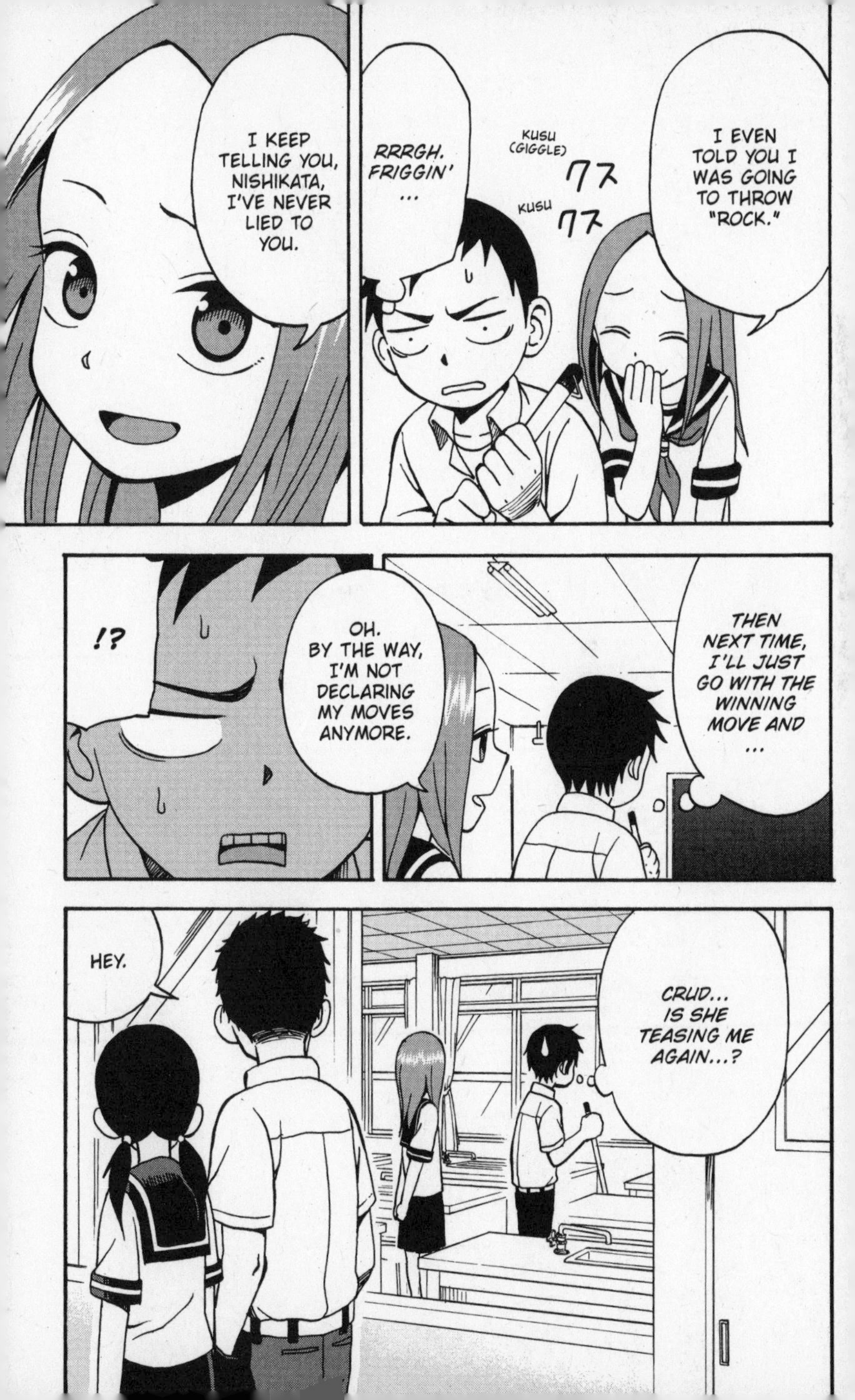
I EVEN TOLD YOU I WAS GOING TO THROW "ROCK."
KUSU (GIGGLE)
クス
KUSU
クス
RRRGH. FRIGGIN' ...
I KEEP TELLING YOU, NISHIKATA, I'VE NEVER LIED TO YOU.
THEN NEXT TIME, I'LL JUST GO WITH THE WINNING MOVE AND ...
OH. BY THE WAY, I'M NOT DECLARING MY MOVES ANYMORE.
!?
CRUD... IS SHE TEASING ME AGAIN...?
HEY.

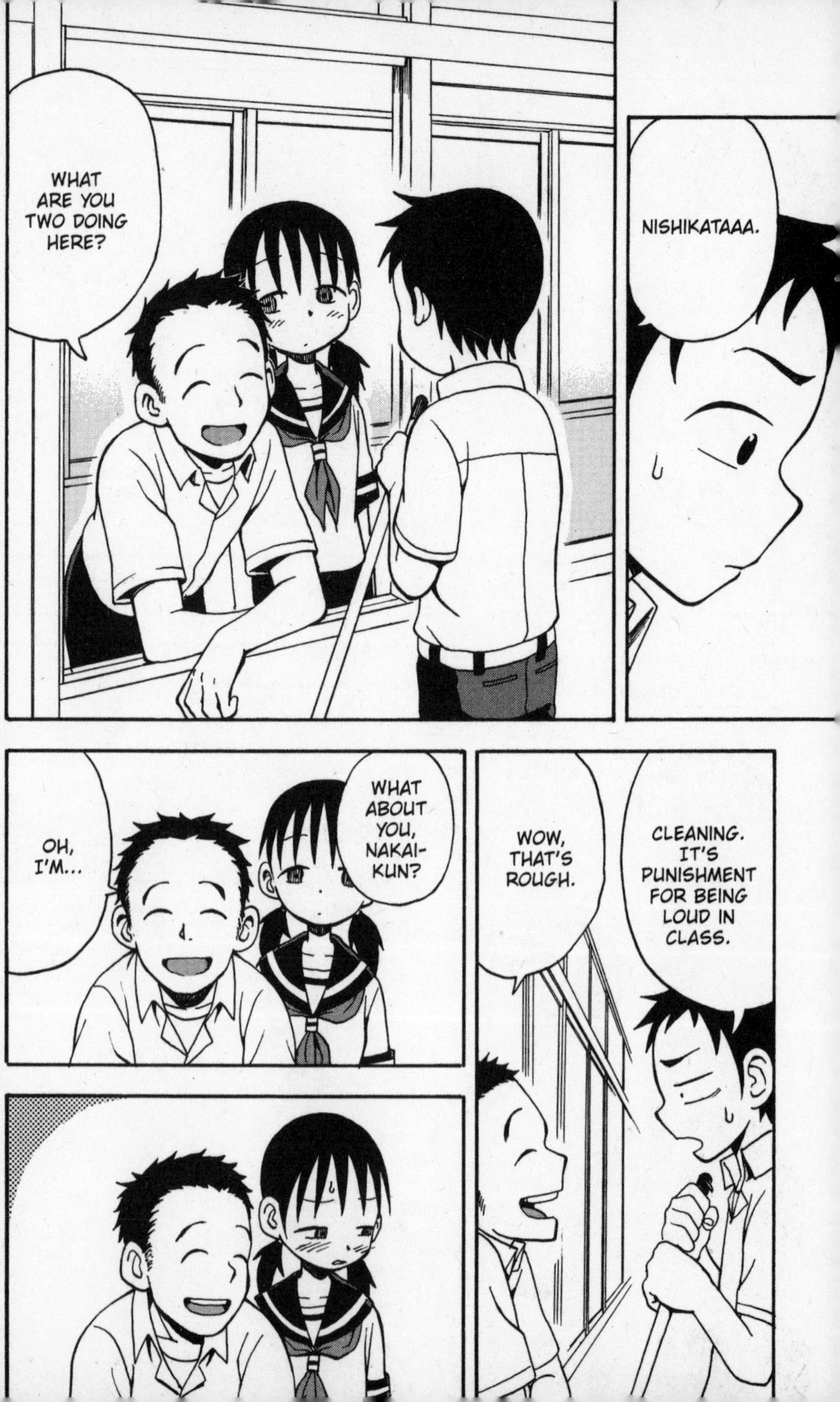
NISHIKATAAA.
WHAT ARE YOU TWO DOING HERE?
CLEANING. IT'S PUNISHMENT FOR BEING LOUD IN CLASS.
WOW, THAT'S ROUGH.
WHAT ABOUT YOU, NAKAI-KUN?
OH, I'M...

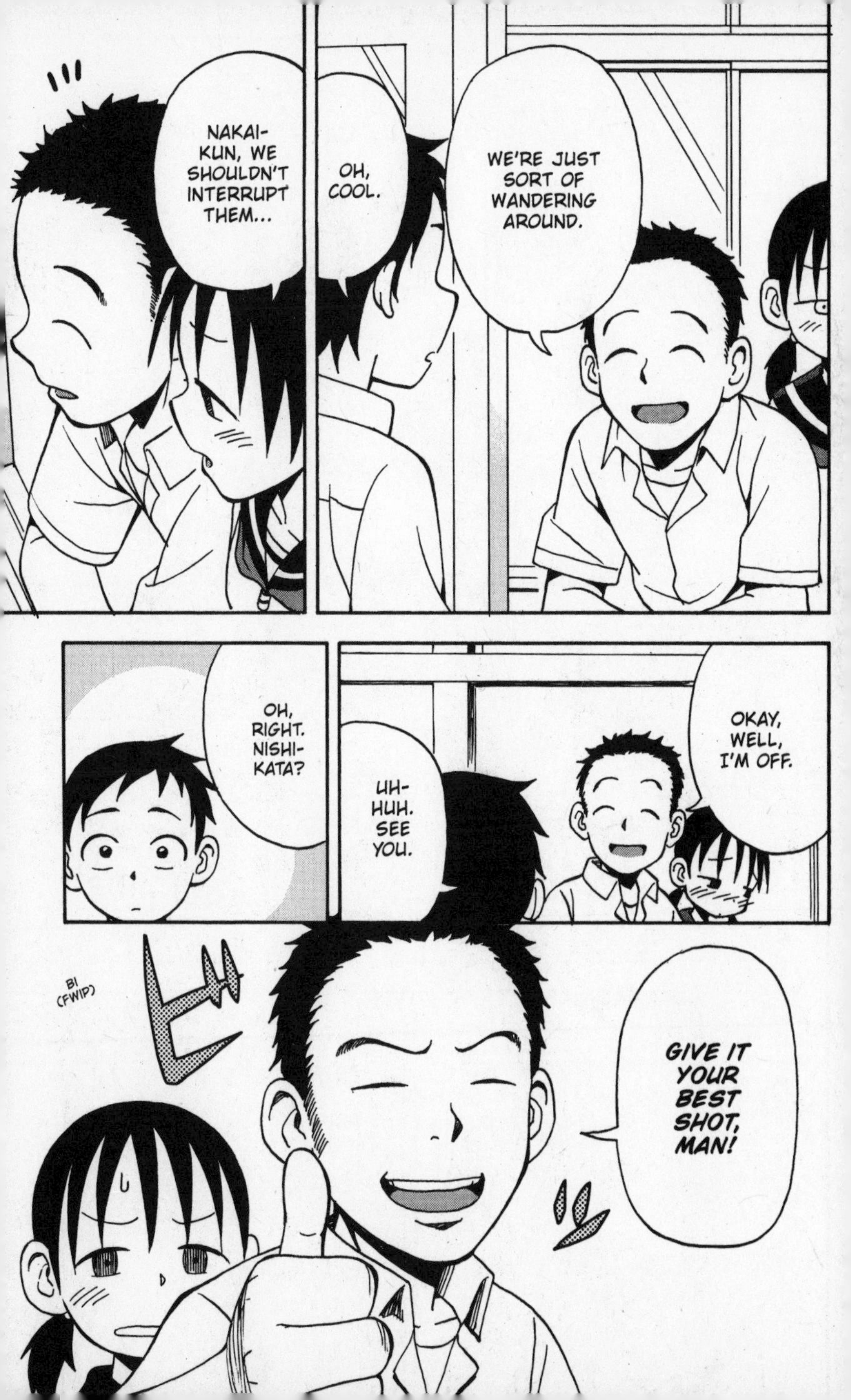
WE'RE JUST SORT OF WANDERING AROUND.
OH, COOL.
NAKAI-KUN, WE SHOULDN'T INTERRUPT THEM...
OKAY, WELL, I'M OFF.
UH-HUH. SEE YOU.
OH, RIGHT. NISHI-KATA?
GIVE IT YOUR BEST SHOT, MAN!
BI (FWIP)

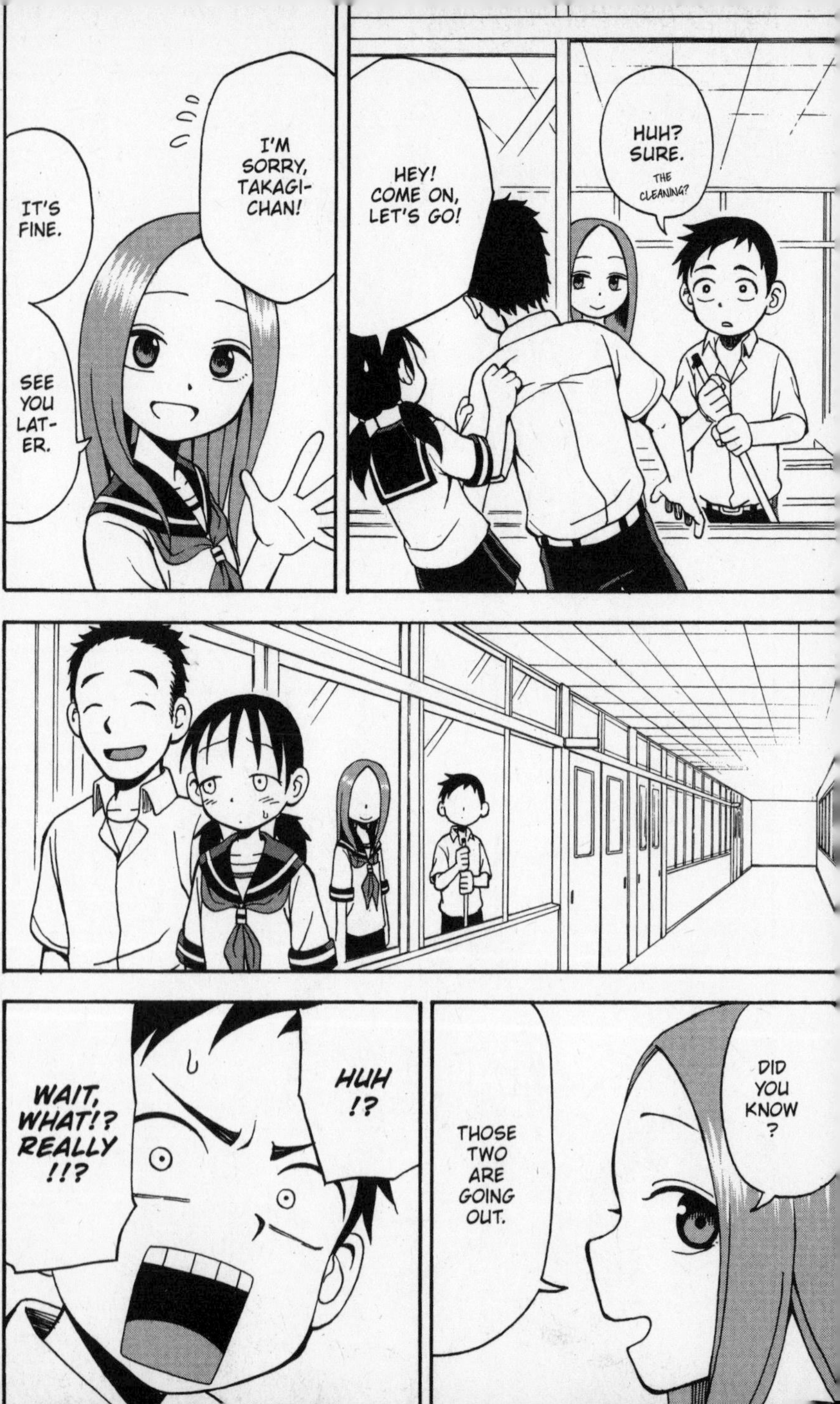
HUH? SURE.
THE CLEANING?
HEY! COME ON, LET'S GO!
I'M SORRY, TAKAGI-CHAN!
IT'S FINE.
SEE YOU LATER.
DID YOU KNOW?
THOSE TWO ARE GOING OUT.
HUH!?
WAIT, WHAT!? REALLY!!?

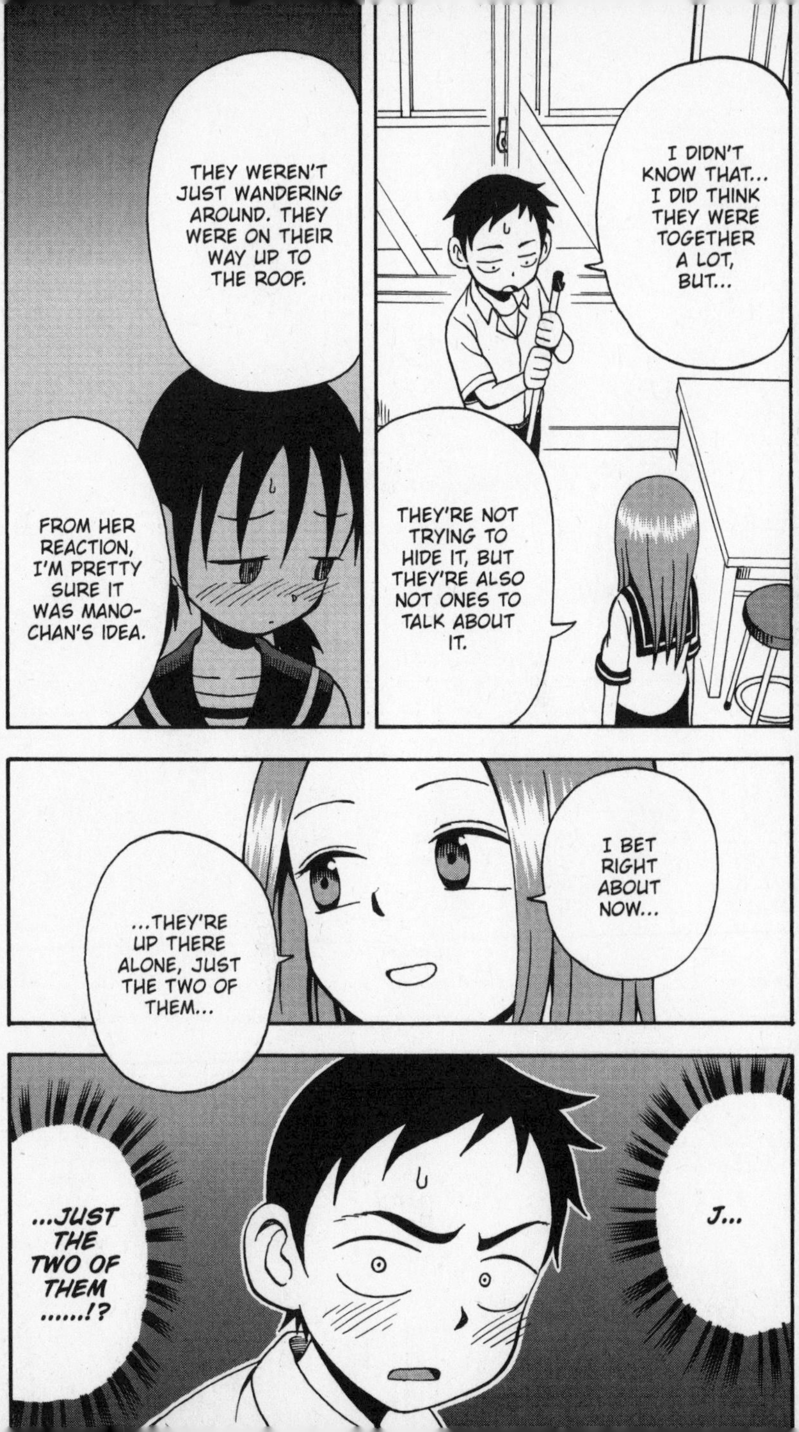
I DIDN'T KNOW THAT... I DID THINK THEY WERE TOGETHER A LOT, BUT...
THEY'RE NOT TRYING TO HIDE IT, BUT THEY'RE ALSO NOT ONES TO TALK ABOUT IT.
THEY WEREN'T JUST WANDERING AROUND. THEY WERE ON THEIR WAY UP TO THE ROOF.
FROM HER REACTION, I'M PRETTY SURE IT WAS MANO-CHAN'S IDEA.
I BET RIGHT ABOUT NOW...
...THEY'RE UP THERE ALONE, JUST THE TWO OF THEM...
J...
...JUST THE TWO OF THEM ......!?

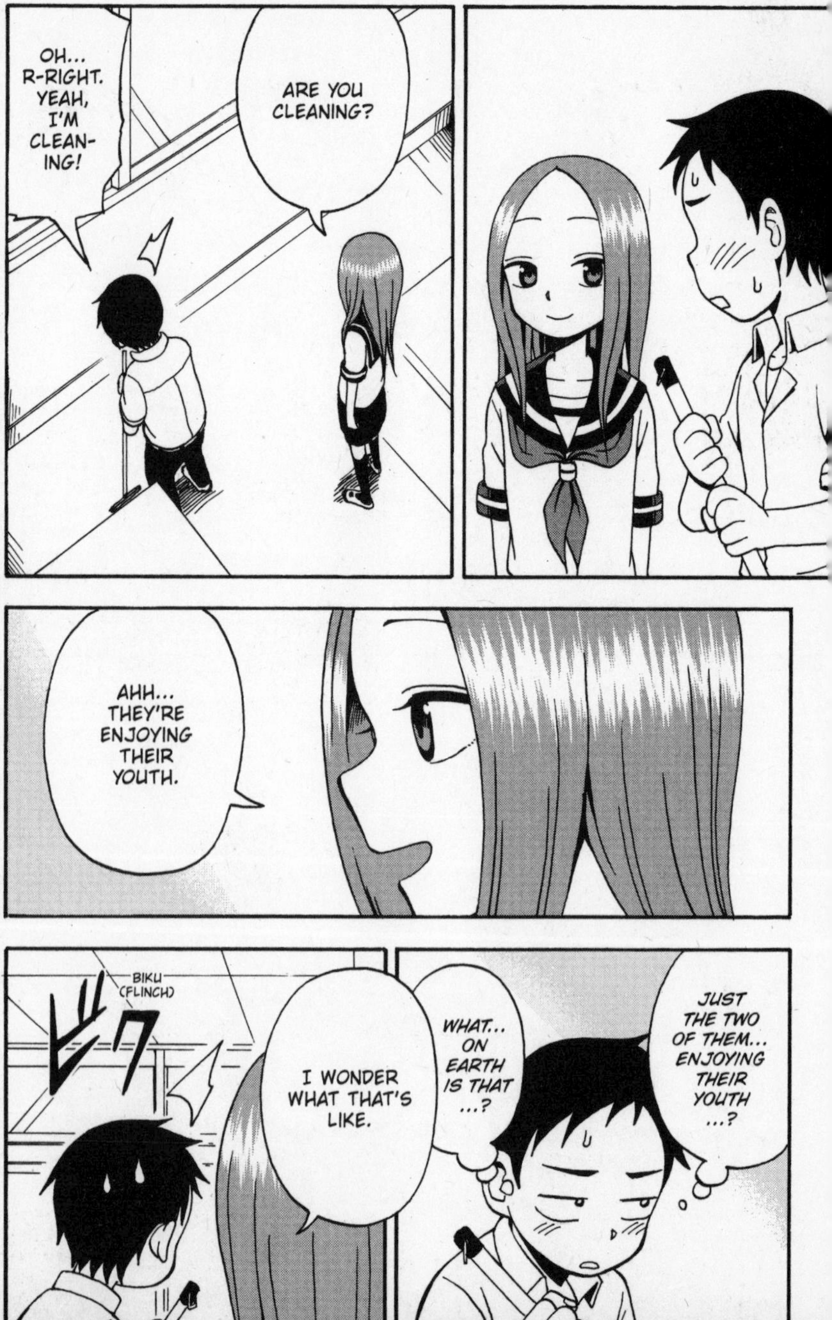
ARE YOU CLEANING?
OH... R-RIGHT. YEAH, I'M CLEAN-ING!
AHH... THEY'RE ENJOYING THEIR YOUTH.
JUST THE TWO OF THEM... ENJOYING THEIR YOUTH ...?
WHAT... ON EARTH IS THAT ...?
I WONDER WHAT THAT'S LIKE.
BIKU (FLINCH)

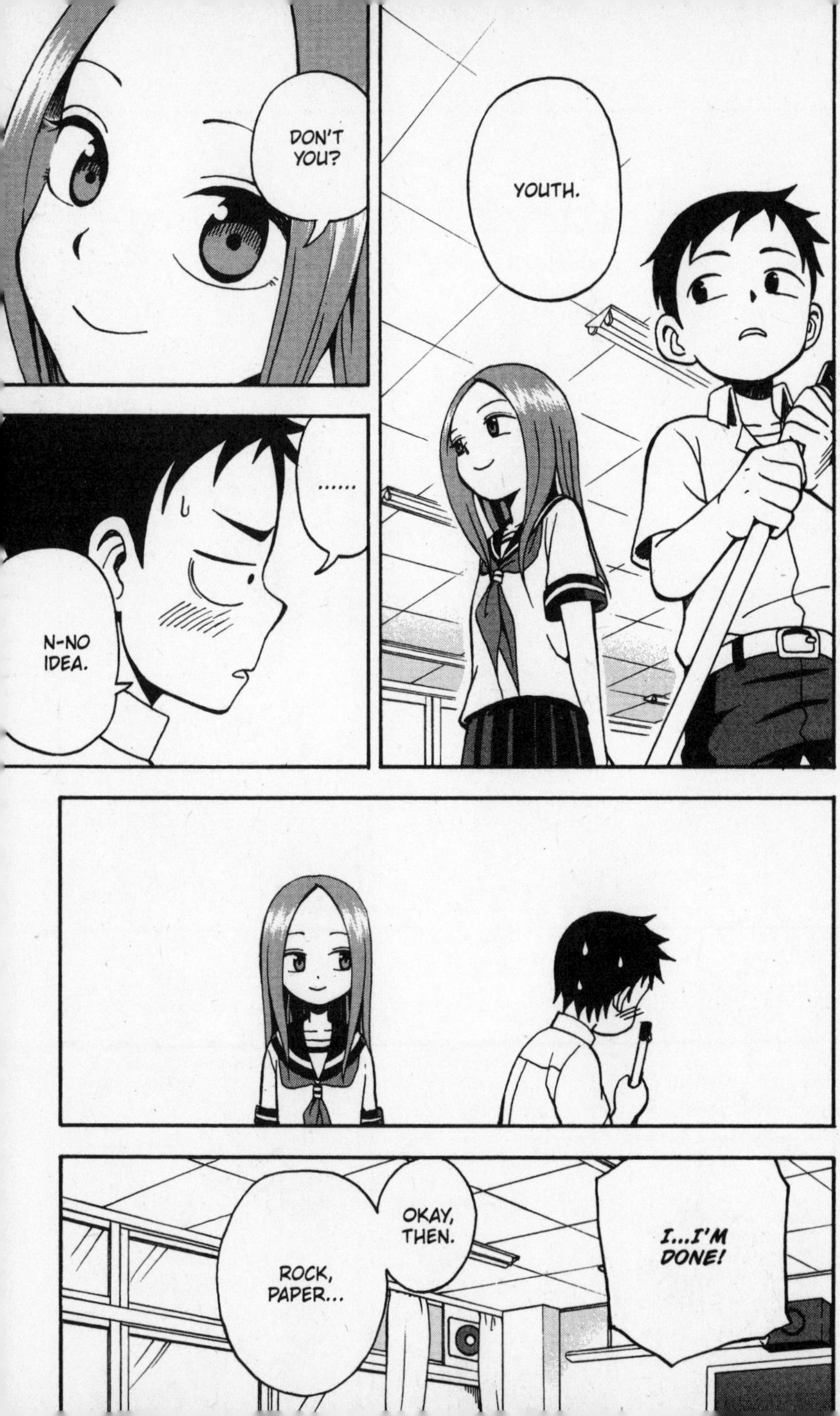
YOUTH.
DON'T YOU?
......
N-NO IDEA.
I...I'M DONE!
OKAY, THEN.
ROCK, PAPER...

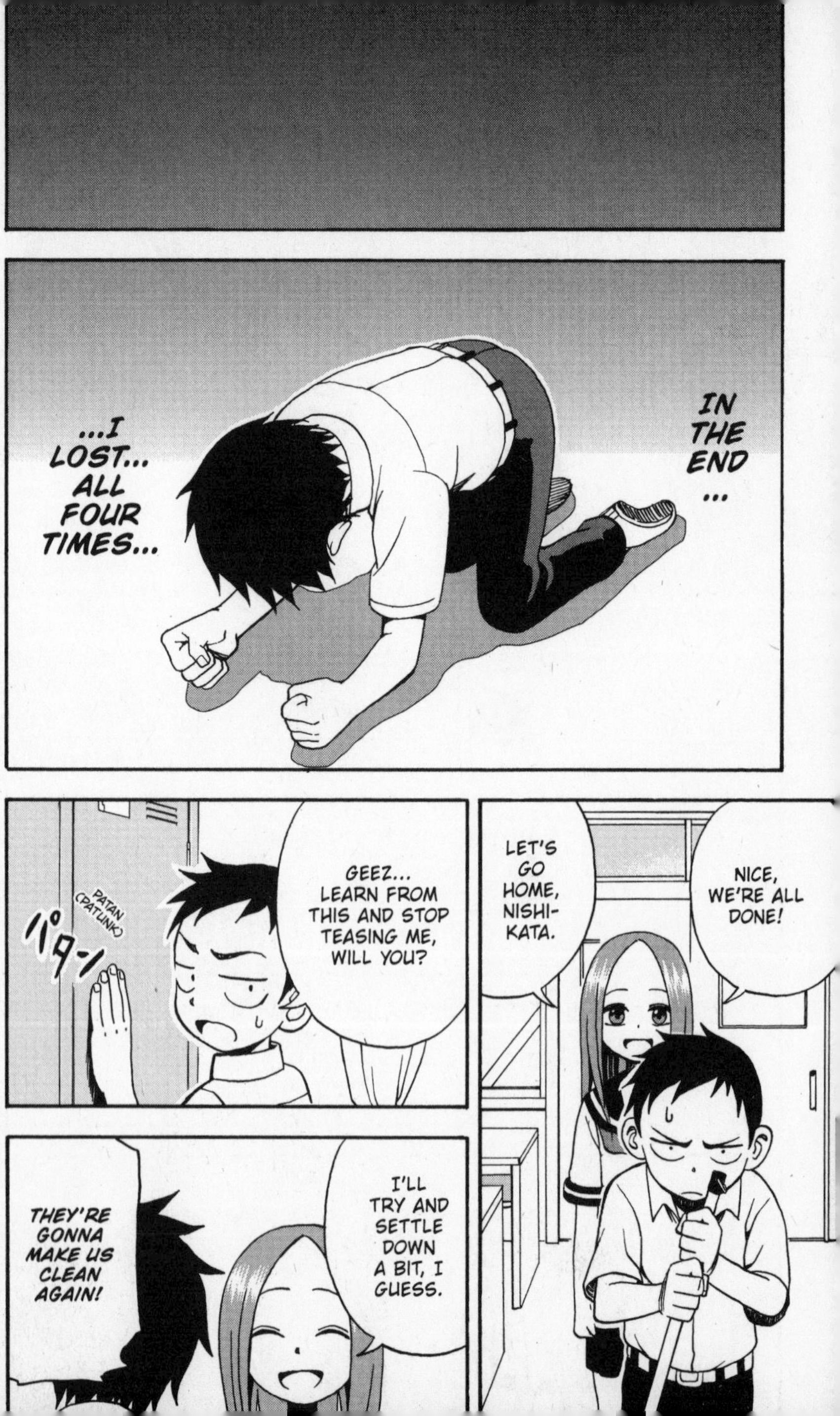
IN THE END...
...I LOST... ALL FOUR TIMES...
NICE, WE'RE ALL DONE!
LET'S GO HOME, NISHIKATA.
GEEZ... LEARN FROM THIS AND STOP TEASING ME, WILL YOU?
パタン
PATAN (PATUNK)
I'LL TRY AND SETTLE DOWN A BIT, I GUESS.
THEY'RE GONNA MAKE US CLEAN AGAIN!

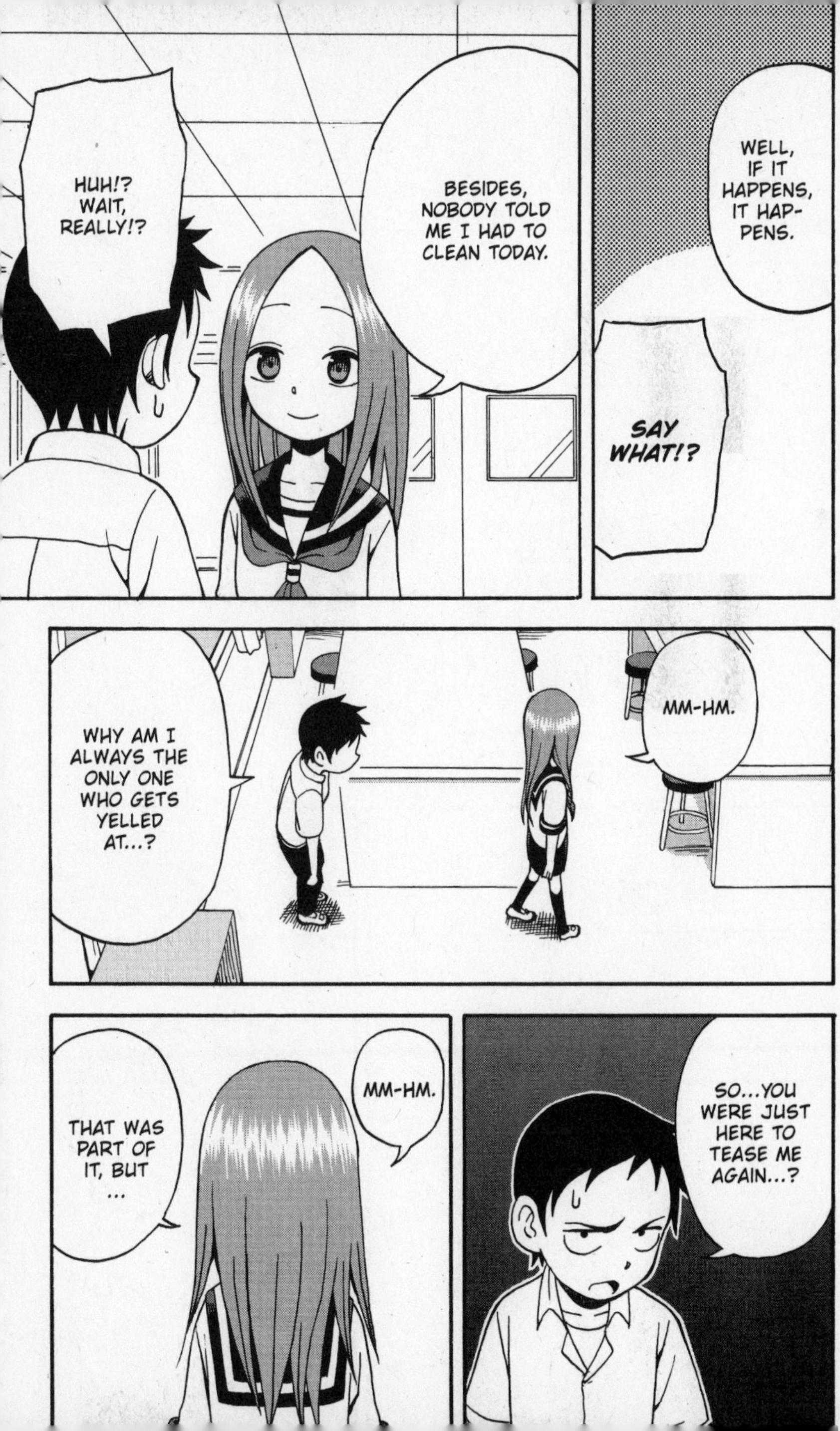
WELL, IF IT HAPPENS, IT HAP-PENS.
SAY WHAT!?
BESIDES, NOBODY TOLD ME I HAD TO CLEAN TODAY.
HUH!? WAIT, REALLY!?
MM-HM.
WHY AM I ALWAYS THE ONLY ONE WHO GETS YELLED AT...?
SO...YOU WERE JUST HERE TO TEASE ME AGAIN...?
MM-HM.
THAT WAS PART OF IT, BUT ...

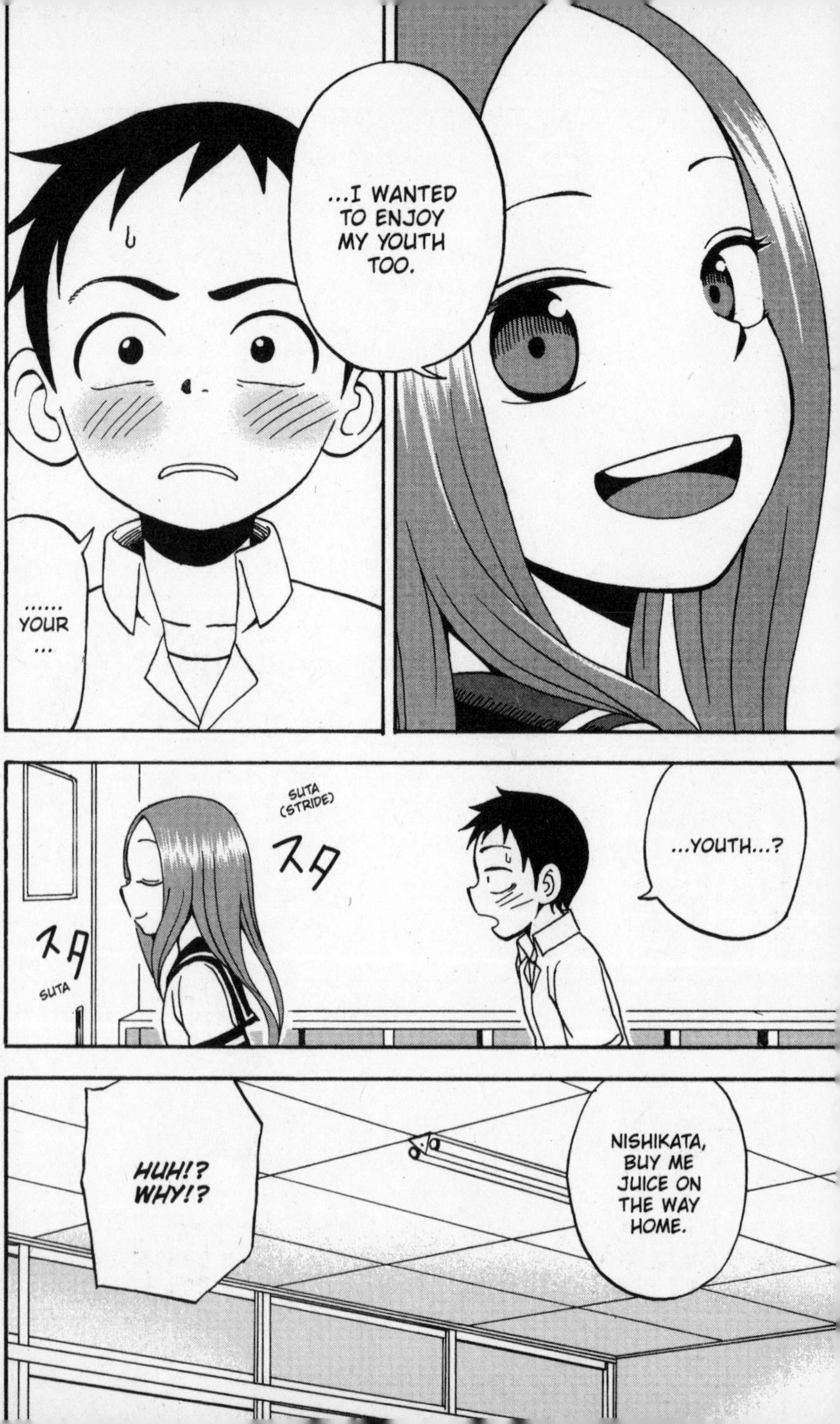
...I WANTED TO ENJOY MY YOUTH TOO.
...... YOUR ...
...YOUTH...?
SUTA (STRIDE)
スタ
スタ
SUTA
NISHIKATA, BUY ME JUICE ON THE WAY HOME.
HUH!? WHY!?

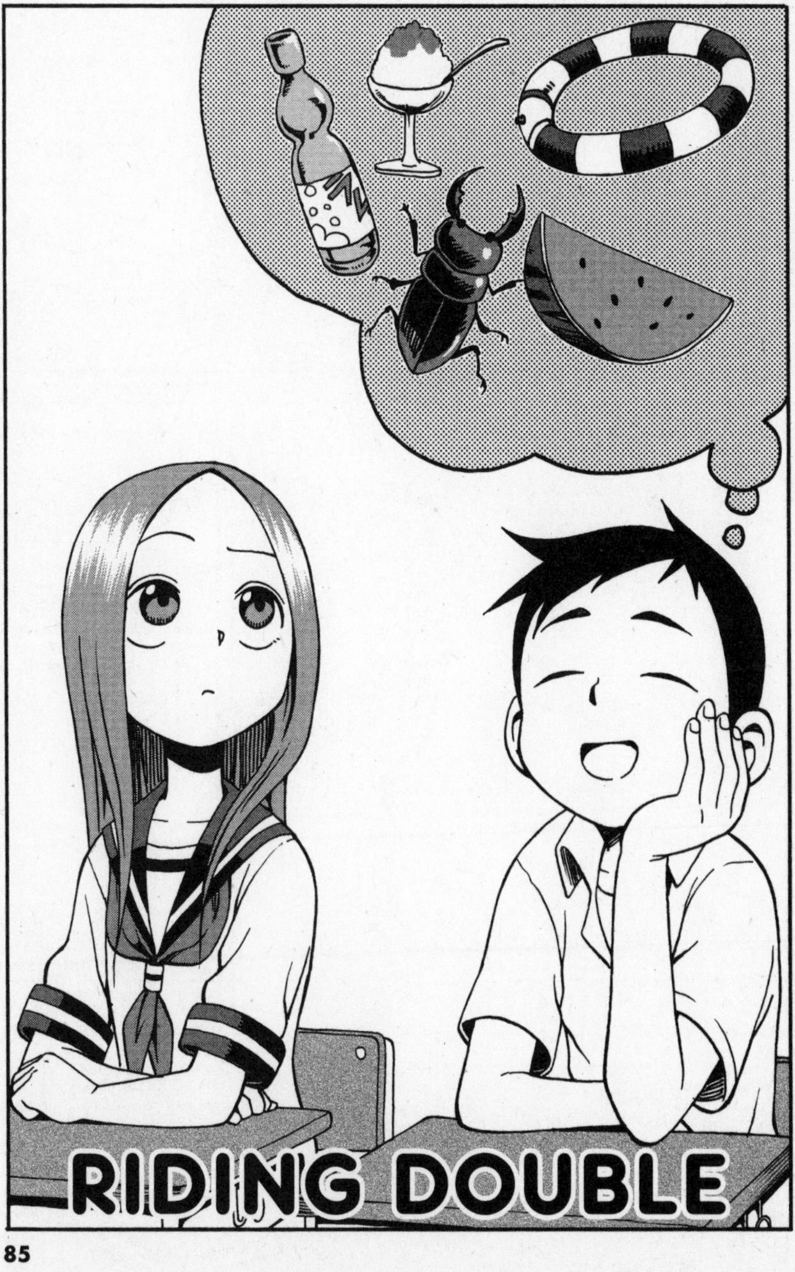
RIDING DOUBLE

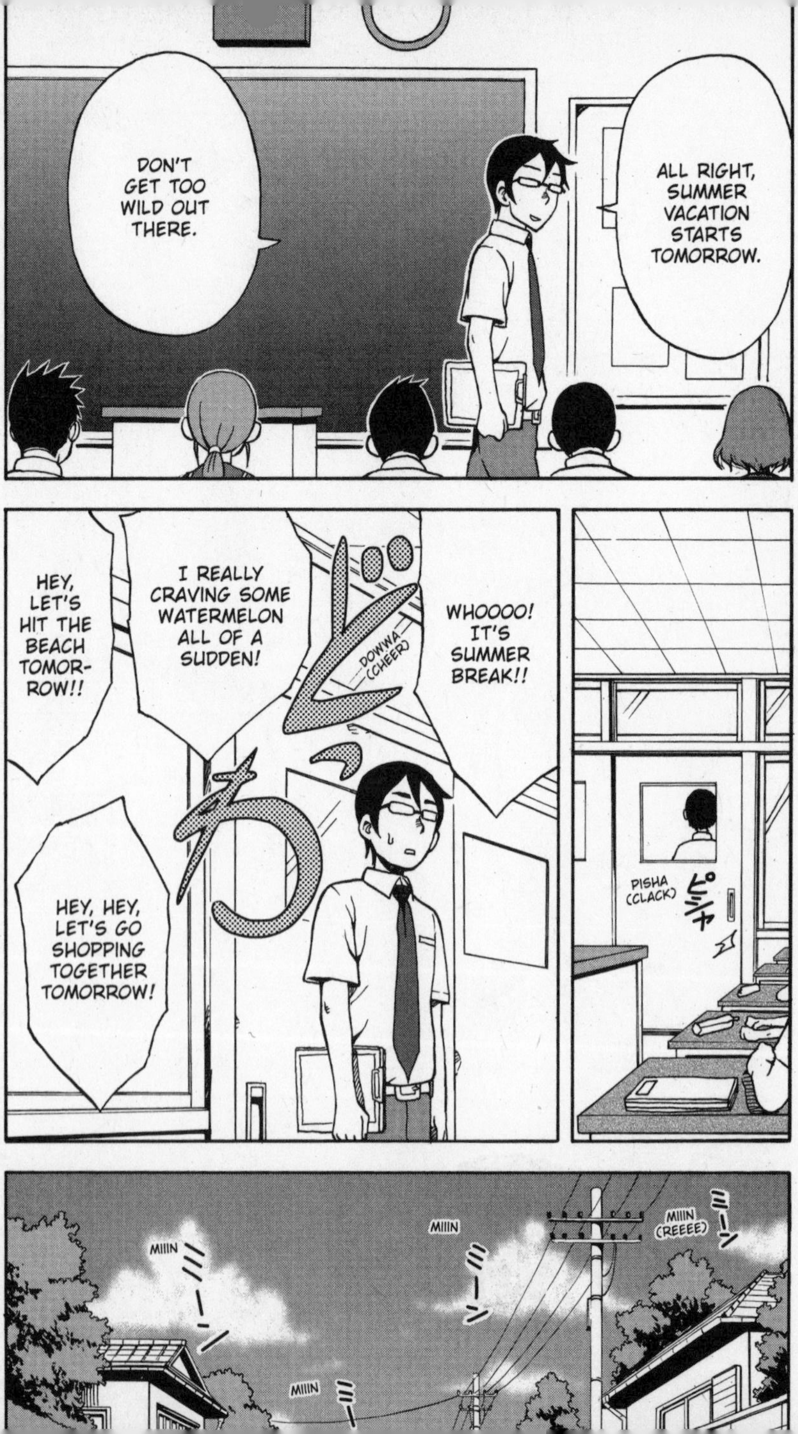
ALL RIGHT, SUMMER VACATION STARTS TOMORROW.
DON'T GET TOO WILD OUT THERE.
PISHA (CLACK)
WHOOOO! IT'S SUMMER BREAK!!
DOWWA (CHEER)
I REALLY CRAVING SOME WATERMELON ALL OF A SUDDEN!
HEY, LET'S HIT THE BEACH TOMORROW!!
HEY, HEY, LET'S GO SHOPPING TOGETHER TOMORROW!
MIIIN (REEEE)
MIIIN
MIIIN
MIIIN

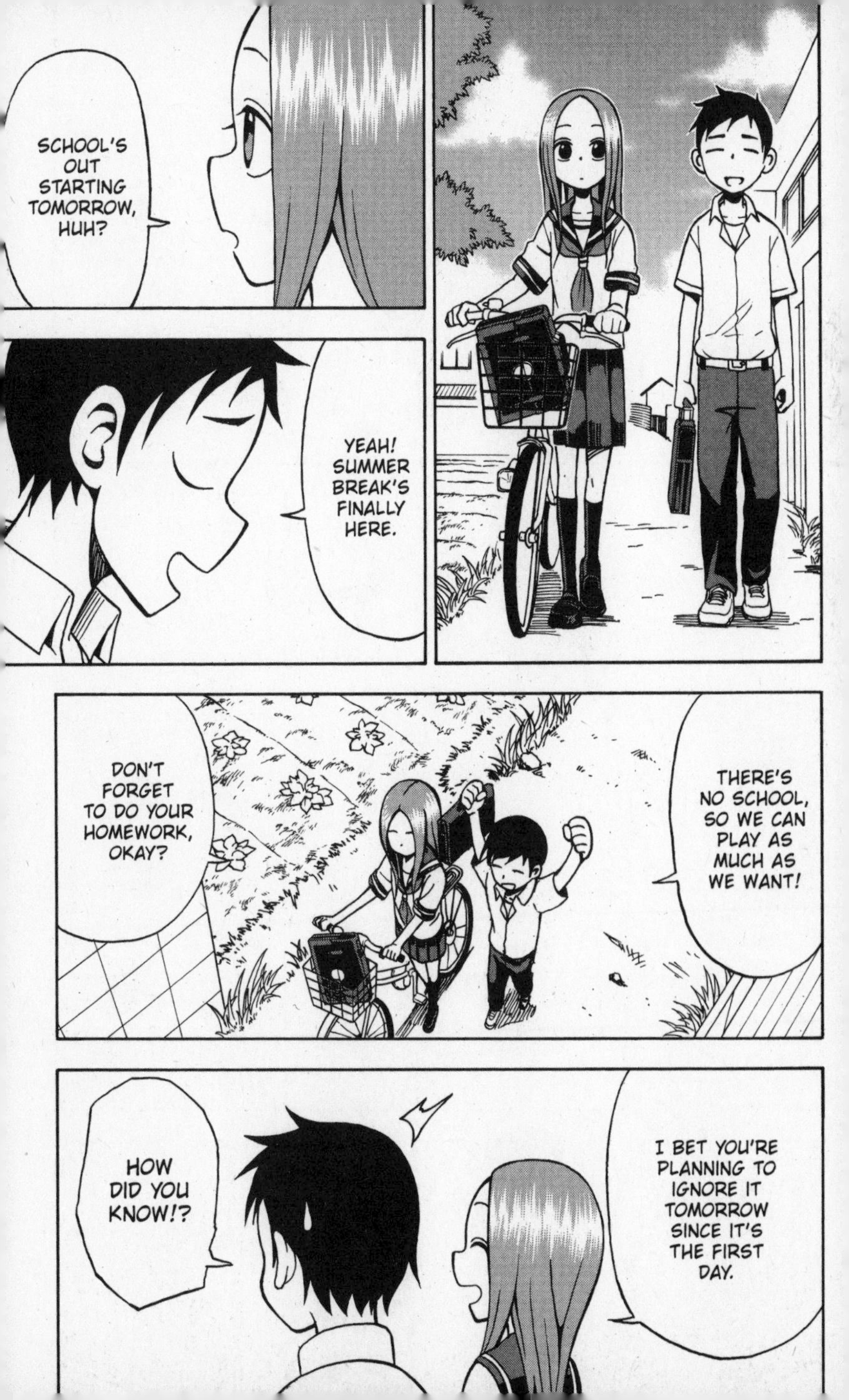
SCHOOL'S OUT STARTING TOMORROW, HUH?
YEAH! SUMMER BREAK'S FINALLY HERE.
THERE'S NO SCHOOL, SO WE CAN PLAY AS MUCH AS WE WANT!
DON'T FORGET TO DO YOUR HOMEWORK, OKAY?
I BET YOU'RE PLANNING TO IGNORE IT TOMORROW SINCE IT'S THE FIRST DAY.
HOW DID YOU KNOW!?

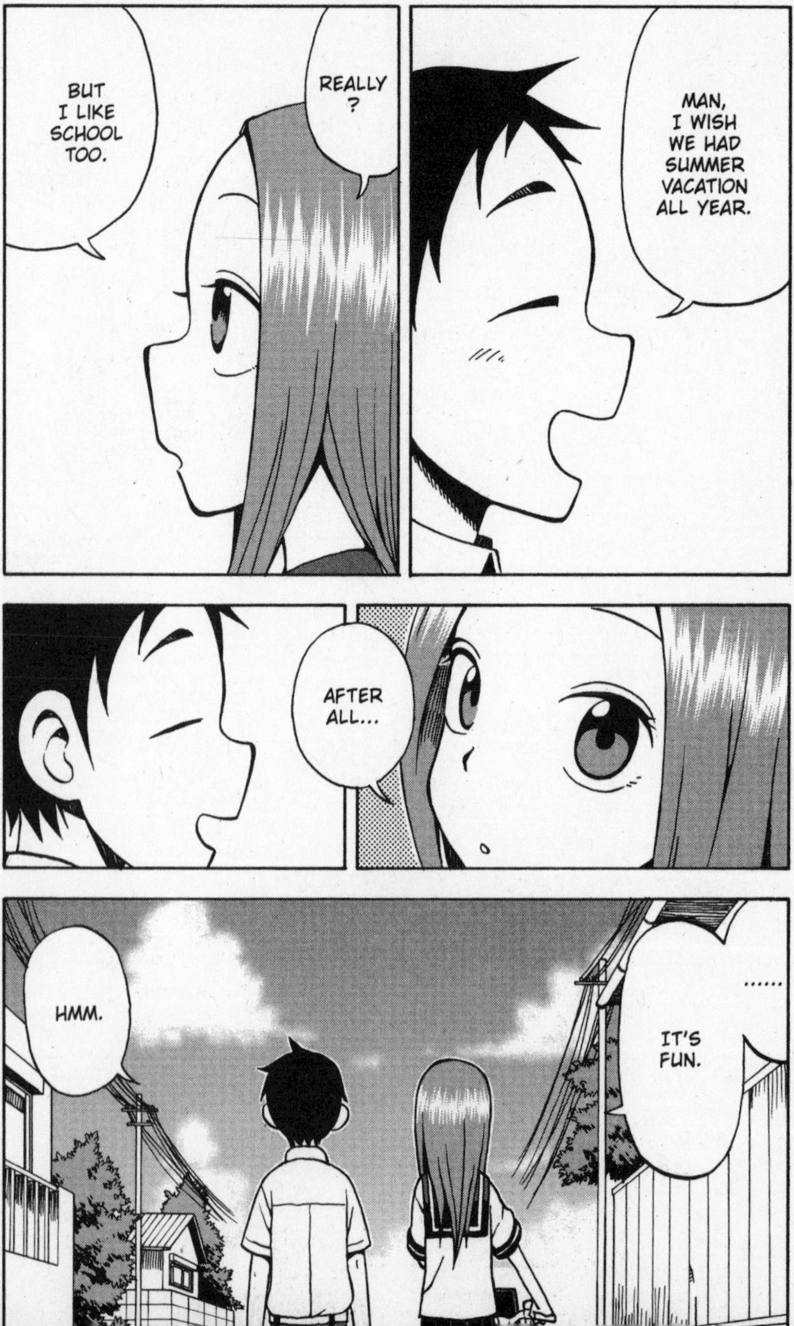
MAN, I WISH WE HAD SUMMER VACATION ALL YEAR.
REALLY ?
BUT I LIKE SCHOOL TOO.
AFTER ALL...
......
IT'S FUN.
HMM.

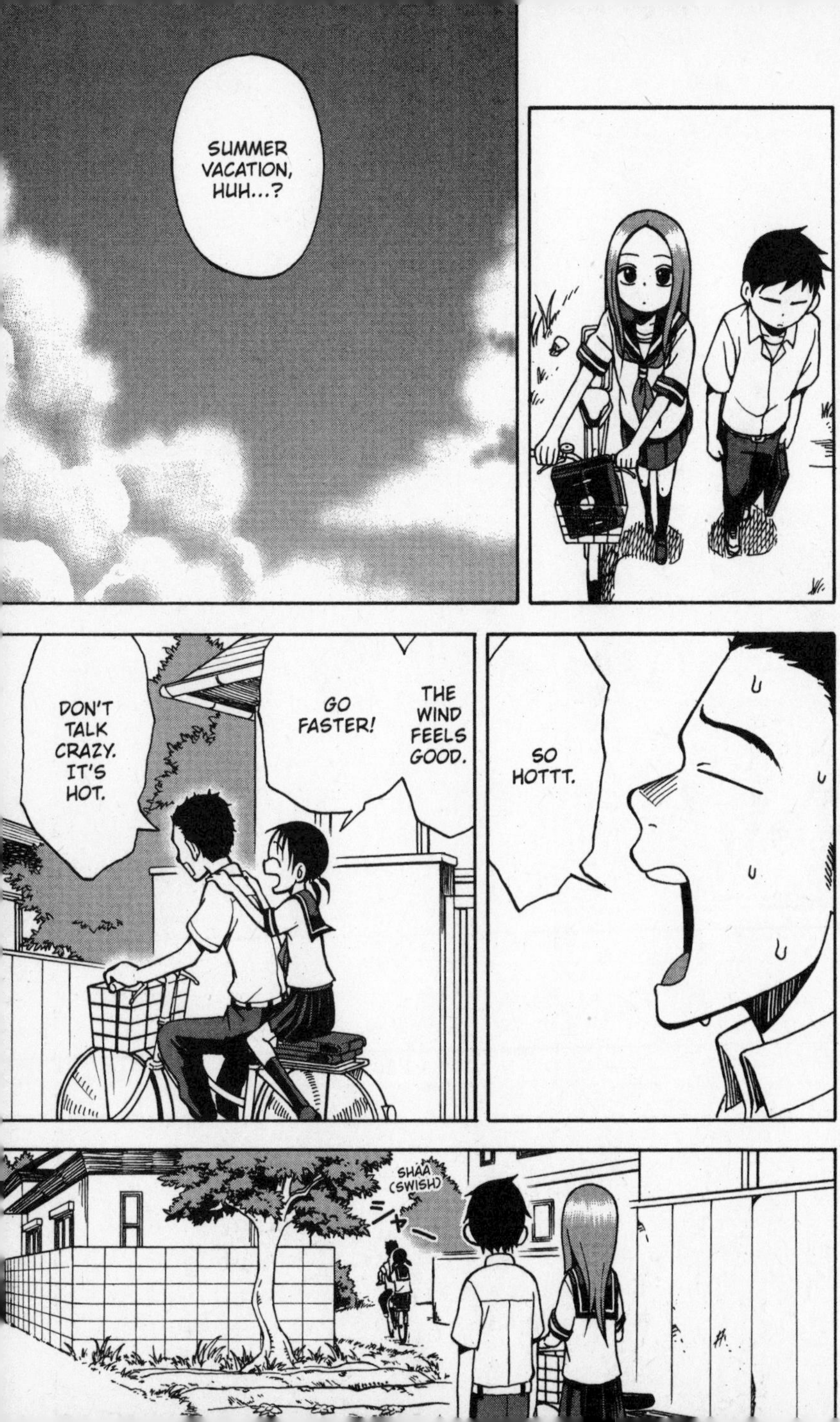
SUMMER VACATION, HUH...?
SO HOTTT.
THE WIND FEELS GOOD.
GO FASTER!
DON'T TALK CRAZY. IT'S HOT.
SHAA (SWISH)

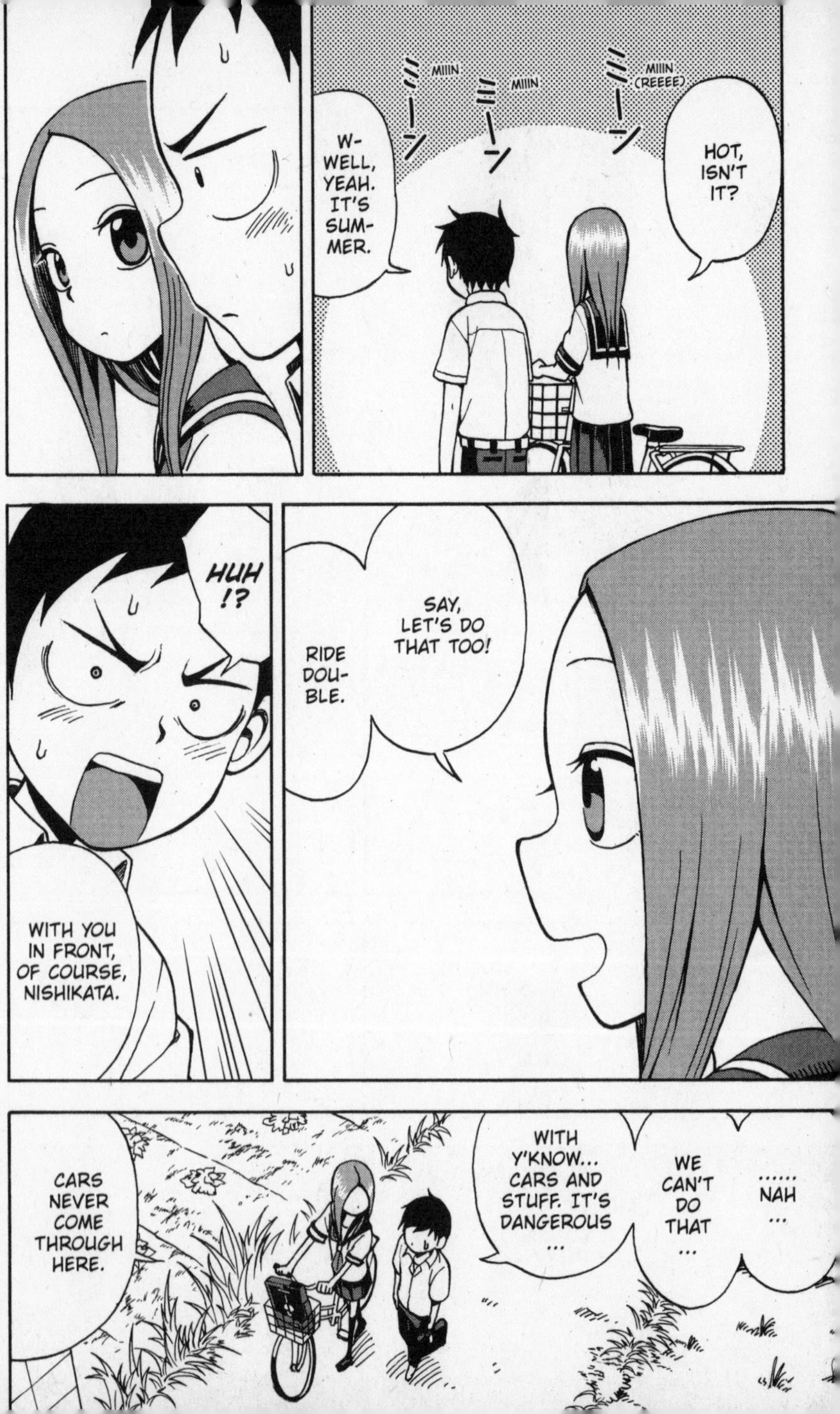

MIIIN (REEEE)
MIIIN
MIIIN
HOT, ISN'T IT?
W-WELL, YEAH. IT'S SUMMER.
SAY, LET'S DO THAT TOO!
RIDE DOUBLE.
HUH!?
WITH YOU IN FRONT, OF COURSE, NISHIKATA.
......NAH...
WE CAN'T DO THAT...
WITH Y'KNOW... CARS AND STUFF. IT'S DANGEROUS...
CARS NEVER COME THROUGH HERE.

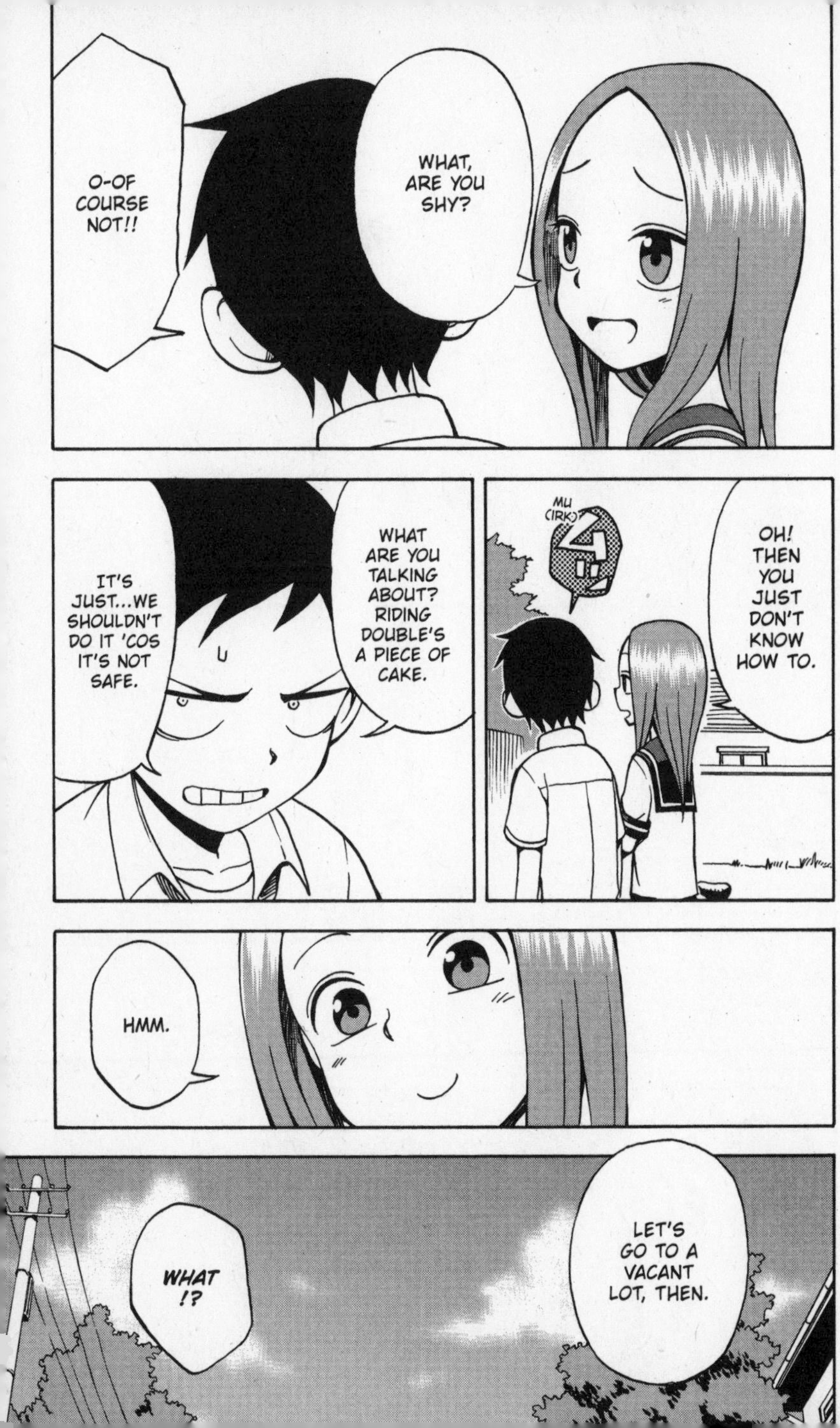
WHAT, ARE YOU SHY?
O-OF COURSE NOT!!
OH! THEN YOU JUST DON'T KNOW HOW TO.
MU (IRK)
WHAT ARE YOU TALKING ABOUT? RIDING DOUBLE'S A PIECE OF CAKE.
IT'S JUST...WE SHOULDN'T DO IT 'COS IT'S NOT SAFE.
HMM.
LET'S GO TO A VACANT LOT, THEN.
WHAT!?

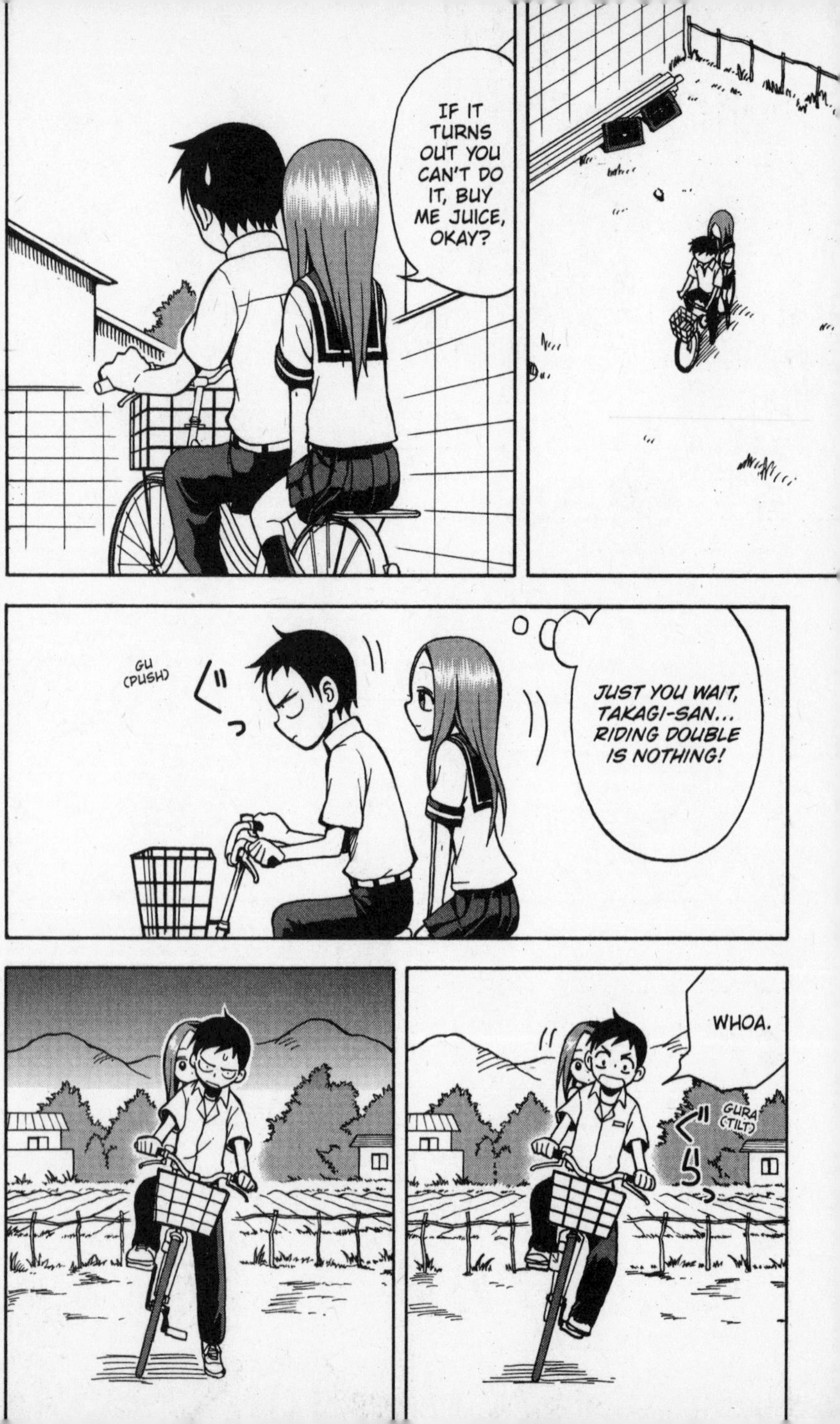
IF IT TURNS OUT YOU CAN'T DO IT, BUY ME JUICE, OKAY?
JUST YOU WAIT, TAKAGI-SAN... RIDING DOUBLE IS NOTHING!
GU (PUSH)
WHOA.
GURA (TILT)

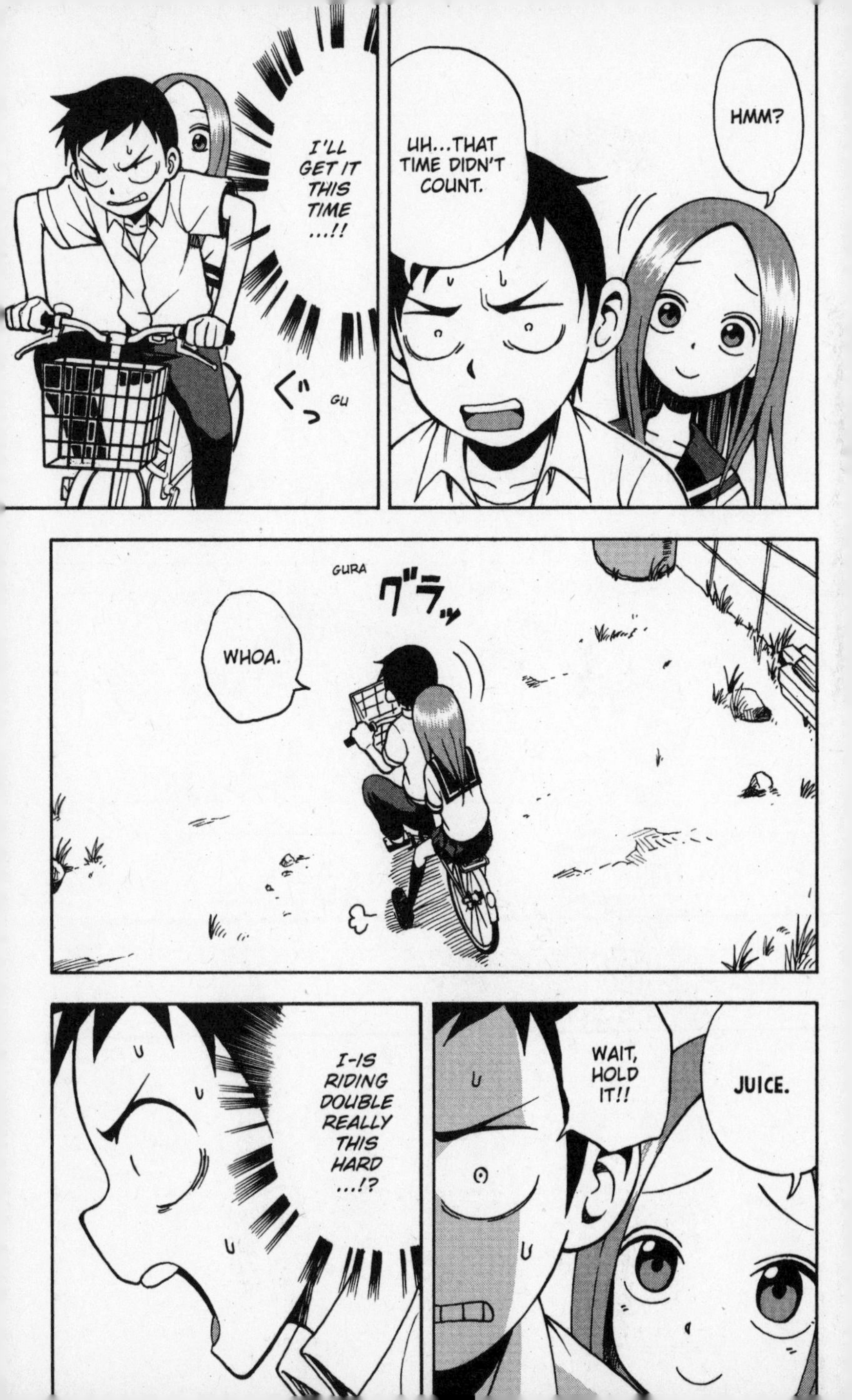
HMM?
UH...THAT TIME DIDN'T COUNT.
I'LL GET IT THIS TIME ...!!
ぐっ
GU
GURA
グラッ
WHOA.
JUICE.
WAIT, HOLD IT!!
I-IS RIDING DOUBLE REALLY THIS HARD ...!?

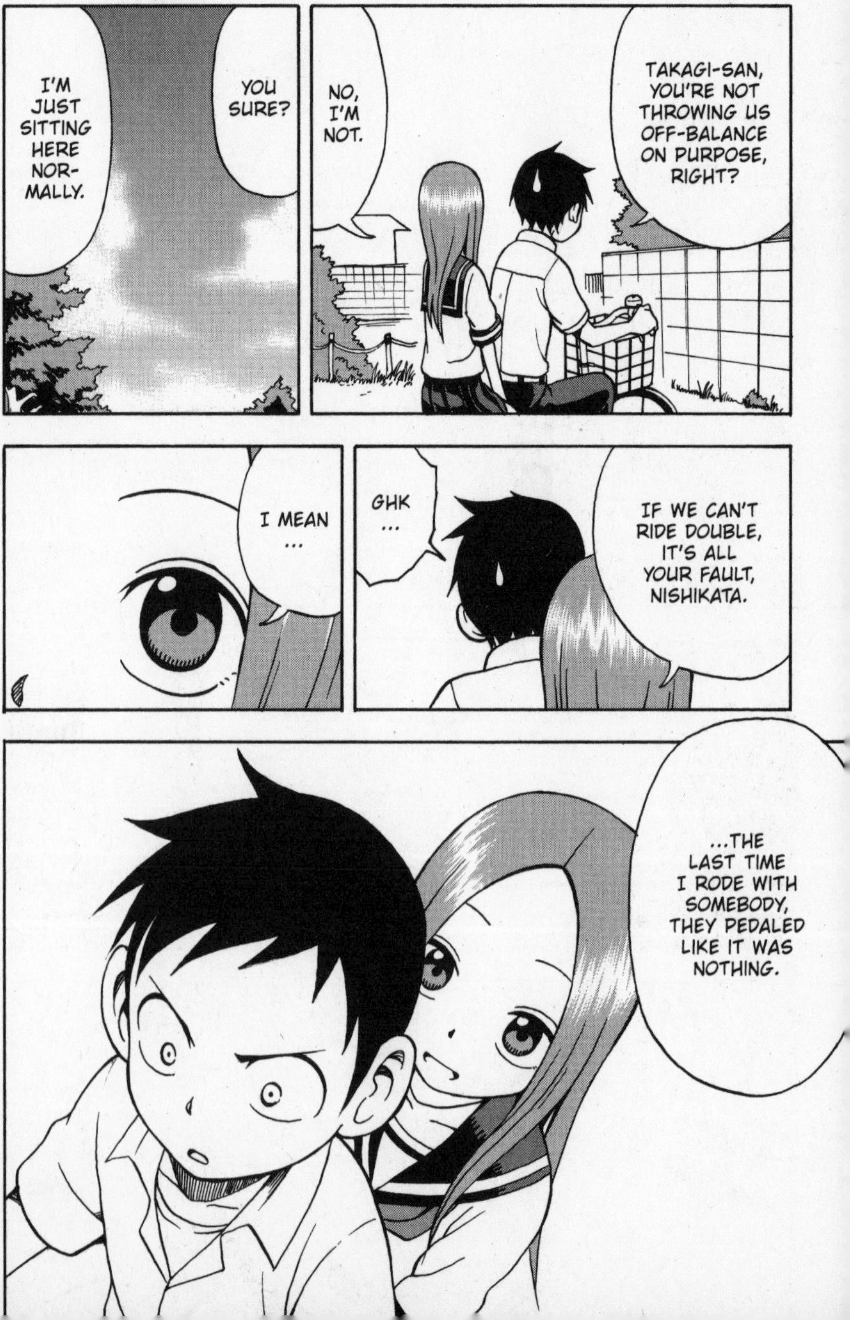

TAKAGI-SAN, YOU'RE NOT THROWING US OFF-BALANCE ON PURPOSE, RIGHT?
NO, I'M NOT.
YOU SURE?
I'M JUST SITTING HERE NOR-MALLY.
IF WE CAN'T RIDE DOUBLE, IT'S ALL YOUR FAULT, NISHIKATA.
GHK ...
I MEAN ...
...THE LAST TIME I RODE WITH SOMEBODY, THEY PEDALED LIKE IT WAS NOTHING.

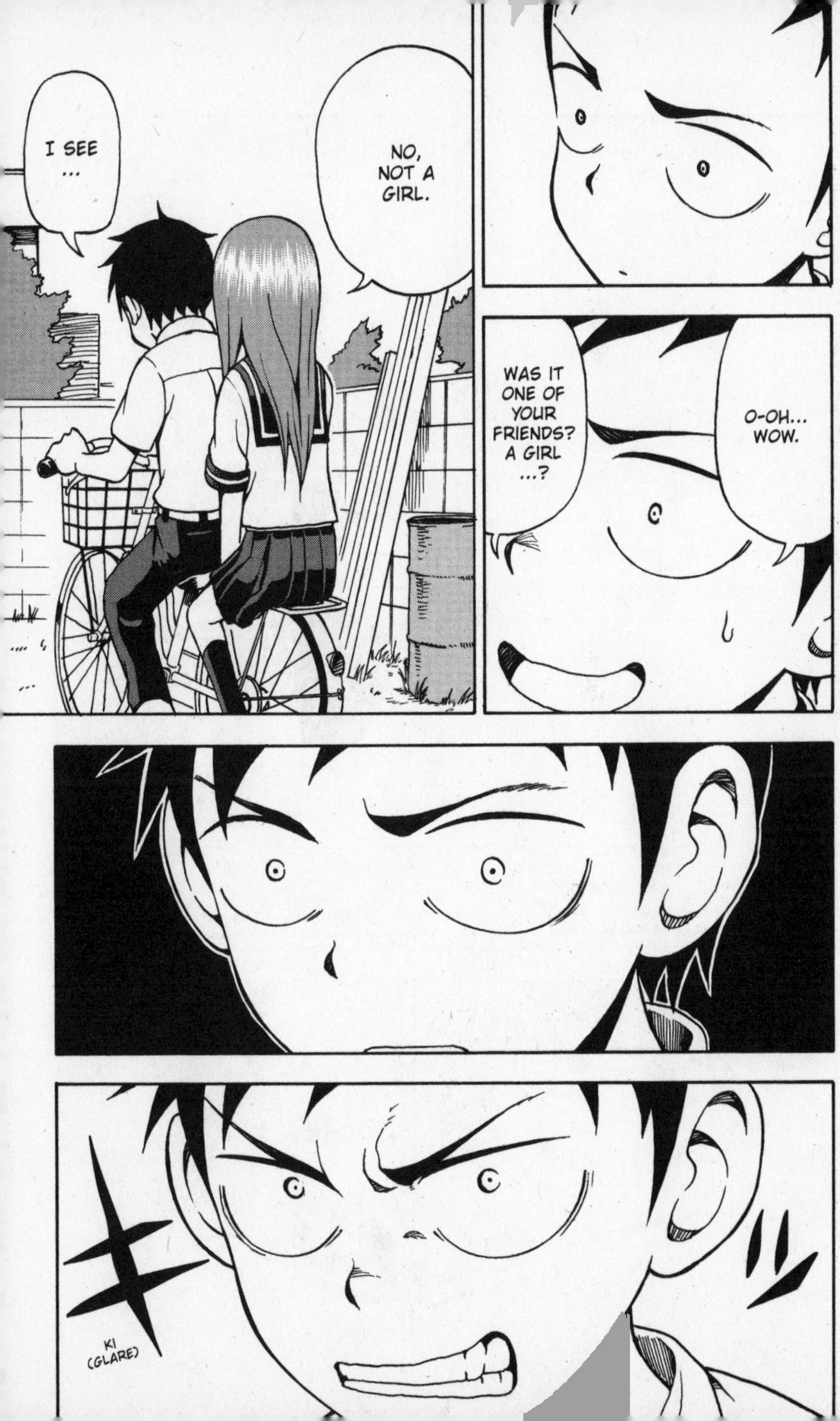
O-OH... WOW.
WAS IT ONE OF YOUR FRIENDS? A GIRL ...?
NO, NOT A GIRL.
I SEE ...
KI (GLARE)

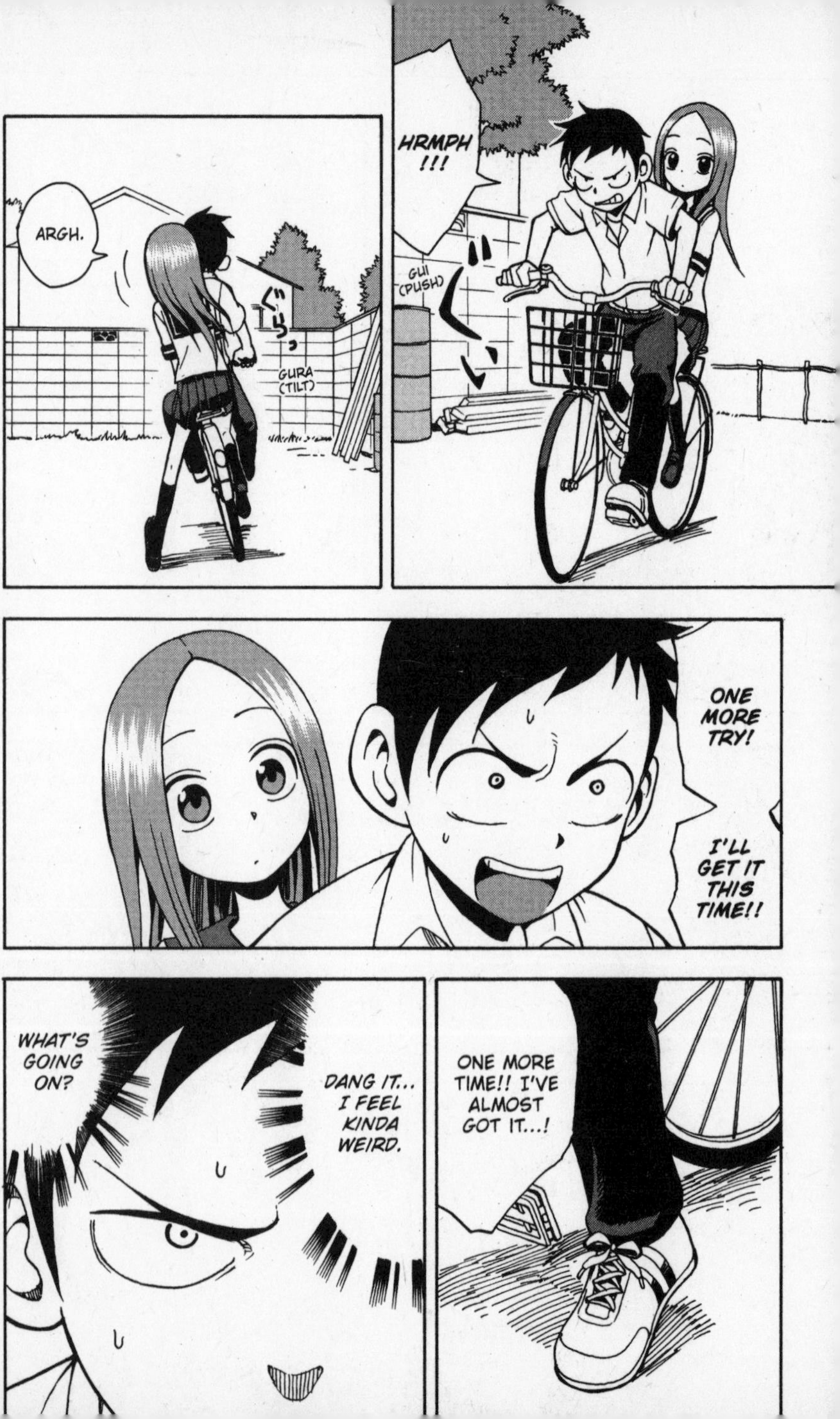
HRMPH!!!
ぐいっ
GUI (PUSH)
ARGH.
ぐらっ
GURA (TILT)
ONE MORE TRY!
I'LL GET IT THIS TIME!!
ONE MORE TIME!! I'VE ALMOST GOT IT...!
DANG IT... I FEEL KINDA WEIRD.
WHAT'S GOING ON?

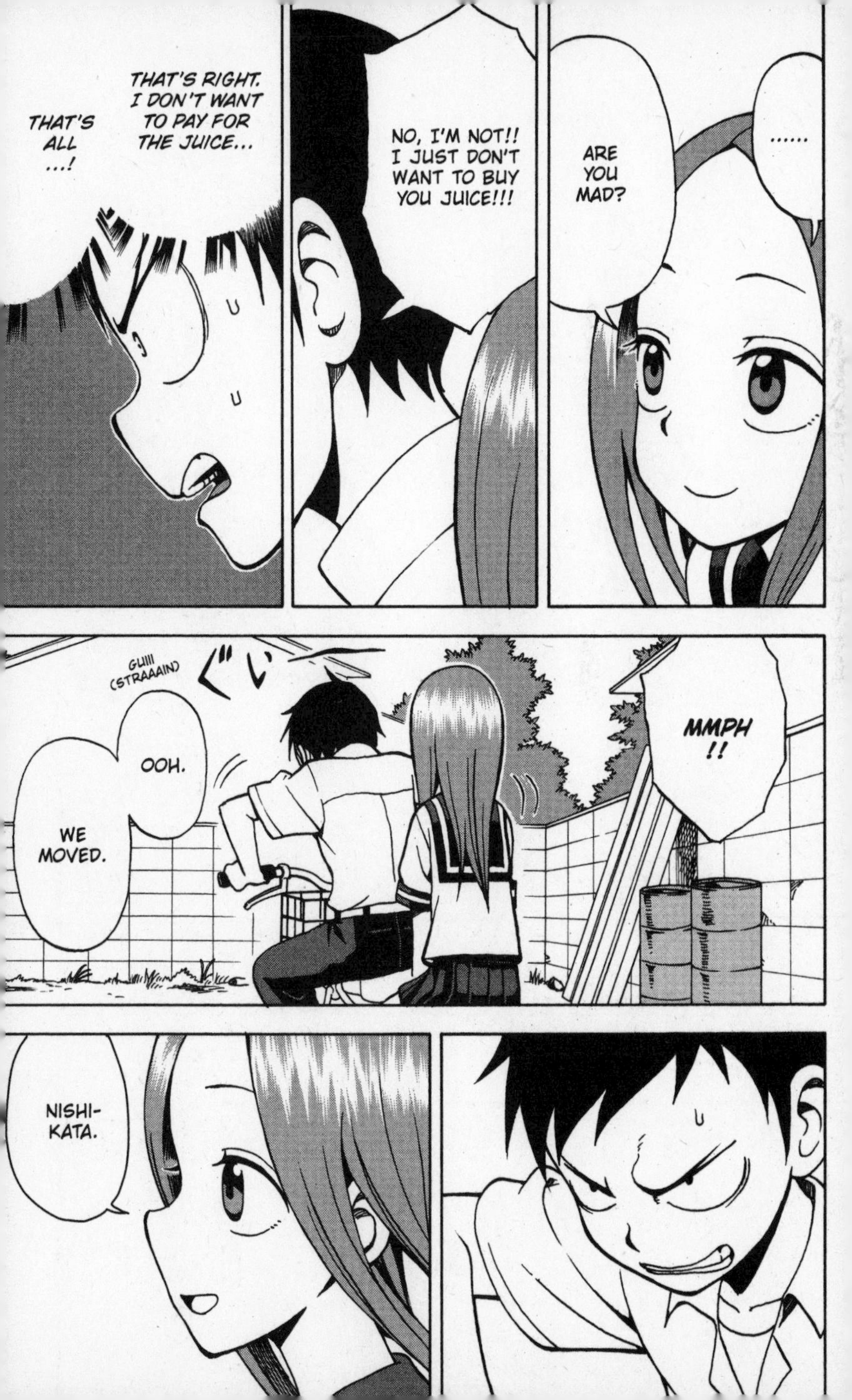
......
ARE YOU MAD?
NO, I'M NOT!! I JUST DON'T WANT TO BUY YOU JUICE!!!
THAT'S RIGHT. I DON'T WANT TO PAY FOR THE JUICE...
THAT'S ALL ...!
MMPH !!
ぐい
GUIII (STRAAAIN)
OOH.
WE MOVED.
NISHI-KATA.

WHA—?

THE LAST TIME I RODE DOUBLE WAS WITH MY DAD.

I THINK I WAS ABOUT FOUR.

ZU (SLIP)

GASHAAAN (CRASH)

ガシャーン

EEK.

WAUGH!

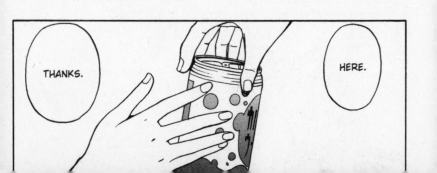

THANKS.

HERE.

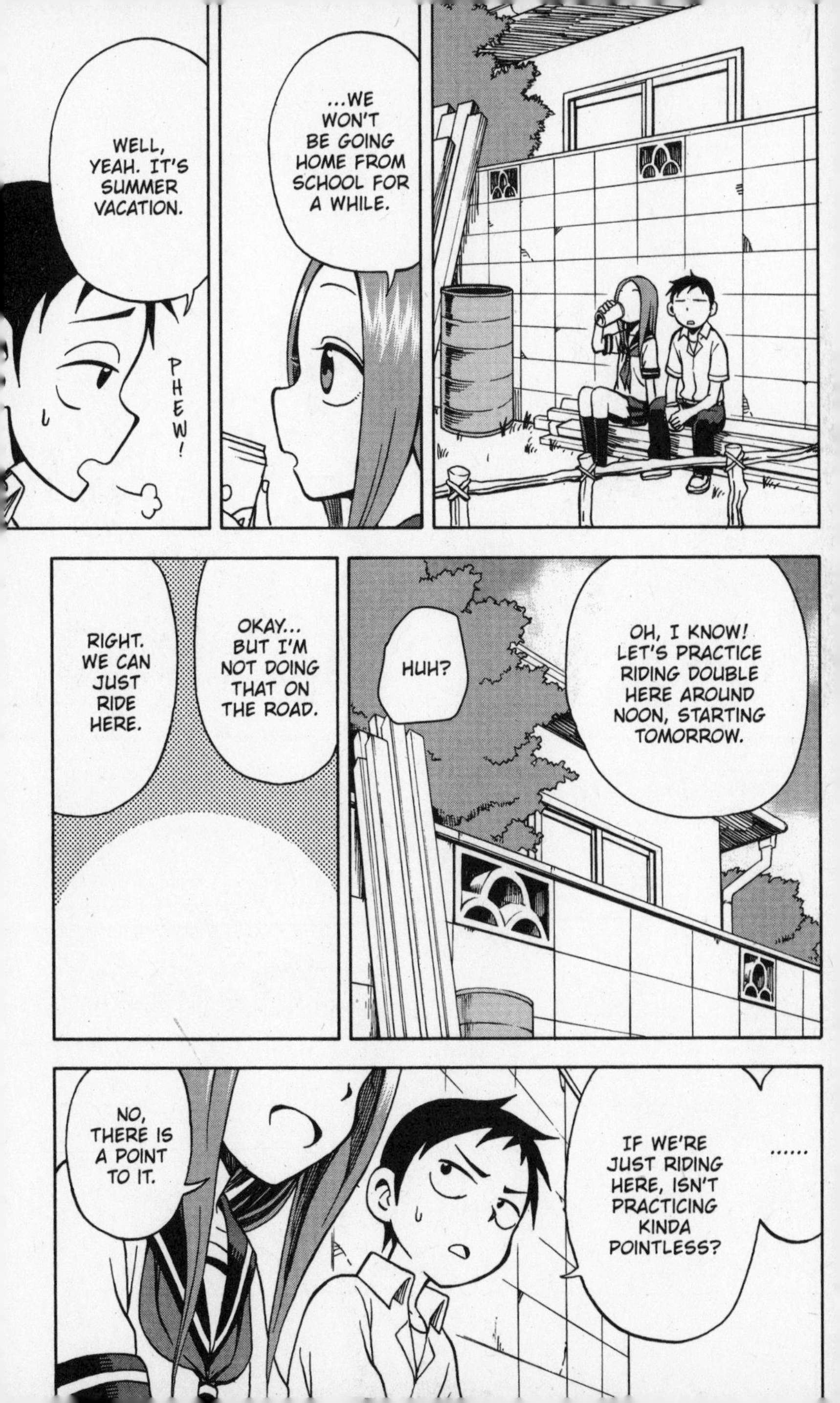
...WE WON'T BE GOING HOME FROM SCHOOL FOR A WHILE.
WELL, YEAH. IT'S SUMMER VACATION.
PHEW!
OH, I KNOW! LET'S PRACTICE RIDING DOUBLE HERE AROUND NOON, STARTING TOMORROW.
HUH?
OKAY... BUT I'M NOT DOING THAT ON THE ROAD.
RIGHT. WE CAN JUST RIDE HERE.
......
IF WE'RE JUST RIDING HERE, ISN'T PRACTICING KINDA POINTLESS?
NO, THERE IS A POINT TO IT.

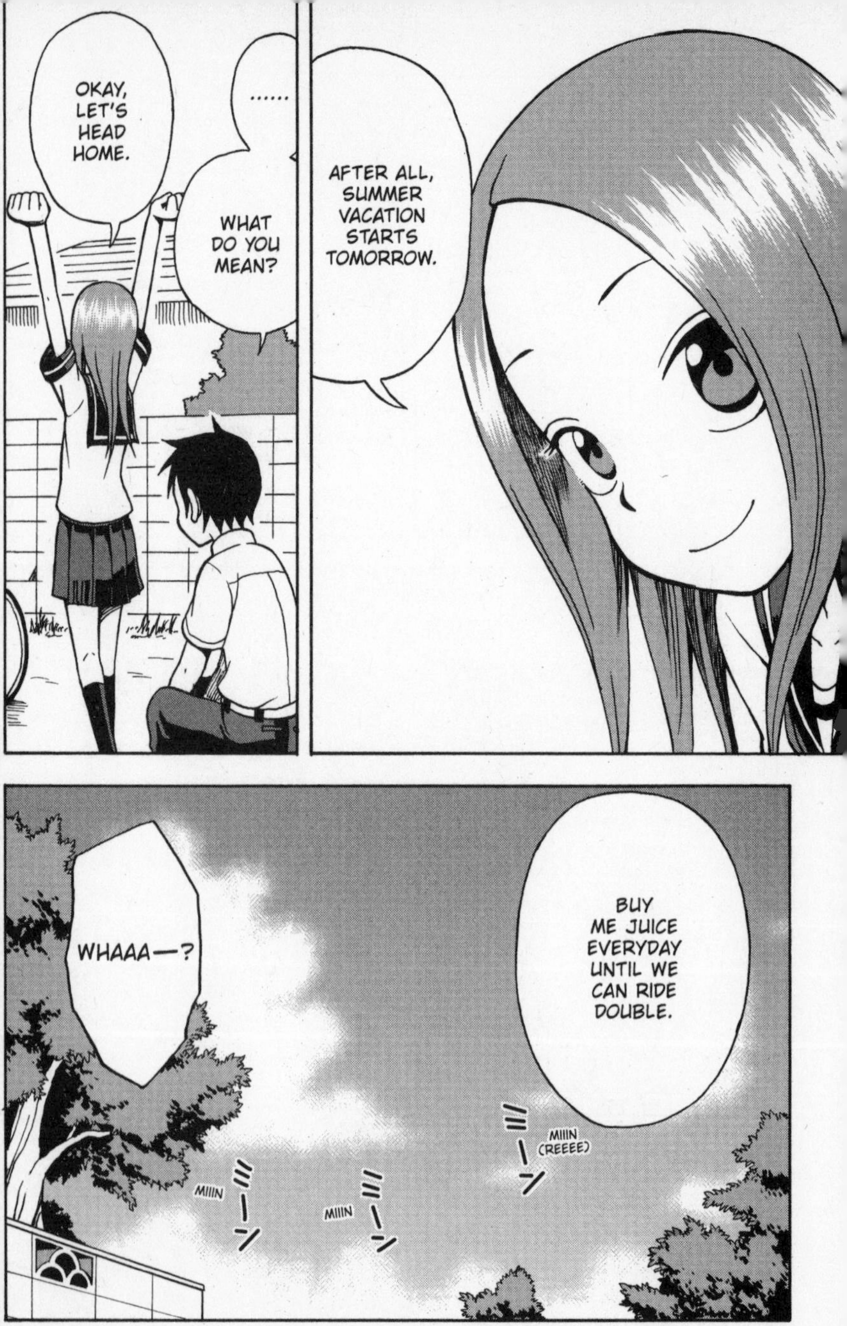
AFTER ALL, SUMMER VACATION STARTS TOMORROW.
......
WHAT DO YOU MEAN?
OKAY, LET'S HEAD HOME.
BUY ME JUICE EVERYDAY UNTIL WE CAN RIDE DOUBLE.
MIIIN (REEEE)
MIIIN
MIIIN
WHAAA—?

Teasing Master
Takagi-san

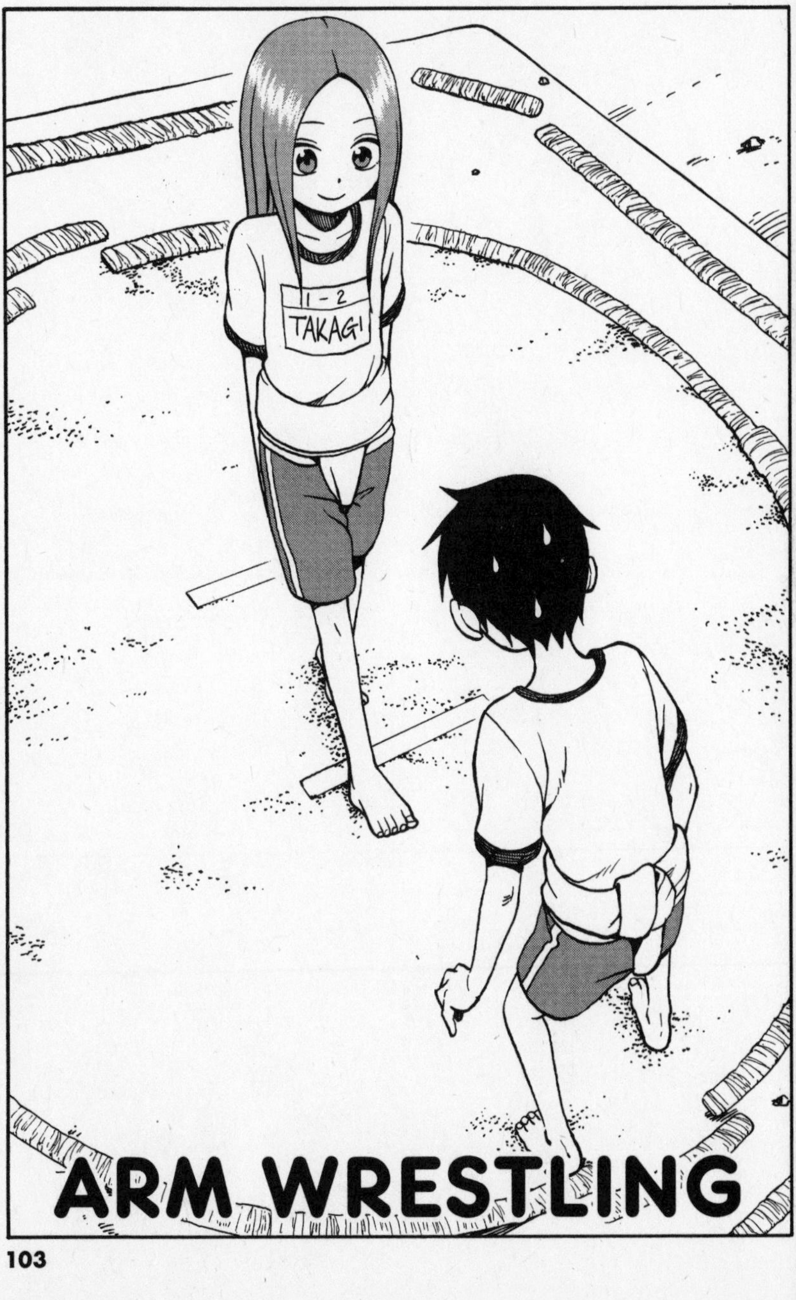
1-2
TAKAGI
ARM WRESTLING

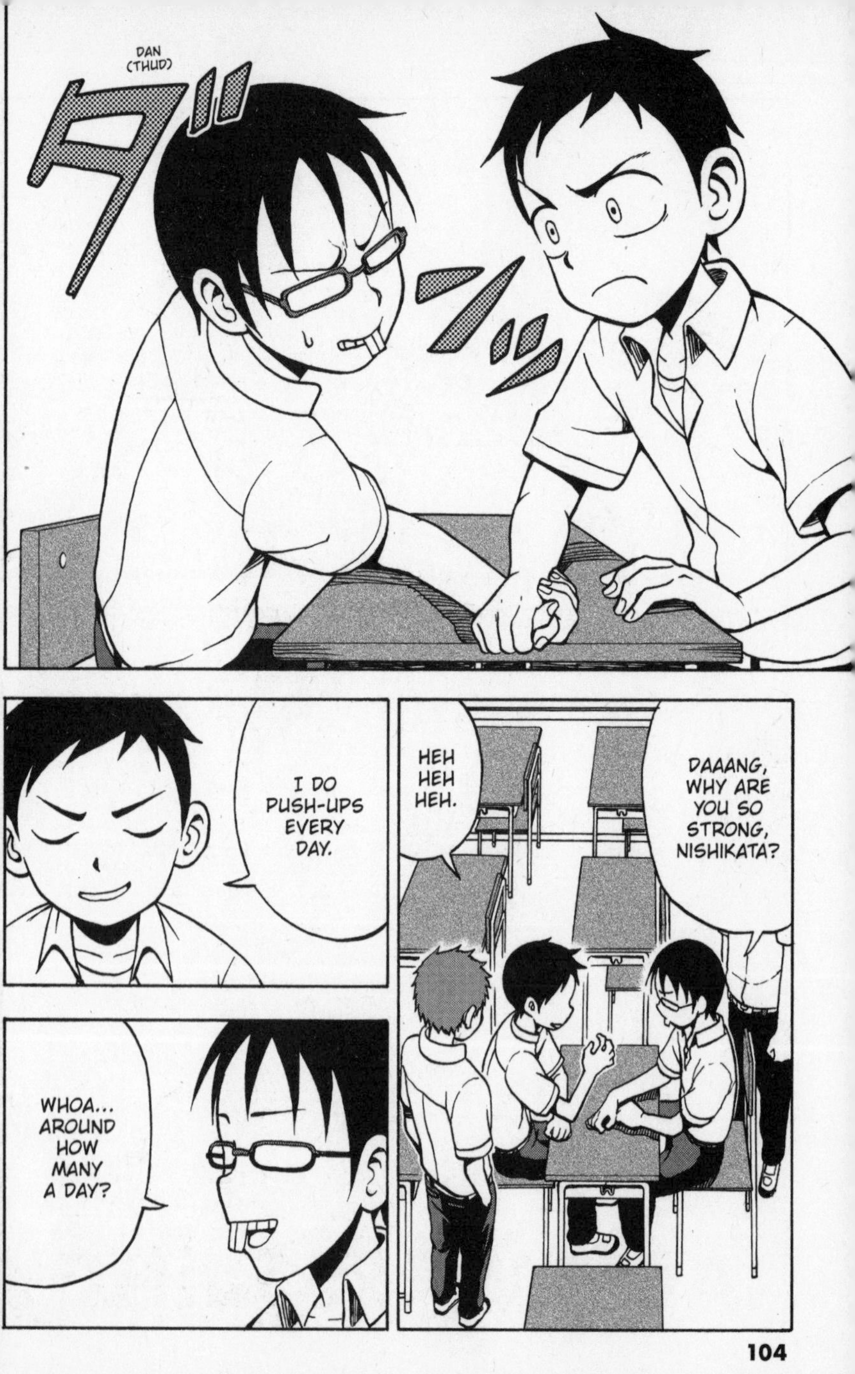
DAN (THUD)
DAAANG, WHY ARE YOU SO STRONG, NISHIKATA?
HEH HEH HEH.
I DO PUSH-UPS EVERY DAY.
WHOA... AROUND HOW MANY A DAY?

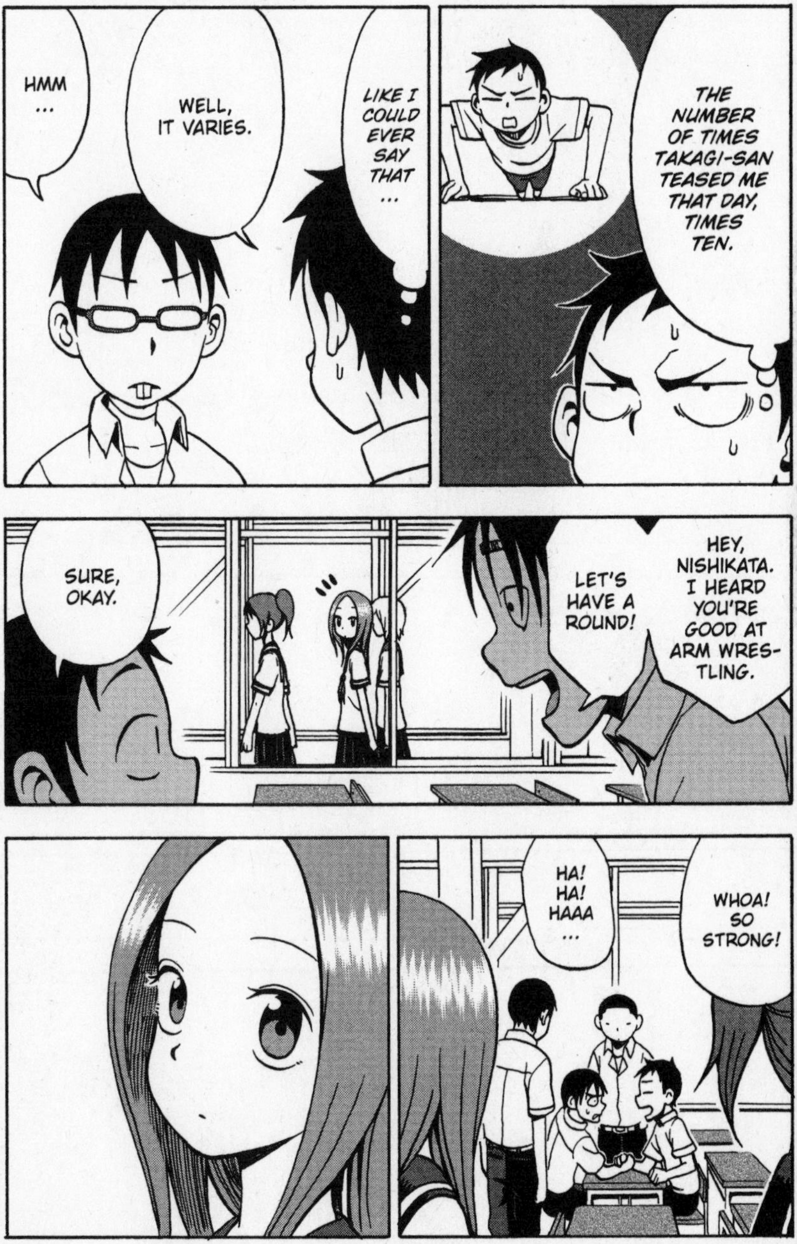

THE NUMBER OF TIMES TAKAGI-SAN TEASED ME THAT DAY, TIMES TEN.
LIKE I COULD EVER SAY THAT ...
WELL, IT VARIES.
HMM ...
HEY, NISHIKATA. I HEARD YOU'RE GOOD AT ARM WRESTLING.
LET'S HAVE A ROUND!
SURE, OKAY.
WHOA! SO STRONG!
HA! HA! HAAA ...

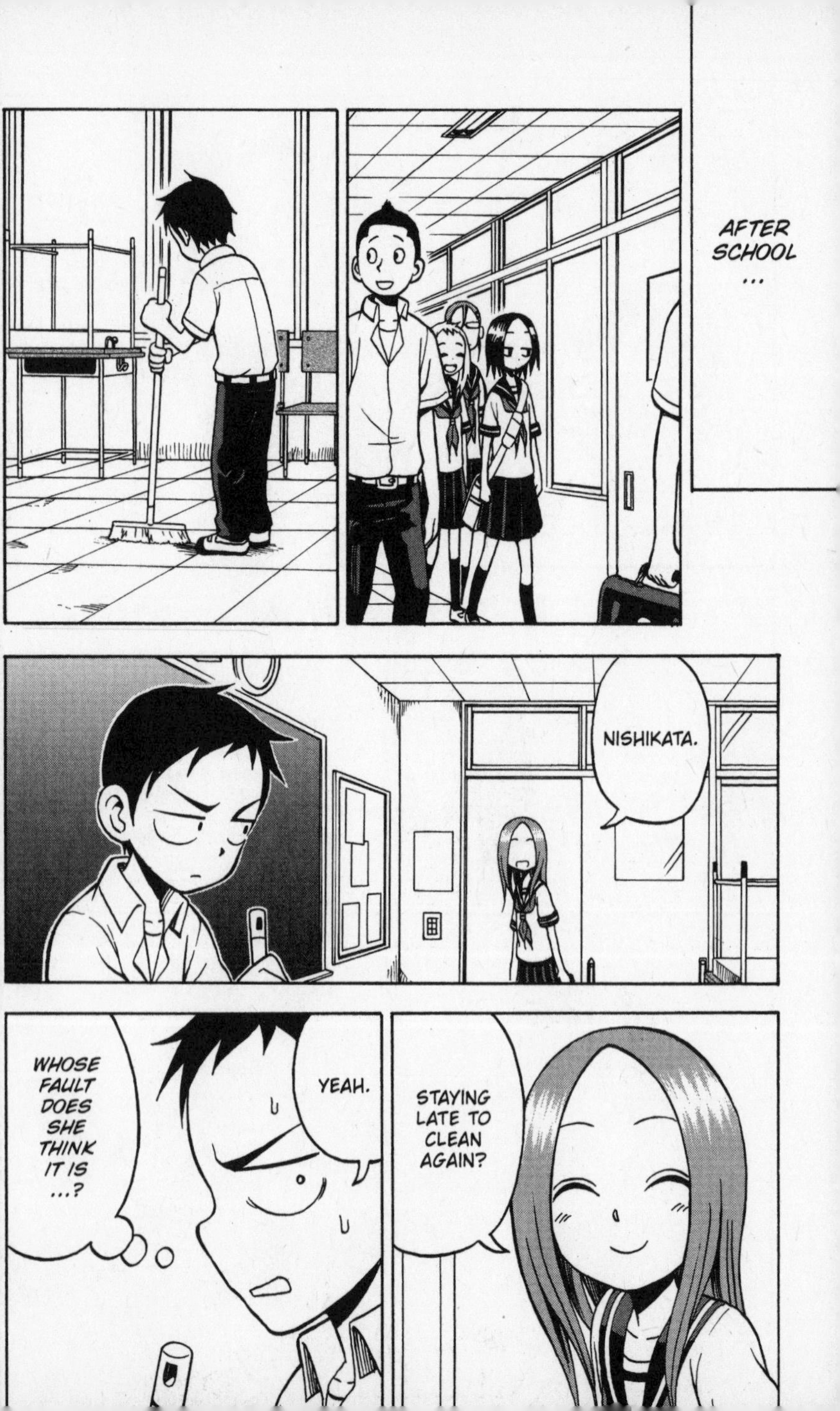
AFTER SCHOOL ...
NISHIKATA.
STAYING LATE TO CLEAN AGAIN?
YEAH.
WHOSE FAULT DOES SHE THINK IT IS ...?

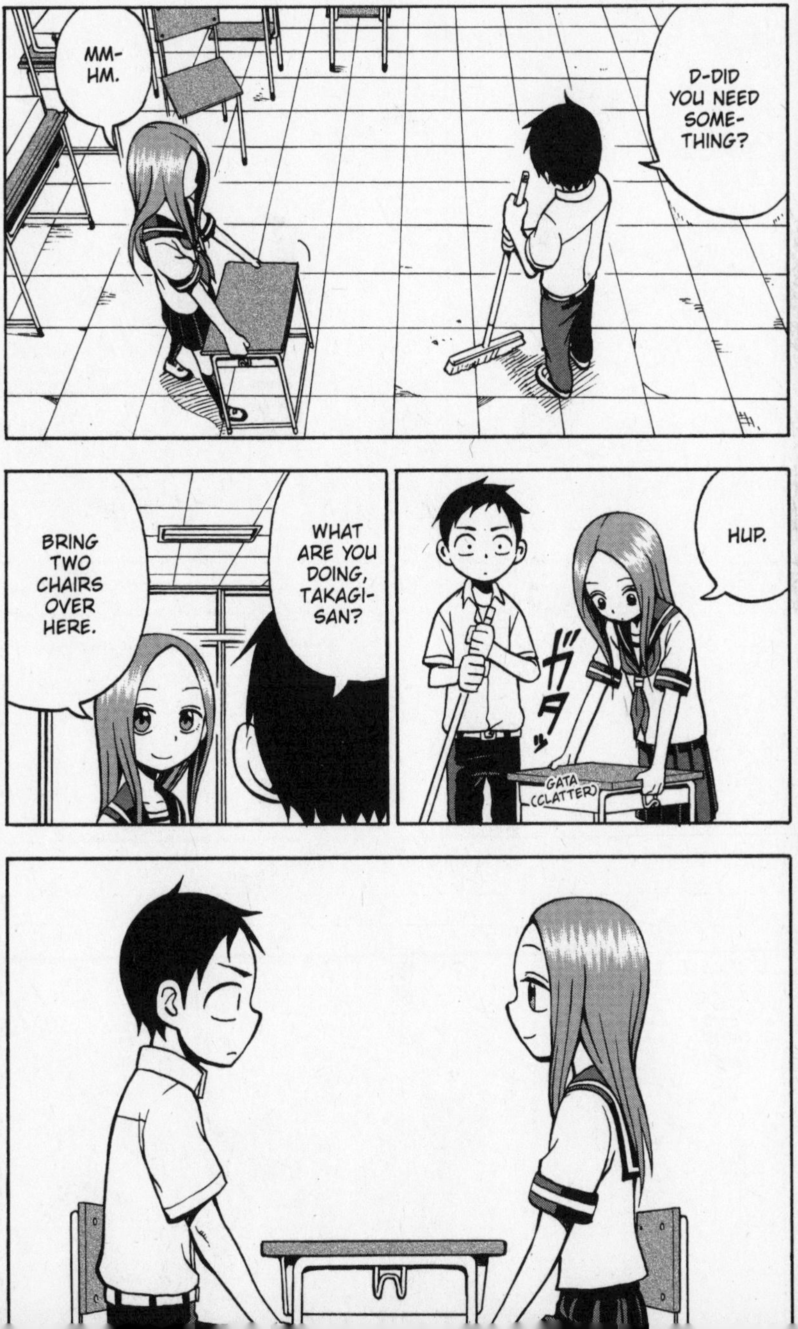
D-DID YOU NEED SOME-THING?
MM-HM.
HUP.
GATA (CLATTER)
WHAT ARE YOU DOING, TAKAGI-SAN?
BRING TWO CHAIRS OVER HERE.

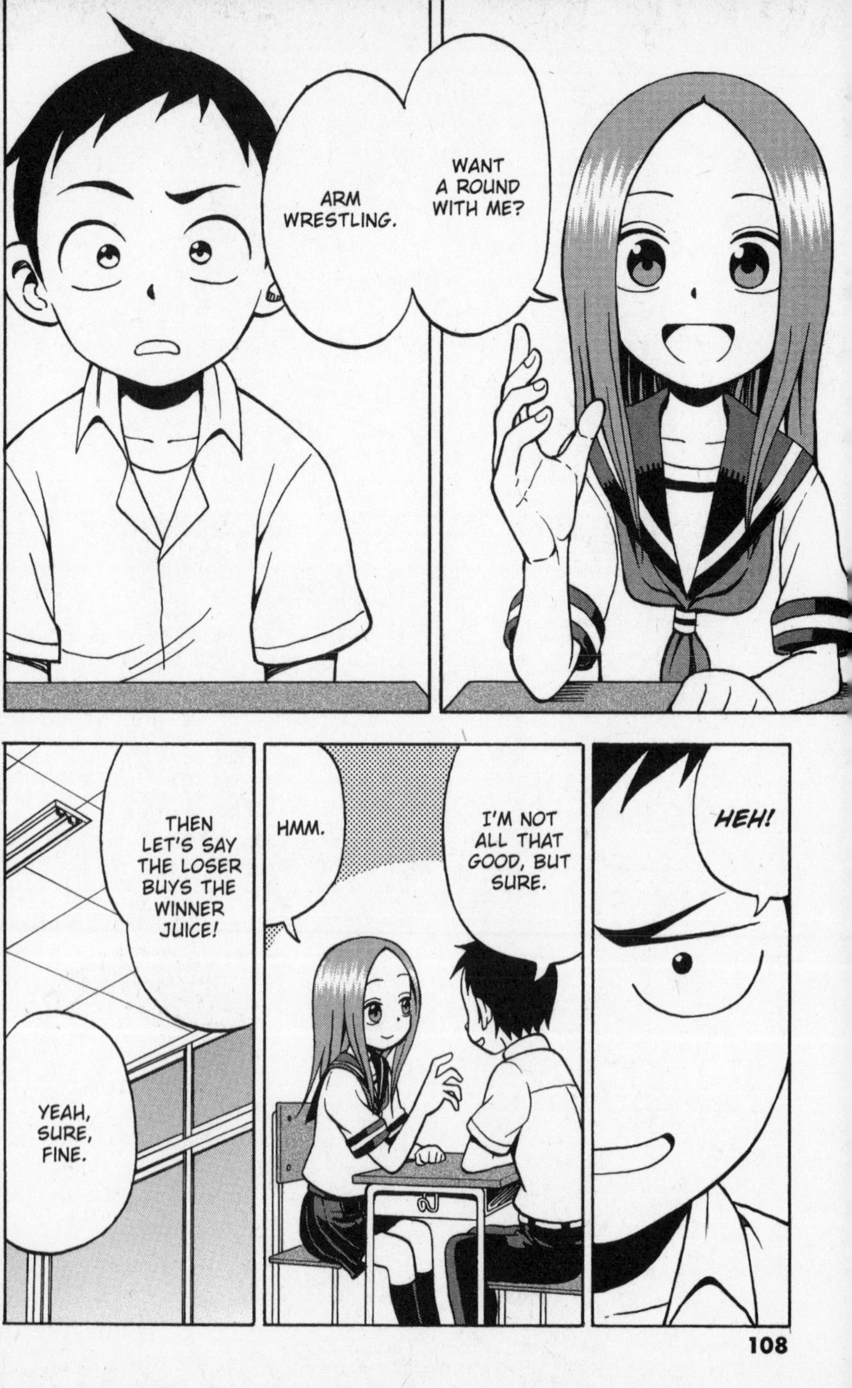
ARM WRESTLING.
WANT A ROUND WITH ME?
HEH!
I'M NOT ALL THAT GOOD, BUT SURE.
HMM.
THEN LET'S SAY THE LOSER BUYS THE WINNER JUICE!
YEAH, SURE, FINE.

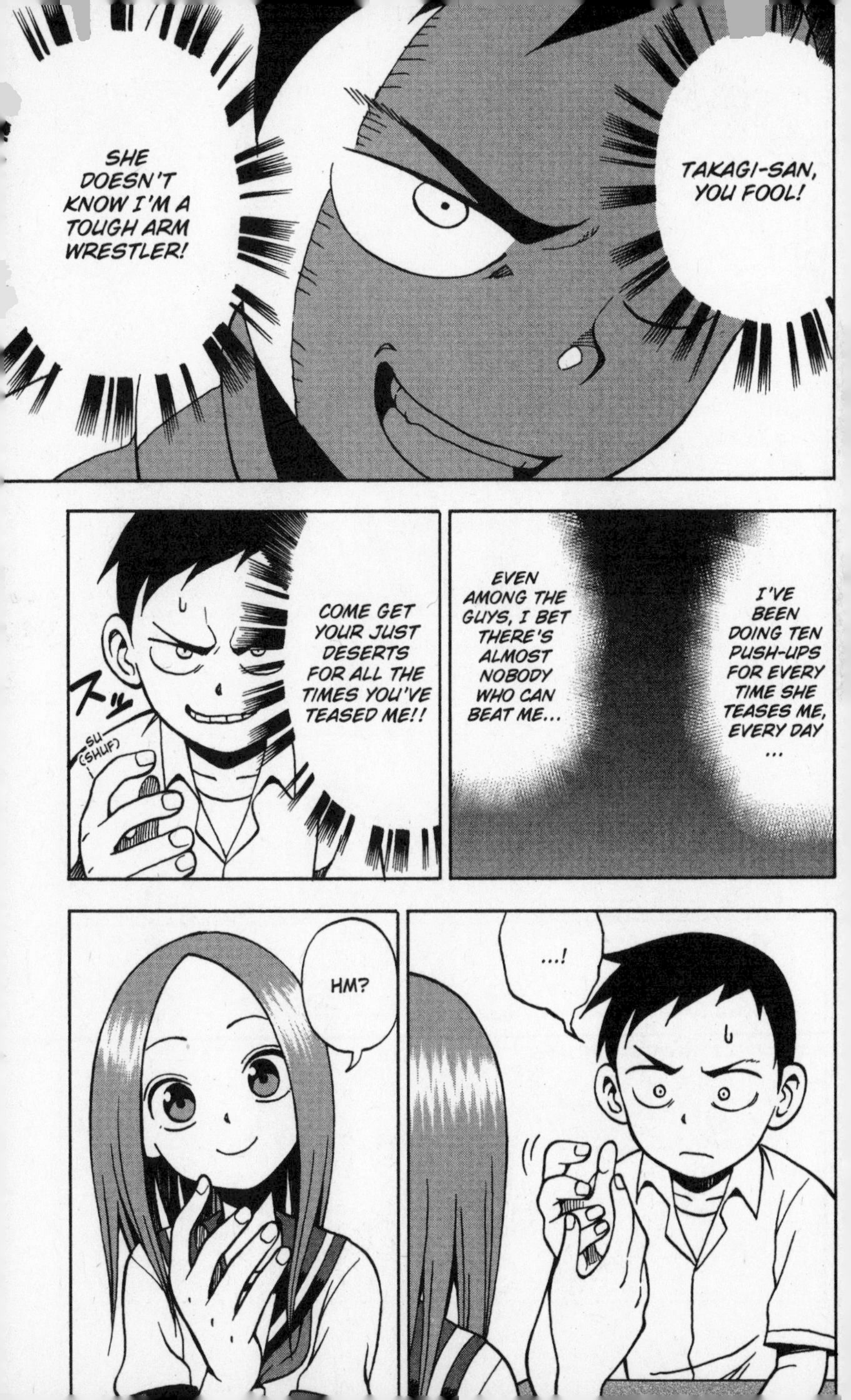
TAKAGI-SAN, YOU FOOL!
SHE DOESN'T KNOW I'M A TOUGH ARM WRESTLER!
I'VE BEEN DOING TEN PUSH-UPS FOR EVERY TIME SHE TEASES ME, EVERY DAY ...
EVEN AMONG THE GUYS, I BET THERE'S ALMOST NOBODY WHO CAN BEAT ME...
COME GET YOUR JUST DESERTS FOR ALL THE TIMES YOU'VE TEASED ME!!
スッ
SU (SHUF)
...!
HM?

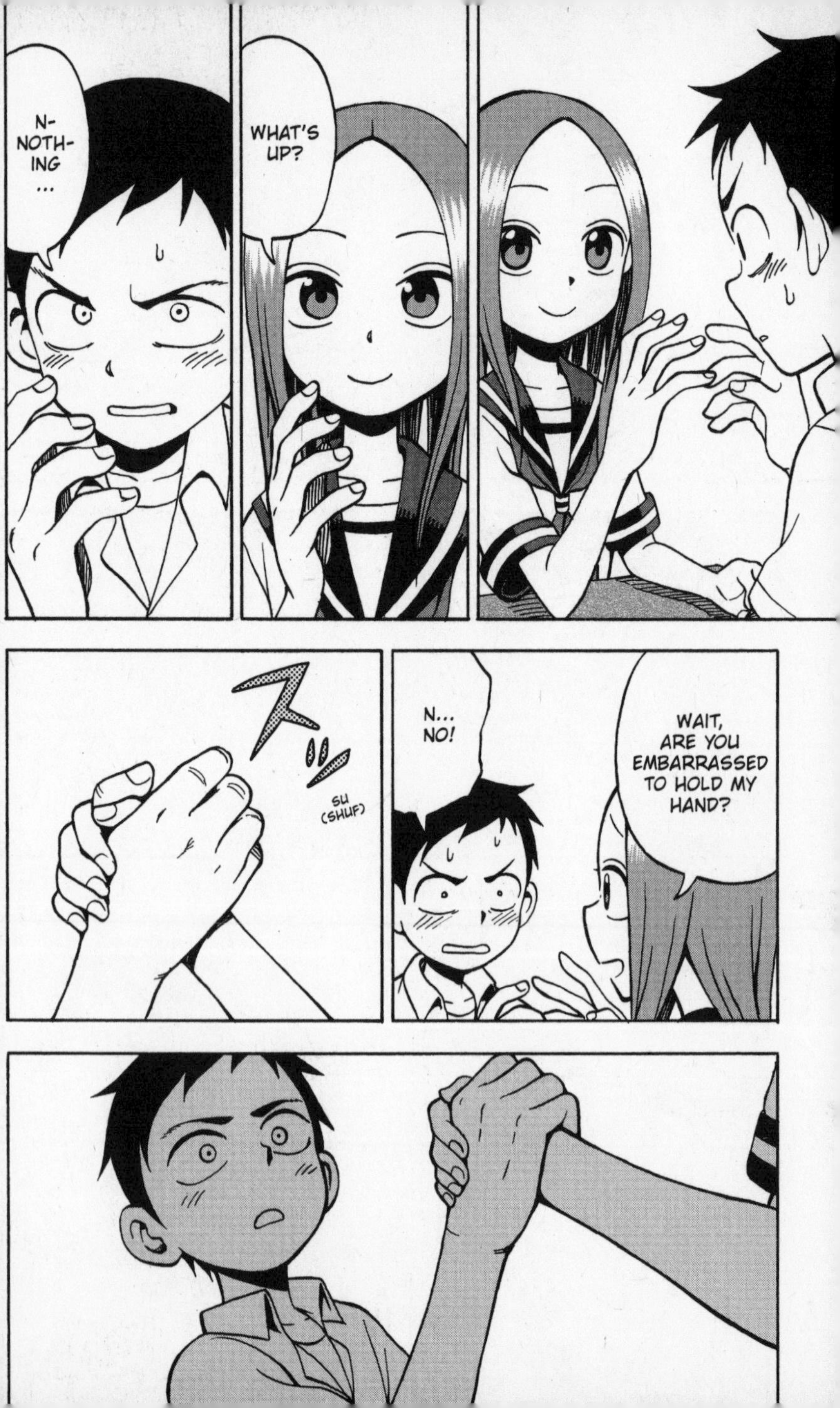
WHAT'S UP?
N-NOTHING-ING...
WAIT, ARE YOU EMBARRASSED TO HOLD MY HAND?
N... NO!
SU (SHUF)

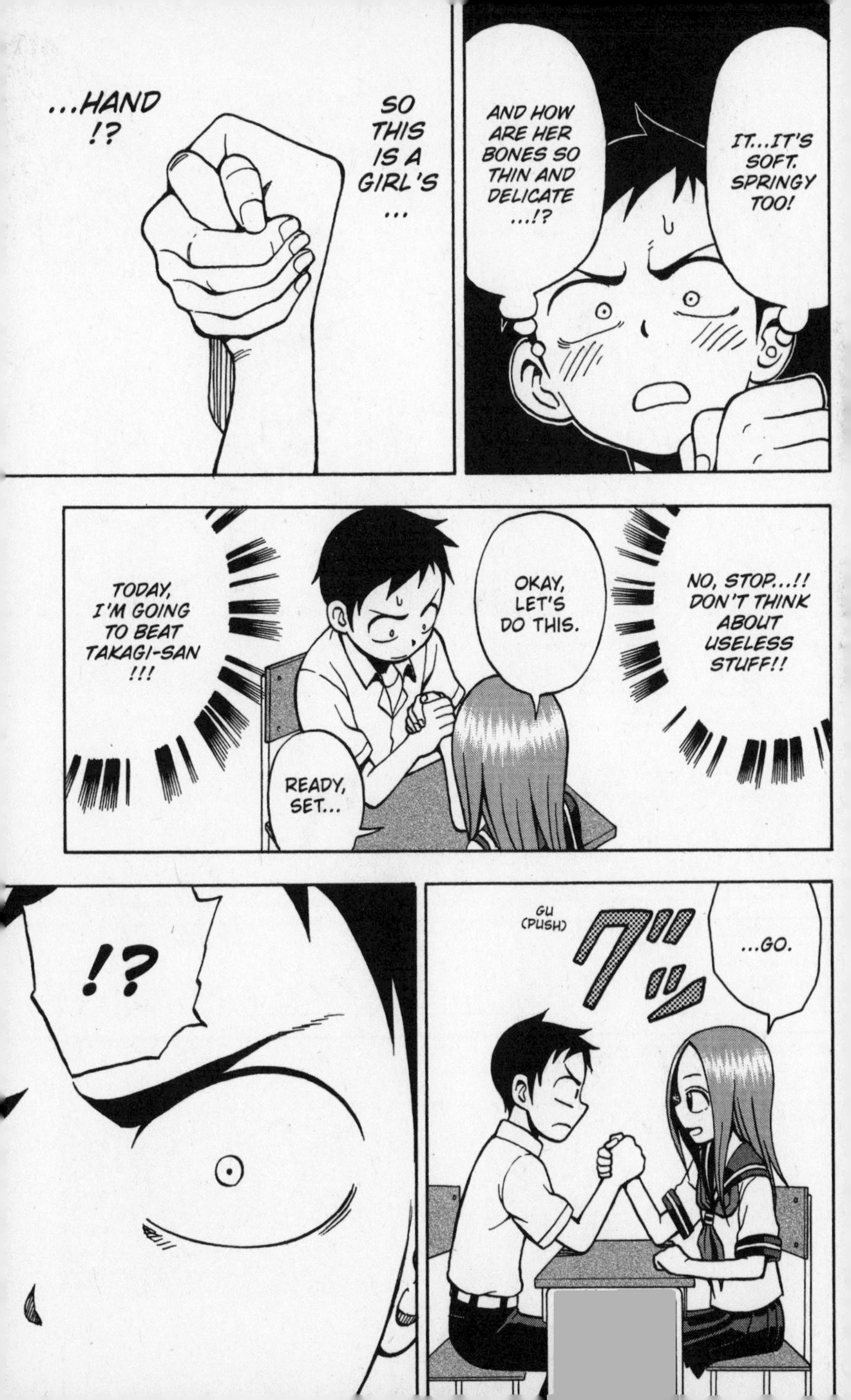
IT...IT'S SOFT. SPRINGY TOO!
AND HOW ARE HER BONES SO THIN AND DELICATE ...!?
SO THIS IS A GIRL'S ...
...HAND !?
NO, STOP...!! DON'T THINK ABOUT USELESS STUFF!!
OKAY, LET'S DO THIS.
TODAY, I'M GOING TO BEAT TAKAGI-SAN !!!
READY, SET...
...GO.
GU (PUSH)
!?

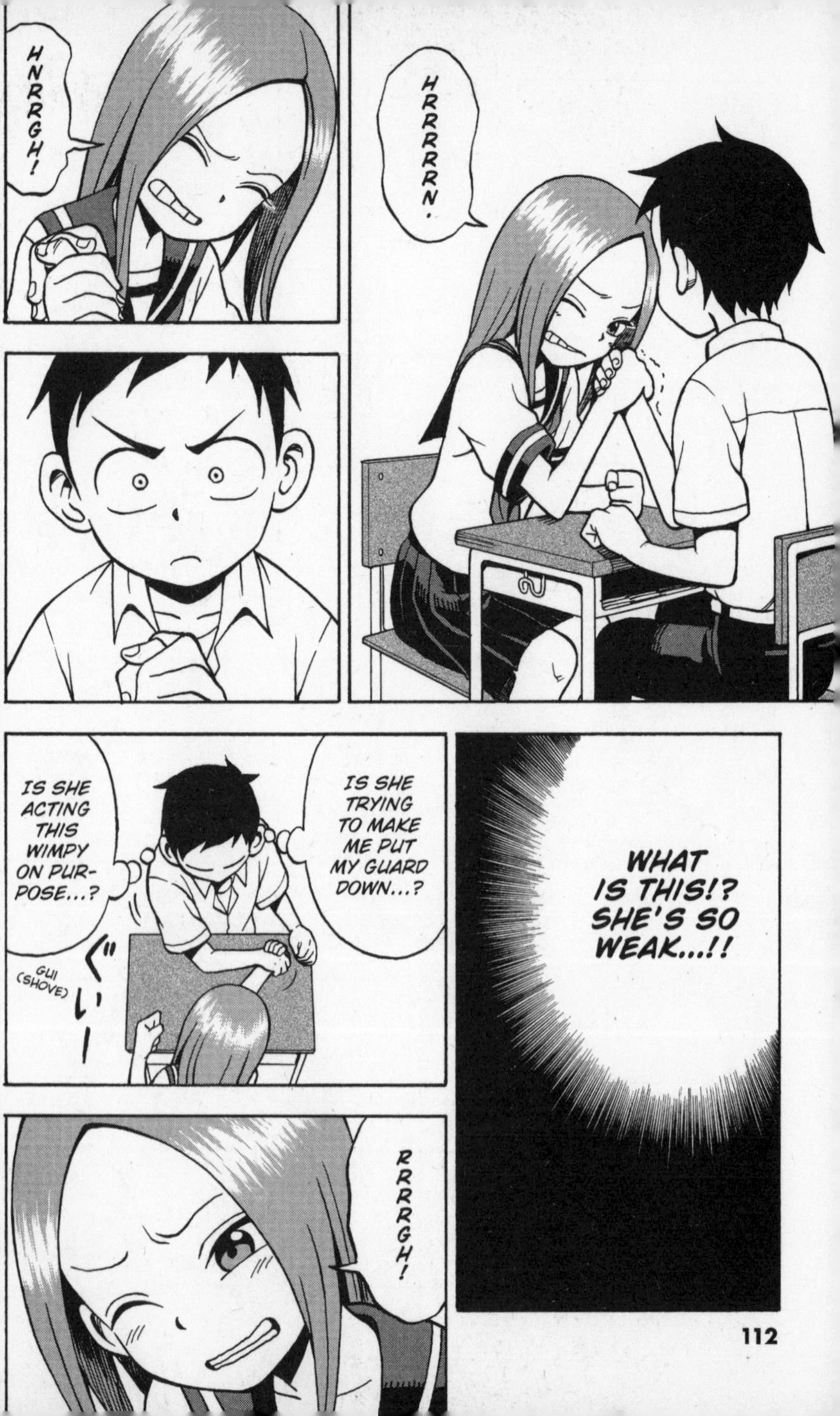
HRRRRRN.
HNRRGH!
WHAT IS THIS!? SHE'S SO WEAK...!!
IS SHE TRYING TO MAKE ME PUT MY GUARD DOWN...?
IS SHE ACTING THIS WIMPY ON PUR-POSE...?
GUI (SHOVE)
RRRRGH!

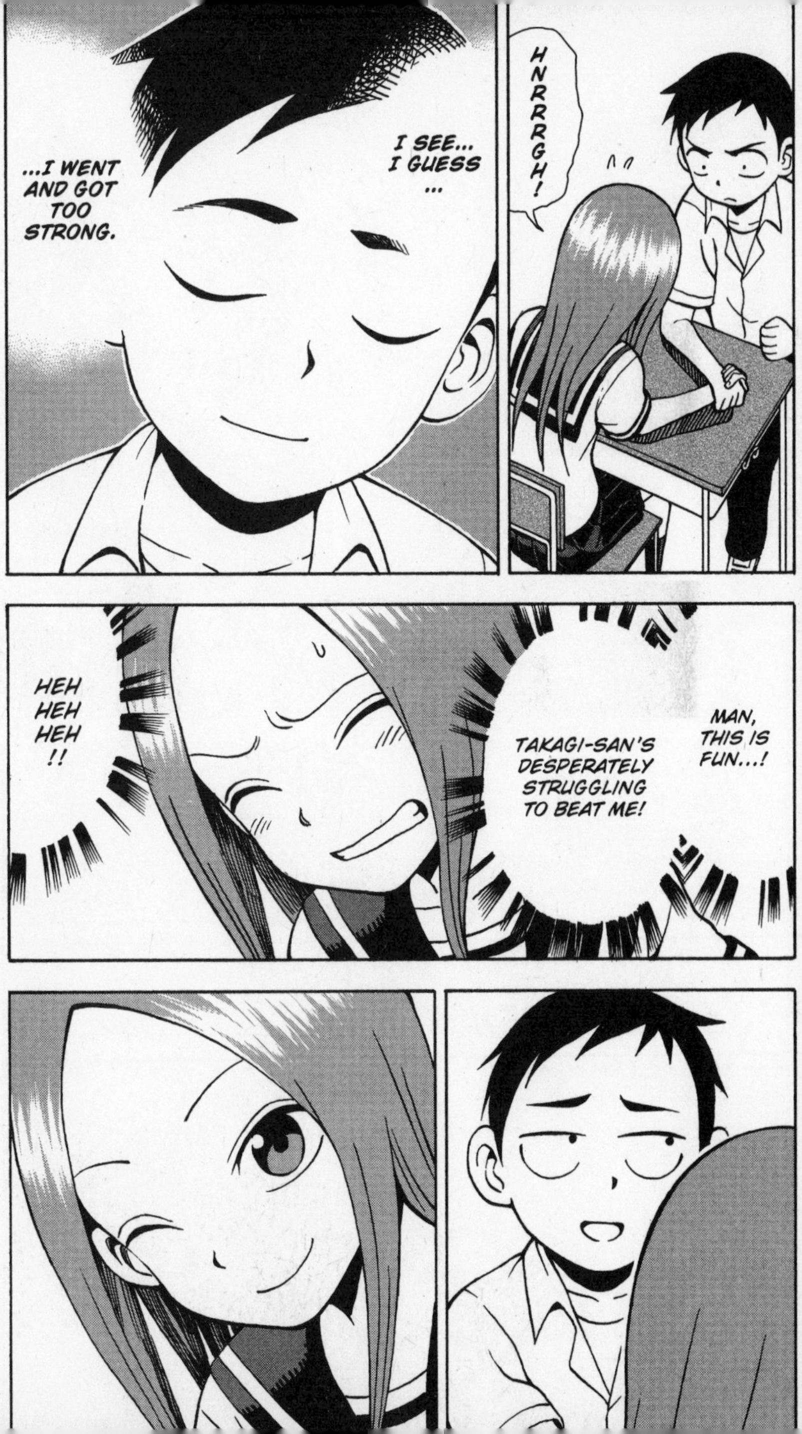
HNRRRGH!
I SEE... I GUESS...
...I WENT AND GOT TOO STRONG.
MAN, THIS IS FUN...!
TAKAGI-SAN'S DESPERATELY STRUGGLING TO BEAT ME!
HEH HEH HEH!!

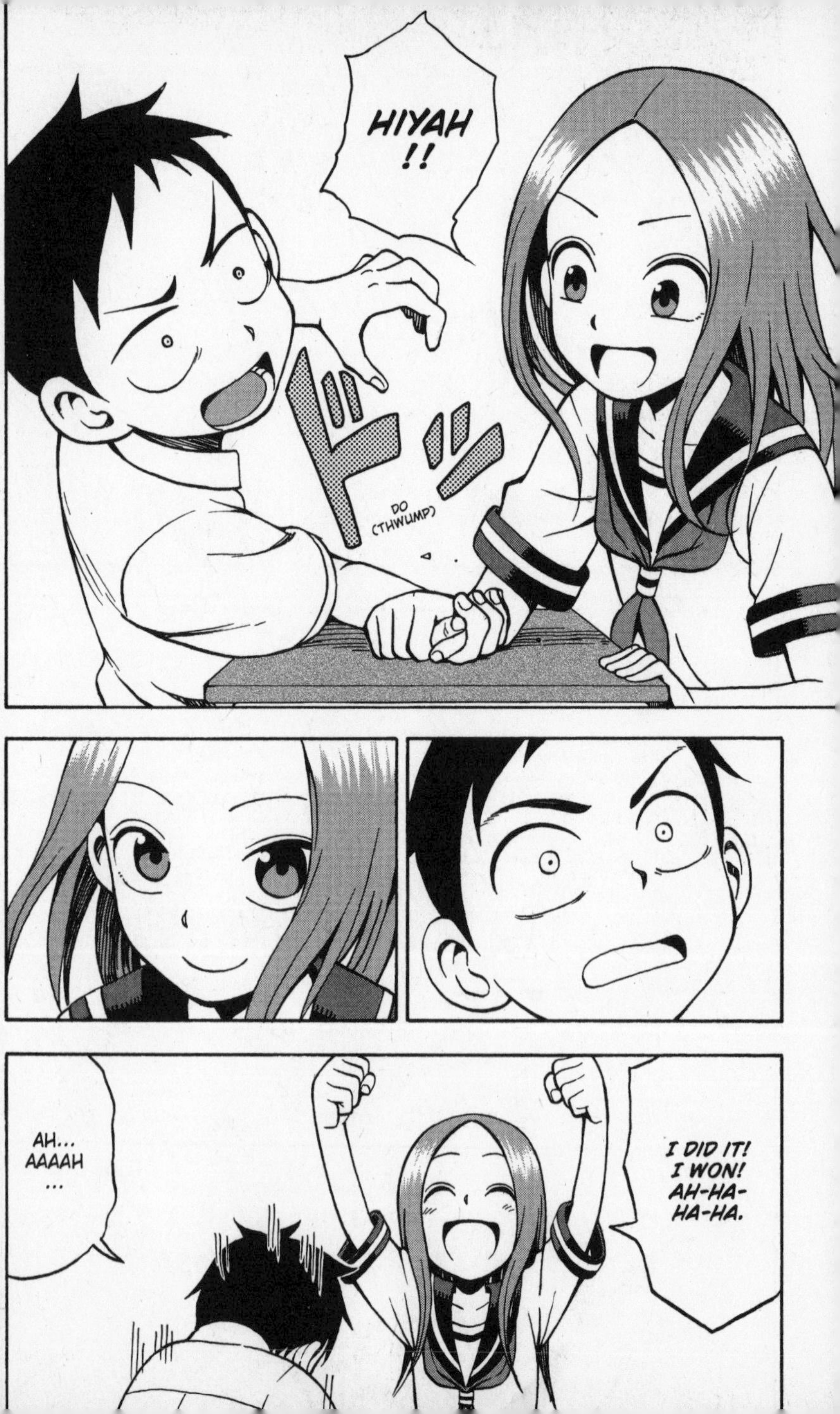
HIYAH !!
DO (THWUMP)
I DID IT! I WON! AH-HA-HA-HA.
AH... AAAAH ...

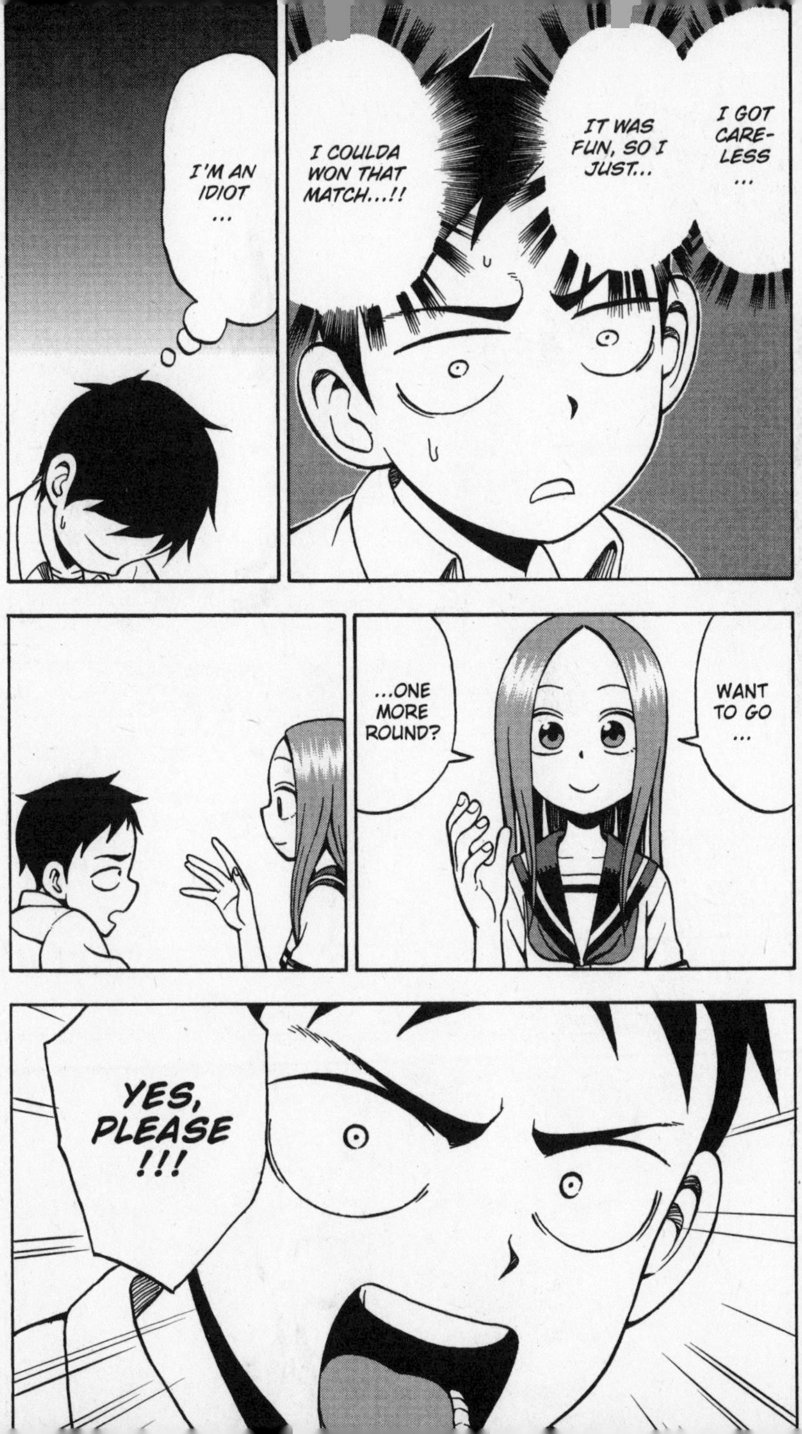
I GOT CARE-LESS...
IT WAS FUN, SO I JUST...
I COULDA WON THAT MATCH...!!
I'M AN IDIOT...
WANT TO GO...
...ONE MORE ROUND?
YES, PLEASE!!!

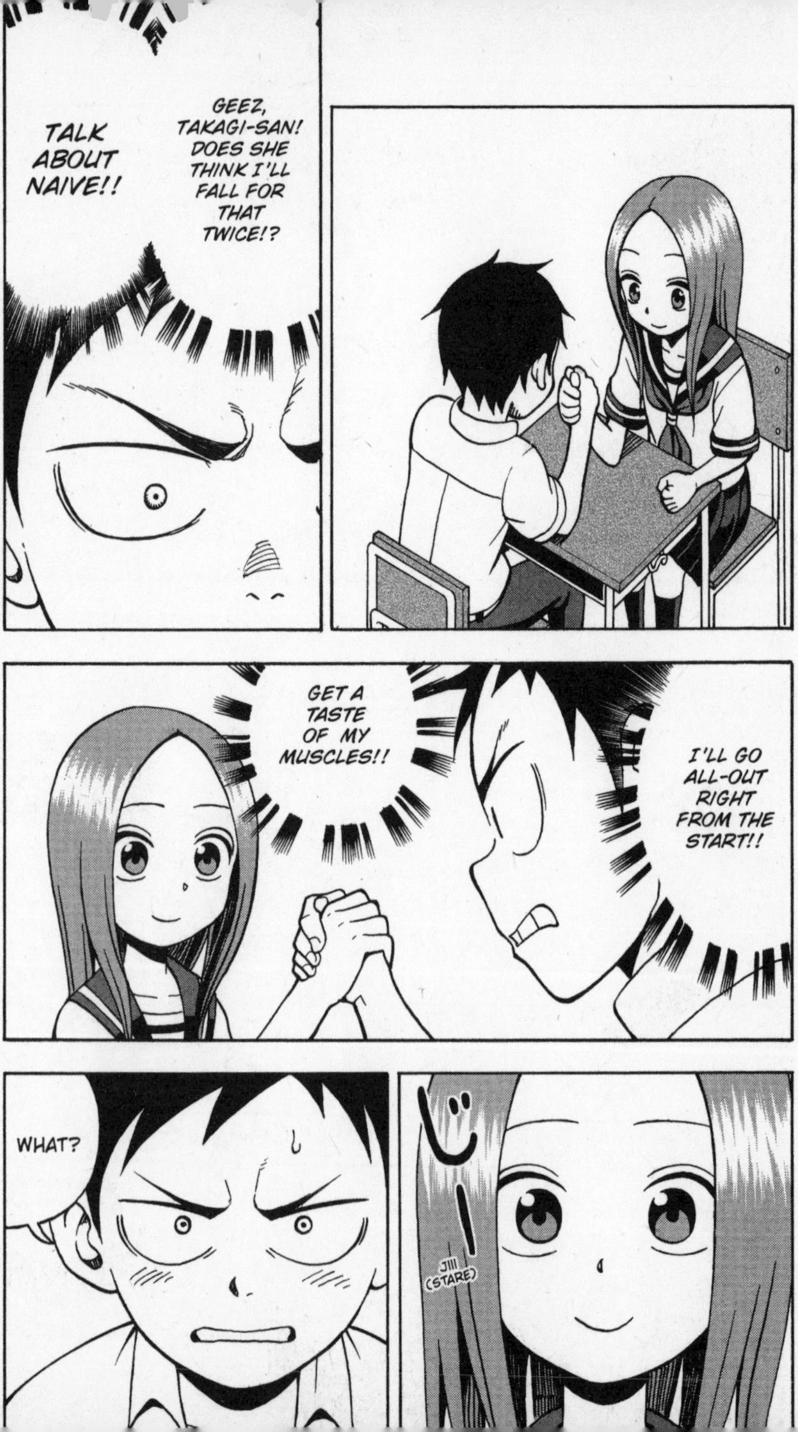
GEEZ, TAKAGI-SAN! DOES SHE THINK I'LL FALL FOR THAT TWICE!?
TALK ABOUT NAIVE!!
I'LL GO ALL-OUT RIGHT FROM THE START!!
GET A TASTE OF MY MUSCLES!!
JIII (STARE)
WHAT?

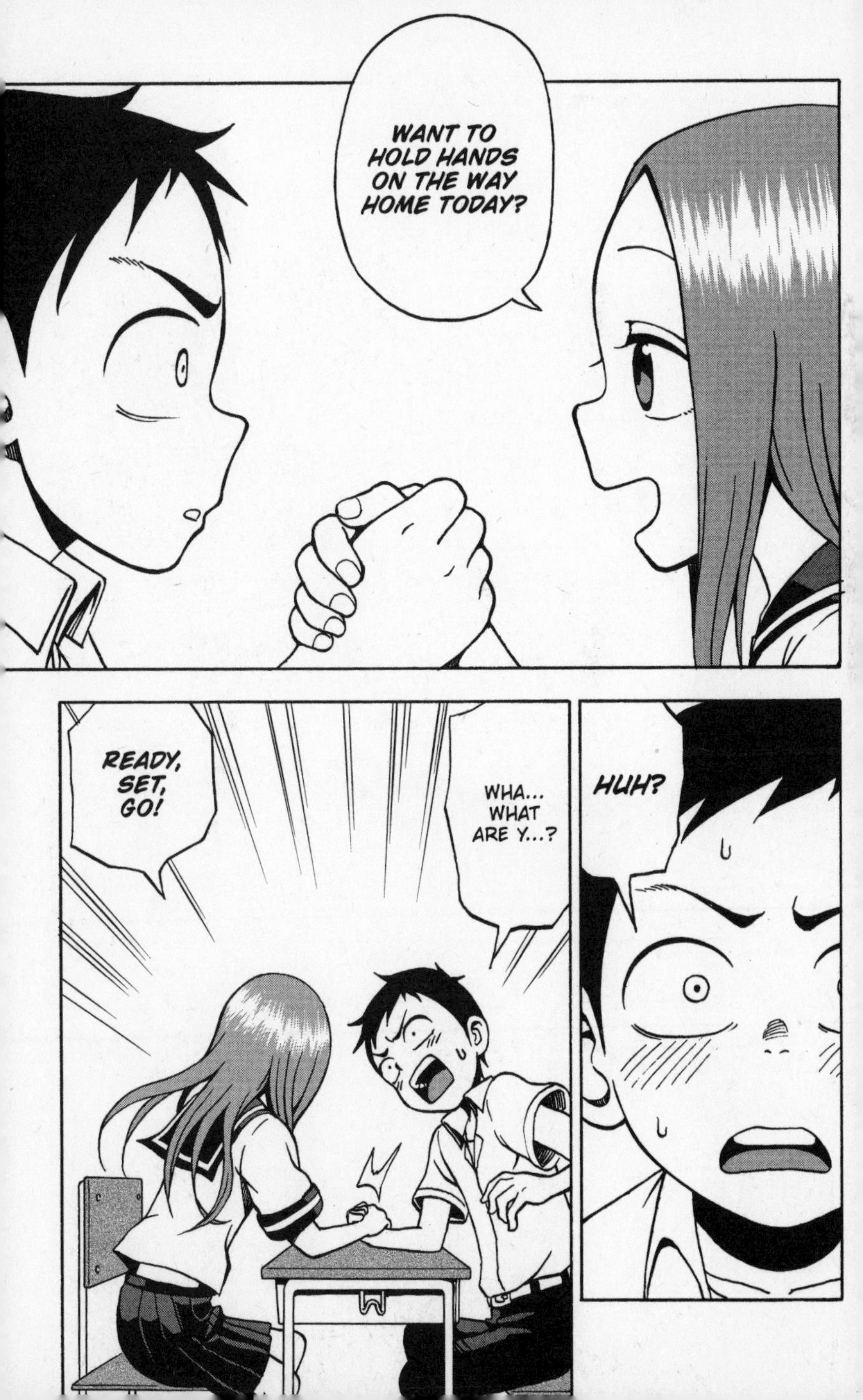
WANT TO HOLD HANDS ON THE WAY HOME TODAY?
HUH?
WHA... WHAT ARE Y...?
READY, SET, GO!

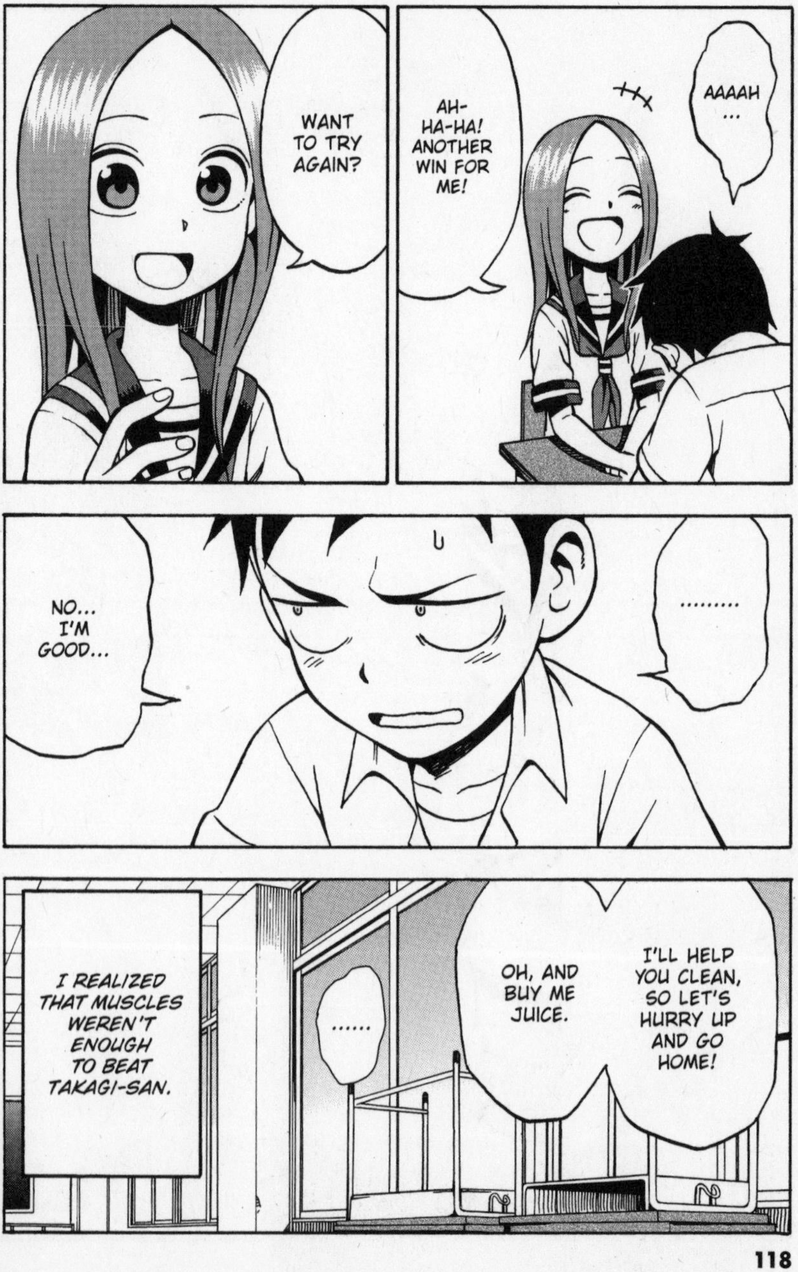
AAAAH ...
AH-HA-HA! ANOTHER WIN FOR ME!
WANT TO TRY AGAIN?
.........
NO... I'M GOOD...
I'LL HELP YOU CLEAN, SO LET'S HURRY UP AND GO HOME!
OH, AND BUY ME JUICE.
......
I REALIZED THAT MUSCLES WEREN'T ENOUGH TO BEAT TAKAGI-SAN.

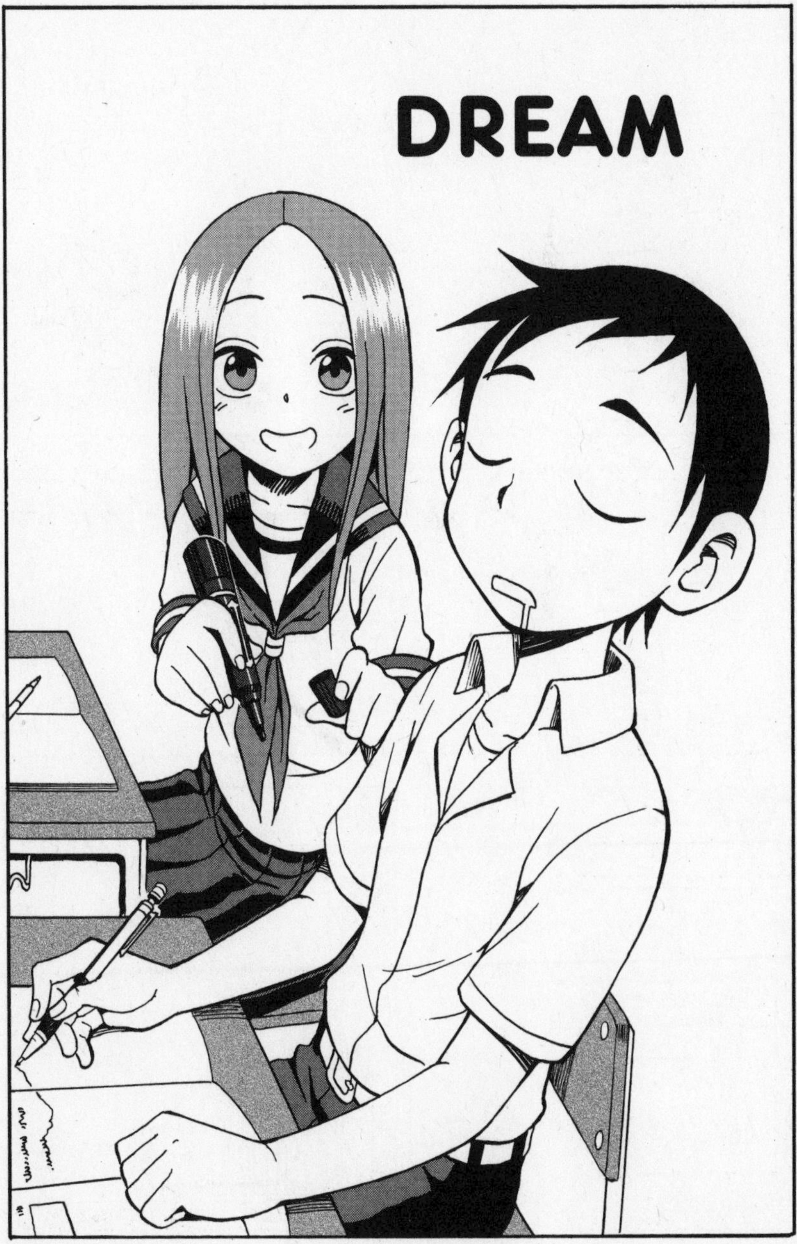
DREAM

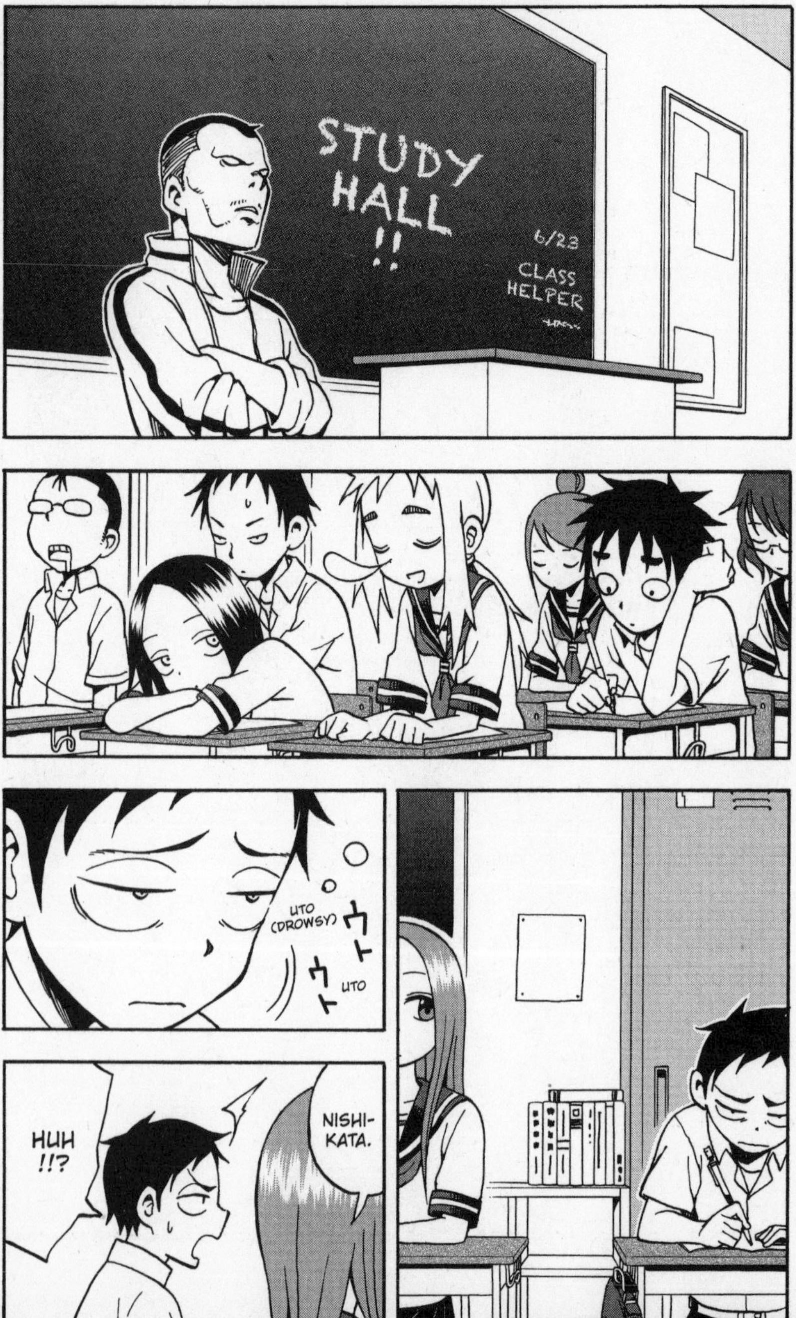

STUDY HALL !!
6/23
CLASS HELPER
ウト
UTO (DROWSY)
ウト
UTO
NISHI-KATA.
HUH !!?

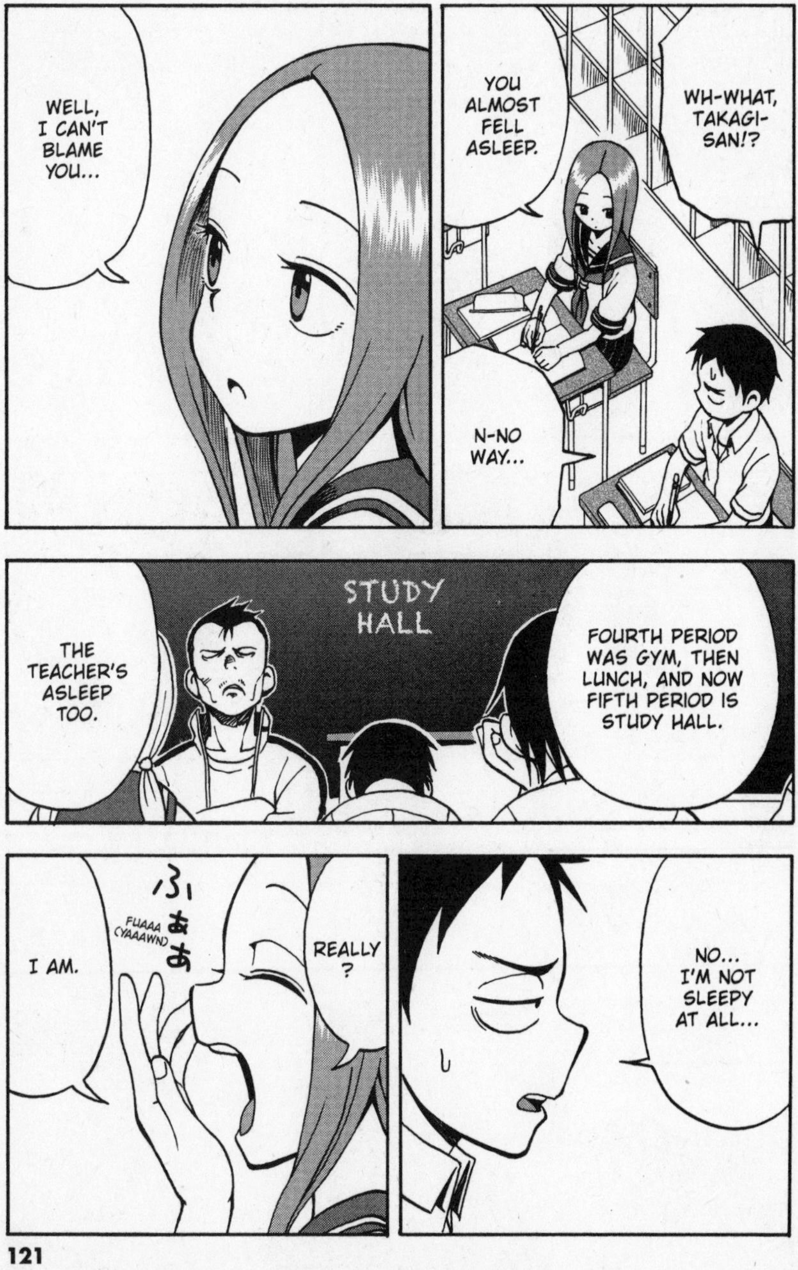
WH-WHAT, TAKAGI-SAN!?
YOU ALMOST FELL ASLEEP.
N-NO WAY...
WELL, I CAN'T BLAME YOU...
FOURTH PERIOD WAS GYM, THEN LUNCH, AND NOW FIFTH PERIOD IS STUDY HALL.
STUDY HALL
THE TEACHER'S ASLEEP TOO.
NO... I'M NOT SLEEPY AT ALL...
REALLY?
ふあぁ
FUAAA (YAAAWN)
I AM.

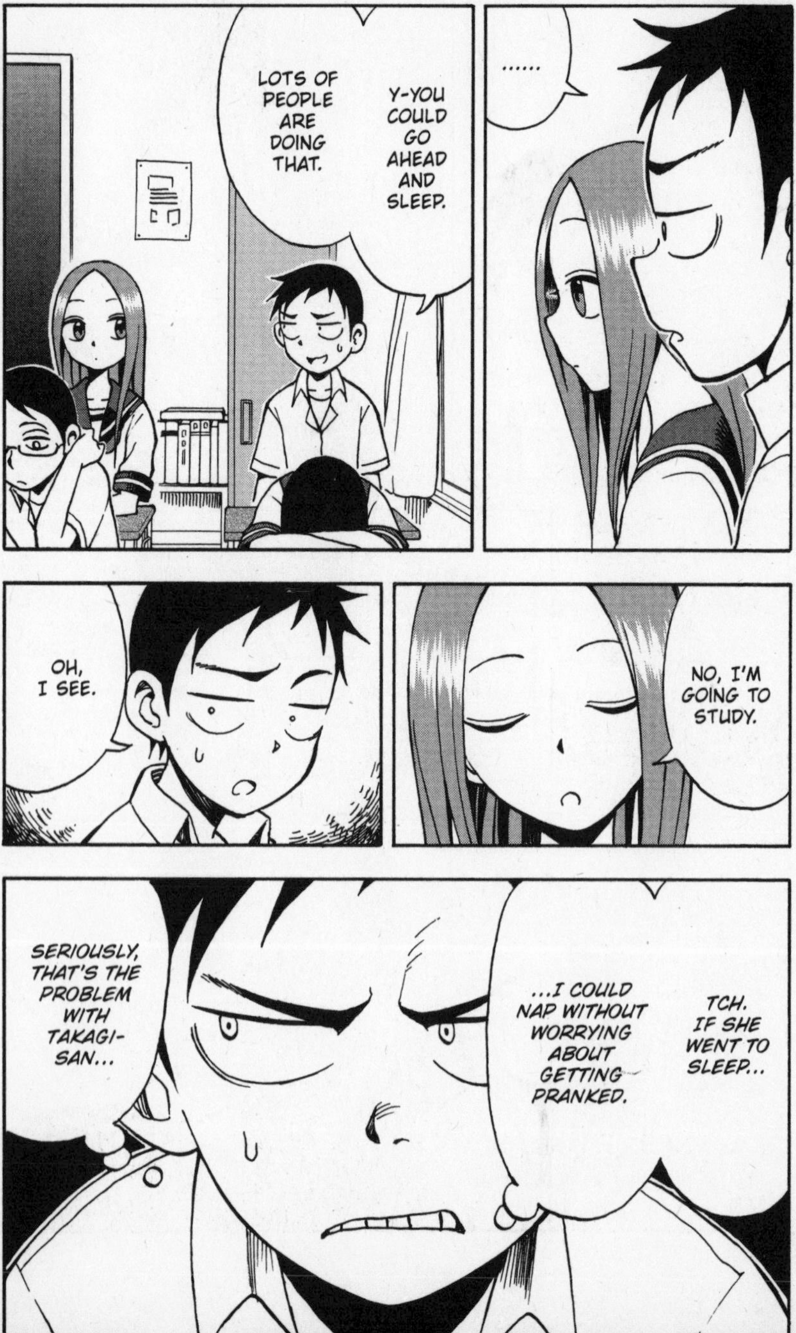
......
Y-YOU COULD GO AHEAD AND SLEEP.
LOTS OF PEOPLE ARE DOING THAT.
NO, I'M GOING TO STUDY.
OH, I SEE.
TCH. IF SHE WENT TO SLEEP...
...I COULD NAP WITHOUT WORRYING ABOUT GETTING PRANKED.
SERIOUSLY, THAT'S THE PROBLEM WITH TAKAGI-SAN...

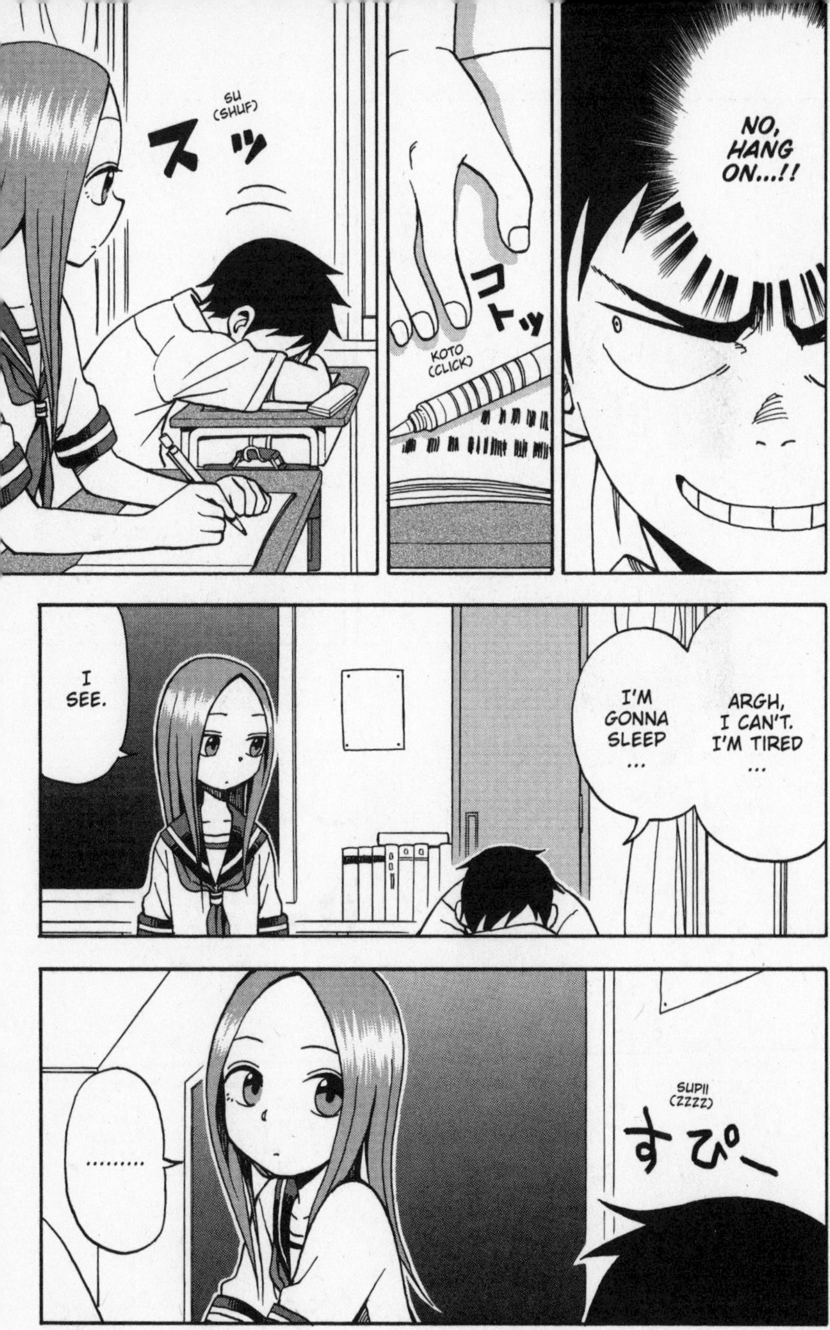
NO, HANG ON...!!
コトッ
KOTO (CLICK)
スッ
SU (SHUF)
ARGH, I CAN'T. I'M TIRED ...
I'M GONNA SLEEP ...
I SEE.
すぴー
SUPII (ZZZZ)
..........

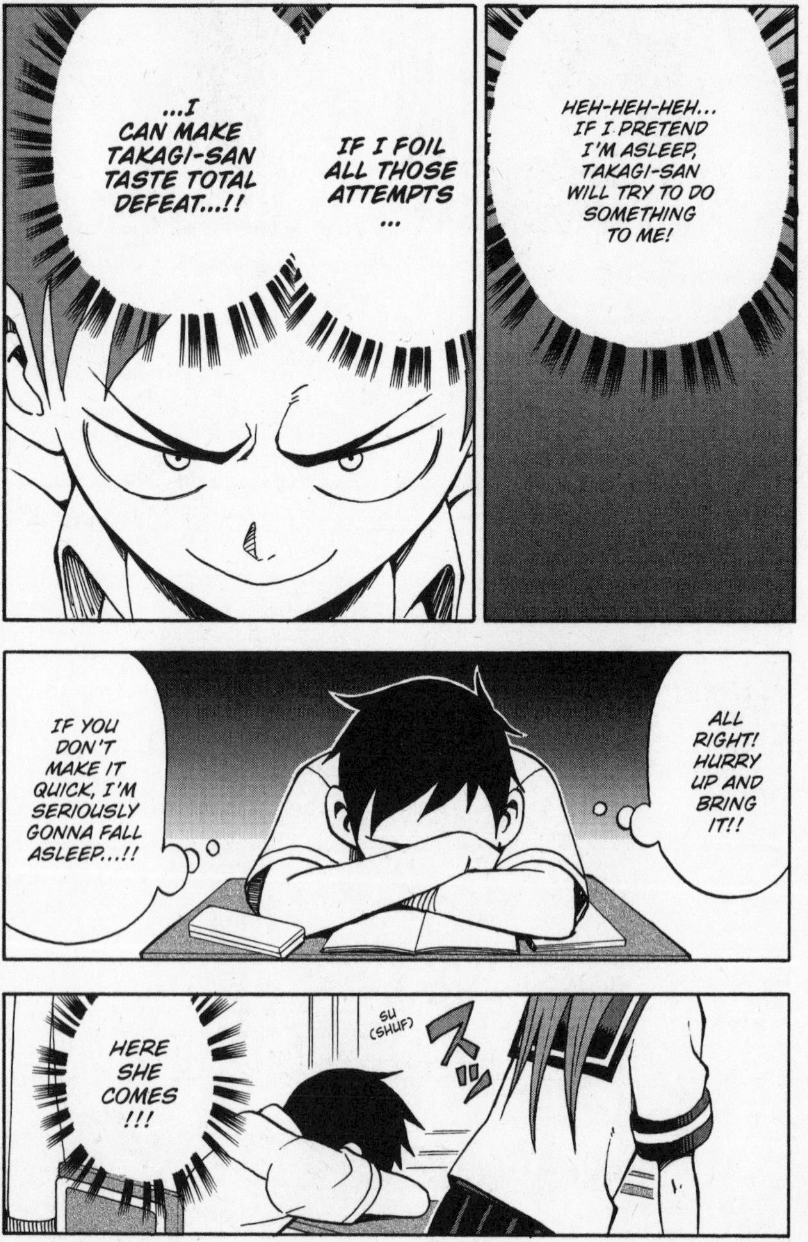
HEH-HEH-HEH... IF I PRETEND I'M ASLEEP, TAKAGI-SAN WILL TRY TO DO SOMETHING TO ME!
IF I FOIL ALL THOSE ATTEMPTS ...
...I CAN MAKE TAKAGI-SAN TASTE TOTAL DEFEAT...!!
ALL RIGHT! HURRY UP AND BRING IT!!
IF YOU DON'T MAKE IT QUICK, I'M SERIOUSLY GONNA FALL ASLEEP...!!
SU (SHUF)
HERE SHE COMES !!!

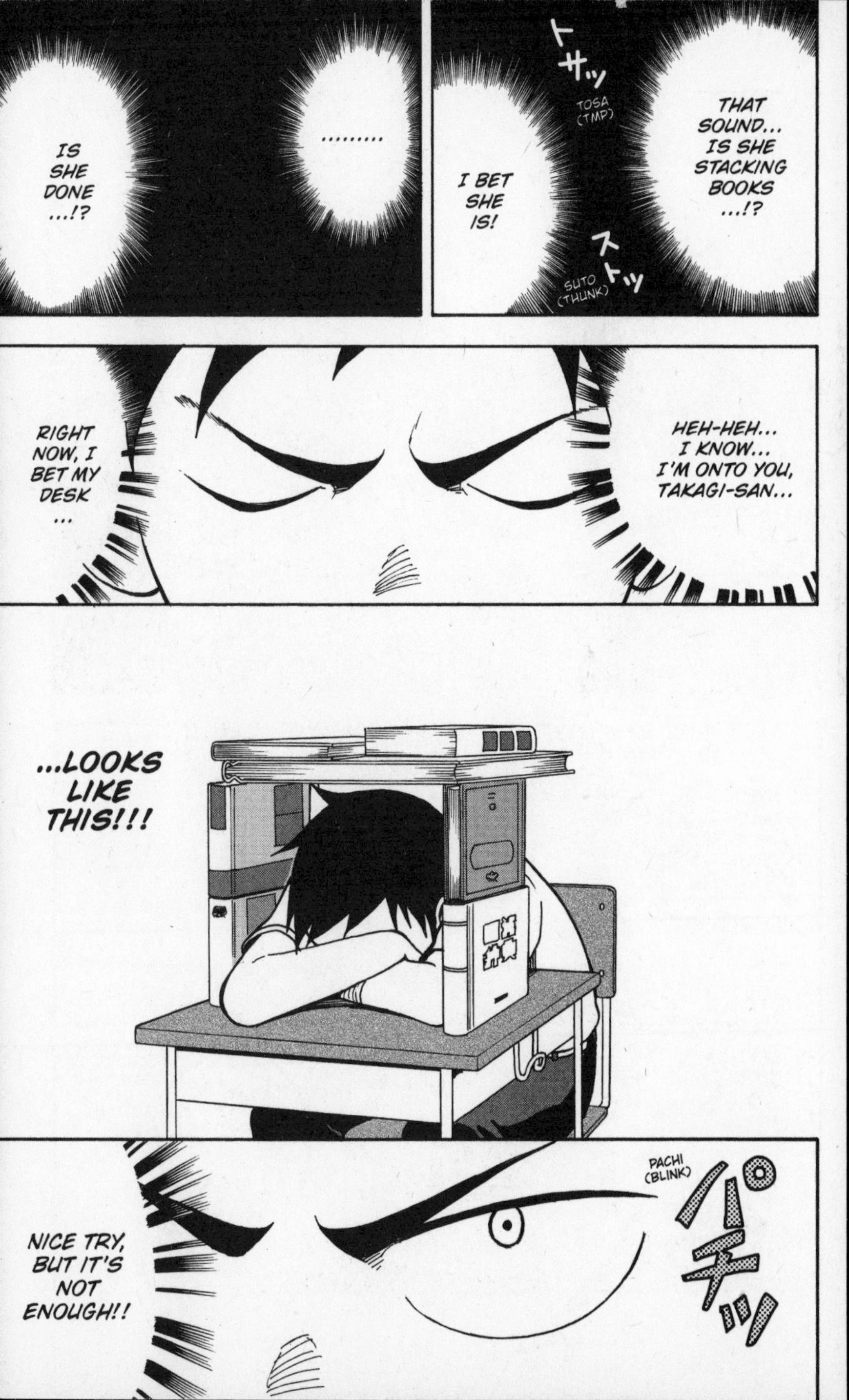
トサッ
TOSA (TMP)
THAT SOUND... IS SHE STACKING BOOKS ...!?
I BET SHE IS!
ストッ
SUTO (THUNK)
.........
IS SHE DONE ...!?
HEH-HEH... I KNOW... I'M ONTO YOU, TAKAGI-SAN...
RIGHT NOW, I BET MY DESK ...
...LOOKS LIKE THIS!!!
パチッ
PACHI (BLINK)
NICE TRY, BUT IT'S NOT ENOUGH!!

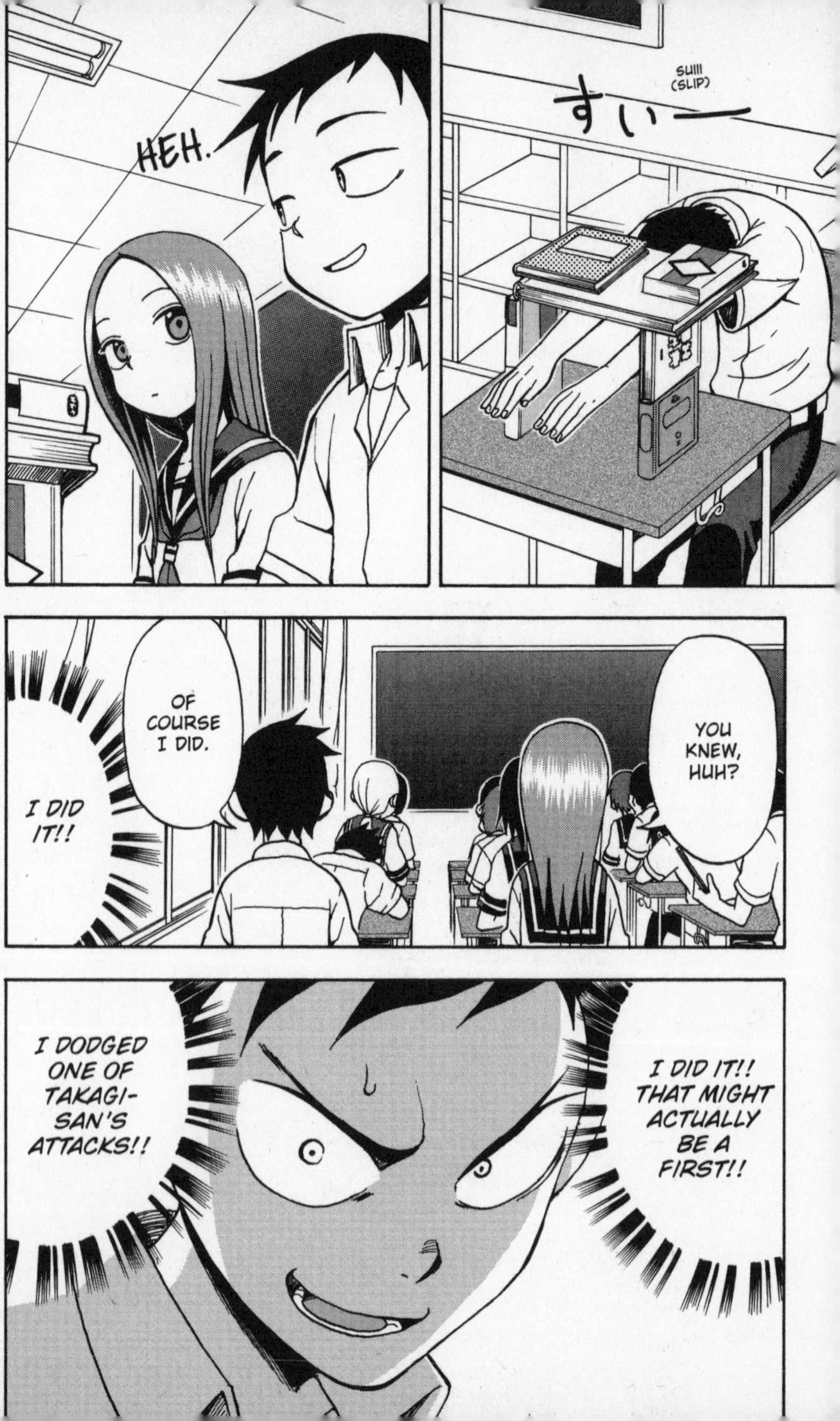
SUIII (SLIP)
すいー
HEH.
YOU KNEW, HUH?
OF COURSE I DID.
I DID IT!!
I DID IT!! THAT MIGHT ACTUALLY BE A FIRST!!
I DODGED ONE OF TAKAGI-SAN'S ATTACKS!!

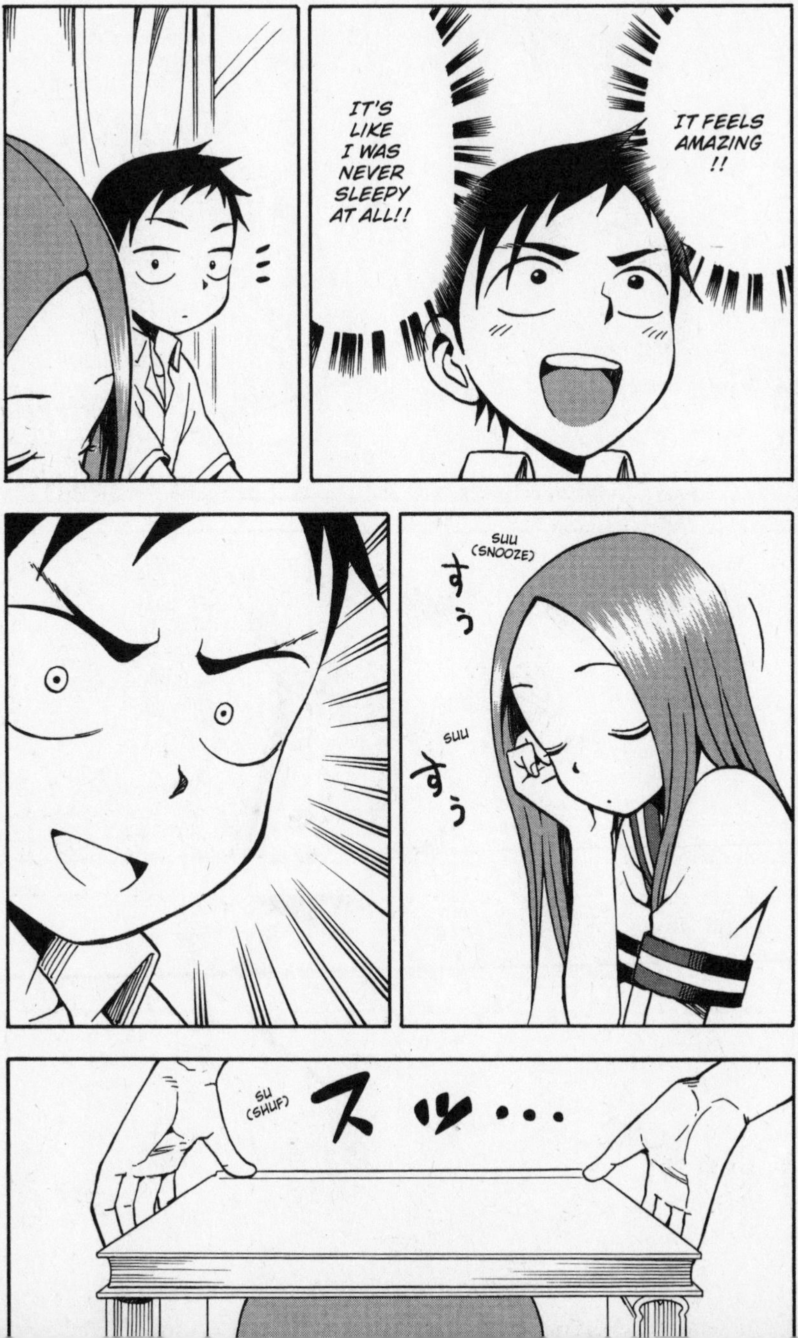
IT FEELS AMAZING !!
IT'S LIKE I WAS NEVER SLEEPY AT ALL!!
SUU (SNOOZE)
すう
SUU
すう
SU (SHUF)
スッ…

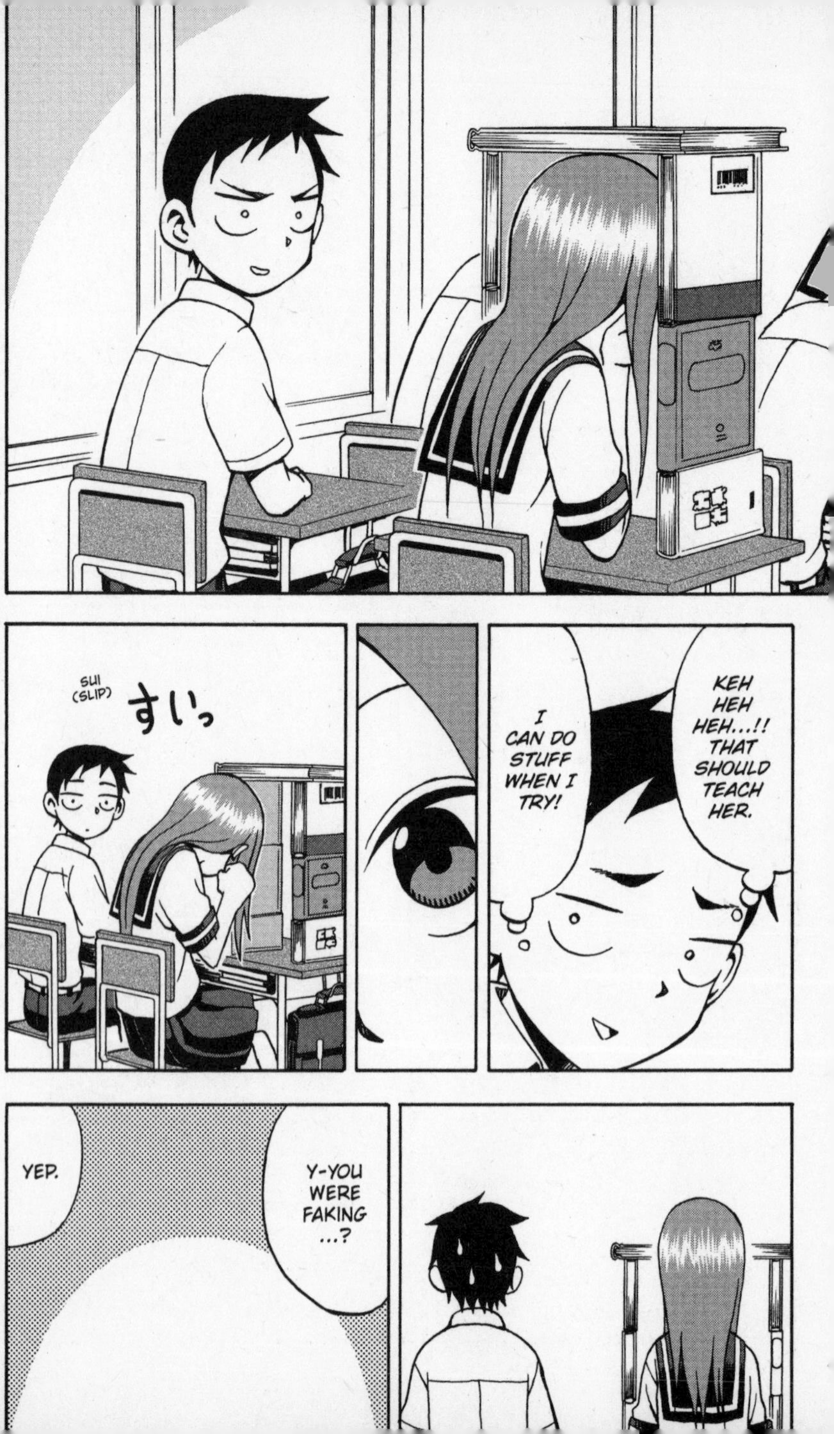
KEH HEH HEH...!! THAT SHOULD TEACH HER.
I CAN DO STUFF WHEN I TRY!
すいっ
SUI (SLIP)
Y-YOU WERE FAKING ...?
YEP.

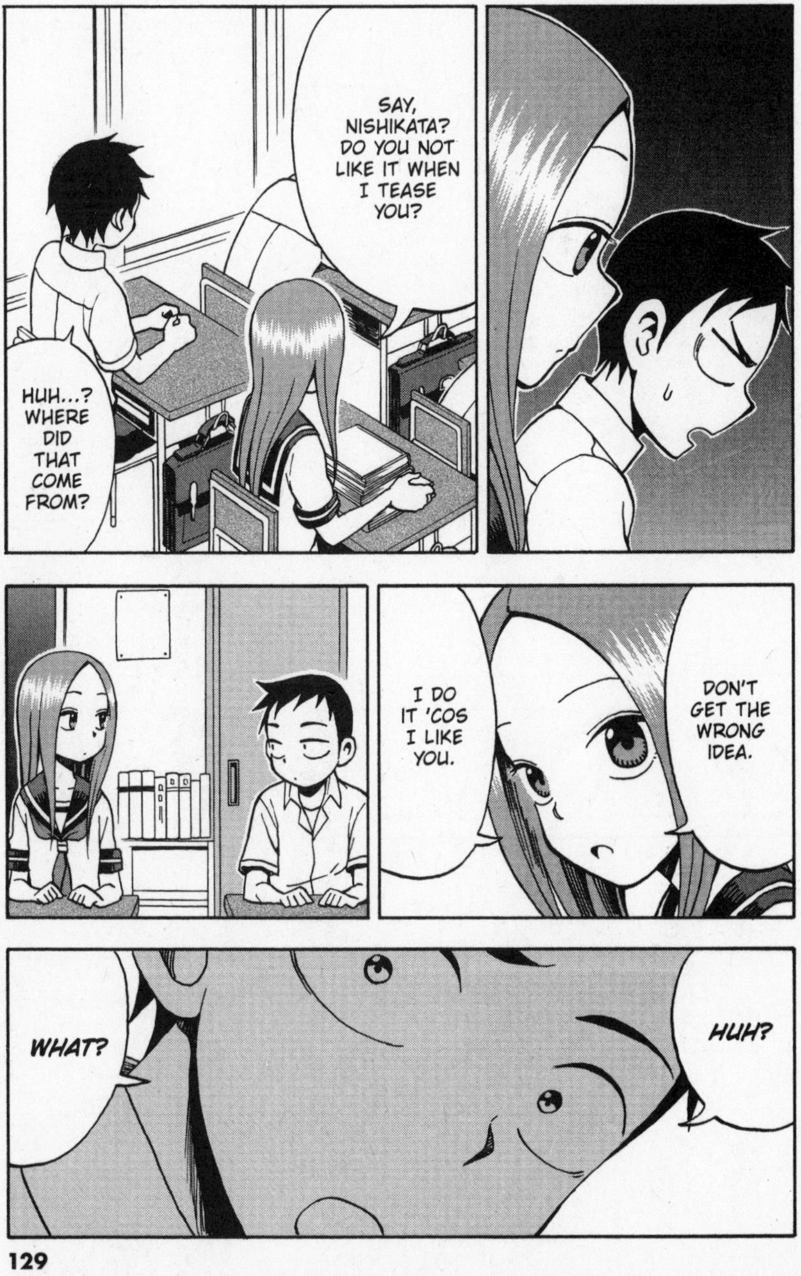
SAY, NISHIKATA? DO YOU NOT LIKE IT WHEN I TEASE YOU?
HUH...? WHERE DID THAT COME FROM?
DON'T GET THE WRONG IDEA.
I DO IT 'COS I LIKE YOU.
HUH?
WHAT?

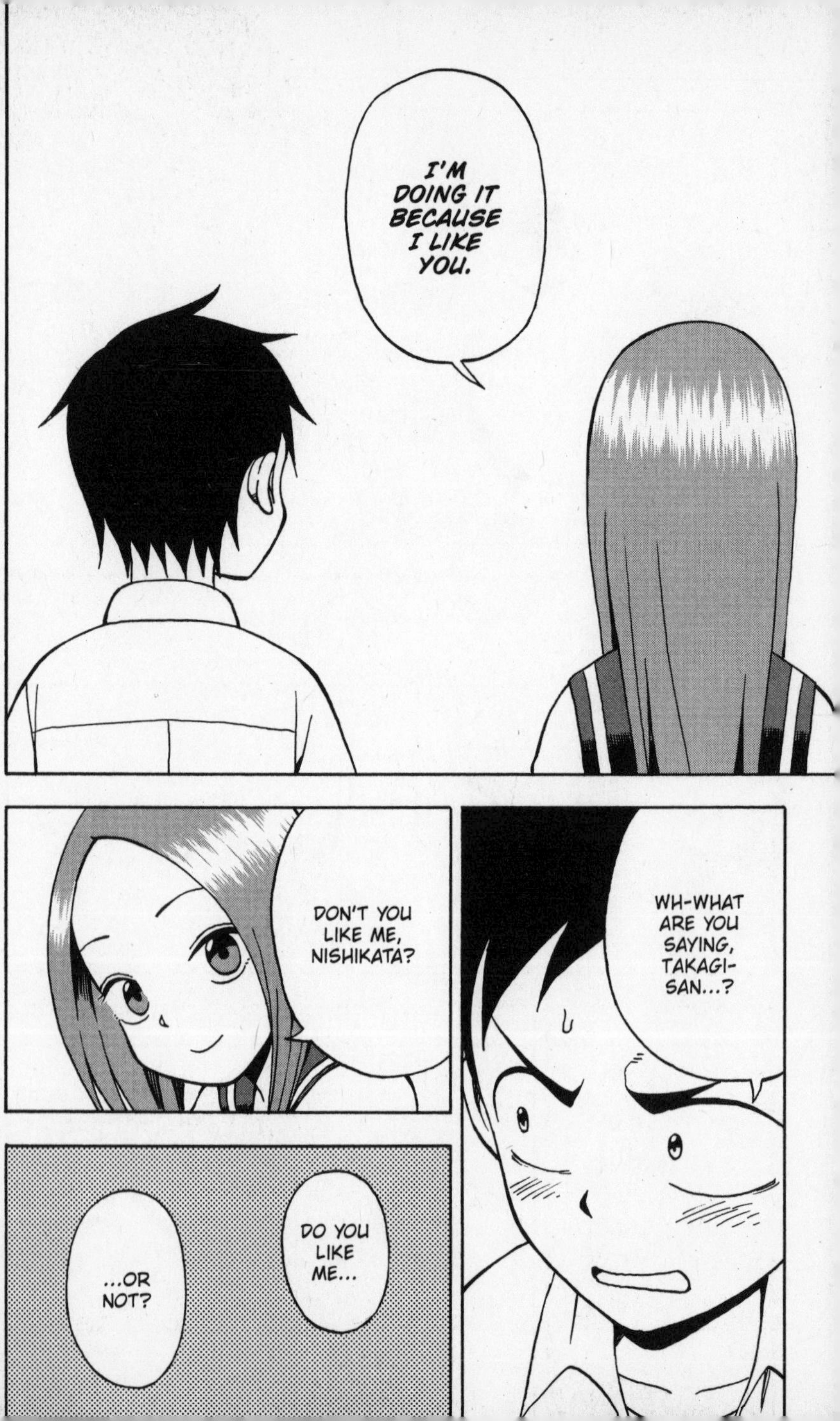
I'M DOING IT BECAUSE I LIKE YOU.
WH-WHAT ARE YOU SAYING, TAKAGI-SAN...?
DON'T YOU LIKE ME, NISHIKATA?
DO YOU LIKE ME...
...OR NOT?

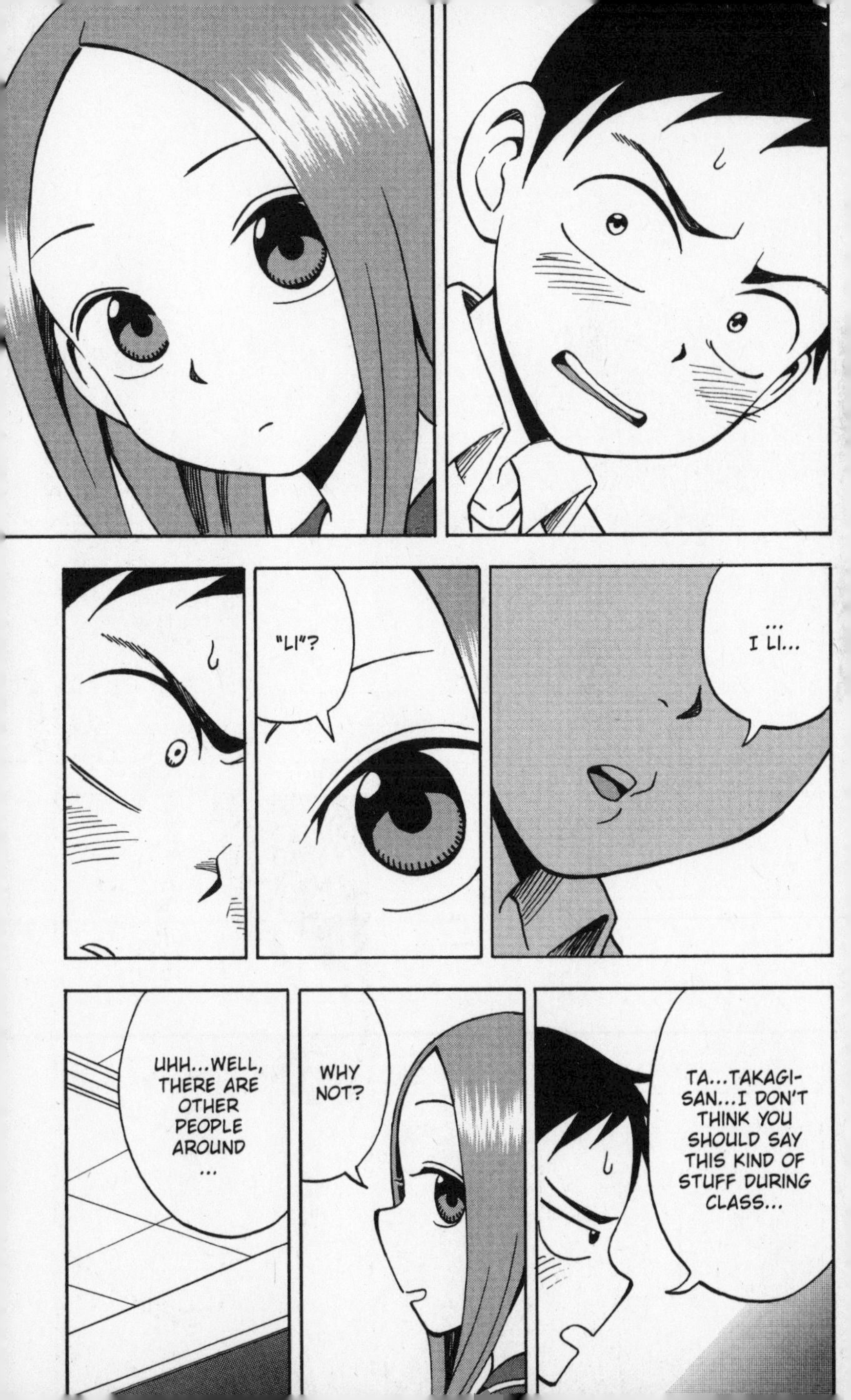
... I LI...
"LI"?
TA...TAKAGI-SAN...I DON'T THINK YOU SHOULD SAY THIS KIND OF STUFF DURING CLASS...
WHY NOT?
UHH...WELL, THERE ARE OTHER PEOPLE AROUND...

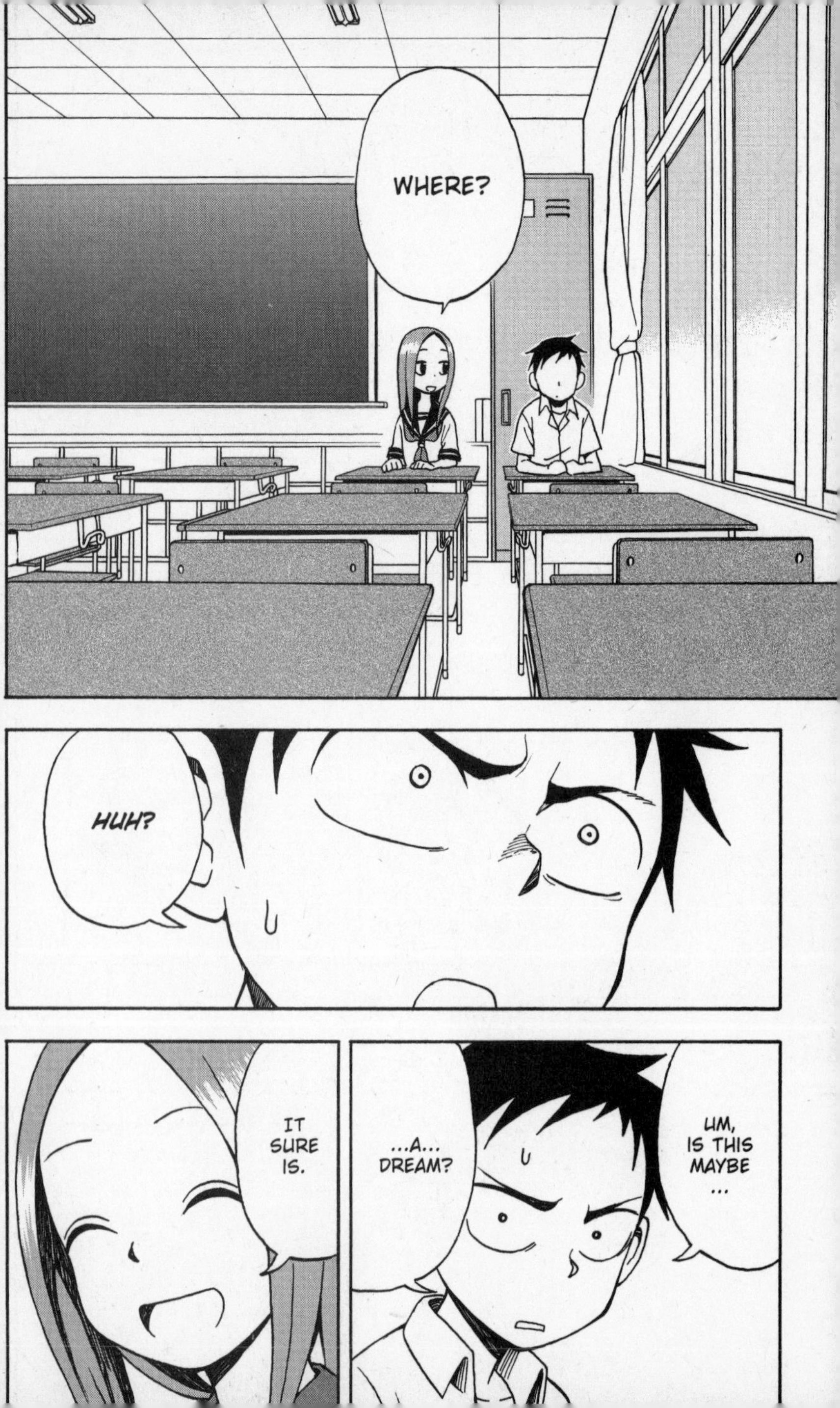
WHERE?
HUH?
UM, IS THIS MAYBE ...
...A... DREAM?
IT SURE IS.

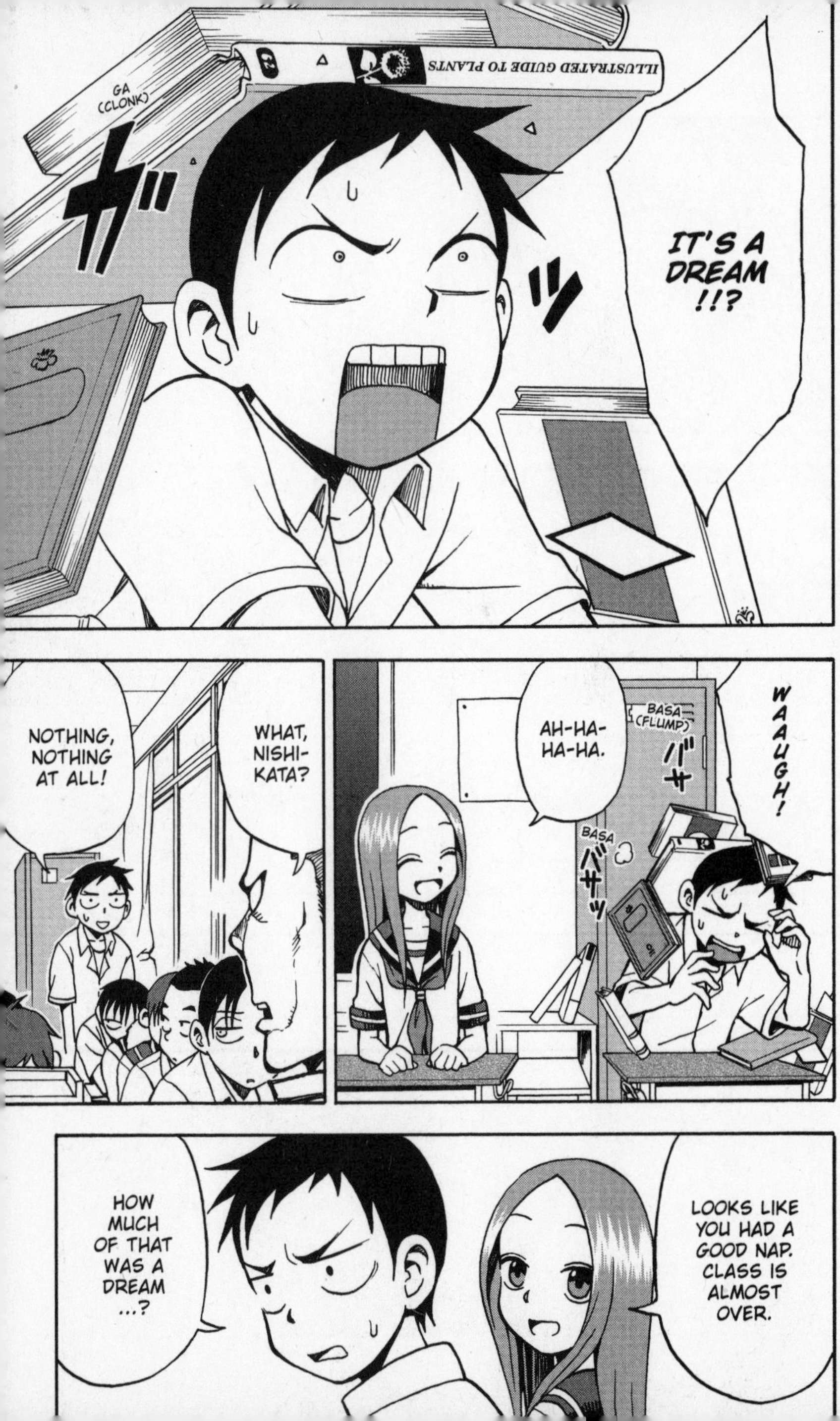
ILLUSTRATED GUIDE TO PLANTS
IT'S A DREAM !!?
GA (CLONK)
WAAUGH!
BASA (FLUMP)
BASA
AH-HA-HA-HA.
WHAT, NISHI-KATA?
NOTHING, NOTHING AT ALL!
LOOKS LIKE YOU HAD A GOOD NAP. CLASS IS ALMOST OVER.
HOW MUCH OF THAT WAS A DREAM ...?

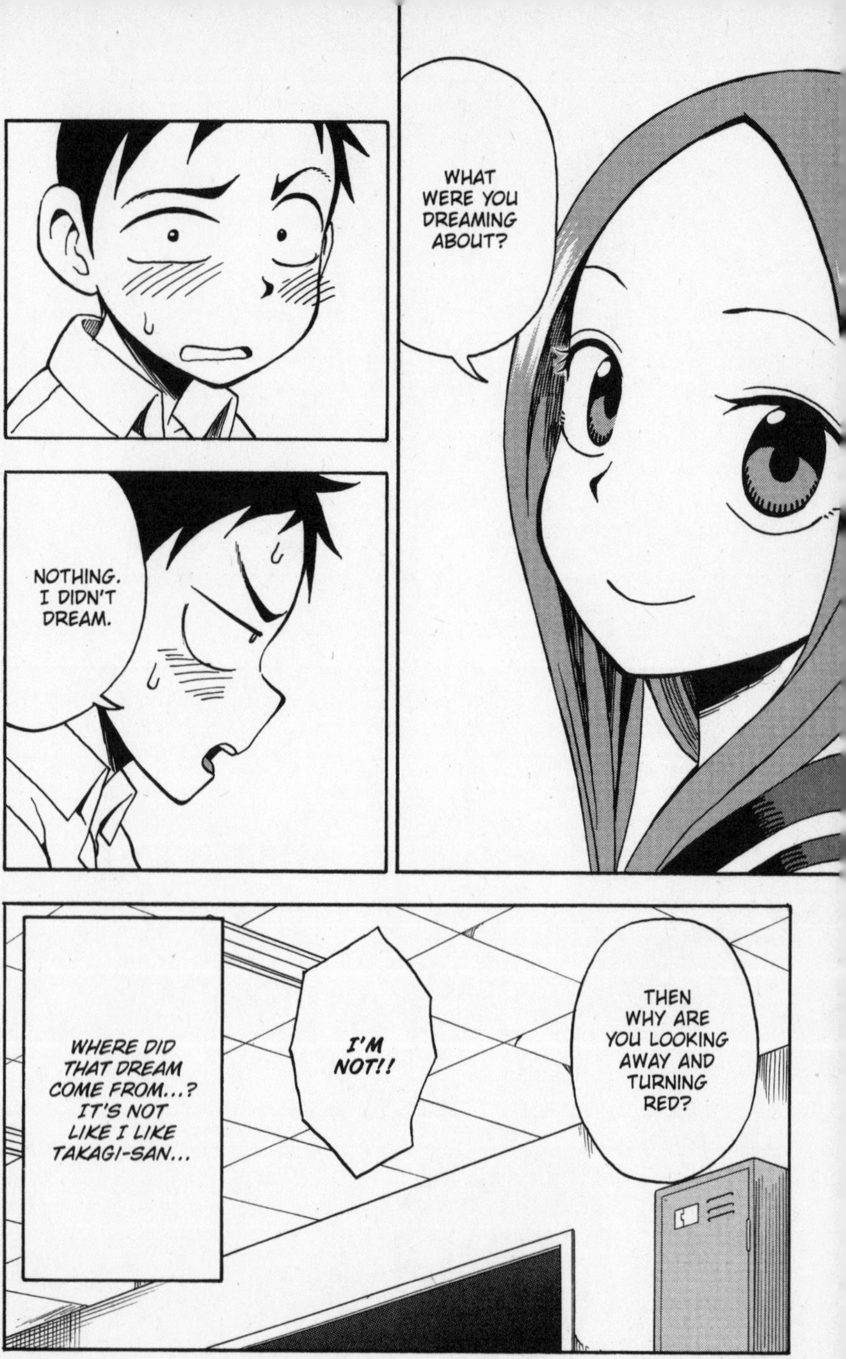
WHAT WERE YOU DREAMING ABOUT?
NOTHING. I DIDN'T DREAM.
THEN WHY ARE YOU LOOKING AWAY AND TURNING RED?
I'M NOT!!
WHERE DID THAT DREAM COME FROM...? IT'S NOT LIKE I LIKE TAKAGI-SAN...

Teasing Master
Takagi-san

THE NEXT PAGE IS A MINI ONE-SHOT THAT RAN IN THE GESSAN JULY 2012 ISSUE. SEVERAL THINGS ARE DIFFERENT FROM THE WAY THEY ARE NOW. TAKAGI-SAN'S FACE IS PRETTY MEAN LOOKING, AND THE TWO OF THEM SIT IN A DIFFERENT SPOT, BUT I HOPE YOU ENJOY IT FOR WHAT IT IS.

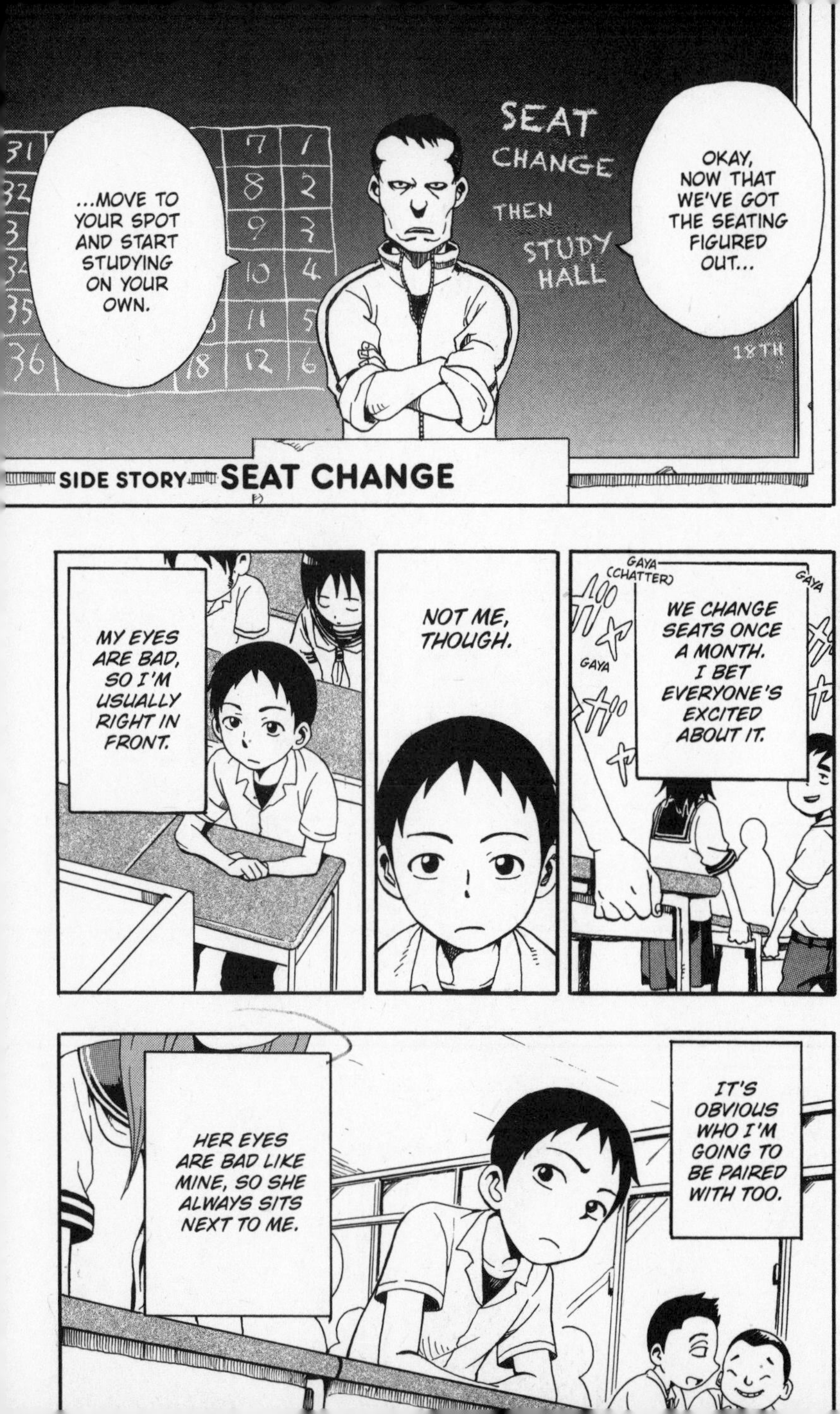
OKAY, NOW THAT WE'VE GOT THE SEATING FIGURED OUT...
SEAT CHANGE
THEN
STUDY HALL
18TH
...MOVE TO YOUR SPOT AND START STUDYING ON YOUR OWN.
SIDE STORY SEAT CHANGE
GAYA (CHATTER)
GAYA
GAYA
WE CHANGE SEATS ONCE A MONTH. I BET EVERYONE'S EXCITED ABOUT IT.
NOT ME, THOUGH.
MY EYES ARE BAD, SO I'M USUALLY RIGHT IN FRONT.
IT'S OBVIOUS WHO I'M GOING TO BE PAIRED WITH TOO.
HER EYES ARE BAD LIKE MINE, SO SHE ALWAYS SITS NEXT TO ME.

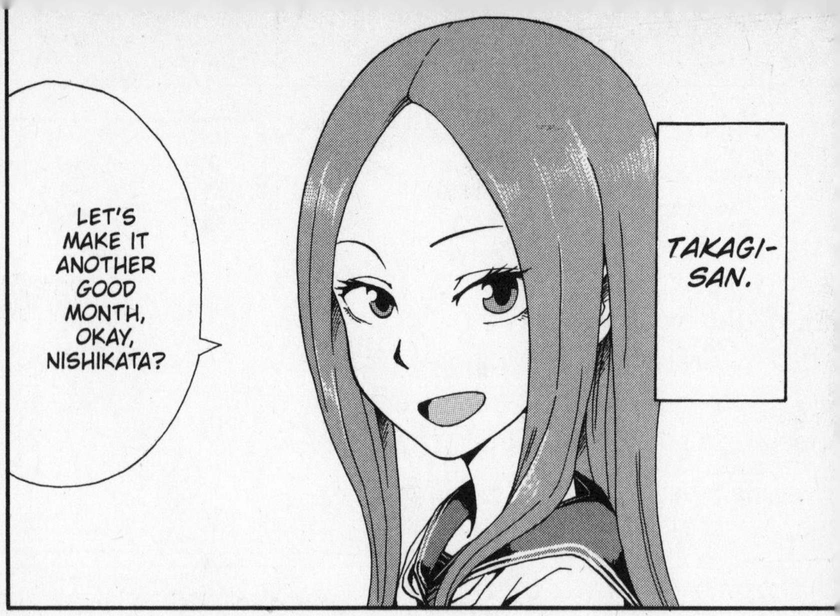
TAKAGI-SAN.
LET'S MAKE IT ANOTHER GOOD MONTH, OKAY, NISHIKATA?

## SIDE STORY

# SEAT CHANGE

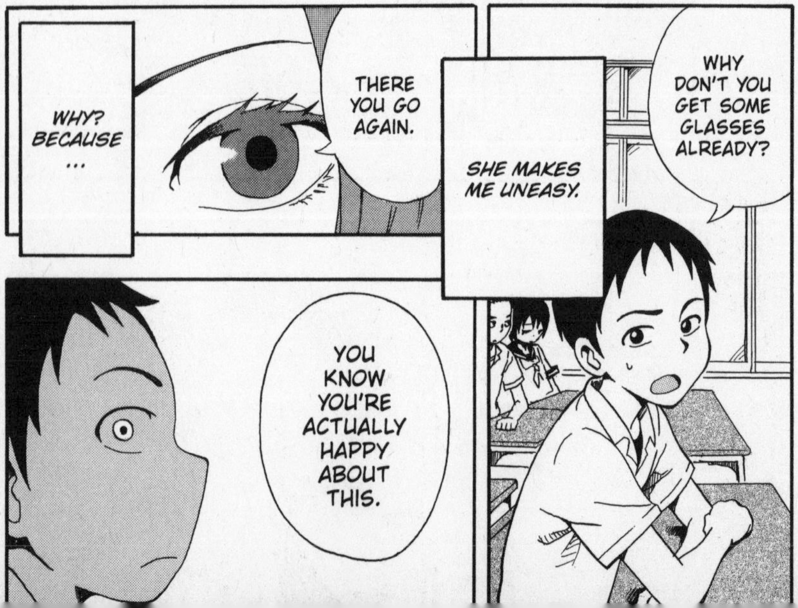
WHY DON'T YOU GET SOME GLASSES ALREADY?
SHE MAKES ME UNEASY.
THERE YOU GO AGAIN.
WHY? BECAUSE ...
YOU KNOW YOU'RE ACTUALLY HAPPY ABOUT THIS.

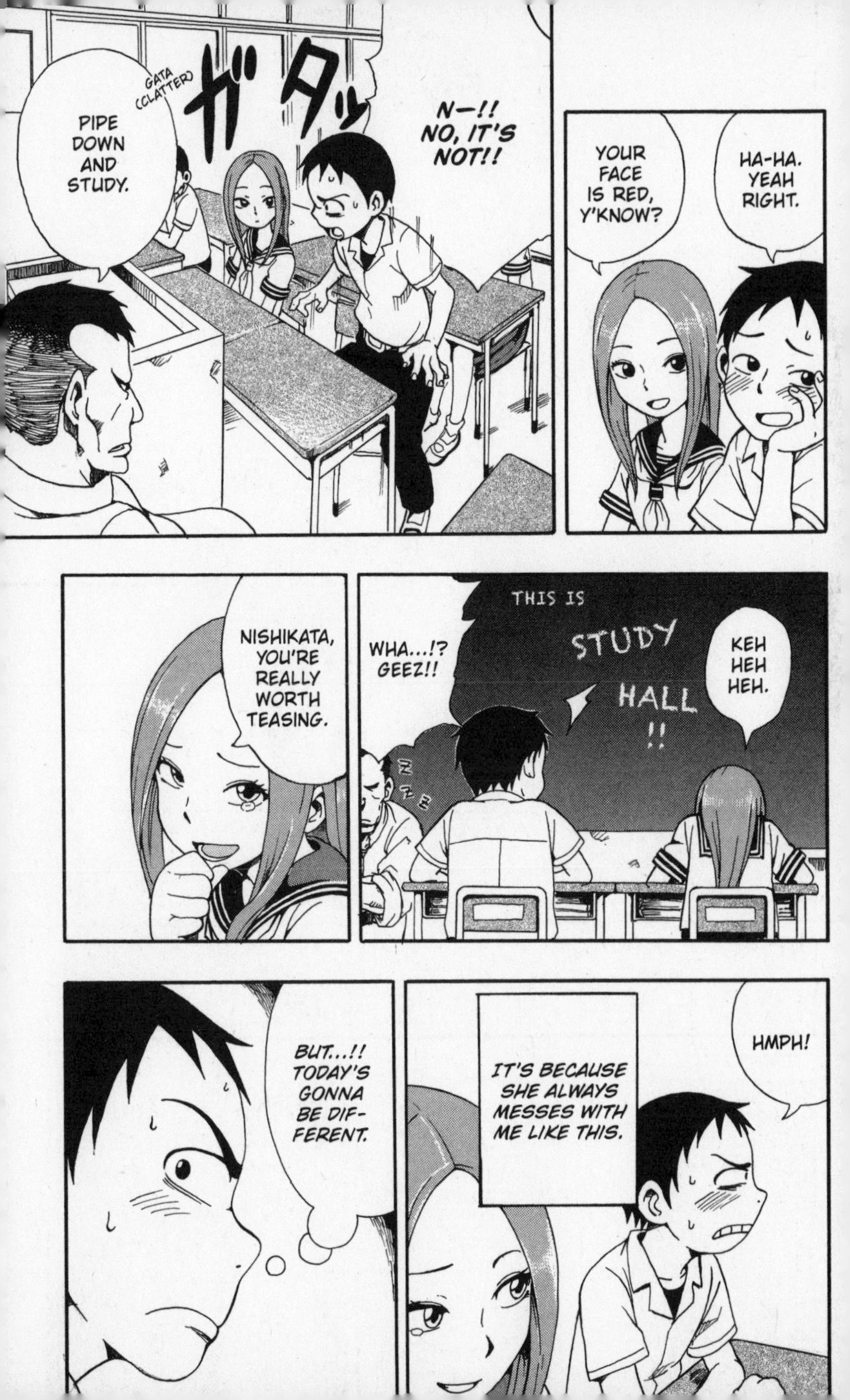
HA-HA. YEAH RIGHT.
YOUR FACE IS RED, Y'KNOW?
N—!! NO, IT'S NOT!!
ガタッ
GATA (CLATTER)
PIPE DOWN AND STUDY.
KEH HEH HEH.
THIS IS STUDY HALL !!
WHA...!? GEEZ!!
Z Z Z
NISHIKATA, YOU'RE REALLY WORTH TEASING.
HMPH!
IT'S BECAUSE SHE ALWAYS MESSES WITH ME LIKE THIS.
BUT...!! TODAY'S GONNA BE DIF-FERENT.

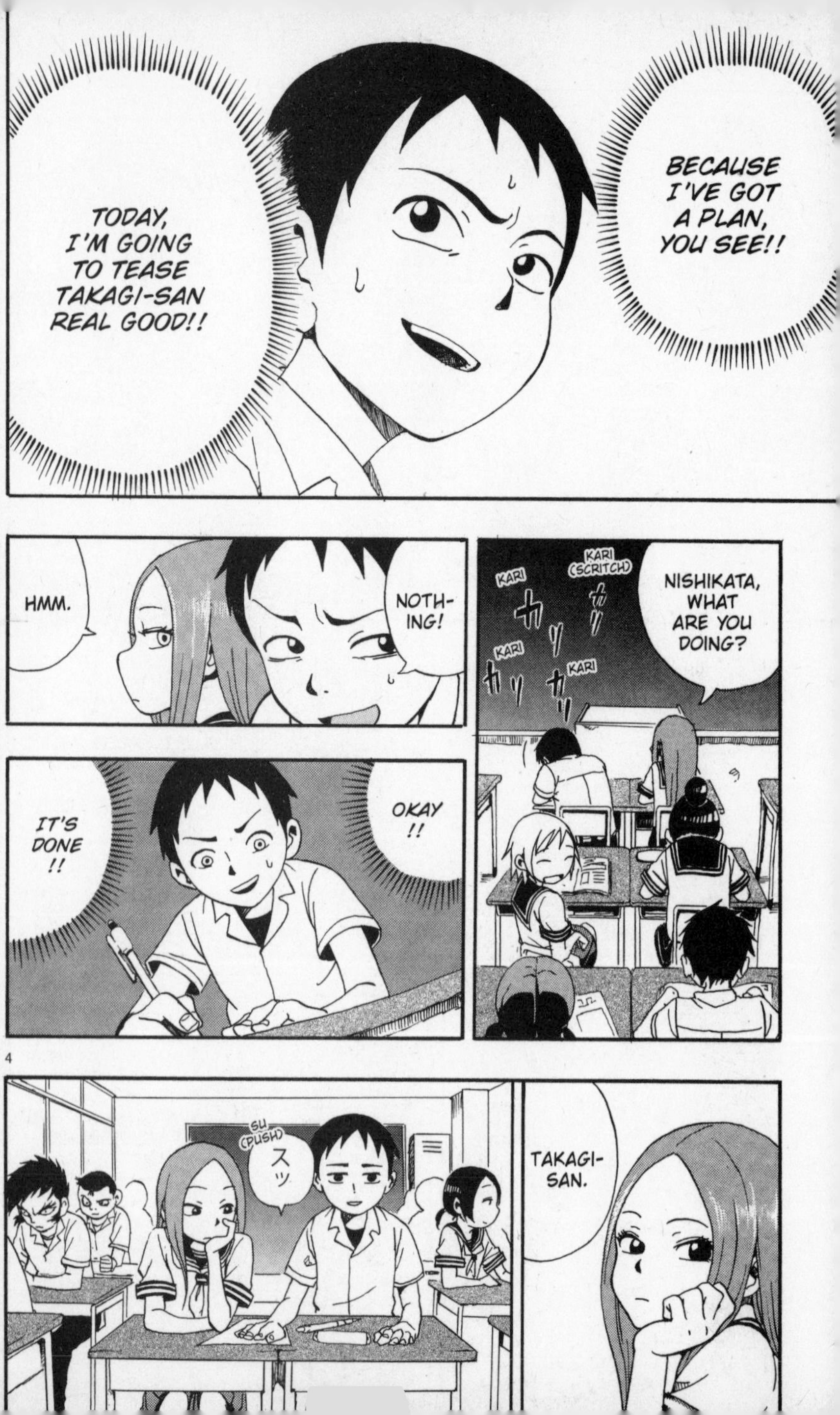
BECAUSE I'VE GOT A PLAN, YOU SEE!!
TODAY, I'M GOING TO TEASE TAKAGI-SAN REAL GOOD!!
KARI (SCRITCH)
NISHIKATA, WHAT ARE YOU DOING?
KARI
KARI
KARI
NOTH-ING!
HMM.
OKAY!!
IT'S DONE!!
TAKAGI-SAN.
SU (PUSH)
スッ

4

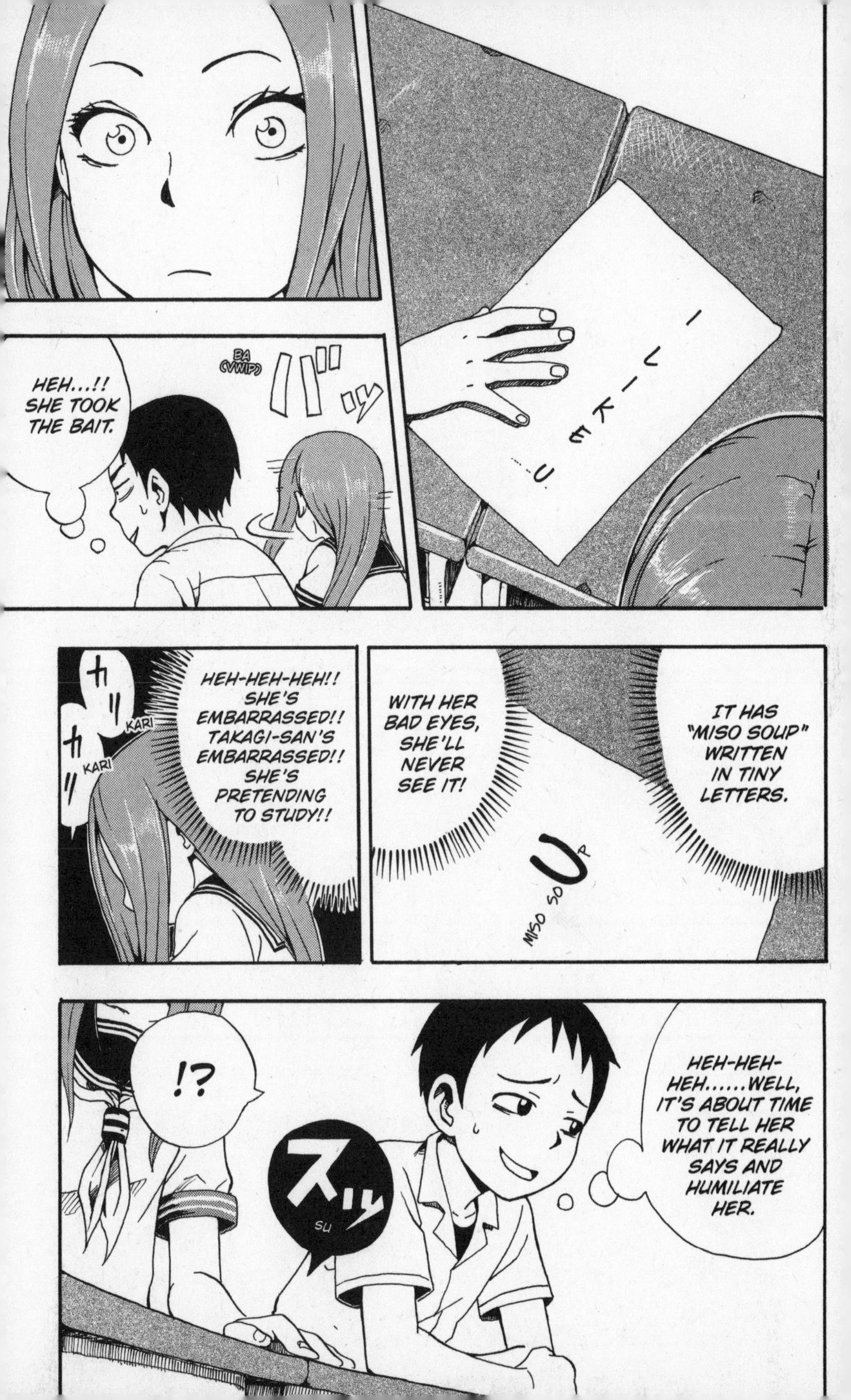
I LIKE U.
BA (VWIP)
HEH...!! SHE TOOK THE BAIT.
IT HAS "MISO SOUP" WRITTEN IN TINY LETTERS.
WITH HER BAD EYES, SHE'LL NEVER SEE IT!
MISO SOUP
HEH-HEH-HEH!! SHE'S EMBARRASSED!! TAKAGI-SAN'S EMBARRASSED!! SHE'S PRETENDING TO STUDY!!
KARI
KARI
HEH-HEH-HEH......WELL, IT'S ABOUT TIME TO TELL HER WHAT IT REALLY SAYS AND HUMILIATE HER.
SU
!?

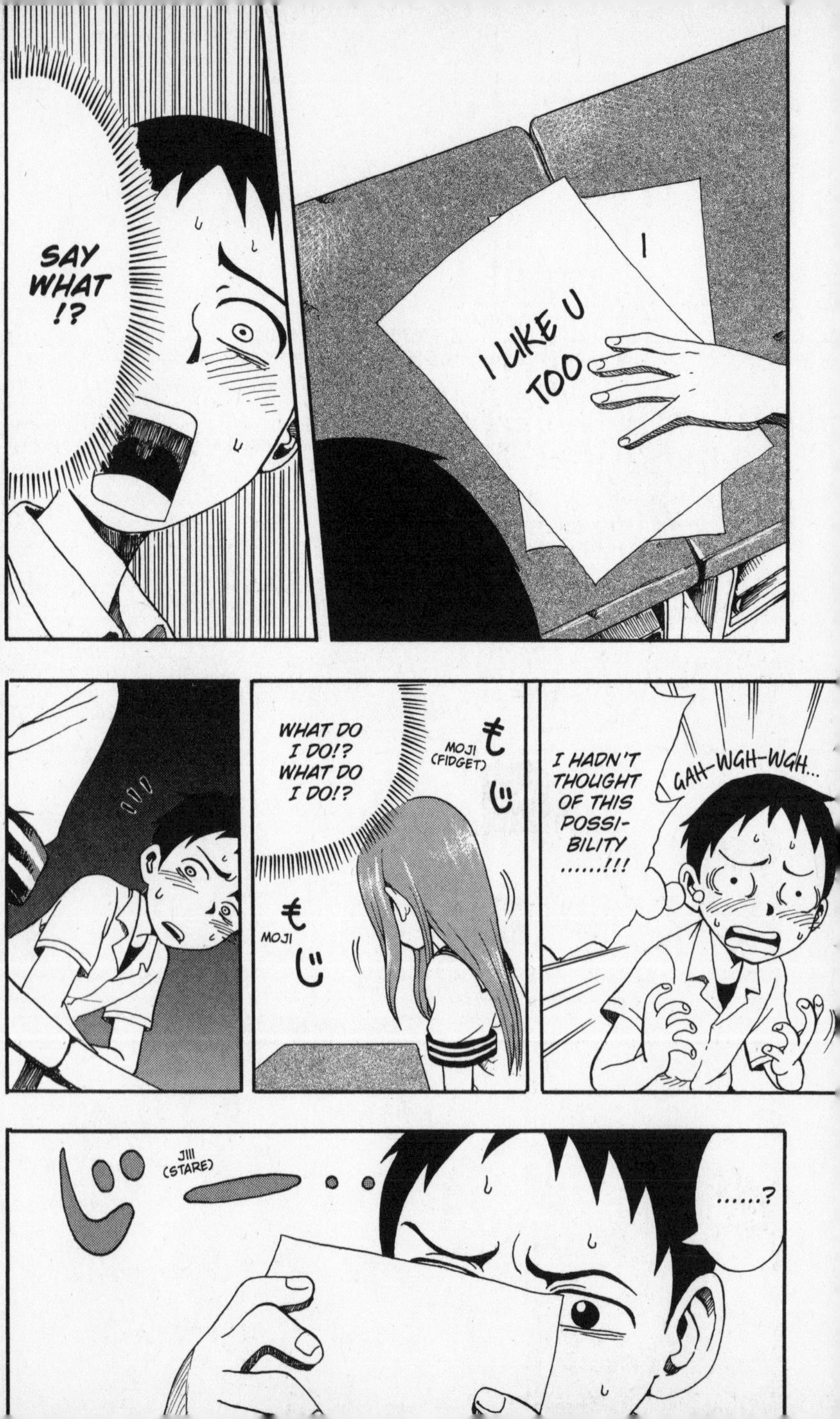
I
I LIKE U TOO
SAY WHAT!?
GAH-WGH-WGH...
I HADN'T THOUGHT OF THIS POSSI-BILITY ......!!!
もじ
MOJI (FIDGET)
WHAT DO I DO!? WHAT DO I DO!?
もじ
MOJI
......?
じーー・・
JIII (STARE)

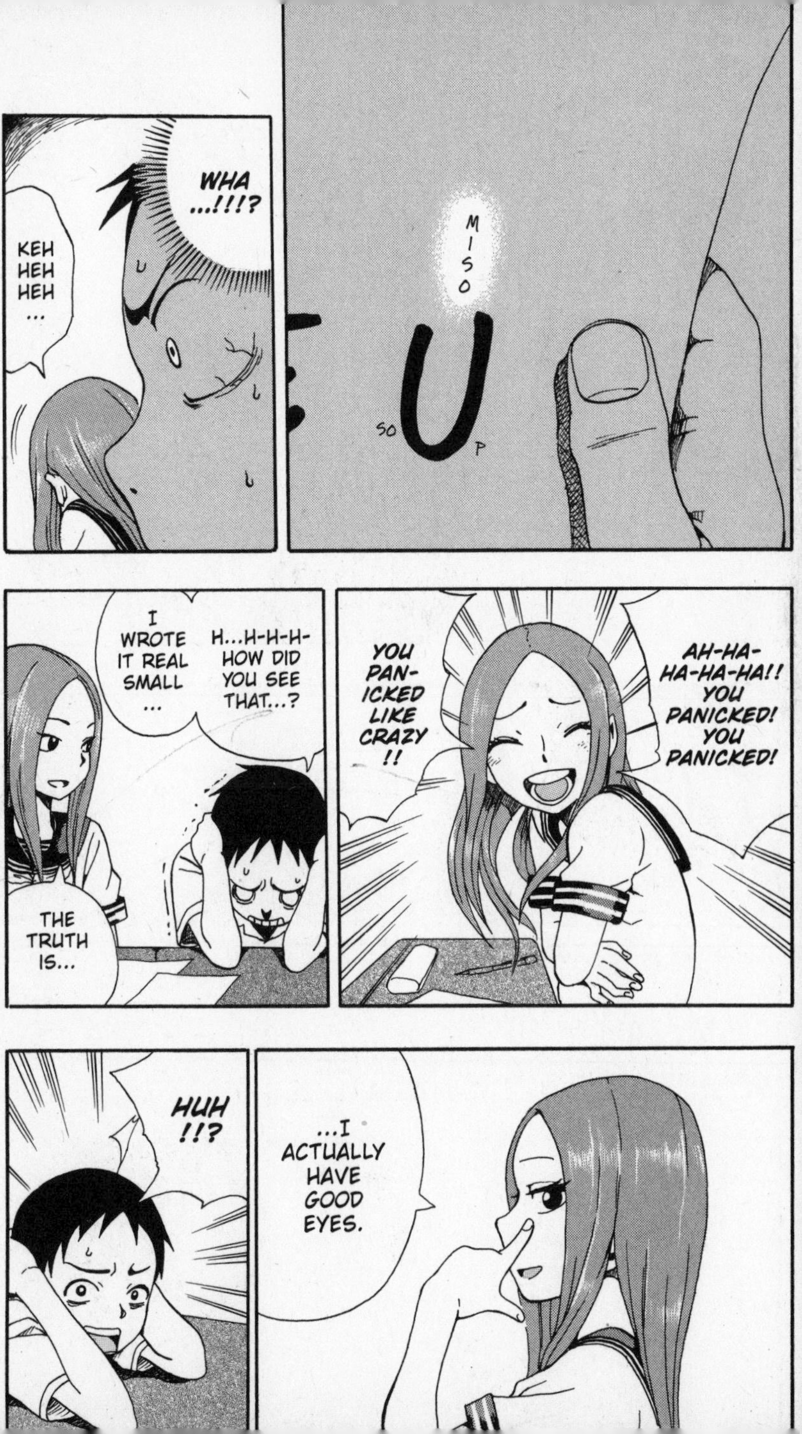
MISO
SO P
WHA...!!!?
KEH HEH HEH...
AH-HA-HA-HA-HA!! YOU PANICKED! YOU PANICKED!
YOU PANICKED LIKE CRAZY!!
H...H-H-H-HOW DID YOU SEE THAT...?
I WROTE IT REAL SMALL...
THE TRUTH IS...
...I ACTUALLY HAVE GOOD EYES.
HUH!!?

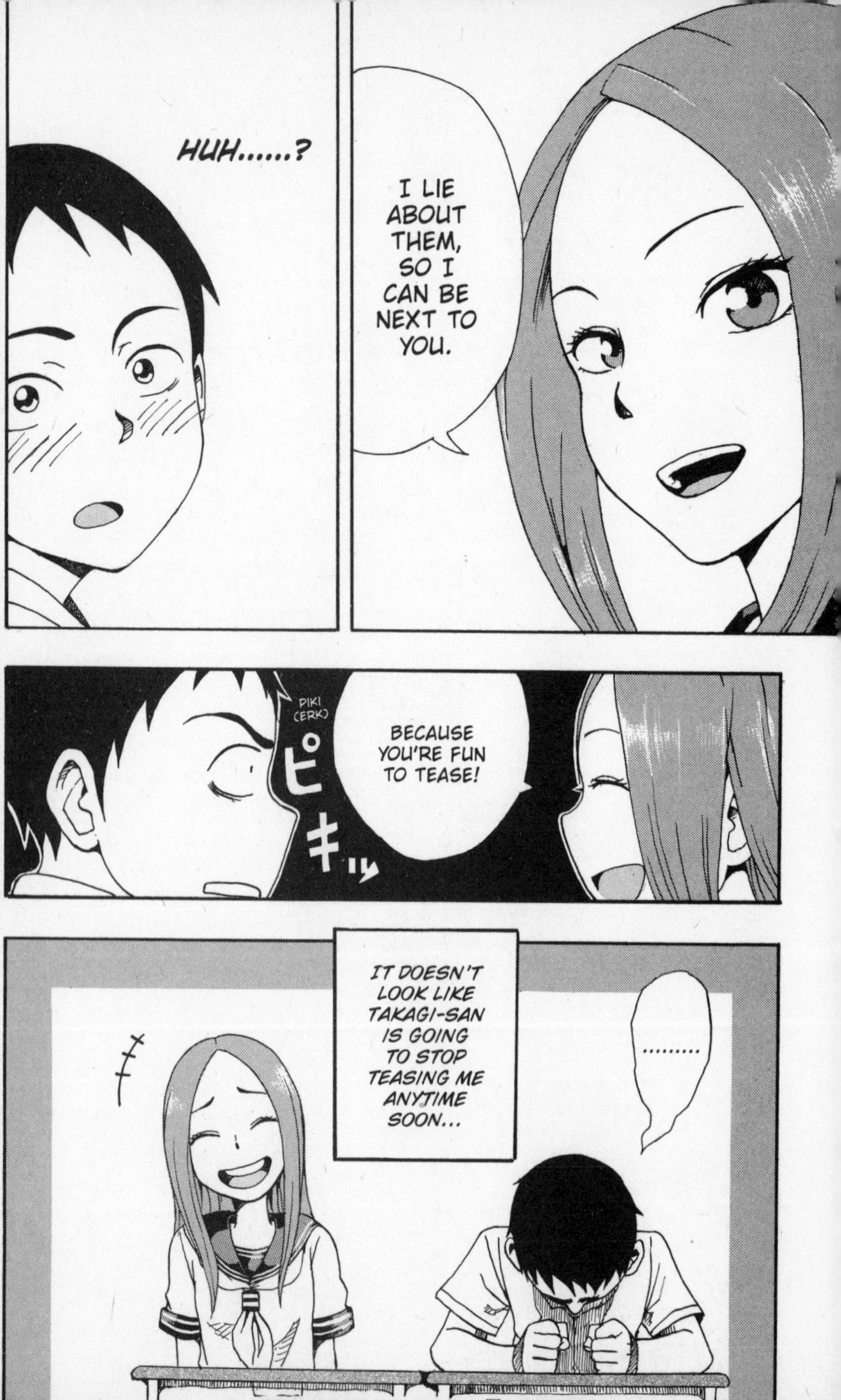
I LIE ABOUT THEM, SO I CAN BE NEXT TO YOU.
HUH......?
BECAUSE YOU'RE FUN TO TEASE!
PIKI (ERK)
.........
IT DOESN'T LOOK LIKE TAKAGI-SAN IS GOING TO STOP TEASING ME ANYTIME SOON...

Teasing Master
Takagi-san

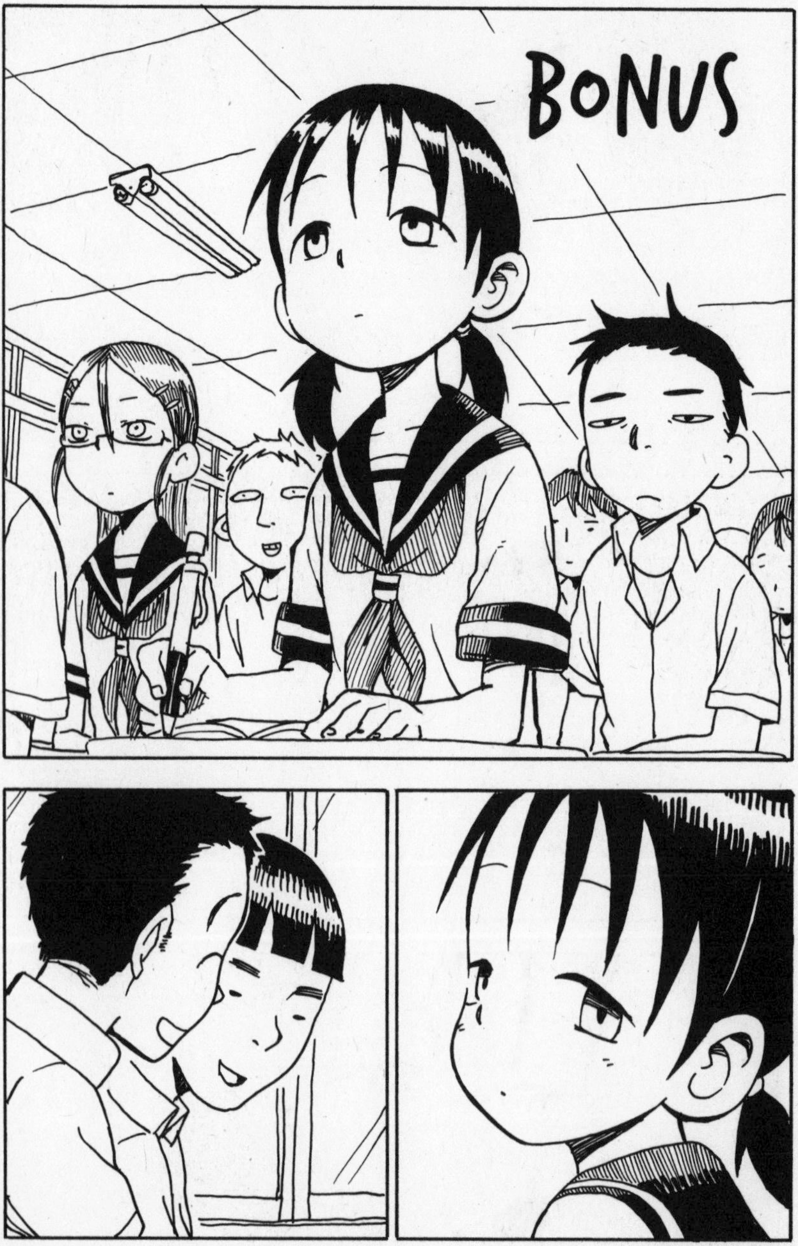
BONUS

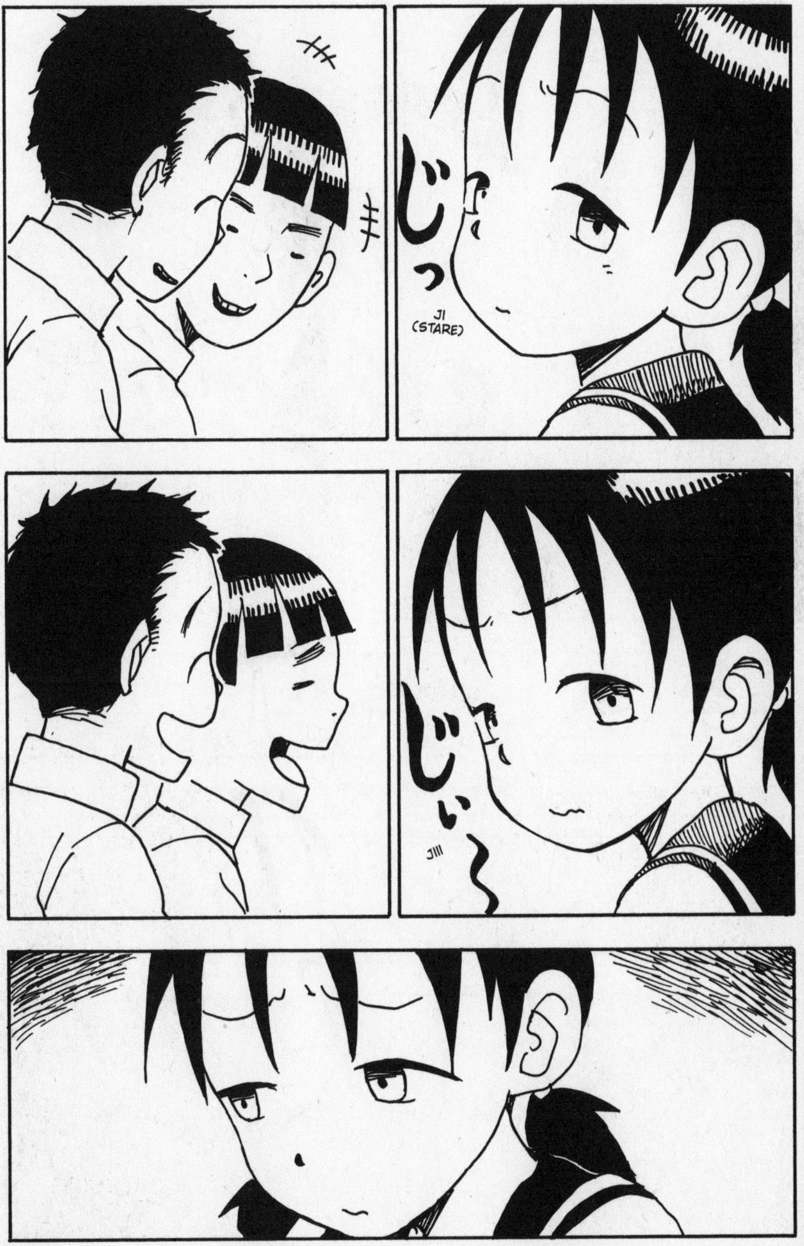
じっ
JI
(STARE)
じぃ〜
JIII

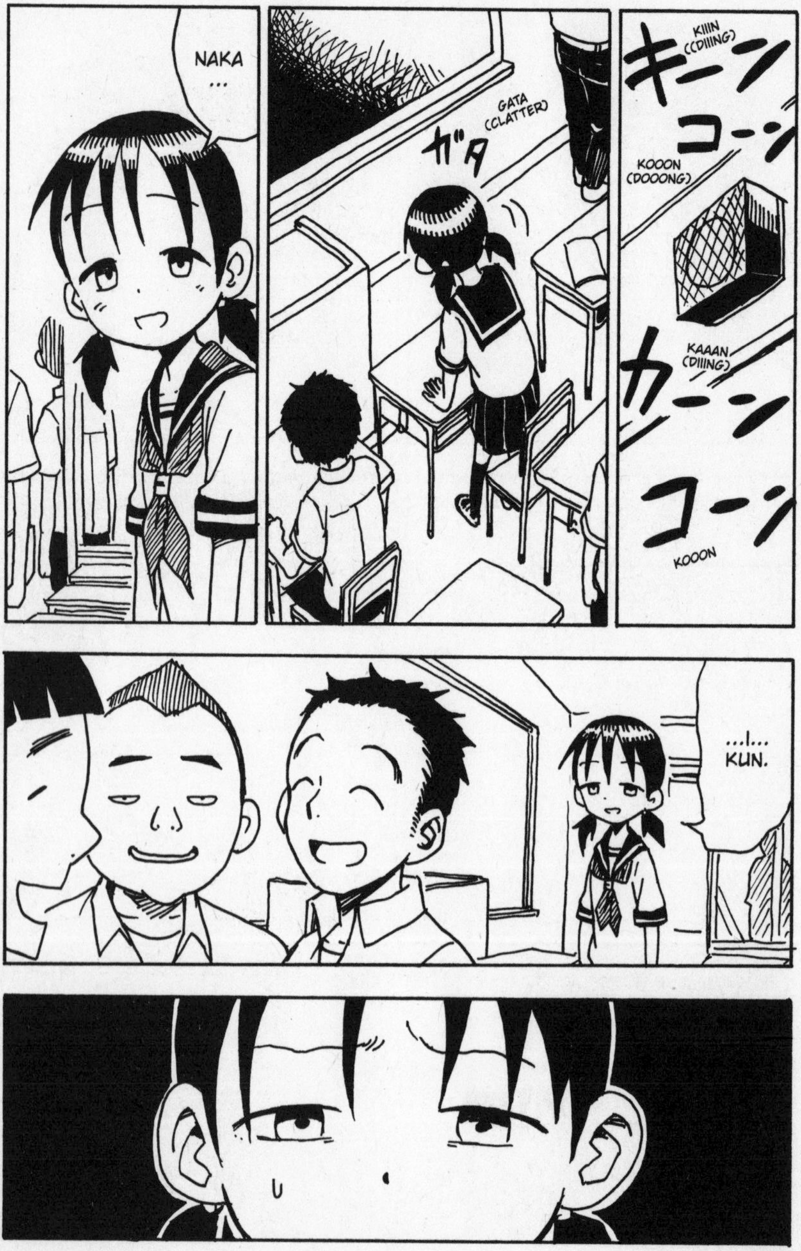
キーン
KIIIN (DIIING)
コーン
KOOON (DOOONG)
カーン
KAAAN (DIIING)
コーン
KOOON
ガタ
GATA (CLATTER)
NAKA ...
...I... KUN.

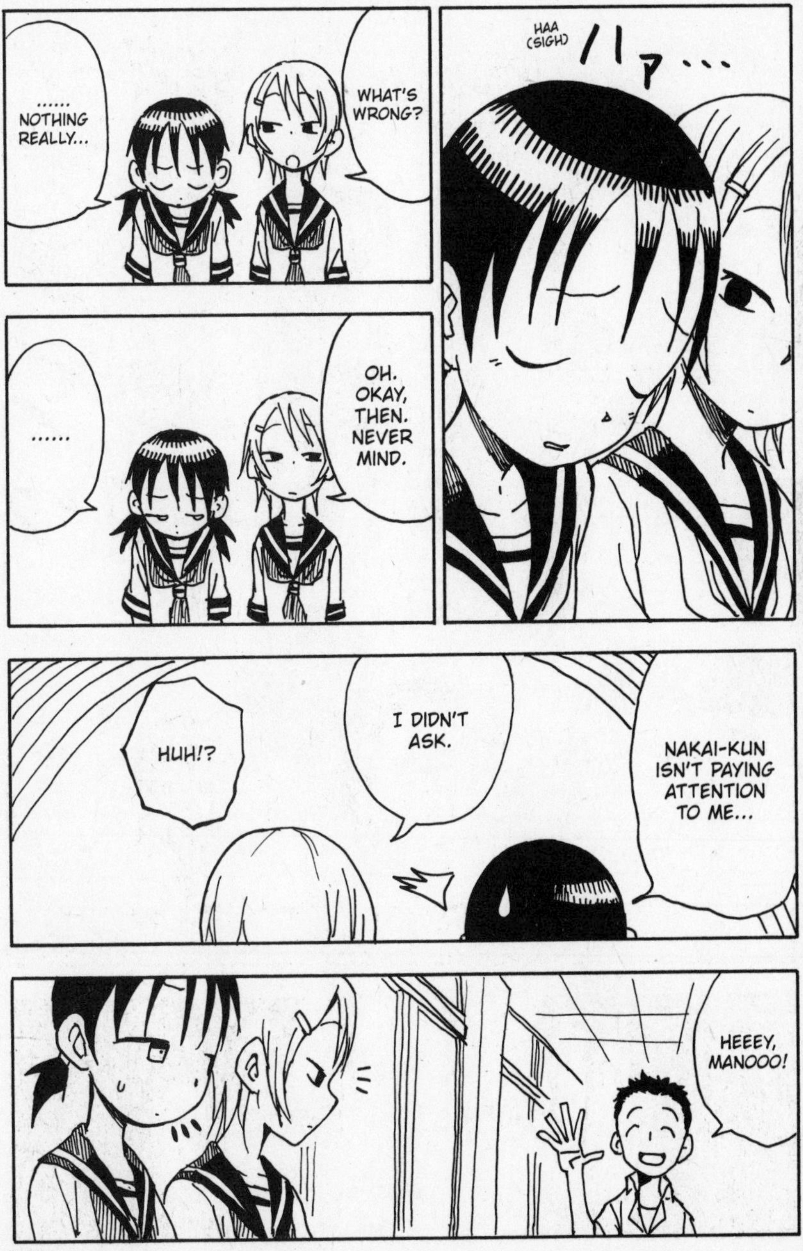
HAA (SIGH)
ハァ…
WHAT'S WRONG?
...... NOTHING REALLY...
OH. OKAY, THEN. NEVER MIND.
......
NAKAI-KUN ISN'T PAYING ATTENTION TO ME...
I DIDN'T ASK.
HUH!?
HEEEY, MANOOO!

I'M MAD AT HIM.

HMPH.

NAKAI-KUN'S CALLING YOU.

......

HELLOOO, EARTH TO MANO.

......

MANO, LISTEN...

NO. I. AM. NOT!!

ARE YOU ASLEEP?

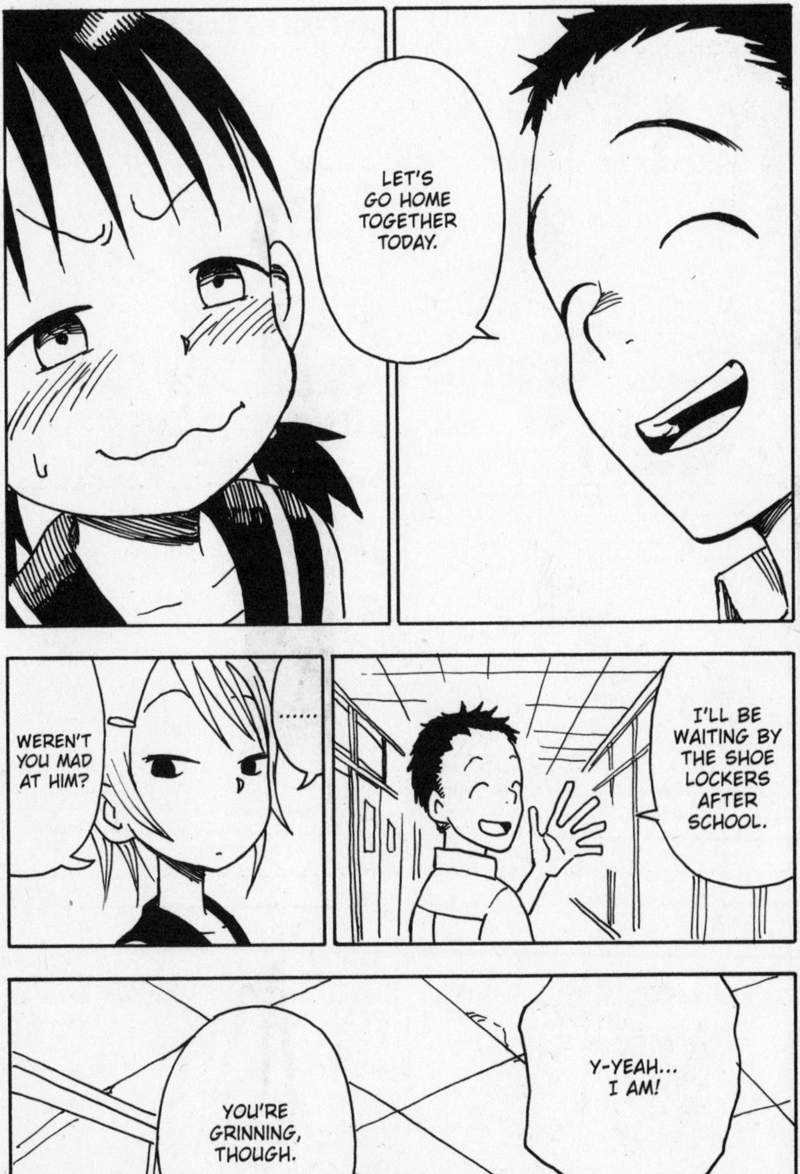
LET'S GO HOME TOGETHER TODAY.
I'LL BE WAITING BY THE SHOE LOCKERS AFTER SCHOOL.
......
WEREN'T YOU MAD AT HIM?
Y-YEAH... I AM!
YOU'RE GRINNING, THOUGH.

**THE END**

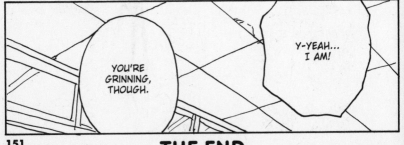

# Translation Notes

## COMMON HONORIFICS

**no honorific**: Indicates familiarity or closeness; if used without permission or reason, addressing someone in this manner would constitute an insult.

**-san**: The Japanese equivalent of Mr./Mrs./Miss. If a situation calls for politeness, this is the fail-safe honorific.

**-kun**: Used most often when referring to boys, this indicates affection or familiarity. Occasionally used by older men among their peers, but it may also be used by anyone referring to a person of lower standing.

**-chan**: An affectionate honorific indicating familiarity used mostly in reference to girls; also used in reference to cute persons or animals of either gender.

**-senpai**: A suffix used to address upperclassmen or more experienced coworkers.

**-sensei**: A respectful term for teachers, artists, or high-level professionals.

## Page 81

Takagi-san uses the word *seishun*, or literally "blue spring," which means "the springtime of one's youth" or "the prime of youth." It is a word commonly used toward young people because they have the most energy to enjoy their lives to the fullest.

## Page 103

Arm wrestling in Japanese is referred to as *udezumou*, or "arm sumo." Takagi and Nishikata are standing in a type of ring used for regular sumo wrestling and are wearing the traditional loincloths that the wrestlers usually wear. In sumo, stepping out of the ring is one way to lose, and Nishikata appears to already be perilously close to the edge.

## Author's Note

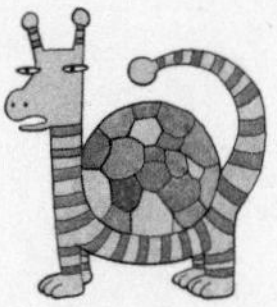

I DIDN'T DO A SINGLE
"SUMMERY" THING THIS
YEAR, SO I WENT FOR A
SUMMERLIKE COVER DESIGN
INSTEAD. PLEASE SHOW
YOUR SUPPORT FOR
VOL. 2 AS WELL.

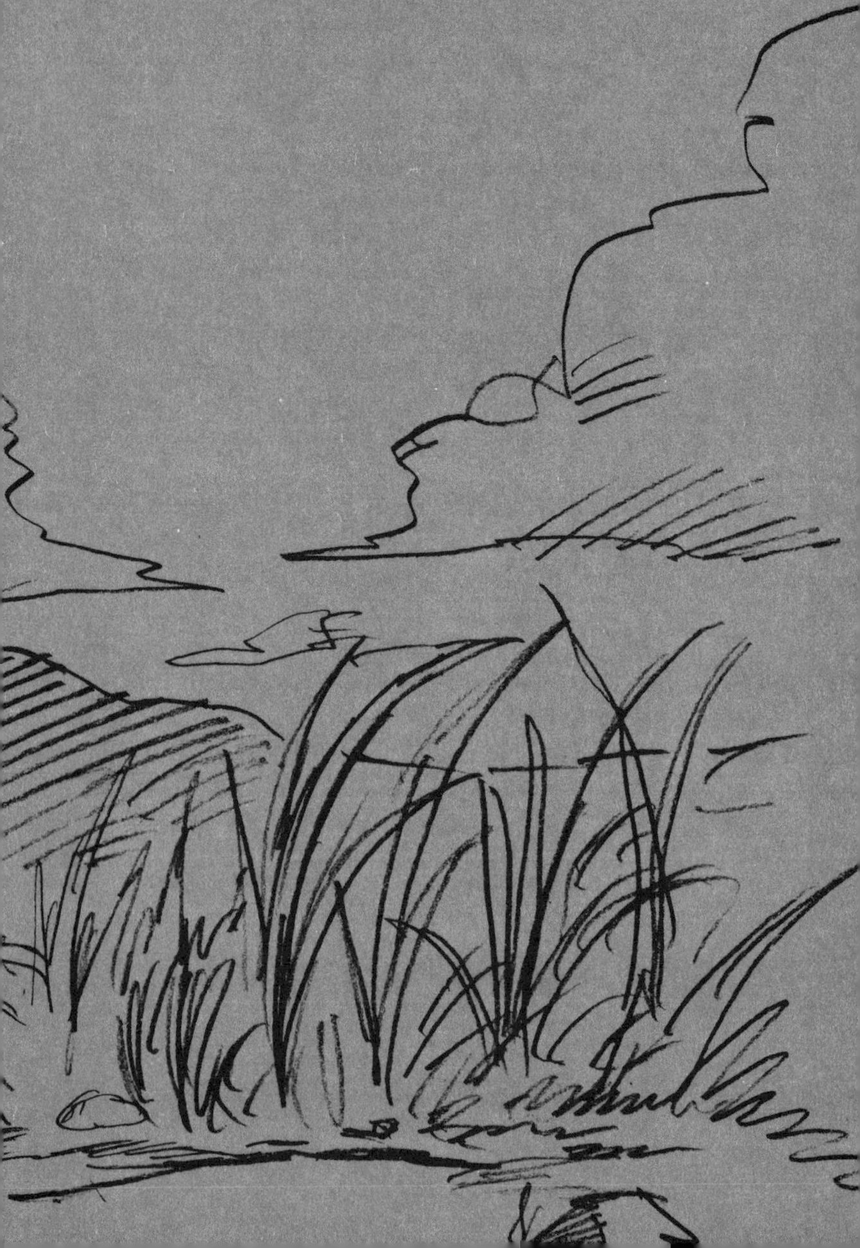

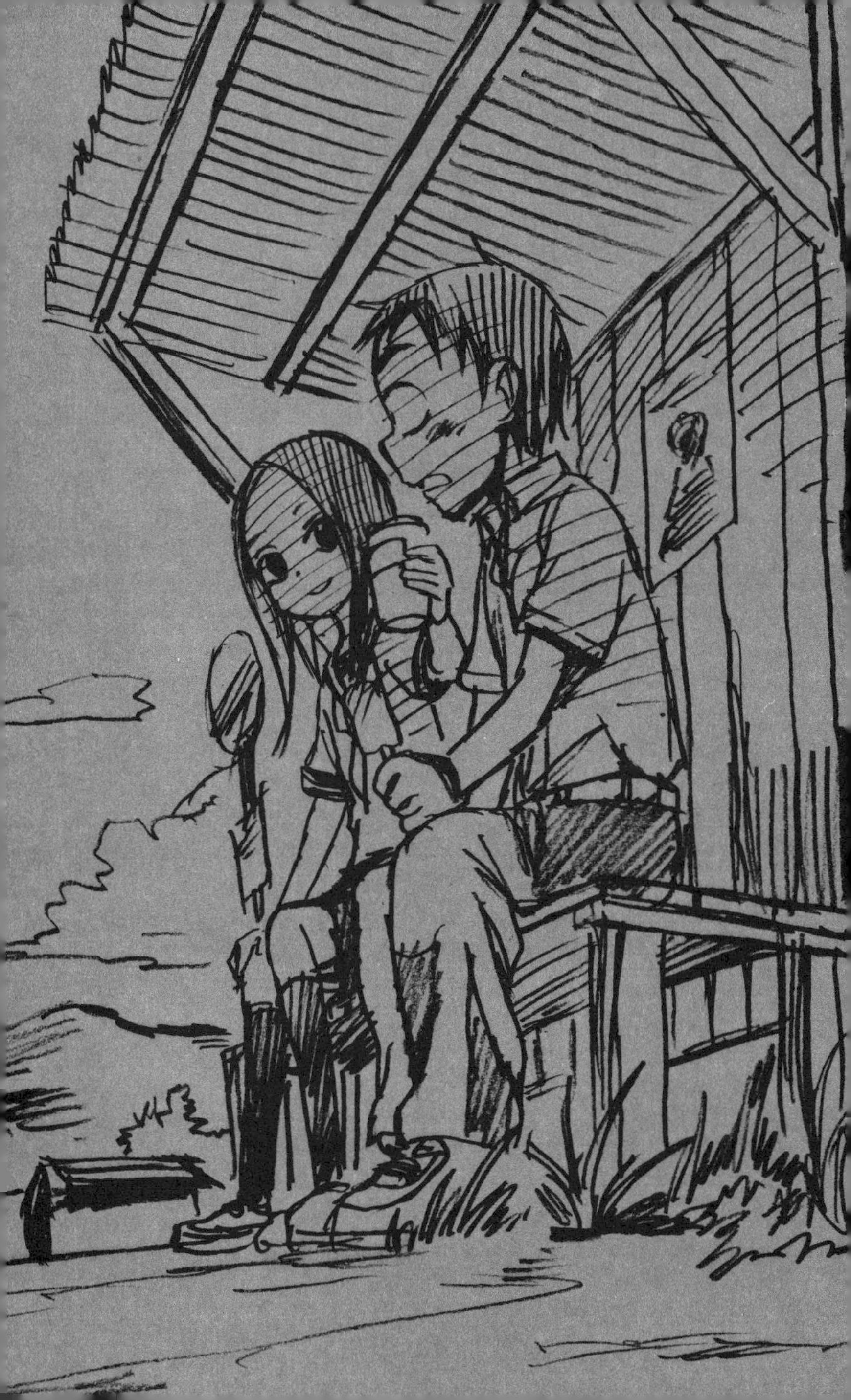

# A Loner's Worst Nightmare: Human Interaction!

# MY YOUTH R♥MANTIC COMEDY iS WRØNG, AS I EXPECTED

Hachiman Hikigaya is a cynic. He believes "youth" is a crock—a sucker's game, an illusion woven from failure and hypocrisy. But when he turns in an essay for a school assignment espousing this view, he's sentenced to work in the Service Club, an organization dedicated to helping students with problems! Worse, the only other member of the club is the haughty Yukino Yukinoshita, a girl with beauty, brains, and the personality of a garbage fire. How will Hachiman the Cynic cope with a job that requires—*gasp!*—social skills?

# ENJOY EVERYTHING.

# Hello! This is YOTSUBA!

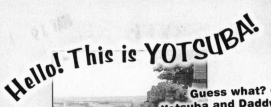

**Guess what? Guess what? Yotsuba and Daddy just moved here from waaaay over there!**

**And Yotsuba met these nice people next door and made new friends to play with!**

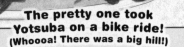

**The pretty one took Yotsuba on a bike ride!**
(Whoooa! There was a big hill!)

**And Ena's a good drawer!**
(Almost as good as Yotsuba!)

**And their mom always gives Yotsuba ice cream!**
(Yummy!)

**And...**
**And...**

**OHHHH!**

# Teasing Master Takagi-san ②

## Soichiro Yamamoto

TRANSLATION: Taylor Engel ♦ LETTERING: Takeshi Kamura

KARAKAI JOZU NO TAKAGI-SAN Vol. 2
by Soichiro YAMAMOTO
© 2014 Soichiro YAMAMOTO
All rights reserved.
Original Japanese edition published by SHOGAKUKAN.
English translation rights in the United States of America, Canada, the United Kingdom, Ireland, Australia and New Zealand arranged with SHOGAKUKAN through Tuttle-Mori Agency, Inc.

English translation © 2018 by Yen Press, LLC

Yen Press
1290 Avenue of the Americas
New York, NY 10104

Visit us at yenpress.com

facebook.com/yenpress
twitter.com/yenpress

yenpress.tumblr.com
instagram.com/yenpress

First Yen Press Edition: October 2018

Yen Press is an imprint of Yen Press, LLC.
The Yen Press name and logo are trademarks of Yen Press, LLC.

# Teasing Master Takagi-san 5

## Soichiro Yamamoto

TRANSLATION: Taylor Engel ♦ LETTERING: Takeshi Kamura

KARAKAI JOZU NO TAKAGI-SAN Vol. 5
by Soichiro YAMAMOTO
© 2014 Soichiro YAMAMOTO
All rights reserved.
Original Japanese edition published by SHOGAKUKAN.
English translation rights in the United States of America, Canada, the United Kingdom, Ireland, Australia and New Zealand arranged with SHOGAKUKAN through Tuttle-Mori Agency, Inc.

English translation © 2019 by Yen Press, LLC

Yen Press
150 West 30th Street, 19th Floor
New York, NY 10001

Visit us at yenpress.com

facebook.com/yenpress
twitter.com/yenpress
yenpress.tumblr.com
instagram.com/yenpress

First Yen Press Edition: July 2019

Yen Press is an imprint of Yen Press, LLC.
The Yen Press name and logo are trademarks of Yen Press, LLC.

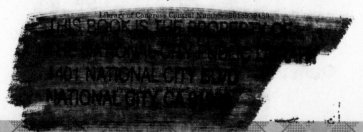

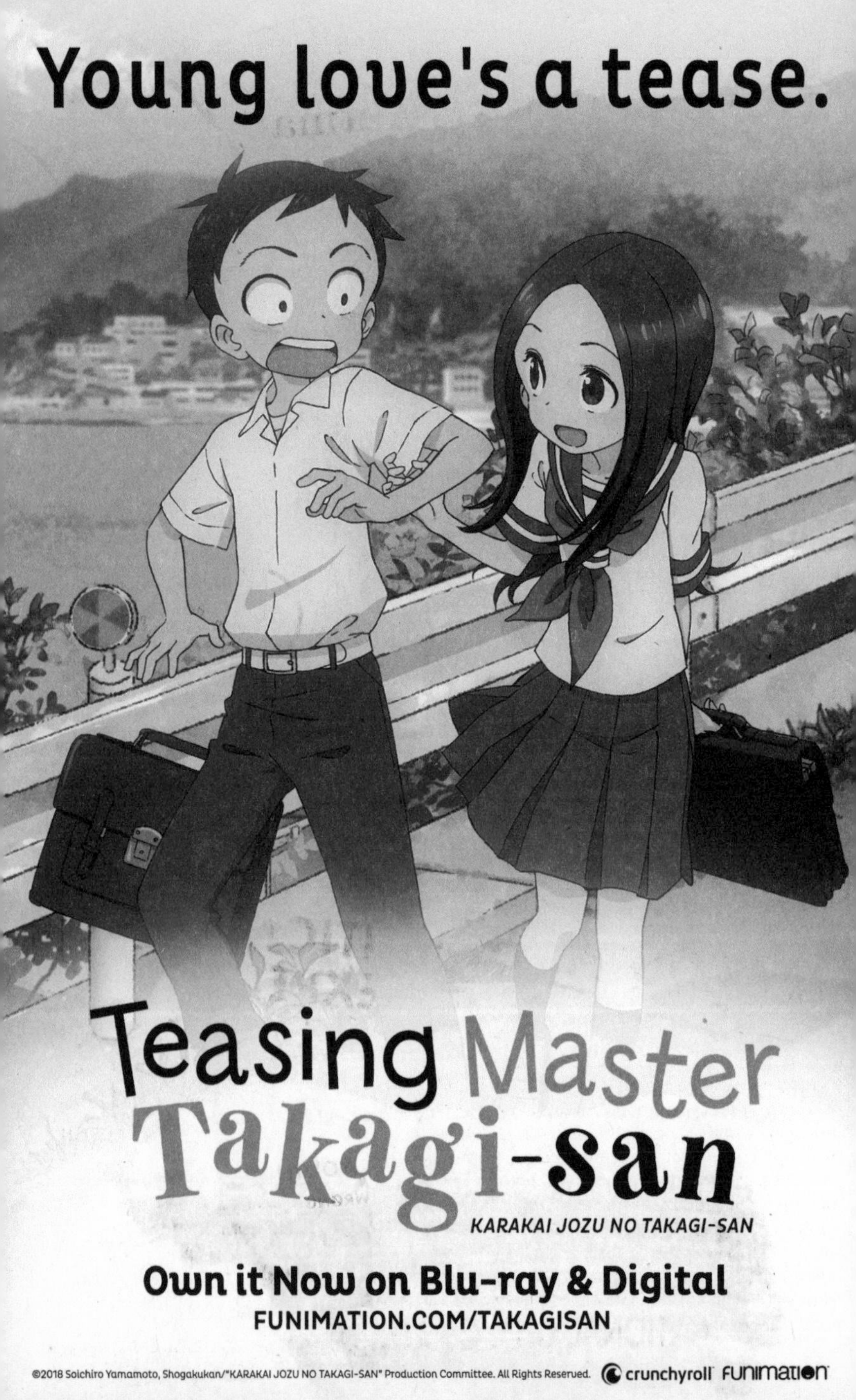
Young love's a tease.
Teasing Master Takagi-san
KARAKAI JOZU NO TAKAGI-SAN
Own it Now on Blu-ray & Digital
FUNIMATION.COM/TAKAGISAN
©2018 Soichiro Yamamoto, Shogakukan/"KARAKAI JOZU NO TAKAGI-SAN" Production Committee. All Rights Reserved.
crunchyroll
FUNIMATION